say

that

again

Also by N. Gemini Sasson:

Say No More (The Faderville Novels)

Memories and Matchsticks (Sam McNamee Mysteries)

The Crown in the Heather (The Bruce Trilogy: Book I)

Worth Dying For (The Bruce Trilogy: Book II)

The Honor Due a King (The Bruce Trilogy: Book III)

*Isabeau: A Novel of Queen Isabella
and Sir Roger Mortimer*

*The King Must Die:
A Novel of Edward III*

*Uneasy Lies the Crown:
A Novel of Owain Glyndwr*

In the Time of Kings

say

that

again

A Faderville Novel

N. GEMINI SASSON

cader idris
press

SAY THAT AGAIN

ISBN 978-1-939344-09-0 (paperback)

Library of Congress Control No. 2015904198

For more details about N. Gemini Sasson and her books, go to:
www.ngeminisasson.com

Or become a 'fan' at:
www.facebook.com/NGeminiSasson

You can also sign up to learn about new releases via e-mail at:
http://eepurl.com/vSA6z

Cover art by Ebook Launch

This book is dedicated to Domino, my original black bi Aussie. She once saved my life. Now *there's* a story...

SAY THAT AGAIN

A little girl's love.
A dog's courage.

Echo's life hasn't been easy so far. Mistreated by one owner after another, he'd rather just learn to get by on his own. Still, he longs for his 'forever home'. Not until he meets young Hannah McHugh does he learn to trust again. Hannah not only understands him — she *hears* him.

Before the accident, Hannah already knew she was different from other kids. Now, animals are speaking to her — and no one believes her. Her sister calls her a liar. The kids at school make fun of her. Her teacher labels her as imaginative. And the psychologist hints that she's troubled. Even her own father, Hunter, tells her she should keep it to herself. Only with her dog Echo, an Australian Shepherd, at her side does she feel truly safe and accepted.

Then, the reclusive Heck Menendez moves in next door. The last thing he wants is a little kid and her dog hanging around. Yet Heck is the only one her family can rely on to keep an eye on her.

When Hannah and Echo disappear, rumors run wild about old Heck. Hunter wants to trust his gut, but time is ticking away.

chapter 1

Hannah

Hannah McHugh placed one small foot in front of the other without knowing exactly where it was that she was going. Her purple sneakers left barely visible imprints in the damp clay of the path as the airy trilling of the bluebird beckoned her onward. To Hannah, the notes were like a song sung only for her. It filled her with happiness. Lifted her heart, all the way up to heaven.

Every now and then, she saw a flash of bright blue feathers, flittering against a glass-blue sky.

Laughing, she followed the bird. Down a steep slope littered with loose slabs of stone. Up a long incline through a towering stand of trees. Along a narrowing trail that wound between boulders bigger than her sister's school bus.

The bird danced from limb to limb. Higher, faster. Happy, singing.

Follow me, it said. *This way. Over here. Hurry!*

Her steps quickened. Her breaths came in puffs, her heart pattering against her sternum as she lifted her knees and pumped her tiny arms to keep up. Her stuffed giraffe, Faustine, swung in her grip, its yarn tail tattered and one beaded eye missing. Part of the stuffing in Faustine's neck had long since been compressed into her slender body, and so her head flopped helplessly at the end of her too long neck whenever Hannah carried her about, or leaned precariously to the right when Hannah set her on all fours, as if the little giraffe had a question she was always waiting to ask.

Just as Hannah topped a hill, the bird dove into a tangle of branches in the valley below, its song muted. Hannah stopped, peered intently at the place where it had disappeared, saw nothing.

Patiently, she stood at attention, eyes and ears keened. But there was no more sign of the bird. Nothing but silence. Deep, empty silence all around. Not even a breeze to rustle the last of autumn's papery leaves.

Then it occurred to her that she had no idea where her family was. Or how far she had come. Or from where.

Panic constricted her ribs. She'd get in trouble for wandering off from their cabin. Her daddy would frown at her and cross his arms. Her mommy would shake a finger in her face and speak to her sternly. She wouldn't be allowed to watch her princess movies or go to Gramma's. Maybe for a whole week. It would be boring sitting in her room alone.

A tear squeezed from the corner of Hannah's eye, tracing a trail of regret as it slid down her cold-kissed cheek. She shouldn't have wandered away from the cabin before everyone else had woken up. They would be worried to find her gone. Frantic. And mad.

But she had only wanted to see what was beyond the little clearing. To search for one of *them*. Her older sister, Maura, had told her there were fairies in the woods and that they took naps beneath mushroom caps and bathed on leaves dappled with morning dew and made their homes in the hollowed trunks of giant oak trees. From a distance, Maura told her, they looked exactly like little white

2

butterflies.

Yet she hadn't seen any fairies. Or butterflies, even. Just the bluebird. And trees. Lots and lots of trees. Millions, maybe gazillions.

She had to get back. But to where? And how?

As she turned in a circle, searching for a familiar sight, fear crept up her spine. She clutched Faustine to her chest and held her tight. This place looked different, not at all like the forest clearing where their cabin was. They had come to the state park for Hannah's fifth birthday. She hadn't wanted a party with lots of other noisy children. Or a pile of presents. Or a fancy restaurant dinner, where waiters wearing sombreros would sing and clap for her, drawing everyone's attention. Those things were all too much, too noisy. She had only wanted this: a weekend with her family, just the four of them, in the faraway woods of southeastern Kentucky, where she could watch the birds and look for wild animals.

What she'd really wanted, though, was a dog of her own. But they had told her she was too young for that and would have to wait, probably until she was Maura's age. And so she'd settled for a camping trip. Now that they were here, she wasn't sure why she'd wanted to come in the first place. It had sounded like fun, but there really wasn't much to do.

Christmas was only a week away and although it was still cool, the weather promised to be good. So Daddy had thrown their suitcases in the truck he used for his veterinary business and put Maura and Mommy in charge of packing the food. Hannah had only been responsible for her own things. But when she went outside this morning, she'd forgotten to grab her coat off the peg by the door and now she was shivering so hard that her teeth clacked. It hadn't felt that cold when she first stepped outside.

Far off, a sparkle caught her eye. She looked down below and noticed, amid a drifting sea of fog, a shimmering silver ribbon. A big creek. What her daddy called a river. Beyond it, the ground rose up again to more hills, bigger hills, taller and broader than those behind her. Hills embraced by wispy clouds.

Hannah started downward, toward the water. She was thirsty. And hungry. She hadn't had breakfast yet, and although she doubted she would find food anywhere near here, she could at least get a drink of water before she tried to find her parents and Maura.

She raced downhill, her short legs wearying not halfway down. She stumbled, falling to her knees. Undeterred, she stood, brushed the dirt from her leggings, and continued on. The ground flattened out. Leaf-littered dirt gave way to winter-dead grass, anchored in the mud of a recent rain.

At water's edge, she knelt and made a scoop with her hands. The water froze her fingers when she dipped them in. She brought the cool liquid to her mouth and sipped, then spat it out. It tasted icky. Like sand.

Farther along the bank, an animal with a black mask and a ringed tail winked at her. It waded into the shallows. Hannah recognized it as a raccoon, the same kind of animal that tipped their trashcans over and made her daddy angry. She smiled and waved. It chattered in response, then plunged its front paws into the water, up to its elbows.

Bit by bit, she scooted closer. The raccoon eyed her curiously and went back to washing its face. Careful not to get too close and scare it away, Hannah sat, crossing her legs. She would try to find her way back to the cabin in a little while. After she was done watching the raccoon. She couldn't be that far away. Maybe if she stayed here, they would find her.

But what if they went the wrong way? What if they searched and searched and just gave up?

No, they'd look. They'd find her. They would.

Hannah kissed Faustine on the head and noticed a dab of mud there. If she dipped Faustine's head in the river, maybe it would rinse away the dirt. Holding Faustine's back legs, she stretched out on her

4

tummy and leaned out from the bank, reaching toward the water.

She wiggled forward a few inches and Faustine's head flopped into the water. She held her there awhile, giving the dirt time to wash away. As she began to pull Faustine back, a flurry of chirps sounded above her. She looked up to see the bluebird alight on a branch on the other side of the river.

You should listen more closely, it said.

"What?"

Just listen!

Hannah didn't understand. She was sure she'd heard the bird, but what was it talking about? Listen to what? To whom?

Fast water. Bad.

"But I need to give Faustine a bath, silly bird."

Not silly.

The bird burst skyward. Hannah tilted her head up to watch, but as she did so, she felt Faustine slip from her fingers. The stuffed animal fell with a splash, floating on the surface a few moments before an eddy engulfed it and pulled it under. Then, a surge pushed Faustine back to the top.

Hannah flailed a hand outward, stretching far. Her body, small though it was, tipped over the edge of the bank. She gasped in shock as her hands hit the cold, cold water. Then as her head plunged beneath the surface, she captured a final gulp of air in her lungs and shut her eyes tight.

chapter 2

Echo

It was something in the eyes. Somehow I just *knew*, even though I wasn't sure what it was that I knew. Deep inside me, there was this ... knot, I guess. Like the more he invaded my space, the tighter my insides coiled. As if I could draw into myself and become so small as to be invisible.

Hands plunged at me. Too fast. I flattened myself to the ground. Held my breath. Fingers clamped around my ribs. I went limp, as if I could melt between the sieve of his fingers and flow away, unattainable. But he lifted me up — high. So high the floor disappeared from sight. I was afraid to look down. Afraid, deathly afraid of falling.

And dying.

Call me morose, but I have always had this innate fear of death. Which is an awful burden to carry around every day, when you think about it. Especially when you're only three months old. Still, it's a perfectly reasonable fear. If you're not afraid of dying, then you're apt to do any number of stupid things that will certainly ensure your death.

I was the last of my litter. The small puppy. The plain one. The shy one. The one nobody wanted. Didn't matter that I was the smartest. Or the fastest. Or stealthiest. That I was first out of the box. That I had a nose that could locate the single piece of kibble that had skittered under the work bench when all the other puppies were oblivious to it.

They were all so reckless. Running to greet the strangers. Falling all over each other like drunken buffoons. Their plump little nubs wagging deliriously. Each time, I hung back, observant. Not afraid, but cautious. The Tall Ones called me fearful; they couldn't have been more wrong. I was simply thoughtful.

One by one, the others had left. I was glad for that. No more razor sharp fangs piercing my ear flaps. No more being dragged around by the scruff, even as I protested. It was my dream come true. But even as I bade my brothers and sisters good riddance, I looked on with envy.

They had been chosen. They had a home.

Secretly, I craved what I had so long eschewed: a Forever Home. That place where you are surrounded by your own family of Tall Ones who shower you with love, play with you, rub your tummy, keep your kibble bowl endlessly full, and lay biscuits on your bed at night.

Maybe it was foolish of me to dream of such a thing when I had never known anything like it, but I was sure such a life existed. That somewhere out there was someone for me. A person I could call my own. This need to attach myself to a human was, I'm sure, programmed into my genetic code.

So when the last set of strangers came that day, I tried. With all my heart, I tried. This was my chance to become an 'only'. To perhaps go off to a place better than the dark, cluttered garage I had known, filled with the odor of engine oil and gasoline, fertilizer and molded grass clippings. Somewhere besides the muddy confines of our cramped pen, where the wind blew cold and sharp through the tall weeds outside the ramshackle fence.

I dreamed of being inside, where it was bright and warm and always dry. The Tall Ones had taken us there whenever the strangers came. Inside, in a place they called the kitchen. A place smelling of food and filled with unfamiliar sounds. It both intrigued and terrified me. Given time, though, I might have grown accustomed to it. Given time, I could have proven myself capable of so much.

Right now, I just wanted *down*!

I kicked my legs and let out a howl. The stranger's hands clamped tighter around me, compressing my ribs. He brought my face close to his, breathing stale breath into my precious air.

"Don't like that, do you?" He pressed his warty nose to mine.

I took it as a challenge, growling. Which, I have since learned, was perhaps the wrong thing to do. Hindsight and all that. But I was trying to send a message, which he didn't seem at all interested in listening to. So I took it as my place to teach him something new. You squeeze; I warn you to stop.

He plopped me down so fast the air whooshed from my lungs with a visceral grunt. Message received, then. Certain that death was imminent, I scrambled under the table legs to tuck myself against the wall.

The stranger turned his back on me and mumbled at the woman who fed me every day.

"Wait!" She shuffled after him as he went from the kitchen. "You can have him for free. No charge, really. We just want him to have a good home — and you seem like such a nice man. A dog lover, for sure."

Stopping in the front doorway, he pulled a rough hand down over his beard and looked my way. "I'll talk to my wife and let you know.

She kinda wanted one of them spotted ones."

The door groaned shut. The woman leered in my direction, stomping toward me, and then peered under the table. Her mouth pressed into a scowl. "What are we going to do, Ed? No one wants him."

"Told you — everybody wants the merles. Told you that when you got the bright idea of buying the mother from that gal in Campbellsville and breeding her to Toby Updegraff's boy."

Straightening, she turned toward Ed. "He's a pretty dog."

"He's got no papers. Papers matter."

"Folks don't care about papers. They just want purebreds."

Snorting, Ed pulled out a chair and sat. "Purebred Australian Shepherd? Who could tell? The runt sure doesn't look like one to me. You sure that bitch didn't get loose and get herself bred by a black Lab or something?" He popped open the tab on his beer and guzzled. "Anyway, can't blame that guy for leaving just now. The little one's always watching me. I bet he turns out meaner than snot."

"Scared of his own shadow, more like." She paced about, banging drawers and clanging pots. "Shame the mother ran off."

"I say we're lucky she did."

Every chime of metal reverberated down to my bones and scraped at my nerves. Overcome by the noise, I quivered uncontrollably. Growing up in the garage, except for our mother's barking and the squeals of my littermates, there had been abounding quiet. If I was afraid now, it was only because there was so much I didn't know. Everything here was new to me. My senses were assaulted every second. I was acutely aware of every movement, every scent, every boom and screech and bellow. Without knowing what any of these things meant, I had only one instinct — and that was to stay safe.

But when Ed reached for me, there was no safe place. No retreat, no recourse. Gruff fingers pinched the skin at the back of my neck,

9

yanking me across the slick floor. He hoisted me by the scruff, swinging me under his arm.

"Tell you what, Carol," he said to the woman. "I'll take care of him. I'm damn tired of cleaning up after the rodent."

Carol followed us to the back door, concern furrowing her ragged brow. "Where are you taking him?"

"For a ride." He chuckled and kicked the door open.

The knot inside my stomach drew tighter.

—oO0o—

He didn't stop driving until I upchucked my breakfast. Had I known he would take that as a signal, I would have done it sooner.

I'd never been in a car and couldn't say I liked it. Too much noise. Too much vibration. Too much of objects flying by at impossible speeds. Too much of too much.

I was thankful when we stopped and he pulled me out.

Until I saw the water, far, *far* below. Big water. Dark water. Fast water.

I stole one last look at his face before he dropped me inside the crinkly white bag. In the constriction of his eyelids, the hollowness behind his pupils, I saw my first glimpse of cruelty. It was a glance through a tunnel that led to a heart of granite.

That was when I knew that not all humans were the same. Still, I clung to the hope, however unproven, that some were good — and that I would come to know them, even as the bag closed above my head and I felt the rush of air beneath me as gravity carried me down.

Down, down, down. Down to the water.

And the end of my beginning.

chapter 3
Echo

Cold blasted through me. Infiltrated every cell, every molecule of my bodily existence. Like rubble bearing down in an avalanche, water surrounded me. Sucked the oxygen from my lungs and squeezed the blood from my heart.

When you dunk your paw into a bowl of water, water is fluid and soft. When you're plummeting from a hundred feet up into a raging river, it is like hitting a concrete barrier at incredible speed. I was sure every bone in my body had been shattered.

Yet if that had been so, I would not have found myself kicking, struggling upward. A little pocket of air had formed at the top of the bag — and that is how I knew which way was up. But the more I clawed, the more air bubbled out through the little hole where Ed had closed the bag up. And the more I fought to free myself, the more my body yearned for oxygen.

I gulped, drawing water into my mouth, flooding my lungs. The river closed in around me and also filled me from within. I was being crushed and suffocated all at once. My heart threatened to burst. My lungs were ready to explode.

The instinct to survive took over. I felt myself pawing. One front leg slipped through the opening. I stuck my nose there, pushing. But it would not loosen. No matter how hard I tried.

I hurt. Everywhere. Outside and inside. Ears, eyes, toes, ribs.

Hurt like I had been beaten with a thorny branch and run over by a car. Every bone pulverized. My skin flayed. Arteries and veins collapsed in on themselves.

But pain, when all-consuming, propels the spirit to another plane. A place where it becomes separate from the body, then fades, gloriously, away.

It was as though I had just laid my pain-riddled body onto a giant leaf and set it adrift on calm waters. With a breath, I blew it away. Let go. Floated through a haze of bliss, my body weightless and free of pain. And drifted to where the light shone down, a cone-like tunnel to up above.

Who are you?

The voice had come from the light. The words, however, were not the language the Tall Ones had spoken. Still, somehow I knew the meaning behind the sounds. I understood.

There's nothing to be afraid of.

"Nothing to be afraid of?" I said, although I hadn't really said it, only thought it. But I heard my words. *Heard* them.

That's right. You're safe.

"Safe?"

You sound like an echo.

"Echo?"

Yes, Echo.

And like that, my name became Echo. Although I still wasn't sure what it was I should be afraid of.

Of not letting go, the voice said.

"Not letting go?"

You want to go toward the light, yes?

"Yes, I do."

Why?

"Because there is no pain there. It's a beautiful place. Peaceful."

It is. But you have to stay.

"Stay ... here? In the water? But I can't breathe. I'm not a fish."

Trust me, you wouldn't want to be a fish. It's very, very boring.

"Then what? I don't understand."

Just stay. Be you. Trust that who you are is who you're meant to be. And trust that you are meant for someone.

The voice trailed away. I blinked at the light as it, too, faded. A silver, forked tailfin flicked before me, then disappeared. Bubbles funneled upward in its place, as a murky wash of bluish-green surrounded me. My legs pulled in toward my body, then stroked the water, pushing it behind me. Green gave way to blue. Brilliant, sparkling sky blue.

My head broke the surface. I swallowed not water, but air, and then coughed up great gobs of phlegm. Foam swirled around me. My legs, numb to the cold, kicked and paddled. The shoreline came into view, rocky banks bordered by sandy mud flats. I strained toward it, but the river carried me farther downstream. So I let it take me. Bobbing and spinning. Until at last it deposited me on a sandy strip, littered with flakes of stone.

I lay sprawled upon the damp earth, the naked arms of trees scratching at a steel gray sky above me. Water lapped at my toes, its sound a steady rhythm, growing in volume. Cold seeped beneath my drenched fur, settling deep in my bones. I began to shiver. My teeth rattled. My muscles cramped, burning with fatigue from my efforts.

I had to go ... somewhere. Anywhere. Just not back there with them, Ed and Carol. So I lifted my head, looked around.

The world tipped and spun. I felt dizzy, nauseated, disoriented. Pulling my elbows beneath me, I rested my muzzle between my front paws and watched the river flow by.

How long had I been down there, beneath the surface? Where was the bridge? And why had Ed thrown me from it? These were things, I realized, I would never know.

What I did know was that I had defied death and survived. And I was no longer afraid of what I did not know, because what we imagine might happen is sometimes far worse than what comes to be.

Trust that who you are is who you're meant to be.

I shook my head to jar the words from my mind. They meant nothing. They were merely a dream.

And trust that you are meant for someone.

Meant for someone? A human? Hah, not likely. What reason did I have to trust any of them?

Slowly, I stood. My legs trembled from weakness. As I walked away, I swayed, my steps twisting along a narrow trail that meandered beside the river.

Pausing, I lowered my nose and inhaled. Others had been here before me. But not humans. Some other kinds of animals I did not know.

A plump form scampered farther ahead across the trail. I hunkered low to hide behind a tuft of grass. It had a ringed tail, ticked fur, and a dark band across its eyes. It stopped, gazed back at me, and chattered in irritation before disappearing into the tangle of trees that spilled down into the valley from surrounding hills. I waited until the creature was long gone before continuing on.

The sun peeked between broken clouds, but it did little to chase the cold away. The only way to get warm was to keep moving. So I did. Mile after mile. Following the river. Going as far as I could from Ed and the bridge.

The promise of food and warmth urged me on. I didn't know where to find those things; only that they weren't here.

Thirsty, I went to the river and drank from it. It tasted of silt and

14

moss and decaying leaves. As I turned back to the path, a lump of fur at water's edge caught my eye. I watched it for a long, long time. It didn't move. It wasn't even breathing. Whatever it was, it was dead.

Crouching low, I crept forward. I had practiced my stealth hunting moves with my siblings many times. I was the best of all of them at it. I had often pounced, but never attacked. I refused to torture them as they had me.

The closer I came to the lump, the more it struck me as odd, out of place. It had one eye, which wasn't really in its skull at all, but attached to the outside by a few loose strands of thread. Its tail and mane were made from thicker cords, tangled and frayed. And it appeared to have no mouth at all. Large brown spots covered its yellow body, its lanky legs almost comical compared to mine.

Aware that it posed no danger, I stood over it, curious as to what it was and how it had gotten there. I sniffed it and detected only the stink of river water. Then I nudged its body with my nose to push it away from the water. When it was safely away from the river, I gently picked it up in my mouth. The neck was oddly angled. I shook it and water flew in a broad arc to patter upon the dead grass. The head flopped side to side, almost separate from the rest of it.

This was my prize, my reward for having survived. In my short life, I had never come across anything quite so fascinating, so desirable, such a fountain of joy. As I trotted along the path, I lifted my head high, proud of this thing I had claimed. It was like having hunted without having maimed or killed.

I would care for it and sleep with it. Guard it at all costs. It was mine. All mine. A source of purpose. An undemanding companion.

For a while, I forgot my hunger and weariness. Renewed, I trotted on and on, following the trail as it veered away from the river and onto a broader plain where the hills parted and the ground rose gradually.

There, at the top of the path, stood a man. Taller than the tallest

Tall Ones I had ever seen. A man of middle years with tawny golden hair. He cupped his hands to his mouth and shouted toward the valley from which I had just come.

"Hannah! Hannaaahhh!"

Slowing, I looked about, expecting a 'hannah' to burst from the underbrush. Maybe that's what the masked creature was? But everything all around was still. There was nothing but me and the man. No sound, no movement. Just the two of us and a bunch of trees and hills and the river in the distance.

I turned, searching for a hiding place. But just as I did so, he spied me. And started running toward me.

A recognition, a sense of 'knowing', sparked deep inside me. I quickly brushed it away and focused.

"Is that ...?" He tossed a look behind him and hooked his arm in the air. "Jenn, here. Hurry! There's a dog down there. He's got Faustine."

Faustine? Was a 'faustine' anything like a 'hannah'?

"What do you mean *'He's got Faustine'*?" a woman's voice called. "Where?"

"This way!"

Heavy feet tromped downhill toward me. Soon, I heard a third set, lighter and more nimble, but no faster.

Frantic, I leaped from the path to bound through grass and weeds. Cockleburs snagged at my fur. Stiff stems of broken weeds poked at the pads of my feet.

"We've got to find her, Dad!" the younger one screeched, her words followed by sobs.

"Don't worry, honey. We will, we will." But he sounded no surer than the others.

The faster I ran, the more my lungs burned for air. My time beneath the water had weakened them and filled my legs with lead. I heaved for air, but as I did so, the furry thing fell from my mouth.

I was several feet beyond it before I could swing around and turn back. Just as I dipped my head to grab it again, the man appeared before me.

We both stopped, staring. I wanted my prize back, but didn't dare risk going closer.

Kneeling, he extended a hand. His voice was soft, soothing, but carried the slightest tremor. "Please, where did you find that? Show us."

Again, that feeling. A sense of familiarity as I met his gaze. I wasn't sure what it meant or why I felt it.

The others came to a stop behind him, faces drawn with concern, almost scared. The younger one was a smaller version of the woman. Tears streaked her face.

"Please," he begged again.

I didn't understand what he wanted. Was he asking to take the thing? Or for me to come to him? Or something else entirely?

Although instinct begged me to trust him, experience told me not to. The last human I was with had done a terrible thing to me.

So I did the smartest thing I could think of.

I ran.

chapter 4

Hannah

Cold. Absolute, piercing, bone-shattering cold. Little Hannah McHugh felt it in her core. Her heart, which at first had raced in fright, now beat sluggishly. Fear had gripped her for only a moment. And then the shock of coldness snatched even that away. She simply existed — frozen, submerged, unable to move or breathe or even think.

Slowly, a question formed in her mind: *Where am I?*

But no answer came. No awareness. No reaction. She saw nothing. Felt nothing. Could not move.

She opened her eyes, blinking hard as tiny particles of silt scratched at them. A murky haze of green swirled around her, lightening, shifting.

What is this place? How did I get here?

She began to remember. Wandering away from her cabin in search of fairies. Following the bluebird. Kneeling beside the river. Faustine falling in. Reaching. Slipping. Plunging …

She was in the river!

Hannah opened her mouth to scream for help. Water rushed in.

Her throat constricted. She gagged. Her chest seized, trying to summon a cough, but her lungs resisted, determined to hold on to what little air they contained.

Desperate to get out, she flapped her short arms like a fish moving its fins. But an eddy was sucking her downward, pulling her farther beneath the surface. A whirlpool had been created by a bend in the river, the bottom scooped deep by countless floods.

Again, she flailed her arms and kicked her legs. The water above her grew deeper, heavier, pushing her down. She closed her eyes. This was not happening. She was not here. She was back at the cabin, safe in her sleeping bag beside the fire, dreaming. That was all.

A weight squeezed her ribs. Her lungs ached. Pressure pushed outward from within.

Once more, she kicked, extending her legs far. Her foot caught on something. She yanked it toward her — or tried to, but the thing held her firm, pressing sharply against the sides of her foot. She'd caught it between two rocks, wedged it there somehow.

Panic gave way to despair and quickly became resignation. Opening her eyes, she looked up. Saw light, white and warm. In that halo of hope, there appeared her parents' faces and beside them Maura, smiling sadly.

Hannah smiled back.

A fish swam by, paused before her face. Its mouth opened, shaping a word: *Listen.*

"I am. I hear you."

It wiggled its head up and down, as if nodding. And then with a flick of its fins, it was gone.

Tranquility filled her. Happiness. She was floating, weightless, no longer tired or afraid.

Out of nowhere, a hand clamped on her wrist and wrenched her free.

19

chapter 5

Echo

Caution isn't the same as fear. To be cautious simply means being alert and careful. Which I always was. Because it kept me safe. To be afraid is to be certain of a bad outcome. And I wished to ensure a good one.

Which was why I ran. Because I would not risk my fate in the hands of a stranger. I trusted myself, not that man I did not know. The river had swallowed me, sucked me into its icy depths. But I had battled for my life and won. And for hours more I had wandered on my own, undaunted, determined. Tired, hungry, yes. But alive. A survivor.

And alone. Which suddenly seemed like not such a good thing. I missed my mother, although my memories of her were vague. For a few short weeks, she had fed and cleaned us. Indifferently, perhaps, but to us she had been our whole world. When we all got our teeth, she had dug under the fence and run, never looking back. As if her freedom meant more than caring for us.

I had heard Ed mutter, as he filled the hole, that she hadn't been worth the trouble and it was a good thing the truck had flattened her just down the road from their house. I knew that meant she wasn't coming back. For the most part, I had had little interaction with Ed, which was a good thing. He was a heartless man.

Carol, however, had shown a trace of kindness. She fed us, patted us on the head sometimes, and cleaned our pen, although not often enough. My siblings had thought nothing of rolling in their own filth. Yet I missed them now, even as smelly as they were. Missed the shared warmth of their bodies when they piled one atop the other to doze contentedly. Missed the joyful yips and growls as they tumbled and played. The way they cleaned my ears and washed the gruel from my face after mealtime.

Yes, I even missed that thin, tasteless slop that Carol had fed us after mother left. It had filled our bellies, although I suspect there was something not quite right with it, as my stools turned from firm and my bowel movements regular, to watery and unstoppable. It felt as though my insides were being scoured out with each poop — or squirt, rather. Every time Carol had to clean up those messes, she cursed at us and pushed us away. She even turned the hose on us. Still, the next time she brought the slop, we devoured it. It was better than nothing. Puppies are always growing and growing means being hungry.

Nothing was what I had in my stomach now as I ran through the woods blanketing the hills above the river. I could endure the cold as long as I kept moving, but hunger sat heavy like a stone beneath my ribs. My stomach twisted in on itself. My bowels cramped. Finding food became my sole objective. If that man, the one who wanted Faustine, were to offer me food right now, I would take it, no matter the risk, because my hunger was becoming so bad that my energy was draining rapidly away. I was already tired from nearly drowning in the river and trying to swim free and all the miles I had covered that morning. But no matter how far I went, I found nothing to eat. I tried chewing on grass, but that only made me retch. I vomited a clear fluid that tasted vaguely of river water.

I had to rest. After a while, I could go on, search some more. So I looked for a place to lie down. Somewhere safe where I could not be seen by others.

A wind began to blow, cold and damp, carrying on it the scent of rain. The sun was now low in the western sky. A blanket of clouds began to obscure its light, driving the chill of early winter deep beneath my fur. But in that fading light, I saw an outcropping of rock halfway up a hill nearby. My feet aching, my legs weary, I climbed that hill, driven by the promise of sleep and safety.

Great slabs of stone, leaning at angles against one another, formed a roof. I ducked beneath the top slab, grazing my head. The first drops of rain pattered upon the frozen ground outside, but in here I was dry, if not warm. I went to the very back of the little overhang and there the wind ceased. After circling around several times, I lay down on a nest of dried leaves. As I tucked my legs in close and rested my chin on my front paws, I thought of Faustine, that droopy scrap of fur that for a short time had belonged to me.

I even missed her.

—o00o—

I awoke sometime in the night. It was a while before I remembered where I was. On my belly, I scooted to the edge of the little cave and watched. Between shifting patches of clouds, moonlight shone down, etching branches in silver. Wind moaned softly through the trees, gathering to a roar as it rushed down to the valley, then dying away as it met the hills' broad swell of earth.

Here, I was safe from wind and rain and cold. But I was still not fed and I was still very much alone. Come morning, I would have to leave.

So I did, when the sun returned, pale and distant, beyond the eastern treetops. This time, after taking a drink from the river, I went straight toward the rising sun. I had grown used to the hunger, but my legs shook with weakness. Slower and slower I went, stumbling often.

Twice before the sun was overhead, I had to stop and sleep. When I woke up again the second time, the sun was hidden behind gray clouds. I was disoriented. And so I picked a place where the hills parted and went that way, even though I was aware that it smelled more and more like humans. But where there were people, there was food.

As I reached the edge of the forest, I paused to gauge my surroundings. In the distance was a cluster of buildings. Cars and trucks rumbled along the road that led there. But well before the town sat a house. A small house where an inside light glowed through drawn curtains. To the side of that house was a shed. With chickens.

Oh, glorious bounty! A buffet of feather-covered meat. Saliva filled my mouth.

Carefully, I wormed my way closer, hiding behind trees, watching to make sure the humans did not see me. A clothesline stretched from a hook at the corner of the house to a rusted metal pole. Bed sheets dangled from clothespins, the damp fabric stiff from the cold, obscuring the view to the house.

When I was within striking distance, I hunkered low next to an empty trash can, twitching with excitement. I studied the pen, trying to figure out how in the heck to get in. There was a gate, but the latch was up high and by the looks of it too sturdy for my puppy teeth. In one corner of the chicken-wire fence, a gap yawned, just big enough for a young dog like me to squeeze if I flattened myself and wriggled through.

Yes, there.

To be truthful, I never thought I would actually need to hunt for my supper. I wasn't sure I could. Yet if I didn't, I could die right here, writhing in hunger, my lips contorted in a snarl of pain. I stepped out from beside the trash can, being as quiet as I could.

23

A gust of wind stirred the sheets. They snapped loudly, then fell. I jumped back, but when I saw there was no one there, I went forward again.

A hen lifted her head, having caught sight of me. I froze. She swiveled her tiny yellow beak side to side, beady eyes glinting in the fading light. Unconcerned, she lowered her head again and scratched at the dirt. Another hen clucked, but did not look my way.

There must have been twenty of them. If I ate one right away and carried another off with me, I would be full enough for a few days, at least. I could return later as needed.

But what if they sounded the alarm well before I was inside? I pondered it. Unlikely. They were all too busy searching for bugs and weed sprouts to eat.

One last time, I glanced toward the house. No cars sat outside it. No voices came from within. No shadows moved across the window. It was possible they weren't even home. In which case, I could feast to my stomach's content.

And while the thought of it revolted me, if I wanted to survive, I *had* to do this.

By the time I pushed my nose into the space between the wire and the dirt, the chickens had gotten used to me. Because I had approached slowly. I took in the distance to the house, how far back from the road it sat, where the back door was, and considered the nearest hiding places for future raids.

Unfortunately, there was no alternate escape route once I was inside the pen. The best course, I decided, was to take one chicken and run. I could eat it elsewhere, then come back later if I didn't find an alternate source of food.

It was all going so well. Bolstered by the thoroughness of my plan and the ease with which it was unfolding, I slid underneath. When my rump was free of the fence, I stood.

Their heads snapped up. They scuttled into a clump. A murmur of clucks rose to a cacophony.

They were on to me. I had to work quickly.

I dove at the nearest pair. They divided, one darting one way, the other bursting upward in a flurry of feathers. A smaller hen flapped frantically before me. I snapped at a wing, but caught only air. Twisting sideways, I scurried after a huddle of them in the corner. But the little monsters were quick, exploding in ten different directions. I slammed a paw down, pinning one to the ground. It squawked, an ear-splitting, gut-twisting sound. I yanked my paw back, startled.

Remorse overcame me, filling me with a sickening feeling. I wanted to nuzzle it, lick the underside of its mouth, and soothe its overblown fears. I could never have killed one of them. Never. I would sooner die of hunger than hurt another creature.

Turning around, I sought my retreat. Confusion and terror reigned. Chickens, once agitated, apparently do not settle easily. They were now in full-blown hysterics. Wings beat frantically. They clucked and clawed and raced around as if their heads had become detached from their bodies.

At last, opportunity appeared. The opening in the fence gaped wide on the other side of the enclosure. I started for it, but pulled up short as a bigger chicken strutted before me. He had a big red comb atop his head that flopped to the side and a wattle beneath his chin that dangled conspicuously. Long shiny tail feathers trailed behind him like the hem of a royal robe. At the back of each foot was a long talon, sharp enough to puncture flesh. Arrogance glimmered in his piercing black eyes. Since he was the only male there, no doubt he had killed the others. This was a creature to be feared and respected.

Averting my eyes, I backed away. Somehow, I had to get around and past him. But the hens were bunched to either side of me. If I forced my way between them, they would raise a ruckus again. Even so, if I was quick enough, I could still get away without being discovered.

I went left, keeping my movements smooth. The hens collided into one another. Which incited the rooster. He came at me, wings outspread as he launched himself upward. I ducked just in time to evade being sliced by one of his talons. He hit the ground and tumbled sideways. I sprinted for the opening before he could recover and come at me again.

Too late.

Because just as I was only a few feet away, a pair of boots stomped before me. The gate slammed shut. I skidded to a halt, the top of my skull smacking squarely into a pair of knees. Rocking back, I looked up.

Just in time to see the trash can swooping down over me.

The metal rim banged down on the ground around me. I had barely pulled my right rear foot inward in time to avoid having it pinched. If my tail had been longer than a stump of two vertebrae, it would have been squashed.

An old woman's cackle rang out. She thumped a hand on top of the trash can, her words garbled by guffaws. The tinny noise reverberated down to my bones. I tried to flatten myself, but I couldn't.

My second impulse was to run, but I sat there in darkness, trapped. My breathing quickened. My heart hammered against the inside of my rib cage.

Then, a slice of light appeared along the ground. A hand groped beneath. I scooted to the back of the trash can, wary. She latched onto a rear foot. I bucked against the side of the can. It toppled backward. But instead of leaping free, as I intended, I tumbled farther inside the trash can.

Thin fingers snagged the fur of my ruff and pulled me close. I had no time to think. A shame I was not given to swifter reactions. Any one of my siblings would have sunk their teeth into her bony hand. But I was too slow, too cautious. Some of the strangers who had come to visit and take a puppy home had referred to me as 'timid'. They had meant it as a weakness, a flaw, which I took offense to.

In this case, I suppose it was.

She clutched me tight, limping toward a smaller building that I had not seen on the other side of the house. Her long gray braid swung before my face, begging to be pulled.

"Think you were gittin' a free supper, did you? Law says I can shoot strays that maraud my chicken coop, if'n I wanna. But you don't look like the sort could do much harm. Damn rooster was about to beat the tar out o' ya." She cackled again, hugging me tighter. Sharp ribs poked at my side. She was old, shrunken, and wiry, yet her grip on me was so strong I could barely breathe.

Before we reached the small building, she reached inside her pocket and tapped something. A large door moved upward, hinges squealing. There, in the hazy half-light, sat an old van. She pulled open the rear door and deposited me inside a cage and latched it shut. It reeked of chicken manure. She climbed into the front seat, pulling herself close to the steering wheel so she could see over it. Two thick pillows were piled beneath her. Her feet barely reached the pedals.

Hands shaking, she fitted a key into its slot and started the engine. It coughed in protest several times before purring to life. She backed the van up and headed out onto the road. The van jerked with each turn or change in speed she made.

If there had been anything in my gut, I would have puked, so she'd stop.

I only hoped this would be a short ride. Because in my limited experience so far, car rides were never good.

chapter 6

Hunter

Hunter McHugh's long legs wheeled uncontrollably as he sped downhill. His heart beat erratically, racing like he was high on amphetamines one moment, then skipping and thudding the next. In his forty-two years, he had never known pure and absolute panic like this. Not even the first time he had died.

Right now, though, that was the furthest thing from his mind. It was his five-year-old daughter, Hannah, who he was thinking about as he plummeted toward the river. The crook formed by the river's abrupt change of course harbored a deep pool, where brownish spume collected in pockets formed by broken branches and large rocks that had tumbled downward from higher up in the valley eons ago. Hunter prayed that Hannah was lying somewhere among those small boulders, on land, with nothing worse than a broken arm or slight bump on her head.

Two men and a woman from the Adair County Fire Department were on the bank at the bend in the river. One of the men had a rope around his waist and scuba gear on. The woman coiled up the slack before handing it to the second man, who clambered up the steep bank and secured the end of the rope to the trunk of a sturdy sycamore.

Hunter faltered in momentary confusion, taken aback by their actions. He checked himself from tumbling into the river by slamming his palm into a boulder. Lungs burning, he sucked in precious air. The muscles of his legs seized and he leaned against the rock for support. His hand wandered to his chest to press against the scar beneath his clothing.

No, she can't be ...

Bile burned the back of Hunter's throat as the man wearing the wetsuit slid from the bank into the water. In one hand, he held a long metal crook. He sank up to his midriff, then began to slog forward. The muck on the river's bottom must have been deep, because he labored like he was marching through quicksand.

Turning his wrist over, Hunter checked his watch. Too much time had elapsed since they discovered Hannah gone from the cabin that morning. His older daughter, Maura, who'd been sleeping in her bunk downstairs had awoken first. Hungry, she'd rummaged around in the coolers they'd packed the day before. Hearing noise downstairs, Hunter crept down from the loft and when he noticed Hannah was not curled up in her bunk, he asked Maura where her little sister was. She looked back at her father and shrugged, perplexed. Immediately, they woke his wife Jenn up and began to call for Hannah. She was not in the cabin or the truck, nor anywhere nearby. They broadened their circle, shouting and whistling for her as they arced outward through the trees, keeping within sight of their cabin.

Despite the dread tightening his chest, Hunter had tried to remain calm. If Hannah was hiding and thought she was in trouble, if there was any trace of tension in any of their voices, she might not come out. She was, in a word, sensitive. Not just emotionally, but she was acutely aware of every sensory input: sounds, smells, tastes, movement. So much so that by the time she turned two, they'd had her tested for autism. The verdict was that she was a highly functioning autistic. Opinions had shifted since then, sometimes almost weekly, but suffice it to say she was in no way ordinary.

Still, the experts had recommended placing Hannah in a special school, which would have meant moving to another state. Hunter thought it would be in Hannah's best interest to relocate wherever their daughter could get the special guidance she needed. It was Jenn who resisted, burying herself in research, insisting that what Hannah needed most was the love of her immediate family and one-on-one attention. Jenn quit her job as the manager at Adair County's largest bank. Schooling Hannah became her primary focus, but she did her best to make sure that Maura's upbringing was as normal as possible, signing her up for softball and 4-H, chaperoning Maura's class field trips whenever she could find someone to look after Hannah, and making a point of scheduling regular family outings like this camping trip. Still, Maura was resentful sometimes, and even though Hannah seemed unaware of it, Maura was often quick to show a spark of jealousy.

On that morning, however, it had been Maura who discovered the imprint of Hannah's small sneakers on the trail leading away from their campsite. And Maura who now came to a crashing halt beside him, hyperventilating as she gulped air in between sobs.

"I'm sorry. I'm so, so sorry, Dad." Maura's whole body trembled. She hugged herself, trying to stop the shaking. It wasn't until Jenn reached them and wrapped her arms around her daughter that she began to settle.

"It's not your fault, Maura." Jenn kissed the top of Maura's head and smoothed the hair that hung down her daughter's back.

Maura shook her head vehemently, dark brown hair whipping across her cheeks. "But it *is* my fault. I was awake for probably fifteen minutes before Dad woke up. If I'd only looked, noticed she wasn't there ..."

While Jenn soothed Maura, Hunter stared on as the diver systematically prodded beneath the surface with his metal crook. Hunter shifted around to the side of the boulder to get a better view. That was when he saw the bright pink cloth floating at the top of the water. The current tugged at it, whipping it left, then right, then pulling it under for a second before spitting it back up.

Like a flag run up the mast of a ship, it was unmistakable: the hood of the sweatshirt that Hannah had gone to sleep in last night.

Please, God, no. Not Hannah. Just let it be her sweatshirt, nothing more. Not her. Please don't let it be her under there.

It seemed to take forever for the rescue worker to reach it. He dipped the crook beneath the water, searching with the end of it. It took far less time for him to discover what was beneath the surface.

"Got something!" he shouted.

Not someone, but some*thing*.

Maura and Jenn went silent, breaths held. A lead shot plunged through Hunter's gut as the realization hit him that they had found Hannah's body. Hunter cursed at himself. This was his fault. He had urged them to remain calm while searching for Hannah, certain she was nearby and not wanting to scare her off. But in trying to be the voice of reason, he had cost them precious time. Twice, Jenn had asked if they should call 911, but Hunter had said 'Not yet. She's got to be around here somewhere.'

When Maura found the tracks leading away from the cabin, it was Hunter himself who made the call. As they waited for help to arrive, he had jogged along the path at the river's edge, searching for any sign of Hannah. The answer came with the sighting of a dog, a young black and white Australian Shepherd, three to four months old, if Hunter was right. The pup held Hannah's stuffed giraffe, Faustine, in his mouth. He looked more afraid than harmful. Evidently, he had found Faustine beside the river, judging by how wet it was. Hoping the pup might lead them to Hannah, Hunter had called to him, but he dropped the stuffed animal and ran, away from the river.

Instinctively, Hunter had turned toward the river. He found Hannah's footprints again. They disappeared beside the river. There, the grass was flattened, as if she'd been lying beside the bank. There were no more footprints in either direction. No further sign of where she might have gone but in the water.

It had taken another fifteen minutes for the rescue workers to reach them and eight more before they stopped at this bend in the river.

Too much time.

If she'd fallen in where her footprints were last found and been swept downriver to here, it could have been as much as forty minutes since then.

Too much damn time.

Suddenly, the man in the wetsuit buried the straight end of his pole in the river's bottom. "Hang on!" he called over his shoulder, before flipping down his scuba mask and diving under.

A cloud of mud drifted up from the murky bottom, obscuring any view the rest may have had of his whereabouts. Only the bubbles emanating from the water's depths betrayed his location. Twice, he emerged, empty-handed. Twice more, he dove down again.

The third time he came up, he was cradling a small, limp form in his arms.

It was Hannah — her skin as blue as glacial ice.

chapter 7

Hunter

By the time the whirr of helicopter blades broke overhead, they had been trying to resuscitate her for six minutes. Hunter meant to stop checking his watch. It was better not to know. But what else was there to do when all you could do was stand by helplessly as your child's life hung by a fraying thread?

"Still no pulse," Hunter heard one of the rescue workers say.

"Keep working," the other replied. "The water was ice cold. There's always a chance."

The chopper landed on a grassy patch about a hundred yards from where they'd found Hannah. The three rescue workers, who'd been alternating CPR the whole time, paused just long enough to hoist her lifeless body onto a stretcher and rush her to the helicopter. Before she was even secure, they resumed chest compressions. One of the chopper medics relayed information to the on-ground first responders, then the door slammed shut and up Hannah went, an angel ascending.

"They're taking her to Somerset Community Hospital," the

female rescue worker said as the helicopter grew smaller and smaller against a grim and wintry sky. "You can follow us there."

"How far is it?" Jenn's hand drifted to Hunter's. She laced her fingers through his.

"By car? Thirty-five minutes normally, but if we turn on the sirens, we can probably cut close to ten minutes off. It's mostly highway."

Twenty-five minutes before they'd know Hannah's fate. Twenty-five minutes before they could see or hold her again. So short a time in the overall scheme of things. And yet so long.

Minutes later, all three were in the truck, Maura gripping the sides of her mother's seat from the back of the crew cab. They left all their belongings behind. Hunter wasn't even sure he'd locked the front door of the cabin or closed it all the way. If the bears wanted to raid their food stores, it was an insignificant sacrifice. Thieves could even take all their stuff. It didn't matter. They had to get to Hannah's side. She would sense that they were there. She would fight. Surely.

Hunter's knuckles whitened as he gripped the steering wheel, trying to keep up with the ambulance as it tore over the dirt road and out onto the two-lane state highway. The journey at first was slow as they navigated the winding road. The shoulder was narrow, dropping off on either side to sheer-sided cliffs or abutting tree-choked hills. One misjudgment and they could plow into a tree trunk or plunge down a ravine.

Soon, they turned onto a divided highway, straight and gently rolling. Cars veered to the shoulder, yielding, as the siren blared. Throughout the trip, none of them spoke. What could they say? That they hoped Hannah would be revived? That they feared she might not? That they were praying for a miracle?

Hunter refused to submit to his worst fears. He, of all people, knew that death was never a given, no matter how bleak the situation.

And bleak it was when they arrived at the hospital. They were herded into a dimly lit, empty doctor's office, their initial inquiries as to Hannah's condition met only with promises that someone would be with them shortly.

Sitting next to each other on the couch, Maura leaned against her mother's arm as Jenn stroked her knee. Hunter sat in a leather armchair next to them, his elbows digging into his thighs, his hands clenched together in a knot.

Every now and then, someone passed by the glass wall separating the office from the corridor and Hunter would launch from the chair, go to the glass, then pace a few lengths of the room before sitting back down. Finally, the door clicked open.

"How is she? Can we see her?" Jenn begged of the nurse who came into the office.

The nurse, who looked almost too young to have even graduated from nursing school, glanced in the hallway behind her. "I'm sorry. I don't know. Really." Frowning, she tilted her head in sympathy, then looked toward the certificates lining the wall in the office. "But she's in the best hands possible. If you need anything, I'm just down the hall at the station."

Then she went, leaving the three of them in profound silence.

The leather of Hunter's chair squeaked as he twisted around to view the framed certificates. They were advanced degrees for a Dr. Danielle Townsley from Cornell and Johns Hopkins, as well as more specific ones indicating specialized training in pediatric surgery and emergency medicine. Credentials enough to merit her being in some bigger hub than Somerset Community Hospital. It made him wonder why she would have chosen to be employed here in small town Kentucky. The pay couldn't be the reason. Maybe she had family around here?

He went to the desk and turned a photo around. It was of a woman with light blond hair, perhaps in her early thirties, with sharp cheekbones and model good looks that hinted at a Scandinavian heritage, her face clean of makeup and her hair pulled back into a loose bun. On one hip, she held a dark-skinned baby with large doe-like eyes. Clustered around her were several more African children, their feet dusty and their smiles big. They stood before a round hut with low walls, its pointed roof fashioned from some kind of reed or grass. They looked happy. She looked happy.

Beside it was a smaller photo of her in a wedding dress, somewhat younger, and her equally attractive groom standing behind her with his arms around her waist, as he planted a kiss in the crook of her neck. Hunter picked it up, studying it, wanting to believe that this was a woman not only of great compassion, but capable of performing miracles.

Footsteps sounded just outside the door. Hunter was still holding the wedding photo when Dr. Townsley walked in wearing scrubs. She paused for a moment, staring at the picture in his hands, her weary face hardening.

Without introduction, she marched past him, pulled out the chair behind her desk, and sat. She folded her hands together on the desktop and gazed at each of them in turn.

Hunter planted his knuckles on the desk and leaned toward her. "Please, don't keep us in the dark any longer. We need to know."

"If she's going to live, you mean?" she said point blank.

Jenn inhaled sharply and pressed herself against the back of the couch.

"Yes," Hunter said. "Were they able to revive her?"

"No." The word fell like a nuclear bomb in the small confines of her office. But upon seeing Jenn start to weep mournfully, Dr. Townsley plucked a tissue from the box on her desk and handed it to her, then returned to her seat. "They weren't able to get her heart beating by the time she arrived here. However ... she was submerged in icy water for well over half an hour. That may just have saved her life."

Hunter glanced at Jenn, but her eyes were scrunched closed, the unused tissue wadded in her fist. He turned back to the doctor. "We don't understand."

"Of course not," she said almost smugly, sighing as if it were too much of a chore to bother explaining. She rocked back in her chair, two fingers pressed to her temple. "By the time your daughter Hannah came to Emergency, she wasn't breathing and she'd been without a pulse for nearly an hour. Our monitors detected no cardiac activity, either. Her pupils were dilated, a possible indication of brain damage, but certainly not definitive."

Inside, Hunter cringed at the news. None of it was good. Why didn't she just get to the point? Tact was one thing; evasiveness was another.

Dr. Townsley reached inside a small fridge next to her chair and pulled out an energy drink, the kind with dangerous amounts of caffeine. Her lips tilted in a smirk. "Allow me this one vice, will you? Bringing patients back from the verge of certain death is very draining."

Hunter wasn't sure if she meant Hannah or someone else — there'd been a young family involved in an auto accident already being treated before they got there with Hannah — so he sat down next to Jenn, prepared for the blow he hoped wasn't coming.

She popped the tab open with long fuchsia fingernails and chugged a few swallows before continuing. "Fortunately for Hannah, her first responders are a stubborn crew. They tend to work harder on children because their bodies are so resilient. Or maybe because they have kids of their own, I don't know. Anyway, they kept forcing air into her lungs and doing chest compressions, effectively massaging her heart and forcing blood to move through her veins.

"We were notified of her impending arrival. Luckily, I happened to be on duty. Had I not been ... Well, we won't go there. Let's just say that not all doctors are equal. We hooked her up to a bypass

37

machine, gradually introducing warmed fluids into her veins and warm air into her lungs."

Alert now, Jenn inched forward on her seat. "So her heart's beating now? She's going to be okay?"

"Oh ... no. Not yet. We're still working on her in ICU. I just wanted to keep you apprised of her treatment."

Jenn gripped her knees murderously. Hunter clamped a hand on her thigh to keep her from leaping forward and throttling the doctor. But it didn't stop her from speaking her mind.

"You're telling us that after an hour she's still not breathing and her heart hasn't beat on its own, yet you've got this all under control? How is that?"

"I urge you to remain calm, Mrs. McHugh. We're using the most advanced science to —"

"I'll calm down" — Jenn shot up from her seat, hands clenched like hammers at her sides — "when you let me see my daughter and tell me what's going on with her!"

Unruffled, Dr. Townsley slowly stood. She tugged her surgical cap farther down onto her forehead and collected her energy drink. "I'll tell you when I know something for sure. Our team is rewarming her gradually from the inside out. It takes time to do it right. And we won't know the full extent of her condition until later. Much later."

She started toward the door, then turned around, her voice sincere and confident. "Anyone else would have given up on her by now. Lucky for you, I'm not anyone else."

chapter 8

Echo

My luck was not going well lately. I'm not sure what I was expecting, but this sure wasn't it.

The old woman who captured me took me to a building on the edge of town. On the outside it was plain, made of cement block. Not a home, or a barn, but some other place with a distinct and perhaps sinister purpose. I sensed it far down in my gut, like a little worm there nibbling at my insides.

She hauled me from the cage and tucked me against her gaunt ribs. The moment she shoved the rear door of the van shut, they started — a chorus of dogs barking with a mixture of fear and excitement. I quivered in response, imagining that inside was a pack of them, ready to devour me whole. I squirmed in her grasp, but she clutched me tighter, her hold surprisingly strong, and shuffled toward the front door.

As soon as she opened it, the stinging odor of urine hit me full force. And not just that of dogs, but cats, too, which repulsed me even more. I had always handled my business neatly, eliminating in the farthest corner of our pen and making certain not to tread in it later. Apparently, the animals in this place had no such manners. They were savages. Wild things. And I did not relish being among them.

Inside, the sounds were even louder and more of them. Barking, nails scrabbling on concrete, the rattling of metal. Behind the counter that the old woman went to, another woman sat. She was broad-framed and wore a sour look as she scratched at a piece of paper with a pen. A phone was pressed to her ear. For several minutes, she ignored the old woman, speaking back into the phone, then writing more, and sometimes stopping to tap at a keyboard.

The old woman cleared her throat as she shifted me to her other hip. I kicked as hard as I could, trying to free myself, but she grabbed the hair at the back of my neck and held on. If I tried to jump, she'd dangle me by my fur.

"Can I —?" the other woman began. Her face relaxed. "Oh, Delores. Not a cat this time, huh?"

"Nope. Think I already got 'em all. This little varmint here was in my chicken coop." She thrust me onto the slick counter. My legs splayed out from beneath me until I was plastered flat on it. "Cute, in an awkward kind of way, don't you think, Evelyn?"

"Did it kill any birds? Because you know what we do with dogs that kill livestock."

I peered over the edge of the counter, judging the drop to the floor and distance to the door.

Delores drew me back to her chest. "Aw, hell no. Pretty harmless little thing. Kind of shy, actually. Rooster Cogburn was beating the holy heck out o' him."

"You don't say? Hang on a minute, will you?" She resumed talking on the phone.

A minute turned into two, which turned into ten. My left leg was going numb where Delores's elbow was pressing into it. Two other people passed through an adjoining hallway, toting bottles of pungent liquid, an armload of towels, and empty buckets. Shortly after that, a mother and her small child were escorted out into the reception area. The little boy clutched a small kitten, which looked absolutely terrified. It hung, mewing and wailing, from his sweater by its nails.

The little boy dragged a sleeve across his runny nose. "I wuv my key cat, Mawmy."

"What are you going to name him?" the mother asked.

He squeezed the kitten so hard its eyes bulged. "I gonna call him Bwocko."

I shuddered in sympathy, wishing I could free the poor kitten from its suffering. Even though I detested cats.

"Brocko?"

"Aft da pres'dent — Bwocko Bama."

She blinked several times. "Ohhh, okay."

Evelyn slammed the phone down in its cradle. Digging her hands through her short, flame red hair, she rolled her eyes. "Some people! You just want to … Never mind." She shook her head, forced a smile. "Anyway … Let me take care of these other folks, Delores, then I'll take this pup off your hands, all right?"

"All right," Delores said, although she didn't look too happy about having to wait even longer.

Delores claimed one of two plastic chairs in the tiny reception area, placing me on her lap. Right next to the door. Which unfortunately opened on the other side. Still, if I timed it just right, there was a chance when the boy and his mother went out that I could make a break for it.

So I sat there calmly, furtively glancing at the door from time to time, calculating my trajectory and speed, and speculating what I would do once I bolted to freedom. First, I had to get as far from this place as possible. Second, I would avoid chickens at all costs. No matter how hungry I was. They could be dead, plucked, and served on a platter. I wasn't ever going to go near them again. Lesson learned.

The mother filled out a lengthy form as Evelyn explained it to her. Beside her, the boy fidgeted. He stroked his kitten as he eyed me with mounting curiosity. I lowered my head and shifted away from him. He was very impolite. His stare made me uncomfortable.

Soon, Delores was leaning against the wall, her eyelids growing heavy. She propped her ruddy cheek against a gnarled fist and closed her eyes. The lightest of snores tickled her lips. Her arm twitched and her hold on me loosened.

Then, opportunity opened wide before me. The mother had grabbed the doorknob and pulled, tugging the boy behind her. A slice of daylight fell across the linoleum floor.

I jumped — and hit the floor sliding. My front legs flew out before me, while my back legs spun sideways. I fell with a thunk on my side, the wind expelling from my lungs.

Momentarily dazed, I struggled upright. A cool breeze from outdoors blew in my face. I sniffed freedom. In this case, it smelled like leaked engine oil and asphalt. Nails curled, I tried to dig into the floor to vault forward, but it was even slicker than the countertop. I couldn't make my legs do what I wanted.

Whether she was unaware of me or ignoring me, I don't know, but the mother continued on out the door, yanking the little boy behind her as he watched me. The door began to drift shut.

Defeated, I relaxed, letting the pads of my paws come in contact with the floor. As they did, I sensed better traction. I staggered forward a step, then two. Delores was still asleep. The door was still open a crack. I scurried forth, sticking my nose out to wedge the door farther open.

Wham!

Evelyn palmed the door shut. Just as I looked up at her, she looped a leash around my neck, winking. "Almost lost you, little guy. Great big world out there. You don't want to be all on your own, do you?"

I strained toward the door to let her know that was precisely what I wanted.

"Awww, are you scared?" Her voice was gravelly and deep for a woman's. She reeled me in. "Poor wittle fing."

I took offense to her condescending tone. Was I supposed to like this place? Why would I want to stay somewhere that smelled *this* bad? And who was she that I should trust her? For all I knew she had a forked tail hidden under that tent-like sweatshirt and a pair of horns concealed beneath that forest of spiky hair.

"Hey, Delores, wake up." Evelyn nudged the old woman.

A snort ripped from Delores's throat. Startled, she sat up and wiped a string of drool from her chin. It took a few moments for her to come to her senses.

"I'm going to take him in back now, all right, Delores?"

Delores flapped a hand at Evelyn, stood slowly, and shuffled to the door, stumbling slightly on the welcome mat. She went outside without one look back.

Suddenly, I felt the loop around my neck tighten and my whole body sliding across the floor.

"Come on now, little guy. I've got just the place for you."

After I hit the small rug in the hallway and it bunched up under me, she scooped me up, squishing me to her ample chest. It was softer than Delores's chest, at least. But her shirt reeked of cigarettes.

She walked past a metal door. From the crack beneath it, barks and yips rang out. Then we went past a room filled with stacks of metal cages. I caught a glimpse of a cat staring out through the wire grid of one of the cage doors, disdain plain on her patched orange and black face. She yawned, as if bored, then stretched, turning her head as she watched us go by.

We had bypassed the place where the big dogs were kept, the room where the cats were crammed. What could be left?

With a grunt, Evelyn pushed open the door at the end of the hall.

43

It was brightly lit and quiet. A private room, perhaps? Sweet solace. The only thing better would be for her to plunk a bowl of food in front of me.

She lowered me to the other side of a low cinder block wall. That was when 'they' woke up. Puppies. A dozen of them.

No. Just … no.

My feet were barely on the floor when they exploded from their sleeping pile and attacked, licking and yapping, running in mindless circles. One of them peed right next to me, then proceeded to pounce on my ribs, knocking the air from my lungs. Gulping in a breath, I crawled on my belly toward the wall. Three or four more pooped in random places; moments later other puppies raced through the mess.

I watched in horror, shocked at their disregard for cleanliness. From behind, someone sank their teeth into my back. I yelped in pain, but they only bit harder. So I whipped around, my teeth gnashing.

"Hey!" Evelyn grabbed me by the scruff, pulling me away. "Don't start anything. Got it?"

I leered at her. What had *I* started? Was I not supposed to defend myself? Should I just let these heathens maul me?

But now she was getting a dose of it. Two pups had latched onto her shoelaces, while a third bit at her pants leg. She grabbed a metal scooper and banged it on the ground. They scattered. She shoveled up their piles of poop, mopped up several puddles, then spritzed it all with some foul-smelling liquid from a plastic bottle. No wonder they all kept pooping in new places. Who would want to go anywhere near where she had sprayed that toxic stuff?

Next, she brought out several bowls of kibble and placed them around the floor. Chaos reigned momentarily as everyone fought for a spot, but very soon each puppy had a place. Even I found a bowl where only two puppies were inhaling their meal, their long tails swinging happily back and forth. Suddenly, I was very conscious of the fact that I had only a nub, but more than embarrassed, I was hungry.

And so I ate. Until my belly nearly burst.

When they were each done, some of the puppies waddled off, yawning. Others played again, but more lazily, as if resisting the pull of sleep. This was a routine they knew well, which made me wonder how long they had all been here and if any ever left.

When Evelyn finally went, I showed my teeth freely. For the most part, they left me alone, but occasionally one forgot my warnings and tested me again. One by one, they wandered off, leaving me in blessed solitude.

From the nearest corner, another pup studied me. She was brown with black streaks, a whip-like tail, and sleek fur. Her muzzle was narrow, her ears folded close to her head. There was nothing aggressive or idiotic in her mannerisms. A little taller at the shoulder than me but lighter in body, she was graceful in her movements, with kind eyes and elegant long legs.

Unassumingly, she drifted closer, walking a few steps, sitting for a while, passing glances at me, yet looking away the moment our eyes caught. When another pup ran up to her, she averted her gaze, ignoring his playful bow.

We understood each other, this pup and I. Kindred spirits. Old souls reunited from some former life. Or so I would have thought if I believed such things. But I saw in her eyes an intelligence that was lacking in the others. And a certain regality, a gentle aloofness. Like that of a cat.

It was then that I decided, for the first time in my life, that I would make a friend.

I ventured closer and closer. We held gazes longer. Eventually, we sat nose to nose. The room was once again quiet. All the others were sleeping soundly. She lowered her head, turned her muzzle sideways, and licked my chin soothingly, but only enough to declare that she submitted to me, even though I had not demanded it of her. To let her know we were on equal terms, I did likewise. Soon, we were curled

45

next to one another, her head resting across my withers.

Gradually, we drifted off to sleep, content in our newfound companionship.

—o00o—

The door latch clicked open. A man ambled in. He peered down at us through thick framed glasses, his glance moving observantly from pile to pile.

Evelyn appeared behind him as the pups raised their heads, yawning and stretching. "You said you don't have any other pets right now?"

"A fish tank, but that's it. A school of tetras, a few angelfish. They're pretty, but more work than company."

"What did you say you're looking for again, Mr. Beekman?"

He pushed his glasses higher up onto his nose. "Something calm and quiet, I suppose. I don't need something that's going to run wild and knock me over, you know? I just want something that will sit next to me while I read in my recliner. Something that won't need to walk miles and miles every day. One lap around the block is enough when the weather's fair. Most of the time it can just do its business in the backyard. I live alone, so it would be nice to have a dog to talk to and take care of."

Evelyn crossed her arms. "Would you like to look at the cats? We have several that —"

"Good heavens, no." Mr. Beekman sucked his chin back, as if the notion was preposterous. "I'm a dog person, through and through. I want a pet that will care whether I come or go and bark when someone comes to the door." His gaze swept from pup to pup as they began to scamper curiously toward him. He bent over the low wall and held his hand out. A fat yellow puppy nipped at his fingers and he pulled his hand back.

"Is there one here you'd recommend? I might even consider an adult. Something more settled. I'm a nurse at Fox Hollow and I was thinking of taking my dog to work with me. The residents always enjoy it when family members bring pets in. I thought it might be good for them to have one that visited more regularly."

"Hmm, maybe an older puppy, then." She scrunched her mouth up. Then her eyes lit. "You'd like Tinker!"

He scratched at his head. "Which one's Tinker?"

"That one." She pointed toward me.

I sat up. My name wasn't Tinker, but if he wanted to call me that, I just might answer to it. It would take some getting used to and was a bit feminine, if I might say, but I could adjust. If he took me, I would have a home, a place all to myself. He'd said he didn't have any other dogs and didn't want a cat. I could be an 'only'. It'd be just me and him. No one else. Maybe he lived out in the country, far from the road with a big, big yard? Yes, that would be better than running loose, cold and alone, never knowing when I would eat next. I could answer to 'Tinker'. I took a step forward.

But then I remembered my new friend. I didn't want to leave her. So I turned around and settled back down next to her. Opening her eyes, she looked up at the man.

He looked down at her adoringly. "That's Tinker? The brindle one?"

"Yes," Evelyn cooed, "it is."

Like that, my hope was snuffed out.

He reached down to pick her up and brought her to his chest. She folded in his arms like an infant being cradled. He rocked her gently as her tongue flicked out to tickle his chin. "I don't know. She's almost cat-like, don't you think?"

"I can see where you'd say that. Aaron said the same thing the day her owner brought her in. It was an elderly woman who was scheduled for surgery that required a long recovery and didn't have anyone to care for her. Sad situation. Not the dog's fault she's here at the shelter."

"I imagine it seldom is." He looked at me for the briefest of moments. "Shame I can't take the whole lot of them. They all deserve a good home, I'm sure."

If there was even a chance he might take us both ...

My ears perked. I trotted over to him and stood on my hind legs, lifting a paw to scratch at the short wall to get his attention. But he had already turned away and the other puppies were clawing at me, pulling me down.

I caught one final glance of Tinker's doleful eyes before I was buried under a tangle of legs.

chapter 9

Hunter

Severe primary accidental hypothermia. A fancy way of saying that the iciness of the river had been what saved Hannah from the quicker death of drowning. Hunter wasn't so sure it had been a mercy. There were risks, complications. The prognosis was not promising.

Technically speaking, hypothermia was termed 'severe' and considered life-threatening when the core body temperature dropped below eighty-two degrees Fahrenheit. At that stage, the chances of cardiac arrest increased dramatically. At its lowest, Hannah's body temperature had been sixty-eight. She had been submerged for more than forty minutes. Forty minutes of her lungs not drawing air, her heart not beating. How was it even possible that she could survive?

As a veterinarian, the only victims of drowning that Hunter had ever seen had not survived. Still, he understood the medical complexities of it all. When Hannah's lungs could not draw air and her body temperature plummeted, her metabolism slowed to a rate just sufficient enough to keep her alive and keep her internal organs — heart, liver, lungs, and brain — from shutting down entirely.

Even if they could get Hannah's heart going again and get her breathing on her own, the real danger lay in the damage already potentially done to her brain. Brain cells deprived of oxygen, especially for as long a time as Hannah had been underwater, can suffer irreversible harm.

"The possibility of brain damage is very real," Dr. Townsley had told them.

"How real?" Hunter had said pointedly. "Ten per cent, fifty ... ninety?"

"I can't really say. Each case is unique. Young children's bodies are surprisingly resilient. But to be honest, I'd be surprised if she didn't suffer some detrimental effects, given the length of time she was without oxygen. That could be anything from a slightly delayed recovery to permanent brain damage."

"You mean ..." Jenn said hoarsely, "she could be a vegetable?"

"It's possible."

When neither Hunter nor Jenn said anything more, Dr. Townsley added, "If you want us to discontinue resuscitation efforts, we will."

"No, don't stop," Jenn pleaded. "Whatever you do, don't stop."

Hunter took it all in as if from a distance. He wondered if Hannah could hear those around her — or if her soul had already departed and they were only putting off the inevitable. Again, his hand drifted to his chest. He had died before — and survived.

By all accounts, Hannah *should* have been dead, well beyond the point of return. When they pulled her small, limp body from the river, Hunter thought for sure she was. She had looked like the remains of a water nymph, hauntingly beautiful in a morose way — her wet hair hanging lank, her skin translucent, her lips an icy blue. That had been late morning. It was now approaching evening.

Hunter's mother, Lise, and his stepfather, Brad Dunphy, had come to the hospital and taken Maura home with them hours ago. Jenn had been beside herself with worry, pacing the corridor outside

Intensive Care, stopping at the end to stare through the glass window of the door through which Dr. Townsley would occasionally appear to give them updates. Two hours had passed since the last report. Not knowing how she was doing was more unbearable than the first unpromising reports.

Jenn flattened her palms against the door leading to ICU. "She's coming." She spun around and dropped into the chair where she'd left her coat, as if she'd been sitting there all along. Her head folded forward into her hands. "Hold me, Hunter. I'm not sure I'm ready for this."

Watching the door, Hunter draped an arm over his wife and placed a kiss beside her ear. "We'll get through this, honey. It's going to be okay."

Raising her head, she bit her lip and nodded, barely holding back a fresh spate of tears.

The doors swung open. Dr. Townsley trudged toward them, dark smudges of fatigue beneath her eyes, her hair a disheveled mess. She inhaled slowly, let it out.

"Is she going to make it?" Jenn prompted, hands clenched in her lap.

Dr. Townsley untied her surgical mask and stuffed it in a pocket. "Yeah … she is."

With a sob of relief, Jenn collapsed against Hunter. He stroked her back soothingly. But one glance at the doctor's face told him that wasn't necessarily good news.

"So her heart and lungs are working on their own now?" he asked.

Dr. Townsley directed them to follow her into her office around the corner. Once inside, she shut the door and gestured for them to sit.

"She's breathing without help, yes. Her heartbeat's growing stronger. We had to inject her with heparin during rewarming to

51

prevent clots from forming. Fortunately, she didn't suffer any broken bones or a head injury during her accident. Either of those would have exponentially increased the potential for internal bleeding. She opened her eyes momentarily, but we haven't been able to get her to respond yet. Not surprising, though. There is some dilation in her pupils now, which tells us she is regaining some brain function."

She rifled through a stack of papers on her desk, pulled out a few, and hastily signed them. "I want to caution you, however, that she still has a long way to go. We won't know the extent of the effects on her brain for days, or weeks even. She has an extended recovery ahead of her — and I can't make any promises as to which way things will go. Anything could happen still."

"Such as?" Hunter said.

"Well, possible complications include pneumonia ... arrhythmia and ventricular fibrillation ... She could still go into cardiac arrest."

Jenn stood. "You mean, after all this, she could still die?"

"She's been through a lot, Mrs. McHugh." Dr. Townsley straightened, her eyes flashing with indignation. "It's a miracle she's gotten this far. May I remind you that —"

"When can we see her?" Hunter placed himself between Jenn and the doctor. More than anything he wanted Hannah back just as she'd been a day ago: a happy, healthy child, even with all her inherent challenges. But he wasn't sure how much of this roller coaster Jenn could take.

When Dr. Townsley hesitated to answer, Hunter said, "We know she won't be able to respond, but we feel it's important to be with her. We need to see her." *Before it's too late*, he almost added.

Dr. Townsley turned her face toward the door, as if attempting to conceal the sigh that escaped her. "All right. Follow me."

—o00o—

"She looks like an angel," Jenn whispered.

The reference sent a stab of long ago memories through Hunter. When he was a boy, the age Hannah was now, he'd had his first cardiac event. He'd been playing ball with his Australian Shepherd, Halo, in the yard, when suddenly he felt faint. After that, he wasn't aware of anything going on around him. They rushed him to the hospital and in the time that his heart was not beating, Hunter had heard things, seen people. People who had died. He had a sense they were waiting for him, yet were surprised to see him so soon.

The doctors had brought him back from cardiac arrest four more times before he turned nineteen. It was a condition called hypertrophic cardiomyopathy. Simply put, his heart didn't work right, so he was given a pacemaker in his twenties and his health improved.

Still, dying hadn't been as bad as most people feared. The experience for him had been precisely like so many others reported: a light at the end of a tunnel, voices calling, speaking to him, then telling him to go back. It was as if he were waiting for a bus, but whenever one came by he realized it was not the one he was supposed to get on.

It was all so long ago now. His recollections had blurred. Sometimes, he wondered if he had only imagined it all. The mind was a powerful thing.

As he gazed at Hannah, his heart filled with love. She looked so … delicate. Someone had taken the time to brush the snarls from her hair. Gone was the pink hooded sweatshirt with cartoon characters holding hands on the front. Shiny foil blankets wrapped her body, except where tubes and wires were attached. The heart monitor next to her bed beeped at a constant rate. Her pulse was still sluggish, her blood pressure on the low end, but her chest was moving up and down steadily.

They sat with Hannah for a long time, holding her hand, stroking her hair, speaking softly to her. The nurses drifted in and out to record her vital signs and change the IV drip.

"She's doing well, relatively speaking," Dr. Townsley said from the doorway. She was dressed in street clothes, trendy and tight fitting, and wearing a pair of three-inch-high silver heels, her hair freshly washed but hanging damp down her back. A jacket dangled from her fingers, sleeves trailing the floor. "I'm on my way home for the time being. Dr. Pruitt has been apprised of her condition. I told him to call me immediately if anything changed."

"Thank you," Jenn said. "For everything."

She shrugged. "I know it sounds cliché, but I'm just doing my job."

"But not just anyone could have given her another chance, Doctor," Hunter said, going to her and offering his hand.

Dr. Townsley stared at it for a moment before shaking it once lightly, then pulling her hand back and sticking it in her jeans pocket.

"If you don't mind my asking," Hunter said, "what brought someone as brilliant as you here?"

She narrowed her eyes at him, her voice flat. "I do mind. It's personal." She turned, went a few steps out into the corridor, then came back. "Maybe I go where I do because in places like this, Dr. McHugh, people aren't used to seeing miracles every day. I've worked in facilities where the brightest minds in the medical world are on staff. Fact is, nobody appreciates brilliance if it's commonplace. Go someplace like Sierra Leone or Namibia, save a life, and they think you're a god among men." She flung her leather jacket over her shoulder, smirking. "Or goddess."

She marched off down the hall, her steps ringing in the empty corridor. Hunter and Jenn exchanged a glance.

"Personable, isn't she?" Jenn remarked.

He returned to Hannah's bedside. "I wasn't going to say it."

"Yeah, but you were thinking it."

"You always could read my mind."

Jenn drooped back in the chair, staring wistfully at Hannah. "But you were always crap at reading mine. Right now, I'm thinking how tired I am and what a long day this has been. I need to sleep. So do you."

"So what do you propose we do? Take shifts?"

"I don't see any other way. Do you?"

"I'll go first." Hunter patted his pocket to locate his phone. He took it out and checked the battery. "I'm good till morning. You can talk to Maura. She always did listen better to you."

"Yeah, give me the hard job." Standing, she kissed Hunter on the cheek. "Before I go, I thought I'd grab a bite in the cafeteria. It should still be open, don't you think? I can bring you something."

The view through the lone window in the room revealed a half empty parking lot ringed by tall lampposts. The sun was long gone, but the clock on his phone had said only 6:15 p.m. It seemed to Hunter like it was closer to midnight, the day had been that long. Yet in so many ways, time had lost all meaning.

"Hunter, do you want me to bring you anything?" she prodded.

"Oh, yeah, sorry. Coffee would be good."

"I'll bring you a sandwich or slice of pizza, too. I know how jittery you get when there's nothing but caffeine in your system."

Jenn went back to Hannah one more time to sweep her fingertips across her small forehead and down her cheek. "I hate to leave her."

From behind, Hunter wrapped his arms around Jenn. "You need your rest. I'll be right here."

She turned in his arms to gaze into his eyes. "If she so much as blinks …"

"I'll call you. Promise." The kiss they shared was one more of desperate hope than deep love.

Shortly afterward, Jenn brought him a cheeseburger, a glass of apple juice, and a large coffee. In truth, she looked tired enough to fall asleep on her feet. Hunter insisted she take the coffee for the drive home.

When she was gone, Hunter flicked on the TV, if only because the noise made him feel less alone. He dozed off for a while, but woke just before 9 p.m. when Dr. Pruitt came in to check on Hannah. He was an older man, polite, but lacking the intensity that Dr. Townsley had. Dr. Pruitt explained that he would now be handling Hannah's case, as Dr. Townsley, who had merely been filling in for another doctor, was moving to Indiana. Not that Hunter would miss her personally, but he knew that if she hadn't been at Somerset Community, Hannah might not have had this second chance.

That night, Hunter would often drift off to sleep, then awaken with a start, thinking it was morning. Usually, no more than an hour had passed. Always, Hannah was the same: silent, inert, unresponsive.

At 7 a.m., Hunter's phone woke him. It was his mother.

"Any change?"

He stretched his legs, pushed the blanket from his lap. "No, Mom, nothing. I'm sorry. I wish ..." His words trailed away. He didn't know what to say.

"At least nothing else bad has happened, right?" Lise offered, filling up the silence. "I mean, Jenn said there could be all kinds of complications and so far, well, she's hanging in there."

"Yeah, I guess so." Standing, he tried to rub the kink from his neck from sleeping in the chair.

After a few more stilted minutes of conversation, Lise told him she'd be by with Jenn in a couple of hours. Another team of nurses shuffled in and out, plus a new doctor who didn't bother to introduce himself.

Hunter was feeling the pull of sleep again, but he didn't want to miss anything, so when yet another nurse cruised in, he asked if she could stay for a few minutes while he fetched himself a cup of coffee. She offered to get it for him.

"I'm going to take a wild guess," she said, "and say you're a two sugar, two cream kind of guy."

"Spot on."

"Be right back. I'll steal it from the break room, just around the corner."

Resisting the comfort of a chair, he squeezed Hannah's fingers lightly and bent close. "Hannah ... listen."

He was about to say more, but he thought he detected the slightest twitch of her facial muscles. Then her eyelids fluttered. And opened.

His heart nearly exploded with joy. He leaned over her, so she could see his face clearly in the morning light, now pouring through the window.

"Hannah, sweet pea, can you hear me? It's Daddy. You're going to be okay. Everything's going to be okay."

Her eyes darted back and forth, unfocused. Her brow folded in confusion. She tried to move her mouth, but the tube they'd inserted down her throat got in the way. It took a few moments for Hunter to realize she wasn't fully cognizant. *It will take time*, he reminded himself. She'd gone through so much. This was merely one of the steps in her recovery.

He waved his hand just inches from her face. There was no reaction. Next, he snapped his fingers beside one ear, then the other. She turned her head slightly. He spoke her name. Nothing.

Soon, her face fell into smooth, relaxed lines. Her eyes drifted shut again.

Hunter sat down and dialed Jenn.

"How is she?" Jenn asked.

He could barely summon his voice. So many emotions were bubbling to the surface. "She woke up."

"She did?" Jenn's breaths became audible, then turned into snuffles of relief.

The nurse walked in, her eyes searching his face. Hunter took the cup of coffee from her and took several sips, even though it burned his tongue.

Jenn, her breathing calm at last, spoke, "Hunter, what *aren't* you saying?"

He set the cup on the windowsill and pinched his eyes shut. "Jenn … she can't see."

chapter 10

Echo

It quickly became clear that being an older puppy in a selection of much younger, pudgier, and cuter ones was a mark against me. My legs were long like a spider's, my movements more awkward than roly-poly, and my once fluffy fur was now sleek and short. I was smarter and of a more reserved nature, while they were playful and outgoing. When people came and looked us over, I hung back, wishful that Mr. Beekman would return for me and reunite me with Tinker, because from the moment I laid eyes on her, I sensed on some level that I already knew her. But he never did.

With every set of visitors, the other puppies rushed forward to tug on pants legs and lap at faces. I, meanwhile, grew more and more despondent.

The number of puppies dwindled at a sporadic rate. Sometimes three or four departed in a day. Sometimes several days went by when no one came to see us. But with time, we became fewer and fewer.

I should have been happy about this, for it meant my odds of being 'adopted', as Evelyn termed it, were greater. But I was twice as big as the remaining pups now. And not at all as attractive. I sensed the pity as people looked past me, the polite disregard. No one ever called me 'cute' or 'pretty', like they did the other puppies. I knew that attractiveness was an important thing, even though I could not fathom precisely what it entailed. I only knew that I was not.

When the Grunwalds showed up, there were only two of us left. The other puppy, too new to have a name, barked and raced around, beside himself with glee. He was miniature in size and fragile-looking, although he didn't seem to notice how small he really was. I sat against the back wall, resigned to a life in the shelter. Although I still didn't like the smells, they had become tolerable. Perhaps in time I would no longer notice them.

The noise was another matter, however. The volume and relentlessness set me on edge. Every bark was a reminder that if I did not find a home by the time I looked full grown, I would be moved to the kennel runs. There, my fate was questionable. Far fewer people visited that area of the shelter. And it seemed to me that more dogs went in there than ever came out.

The Grunwalds — the parents, a grandmother, and no less than six children — were a boisterous lot. Almost a litter, except that they were obviously of different ages. Since humans seemed to keep their young around longer, I could see the advantage of only having one at a time. Although maybe they did have multiples and there was a shelter where they gave their extra children away? I pondered it and decided this was not the case. I had never seen a human mother with more than one infant at a time. And yet... the two youngest of the Grunwalds were mirror images of one another and both the same height, no taller than their mother's hip.

Evelyn explained that we were both up to date on our vaccines — I had taken my shot stoically, while the others had screamed and resisted — and that whichever pup they chose, they would be given a certificate for a free spay or neuter, whatever those were. Some sort of prize, I supposed.

After a brief exchange with Mr. and Mrs. Grunwald, in which Evelyn asked if they were prepared to commit to a dog for the next ten to fifteen years, to which they of course said 'yes', she excused herself, stating that this mythical Aaron, whom I'd never seen, was not in today and she had to man the front desk again.

Instead of staying behind the low wall and observing the puppies at first like most people, the entire Grunwald family poured into the puppy area. The two identical boys zeroed in on the smaller puppy, passing him back and forth as he wagged his silky tail. The grandmother picked me up, scowled, then set me back down. The two middle children, a girl and a boy, punched each other, then whined to their mother, while the oldest two girls leaned against the wall, jabbing their thumbs at small handheld devices.

"Which one do you want?" the father asked to no one in particular. "And hurry up! We ain't got all bloomin' day."

"This one! This one!" the youngest pair shouted as they jumped up and down, the tiny puppy bouncing in the one boy's arms.

Just as he thrust the puppy at his father, the puppy peed right onto the father's boots.

"Aw, God!" The man backed up, waving his hands in front of him. "Put him down, for crying out loud." His face twisted in disgust. "Mavis, grab the other one and let's go. I'm not taking home a piss-pot for a dog."

"But it's a puppy, Earl." She rolled her eyes at him. "Puppies pee. Besides, you said it was going to be an outdoor dog. So what does it matter? If the boys want the Yorkie-Poo, let them have him. He can stay in the garage when it's cold."

"Look at him, Mavis. The thing weighs four pounds. He's a stuffed toy, not a dog. They'll step on him and squash him flat. They need a bigger dog. A sturdy dog that can take a bit of rough and tumble."

"Then why don't we look at the adults? I saw some real pretty ones standing in them runs when we drove up."

"Get a clue, will you? There's a reason those older dogs are in there. It's prison for dogs. I'm not dealing with someone else's problem. These puppies are from accidental breedings. They's mixes. Healthier than those purebreds you pay a thousand bucks for."

Her gaze falling on me, she sneered. "You just don't want me to have that Pekingese I saw at the pet store. That smooshed-in face was sooo adorable."

"I ain't payin' for no Pekingese, Mavis Veronica Grunwald. So get that out of your thick head right now. You think the ATM just magically spits out free money?"

"They have payment plans," she muttered.

"We're *getting* the big one."

Squinting, the oldest girl looked up from her device. "Something happened to his tail. What's wrong with it? Is it tucked between his legs?"

"It's gone," the second tallest girl said. "S'pose he was in an accident?"

"Maybe he was born that way?" the mother said. "Aren't some dogs born like that, Earl? Like bulldogs? My cousin Johnny had a bulldog with a short little screw-tail once."

"He ain't no bulldog, Mavis. He's black and white. Must be part Border Collie."

That was the first time I realized that sometimes dogs are smarter than human beings. It would not be the last. I was born bobtailed. It was common for my breed, the Australian Shepherd. I'd heard Carol say it many times when people came to look at my litter. My mother had been a dark blue merle, a dazzling patchwork blend of gray with black spots. Her chest and legs were white. I remembered that much of her. Carol had told people our father was a red tri, meaning he was three colors: red, copper, and white. Indeed we had been a motley crew of merles and solids, with varying amounts of white trim, four of the seven of us with copper also on our legs, cheeks, and eyebrows.

I had been the plainest of the bunch, dark-faced and with yellow eyes that spooked a lot of people, judging by their wariness. Strangers had a habit of staring at me, remarking on how different I was — how much plainer, how much quieter, how much smaller. Evidently, it was not a compliment. I had grown since then, but I was still plain and quiet. I have never understood why being calm and less barky was considered a flaw, though. 'Still waters run deep' has a lot of truth to it.

The oldest girl flipped her long brown hair over her shoulder and sneered at me. "He's ugly. Just a plain, ugly black dog with a lil' bit o' white on him."

"We're getting the big one."

"He's shy," Mavis protested. "Don't wanna have nothing to do with us."

"He'll get used to us." Earl grabbed the twins by their coat collars and prodded them out of the puppy area. "Let's go, Tristan and Troy. Come on, the rest of you. My shift starts in an hour and I need to get home and change. Last thing we need is for me to get fired, 'cause ain't no one else puttin' food on the table."

"Now you know I'd be working if it wasn't for my bad back. Can't help that I got a bad back."

"You been on your back way too much, woman." Earl shooed the boys out into the hallway. "No job I know of you can work lying down." Snickering, he lowered his voice. "Well, there's one I can think of… That *is* how I met you."

She punched his arm — and not in a teasing way. "You're just with me 'cause no one else would sleep with you. I know I was your first."

"First, but maybe not my only."

"What's that supposed to mean?"

"Means maybe we wouldn't be together if it weren't for the first accident."

Mavis glanced at the twins through the open doorway, then grumbled, "How do you explain the second, third, fourth, and fifth ones, huh?"

They huddled together, sniping at each other. The middle girl picked me up, her arms clamped around my chest, my back legs swinging freely. She was barely strong enough to hang onto me, but no one seemed interested in helping her.

The rest of the day went like that. Bickering and name calling, shouts and curses. My fur being grabbed, my ears tugged. They placed a snug chain collar around my neck with tags on it. Every time I moved, the metal tags plinked. I didn't like the feel of it, or the sound. Torture. Absolute torture.

As soon as we were inside their double-wide trailer and the middle girl, whose name was Tiffany, set me down, I ran and hid behind the couch. The twins dragged me out.

One tossed a ball down the hallway. "Fetch!" Troy commanded.

I watched it bounce over the stained carpet, smack against a door, and come to a stop. Tristan ran to get the ball.

"Not you, idiot!" Troy said. "The dog's supposed to get it."

"I know. But maybe he doesn't know what 'fetch' means just yet."

Ten more times Troy lobbed the ball down the narrow hall. After a while, I refused to even look at it. I didn't like their shouting, the hollow sound of the ball colliding with the closed door, the dimness of the hall, or their rough hands on me. Eventually, they gave up and went outside.

Wary that they might return, I crept into the kitchen and lay beneath the table. The grandmother was there, chopping vegetables and throwing them in a pot. Then she mixed something in a bowl, formed it into a lump on a spoon, and tossed it into a pot of hot grease that sizzled. After that, she washed dishes and set the table, never once looking my way.

My bladder was getting full. This place didn't exactly smell clean — I could tell a lot of food and drinks had been spilled on the floor and left to soak into the rugs and floorboards — but I didn't want to pee inside. That was just … wrong.

So I stared at her, willing her to notice me, wishing she'd take me outside and let me relieve myself. I stared at her so long my eyeballs were swimming.

Making sure the twins were not within sight, I walked up to her and sat, squeezing my hind legs together to keep the pee from leaking out. I nudged her knee with my nose. She swatted at me. I whimpered. She kicked me in the leg with her heavy leather boot.

Limping, I returned to beneath the table. More time passed. She dried the dishes and put them away, stopping now and then to stir the pot of vegetables or scoop one of the greasy, doughy things out of the other pot and adding more. Desperate for relief, I slinked into the living room.

Although it was still daylight out, heavy curtains were drawn across the window, darkening the room. Only bursts of light from the TV lit the over-full confines. Two couches were shoved against opposite walls. In one, Mavis was stretched out, wearing oversized sweatpants and a football jersey. Three empty beer cans sat on the end table next to her. On the other couch, the oldest girl sat with her legs crossed. I called her Scowler, because that's what she did all the time — scowl.

Scowler glanced up from her handheld device, then back down. "What's he doing in here? Thought y'all said the dog was staying outside."

"Soon as your father gets home from work and gets around to putting some water in the bowl and straw in the doghouse."

A loud noise came from the TV and Mavis jerked upright. A moving picture of a car exploding and bursting into flames flashed

65

across the screen. For a moment I thought it was a window to outside, but then I realized the scene lacked dimension. It also lacked scent. How could they spend so much time watching something that wasn't real? Could anything be more boring?

Mavis squinted at me, fighting sleep. "Take him out, will you?"

"In a bit," Scowler said.

"Now!" Mavis barked.

"I said in a bit!" Scowler shouted back without looking up, even as her fingers flew over the device, tapping away. "Movie's almost over, all right? Geesh, get off my back."

Either Mavis believed her or she'd given up arguing. In minutes, she was asleep. Without a glance in my direction, Scowler marched off to a back bedroom, slammed her door, and turned her music up loud.

I could hear the twins yelling outside, but I hadn't seen the others since we arrived. Earl had gone off to work within minutes of getting home. I went and lay by the front door, hoping Mavis or Grandmother would see me. But neither seemed concerned about where I was, what I was doing, or if I might need anything.

Time to leave a message, bold and clear. I squatted over the welcome mat and emptied my bladder. It soaked through, running out onto the tiled floor to seep beneath a row of cardboard boxes. When I was done, I carefully picked my way around the mess and went back to my spot beneath the kitchen table, where I fell sound asleep — until the front door banged shut.

"Oh my God!" Tiffany screamed. "Is that …? Oh, no. Oh, no, no, no. It *is*!"

She stomped into the living room. "Mooommm! The dog peed a river right in front of the front door. My dance costumes are ruined." Her voice pitched to a shriek. "Ruined! Completely and totally ruined!"

Message received. The contents of the boxes were an unfortunate casualty.

The Grunwalds were not, however, quick learners. Or perceptive. Rather than understanding that they needed to let me outside occasionally, they chose to punish me for doing what nature demanded.

Scowler was coerced — Mavis threatened to shut off her precious phone — into spreading straw in and around the doghouse in the backyard and filling an old metal bowl with water for me. I might have enjoyed the separation from the family goings-on, but the bowl still had a layer of algae on its surface and so the water tasted bad. The straw was damp and had a moldy smell. And I had not been fed since early that morning.

There, Scowler tied me, the limit of my world being the length of a chain that went from a hook on the doghouse to a skinny, leafless tree. As the sun dipped behind distant mountains and the cold settled in, I crawled inside the doghouse. I shivered myself to sleep, my belly rumbling for food.

—o0Oo—

Days and then months passed this way. The collar, that had at first been barely big enough to slip past my ears and over my head, grew tighter and tighter. Whenever I swallowed, the metal links dug into my throat. Sometimes, it even made it hard to breathe.

Things weren't all bad. At least I wasn't subjected to the perpetual disorder and uproar of being indoors at the Grunwalds' house. In my isolation, I was able to observe many things: cars speeding down the road in the distance; squirrels leaping from limb to limb in the nearby woods; and crows swooping through the sky in great clouds, then down to dot an adjacent field as they pecked kernels of corn from the furrowed earth. I watched as storms rolled in from the west and snowflakes drifted down to coat the hills in a glistening blanket of white.

And then, as the days warmed, the grass greened, and the tree branches thickened with buds, rain came down to cleanse the world. If only it could wash the unhappiness from the Grunwalds, too …

But all was not peaceful. I dreaded whenever I saw the twins coming. They often taunted me, bouncing stones off the side of my doghouse as I huddled inside, or poking me with a stick when I ventured outside as they pretended to be knights with swords and I was the dragon. I discovered by accident that me playing dead gave them satisfaction. Troy would plant a foot on my ribs as I lay still and declare me 'slain'; then they would run off, laughing. I was grateful when they climbed on the school bus each morning and just as grateful that the other children took no interest in me. As far as I knew, I didn't even have a name, although I heard Tiffany call me Piss-Pot more than once.

Always, though, I thought of myself as Echo. Echo the Survivor. Echo the Wise.

Every morning, I wished for a friend like Tinker or an owner like Mr. Beekman. And at night when I fell asleep, hungry and chilled, I dreamt of the two of them, him in his chair, her curled up beside him, as he read a book, soft music playing from an old radio somewhere.

chapter 11

Hunter

Ten days after the accident, on a Sunday morning, Jenn and Hunter walked into the hospital room to find their daughter staring at a blank wall.

"Look what I have, sweetie. It's Faustine!" Jenn said, taking the giraffe from her oversized handbag. "And see, she's all nice and clean. I even added another eye and fixed her neck so her head doesn't flop around anymore." She held Faustine out. "What do you think, Hannah?"

Hannah's head turned toward the sound of her mother's voice. She smiled and reached out to receive Faustine.

—o00o—

Maura placed a necklace of shells that she'd made herself in Hannah's palm. Two weeks had passed since Hannah had nearly drowned. In that time, Maura had been inconsolable, weighed down by guilt.

"I want you to know I'm sorry about what happened to you,"

Maura said, folding Hannah's fingers over the necklace. "And I hope everything turns out okay." Sniffling, she rubbed the back of her sleeve across her eyes. "I miss you and I want you to come home. The house is so quiet without you."

Hannah's lips moved and a raspy sound came out.

"What?" Maura said, bending closer so her ear was mere inches from Hannah's mouth.

Hunter put down the bag of clean clothes that Jenn had sent with them. Before he could reach Hannah's bedside, Maura drew back and looked at him in disbelief.

"What is it?" he asked.

Maura glanced at her sister. "She said 'thank you'."

"Are you sure?"

"Positive." She flung her arms around her father and squeezed tight.

"What's this for?"

"Just happy, is all. I'd hug her, but she likes to scream whenever someone touches her too hard, so I'm hugging you, instead." Maura tilted her head back and they shared a smile. "Can I call Mom?"

Hunter handed her his phone, but instructed her to make the call in the waiting area down the hall. He watched her go, then sat carefully on Hannah's bed.

She looked at him through a fog, but when he took her hand, she held on firmly.

"Hannah, sweet pea. You know how badly you wanted a dog for your birthday and, well, we told you that you weren't old enough? I'm thinking maybe we were wrong about that. If we had a dog ... *If* we had a dog, you could probably change his water and brush him sometimes. Maura could walk and feed him. You could both play with him. You'd have to share, though. Would that be okay?"

She didn't respond — not that he expected her to — but he went on anyway. "First, though, you have to get better, okay? And I know it's hard, but when people ask you questions, you have to answer. That way we know you hear us and understand. Okay?"

She nodded, barely, and breathed a single word, "Okay."

—o00o—

A month after she spoke again, the Hannah they took home was not the same girl who had fallen into the river that cold December morning. She was quieter, less curious, and more withdrawn. It still seemed like she was having a hard time grasping thoughts and shaping them into words, but as Dr. Pruitt explained, it would take a while yet for her full mental capacity to return — and her personality might never be completely the same. She'd been traumatized and the effects of the tragedy that had very nearly claimed her life could last well into adulthood.

As far as her motor functions went, however, she was almost normal for her age. Almost. Hunter couldn't help but notice the slight shake in her hands when Jenn handed her a drink the morning they were packing her belongings in the hospital room. Hunter paused as he was folding her pajama bottoms, watching. Hannah brought the cup greedily to her lips. It was mango juice, her favorite. Juice dribbled down her chin. Undeterred, she wiped it away and drank until she had emptied the cup.

He glanced at Jenn, but she was chattering away gaily, so happy to be taking Hannah home. A spot of guilt stained Hunter's conscience. Through it all, Jenn had never given up hope, never wavered; while he had been convinced more than once that Hannah would never again draw breath, or look into their eyes, or speak. Perhaps it was because of what he'd been through himself as a child and then as a young man, but he wasn't afraid of death like most people were. It was not a finality, an ending. It was merely a transition. And what waited on the other side was more beautiful than anyone else dared believe. It was a place not of rapture, but of peace and contentment. Where there was no yesterday or tomorrow, no there or that or then, but simply here and this and now.

He had never spoken of his near-death experiences to anyone. Not even Jenn. How do you explain the hereafter to someone who doesn't believe in soulmates or reincarnation or even God? It wasn't about being secular or religious, though. It was about the spiritual. About believing there was more to any living thing than the body or even the soul. Even Hunter didn't fully understand it. He simply accepted it.

Except for Jenn's monologue, the ride home was quiet. A thin layer of snow had fallen over a coating of ice, making the roads treacherous. Hunter gripped the steering wheel, his knuckles white, going slowly. Salt trucks were a rarity this far south in Kentucky, so he kept to the highways as much as he could, where the constant friction of vehicle tires had at least crushed the sheet of ice into a thick slush.

Every once in a while, he glimpsed his youngest daughter in the rearview mirror. Hannah stared out the car window, expressionless. Even when they pulled into their driveway. Their house was on a five-acre plot carved out of his parents' farmstead. The land had once belonged to a sheep farmer named Cecil Penewit. Hunter had never met him, but Aunt Bernie, who was not really his aunt, had gotten engaged to Cecil the same night Cecil suffered a heart attack and died at the Adair County Fair. Bernadette had graciously taken over managing his affairs, even in the wake of his funeral. The farm was slated to be sold to a land development company at auction, but Hunter's mother had stepped in and made a preemptive offer and the deal was done before it ever went on the block. At the time, Lise had just returned to the area after several years in Covington. She needed a place to raise her children, Hunter and Cammie, and someone to help with them. Bernie, recovering from hip surgery, moved in with them. Lise married Brad Dunphy, the sheriff of Adair County, and later they had a child together, Emily.

After Hunter returned from vet school and took over Doc Samuels' practice, Lise and Brad had gifted him a parcel of acreage, where he built his home. Soon after, he and Jenn started their family. It was an idyllic life, even with Hannah's unique issues. One that Hunter would not trade for the world.

If anything, he realized as the car tires crunched over the limestone gravel of his lane, Hannah's near catastrophe had only served to spotlight everything in life that was precious. When your child's life hung in the balance, matters like material possessions and career or financial ambitions paled in comparison. And quibbles, like who forgot to replace the toilet paper, weren't worth bringing up.

What was more, they had all come through it stronger as a family. Before the accident, Hunter had been immersed in his practice, feeling obligated to answer every after-hours voicemail and taking on new clients by expanding his workday. Jenn had buried herself in reading books and blogs on educating special needs children. Late at night, she'd catch up on internet forums, where parents of such children shared their daily challenges and occasional woes, and celebrated each other's triumphs. Hunter was proud of Jenn for what she'd taken on, but he often felt like she had sacrificed too much of herself and gone as far as smothering Hannah with all the latest methods. It was almost as though she felt that if she didn't do absolutely everything possible that Hannah would somehow fall further behind. Hunter, however, kept his thoughts on the matter to himself, even though Jenn's obsession had compromised their marriage. Having thrown himself into his work, he knew he wasn't much better.

Then there was Maura, in the middle of it all. Thank goodness she was a resilient, outgoing child with so many social connections. She may not have liked all the attention heaped upon her little sister at times, but she loved her just the same. Since the accident, she'd become even more watchful of Hannah, as if she somehow felt

73

responsible for her safety now.

When they stopped, Maura pulled open the rear car door. "Hey there, squirt." Reaching inside, she unbuckled Hannah's seatbelt. "I took care of all your stuffed animals while you were gone, except the ones you had at the hospital. I offered to play with them, but they said nope, they'd wait until you got home. They were sooo excited to hear you were coming back today."

Hunter and Jenn unloaded Hannah's bags from the trunk and started toward the front door. Partway there, Hunter cast a glance at Maura. She threw her hands wide, shrugging.

"No luck?" Hunter asked.

Maura shook her head.

"Here, take this." He handed her a backpack full of Hannah's picture books and set the rest on the ground. "Put it in her room. We'll get the rest."

While Jenn and Maura transferred Hannah's things to her room, Hunter took her into the kitchen and made her favorite lunch of grilled cheese, cut diagonally. Triangles, Hunter learned when she was three, were acceptable; rectangles were not. Rectangles were cause for a screaming tantrum. The week before their trip to the cabin, Maura had handed Hannah half a PB&J — in rectangle form. The noise had been enough to bring Jenn and Hunter running inside from the garage, thinking that Hannah was fatally wounded. But no, it was just Hannah being Hannah, communicating her displeasure over some minute detail in her world being out of balance.

As Hunter sat and ate with Hannah at the tall stools on the back side of the kitchen island, Jenn sorted laundry, while Maura busied herself upstairs arranging the stuffed animals on the shelves and dresser tops. Hunter took advantage of the alone time to reach out to his daughter.

He opened his palm and placed it next to Hannah's hand. She stared at it awhile, but did not reach out.

"Hannah, you're home now. Safe. There's nothing to be scared of, okay?"

She kicked at the cupboards beneath the counter, her toes tapping against the door in a soft but monotonous rhythm. If Maura had been doing the same thing at this age, he would have told her sternly to stop, but this was Hannah and sometimes it was better just to let her do her thing. As Jenn had once explained to him after he tried to stop her once from rocking in her chair in the waiting room of the doctor's office and she erupted into full-blown hysteria, these little tics were soothing to her and took her mind off whatever was threatening to overload her senses. But looking around right now, Hunter couldn't figure out what might be bothering her. Had someone moved the fruit bowl? Rearranged the magnets on the refrigerator? Hunter seldom noticed small things like that, but Hannah was acutely aware of every detail. There was no telling what could set her off. Since the accident, though, she'd been abnormally sedate. He wasn't sure yet if that was a good or bad thing.

Hunter tried asking her other things, like what she wanted to do today. He'd taken the whole day off just to be with her and even if all she wanted to do was sit in front of the TV and watch her princess movies, he was good with that. But all she did was munch on her grilled cheese and stare out the kitchen window. There was nothing there to look at except the naked branches of a tree against a wintry sky. The snow and ice had melted off, so there wasn't even that to look at now.

"What do you see?" he asked.

"Waiting for the bluebird," she said softly.

"It's winter now. Not many birds out there except crows and a few sparrows. You might see some of those."

She kicked harder at the cupboards. "No. Bluebird."

Don't push it, Hunter told himself. *She's talking. That's progress.*

"So have you seen any bluebirds lately?"

She swung her gaze on him. "Yah."

"Where?"

"By the river."

A tingle buzzed deep down inside him. He wasn't sure how far he wanted to take this, but maybe it would give him a clue as to what was going on inside her head. "The river by the cabin, you mean?"

Nodding, she stopped kicking the cupboards and stared at her empty plate. Although she was quiet now, Hunter could tell there were thoughts churning inside her and that she was having a hard time remembering the right words.

"Did it fly away?" he prompted.

Her head snapped up, bewilderment in her eyes. "I don't know. I fell in."

No, it was too soon to go there, he thought. For him, at least. He had nearly lost his daughter. Even though he knew there was more beyond this life, the event was still too raw. Time to change the subject. "Hey, Maura picked out all your favorite movies and put them by the big TV. We can hang out on the couch and watch them and eat snacks all day, if you want. How's that sound?"

But if there was one thing Hannah didn't like, it was a one-hundred-and-eighty-degree turn. Her lower lip thrust out. She began huffing — a precursor to hyperventilating.

"I'm sorry," Hunter hurried to say. "The bird, the bird. Did you want to tell me something about the bluebird?"

She swallowed little gulps of air, her head bobbing up and down.

"Tell me, then. Was it pretty?"

"Yah."

"What else?"

"It flewed."

"Yes, birds are good at that. Wouldn't it be cool if we could fly, too?"

She looked at him blankly, as if he were speaking nonsense.

Hannah may have been in her own little world at times, but she was smart enough to know people couldn't fly.

"It flewed to the river," she said.

And Hannah had followed it. That explained how she ended up there. Maybe she was worried that she was in trouble for going down to the river? Hunter knew he couldn't say anything that might infer blame, but he needed to reassure her. "It's okay, Hannah. Birds are interesting. I could watch them for hours, too. Next time you see a pretty bluebird, you come and get me or Mommy, okay? We want to see it, too."

She swung her feet, not quite hitting the cupboards, but to create a rocking motion. "It talked."

"Aha. And what did it say?" Hunter opened a cabinet behind him and took out a box of cheese crackers. He dumped them on Hannah's plate. She immediately started lining the little squares up, side by side. They'd once bought her animal shaped crackers, but they were not symmetrical and held no interest for her. She refused to eat them.

"Listen," she said.

"I am listening, honey. What did it say? Good morning? Hello?"

"It said, 'Listen'." She popped a cracker in her mouth.

"That's what I said to you when you woke up after … after the accident. I said, 'Hannah, listen'. That was me. Don't you remember?"

"Nope."

Hunter was sure she didn't remember a lot of things while she was slipping in and out of consciousness. Still, she probably had heard him. "Did the bird say anything else?"

Her back and forth movement changed to side to side. Normally, she would have kept at the same motion for hours, exhausting herself eventually. But there was a lot about Hannah that wasn't like it used to be. Hunter recalled a distinct shift in his own perception of the world after the first time he had woken up from being transported to the hospital in an ambulance after having been declared 'dead'. And then there'd been the day earlier that same year when he witnessed both his father and grandfather being crushed under the weight of a farm tractor and dying. Months went by before he would talk to anyone; years more before he spoke to someone outside his family.

Hannah resumed rocking back and forth. "Don't r'ember."

Hunter had to resist correcting her. Her speech had been perfect before, but Dr. Pruitt warned them there would be stumbling blocks, that things that used to come easily to her could be a challenge for a while. "That's okay. I forget things that happened to me all the time. Yesterday I put my car keys down when I came in the house and couldn't remember where. Your mom found them next to the computer. Silly, huh?"

Abruptly, she stopped rocking. "Silly bird."

He let it go. Stuff was jumbled around in her head, that was all.

"I r'ember what the fish said."

"What fish?"

"In the water, silly Daddy."

"Okay. What did the fish say?"

She sat tall and pointed a finger toward the ceiling, breaking into a toothy smile. "Listen!"

"What are we supposed to listen to?" Jenn appeared in the doorway of the kitchen.

But Hannah had already withdrawn back into her private world to stare out the window.

Hunter shrugged. "If I figure that out, I'll let you know."

"Ah, the logic of a five-year-old." Jenn winked. "What I wouldn't give to live in her world for a day."

—o0Oo—

From the kitchen window, Hunter watched as Hannah swung a leg over the low bough of the Crooked Tree, which stood between the detached garage and the horse barn. They called it that because, well, it was crooked. Its trunk was formed by the union of two thick boughs. One of them grew straight and tall with many solid branches, while the other bowed low to the ground before curving up. Hannah straddled the bottom bough, the fingers of her hands curled around the looped end of an imaginary set of reins. Kicking her legs against it, she bounced up and down. She spent half an hour like that, her mind taking her to faraway places.

Spring was in full bloom now, green buds bursting from every branch, flowers pushing up through the dirt, songbirds returning. Today the sun burned brightly in a clear blue sky and one could finally go outside without a winter coat on.

When he had finished washing the last of the dishes, Hunter dried his hands and went outside to join Hannah in the backyard. It smelled of lilacs and hyacinth. He stooped down beside Hannah, now sitting with her back against the tree, her pouty mouth weighed down with a frown.

"What's the matter, sweet pea? Did your horse get tired?"

Her head swung back and forth.

"Sad that Maura's busy playing softball today and Mommy's not here?"

Again, she shook her head.

"I'm running out of guesses. You'll have to tell me."

Beneath wispy yellow bangs, she looked up at him. "Am I better enough now?"

"Better enough? For what?"

"A dog."

Oh. He'd entirely forgotten about that. To be honest, he wished he hadn't mentioned it. It was an impulse. A desperate bunt to get her on track for recovery. But Hannah, with her mind like a steel trap, remembered the most seemingly insignificant details sometimes. And he couldn't renege on it. However, there was one major problem.

"Yeah, about that ... See, I haven't talked to Mommy yet and I'm not sure how she's going to feel about it. Remember the guinea pig?"

Hannah averted her eyes. Last year they'd gotten both her and Maura guinea pigs. Hannah hadn't liked how hers squealed. So she'd put it in a shoebox, carried it down to the basement, and piled more boxes on top when it continued to squeal to shut out the noise. Heavy boxes filled with an old set of stoneware dishes. Then she went outside to play. Two days later Jenn discovered the shoebox, squashed beneath the others. Afraid her guinea pig might suffer the same fate, Maura donated hers to her fifth-grade classroom.

Then there were the goldfish. Because they looked hungry, Hannah had dumped half a container of fish flakes into the bowl, which caused them to overeat. Rescuing the last two, Jenn hid the fish food in a cabinet above the refrigerator, then explained to Hannah that they needed to eat just twice a day and only a pinch. That led Hannah to insist on setting an alarm for their feeding times and measuring out their food on a doll's spoon. The big problem arose when the family was away at the fish's designated dinner hour. Hannah would become very upset if the schedule was disrupted in any way to the point that she had a public meltdown in the shoe department at the mall.

Pets had not gone over well and so Jenn and Hunter decided to forego any house pets — a bit ironic when you considered Hunter was a vet in Faderville. They had a few barn cats, still — all too wary of being held to go anywhere near Hannah — and a pair of retired draft horses that Jenn tended to. Although docile, they were big enough that Hannah kept her distance from them.

No, it had been a bad idea to promise Hannah a dog. There was just too much that could go wrong. Maybe if he skirted the topic long enough, she'd forget about it.

Hannah raked her fingers through the newly sprouted grass, a frown tugging at her rosebud mouth. A car turned in the driveway and rolled down the lane. A minute later, Maura jumped out, her softball knickers dusty and a big grass stain on the back of her jersey. Jenn got out and waved to them before herding Maura inside.

When Hunter looked back at Hannah, she'd picked up a twig and was on her knees, drawing something in a patch of dirt.

"What are you making a picture of, Hannah?" He moved to stand above her. "Can I see?"

She sat back on her heels to give him a better view. To Hunter, it looked like a blob with sticks for legs, only slightly more elaborate. Like an early Picasso rendition of … something. He was afraid to ask what it was supposed to be, but he was pretty sure he knew.

"Is that a dog?"

"Yah. My dog."

She wasn't going to let go of this easily. He had to figure out how he was going to divert her from her obsession without breaking his word. He'd been so thankful of her recovery that he'd blurted out the one thing Jenn would never agree to. Even he knew it was a bad idea.

Hunter held out his hand for Hannah and helped her up. Then he swung her atop his shoulders and carried her toward the house, the scent of lilacs growing headier with each step.

As they went, he looked out over the hills and woodlands that had surrounded him since birth. Today, there was a special vibrancy to the greens of the grass and leaves, and a dappling of snowy white or pale pink where flower buds hinted at unfurling. Among the rugged hills, old tobacco barns squatted, a rustic reminder of another time. In patchwork pastures, cows meandered, mud splattered up their hocks.

This was his home, in all its rough and backward beauty. He could never grow tired of the view, no matter how long he lived.

chapter 12

Echo

The view never changed. I was sick of it. If I had to spend the rest of my life staring at the same hills, the same woods, the same decrepit barn in the distance that looked like one strong wind would blow it over, I was going to go barking mad.

When the Grunwalds turned me out from the mobile home, that tin can they called a house, I had taken great fascination in all that there was to see. But even your favorite meal, if served every day, loses its appeal.

My existence had become more mundane than my sanity would allow. I'd long since grown bored of watching the birds and the squirrels, both more abundant now that winter was over. Even the twins had ceased to taunt me. The object of their teasing was now a spotted, miniature potbelly pig. Porkchop spent less than a week in the house, before he was banished to a small pen on the other side of the backyard from my doghouse. For several days, he squealed in my direction. I barked back, but that only invited angry words and the occasional stone flung at me from whoever happened to be closest to the back door.

The collar they'd slipped on my head months ago was now so tight the links had rubbed my flesh open. It itched, but scratching only made it bleed. Soon, a repulsive smell came from the wounds, but in time scabs began to form. Scabs that turned to scars, which made the collar hurt more than before, if that was even possible.

The pain was an aggravation that I lived with daily. It became a part of me, making me more and more irritable. I would have bitten Mavis when she came out to scoop up my waste with the shovel, but when I growled at her she swung it in my direction. I was smart enough to know when I was outgunned.

In frustration, I began to chew at the board to one side of my doghouse opening. My intent was to gnaw it down to nothing, for no other reason than that it was conveniently there and they had never given me any other toys or bones to chew on. Gradually, though, it loosened, and I discovered a new purpose. The hook to which my chain was attached was sunk into that board. If the board came free, I was free. I would visit the pig first, then be on my way to some other life, more exciting than this.

In hindsight, even the shelter was more exciting than this. At least there I was given things to chew on and had regular mealtimes and water that wasn't stagnant and sitting in a rusty, scum-filled bowl. Then again, you should be careful what you wish for.

I sank my teeth into the wood, alternately sawing with my molars and spitting out hunks of splinters. For days I worked on it. One day, Scowler filled up my water bowl, although she didn't bother to clean it, and plunked down a plate of mashed potatoes mixed with a smattering of corn. The Grunwalds had long ago stopped giving me kibble. Too expensive, Mavis had complained. Instead, I was fed the same leftovers as the pig. Which would have been acceptable had they remembered to bring the food out before the fat in the meat congealed or turned rancid and the vegetables began to mold. It was eat or starve, and more than once I regurgitated my dinner, unable to keep it down. I should have learned to trust my nose better, but the stomach is a greedy monster. Thankfully, the mashed potatoes and corn were merely cold, but to me they were a king's banquet.

After filling my belly, I went to work again on the board. Porkchop squealed at me, as if he knew something was afoot. I took it as encouragement, but a part of me suspected he was tattling.

One by one, the lights in the Grunwalds' house went off, until there was only the pale blue flicker of the TV in Mavis and Earl's bedroom. Finally, that window went dark, too. I chomped and chomped, my jaw muscles growing weary. Just when I thought it had finally loosened, I yanked, but the board caught on a pair of nails at the top. Frustrated with how long it was taking, I clamped my teeth into it and put my weight behind it, pulling, pulling, pulling, then twisting the board side to side. Determined, I bucked upward. The board, slick with my saliva, slid from my mouth. I tumbled backwards, rolling first onto my back and then flipping over, feet in the air.

The chain jerked my neck forcefully and I heard a crack and a pop, followed by several clinks. But instead of the cold cut of steel into my skin, I felt an unfamiliar lightness. Carefully, I gathered my legs beneath me and stood.

I was beyond the worn arc of dirt that had been my circumference, the extent of my world. Cool air brushed at my neck, lifting the fur, tickling me there. At my feet in a tangled heap lay the chain and collar. At its end was the board, a big jagged piece of wood with an eye hook screwed into it and that nasty length of chain attached. I turned around once, backed away slowly, expecting the links to trip me. But they were no longer an extension of me, no longer tethered me to the drafty doghouse with its dank straw.

Now what? I was free, but what did that mean? Where would I go? What would I do? Things hadn't turned out so swell before when I crawled from the river and wandered around, all on my own. This was all a bit overwhelming.

A blood curdling squeal cut through the night air. I spun around to see the little spotted pig rooting at the bottom side of the hog panel that formed his enclosure. With furious determination, he dug his hooves at the earth.

For a while, I watched, smug in my newfound freedom. But the more he pawed at the dirt and banged his pink snout against the metal bars, the more I felt a tug at my conscience. Independence, I decided, was highly overrated.

So I went about trying to figure out how to spring him from his pen. I paced around it, testing each panel, scratching at the gate, biting at the latch. But Earl had built his fortress well. As far as I could see, it was impenetrable.

Still, I tried. And when I had exhausted all options, I went to work digging on the outside. If eventually we met, it would form a tunnel, and then the spotted pig and I would race to ... somewhere.

Somewhere far from here.

—o00o—

I hadn't counted on the dirt down deep being so impossibly hard. Or there being so many rocks. *Big* rocks.

When I finally lay down to rest, defeated, the night sky was lightening, a thin crescent of pink showing in the east. Of course, I had worked harder than the pig, but I didn't hold it against him. Porkchop was young and not as strong and certainly not as smart as me.

I resumed my efforts. Just when I thought we were getting close, my claws hit another rock. I scratched around it and dug at the dirt with my nose, expecting another rock that I would need to extract with my mouth. What I discovered was a rock so big there was no hope of moving it. We could have burrowed around it, but that would take more time than we had. Soon Earl would be up, tromping out the door to his truck. The side of the pen where we'd dug was in clear view of the path he'd take.

Undaunted — ignorance is the haven of fools — Porkchop continued to push at the dirt with his snout. I watched in pity, my muzzle resting between my paws. Curious, the little pig came over to where I sat and pressed his flat nose between the bars. He sniffed at me, then snorted a breath.

In the kitchen, a light snapped on. Familiar noises came from inside: the water pump humming, footsteps pounding, a skillet being set on the stove. Through the small kitchen window, I saw Earl go back and forth, a cup of coffee in his hand.

Rain pattered softly upon the earth. I went up to the pig and inhaled his scent. His nose twitched. He wiggled his curlicue tail. I whimpered softly. It was the closest thing to saying 'goodbye' that I could manage.

Before Earl could burst the back door open, I turned and ran, pausing once at wood's edge to take one last look at yet another friend who I'd known only too briefly.

—o0Oo—

It wasn't the rain that wore me down. It was the wind and the cold.

The night had been reasonably warm, but by midmorning a stiff northern wind had changed the weather for the worse. Chilled to the bone, shivers rattled my thin frame. A night without sleep had taken its toll and so, needing rest, I sought shelter in a barn. Gaps yawned between the planks and water dripped through the roof in several places to pool in puddles. An old rusted tractor with flat tires sat in the middle of the cavernous space, like some slain dragon of long ago.

I found a spot behind a large feeding trough that was dry and out of the wind. Mud caked my belly and my fur was drenched through, but it only took a dozen breaths before I fell asleep.

Would that I had placed myself more strategically. Somewhere that I could have seen anyone coming. Somewhere from which I could have escaped.

The rope went around my neck as I still slept. I thought I was dreaming that Earl had slipped a chain on me again.

When I started awake and saw the shadow standing over me, I bolted backward. My rump hit a stool, on which sat an old metal tool box. It toppled to the ground, greasy wrenches and screwdrivers spilling out. I jumped sideways, toward the barn opening. The rope went taut about my neck, gagging me, and I knew for certain this was no dream.

My eyes followed the rope to its end. A man with a long red beard held it, his overalls smeared with oil. He studied me with dull eyes. My impression was one of kind indifference. But it was the rifle propped on his shoulder that threw me.

I pulled with all my strength, even as the rope bit into the raw places in my neck. With a jerk, he lowered the barrel of the rifle … then set it against the trough.

Slowly, he reeled me in. I planted my legs stiffly, but he slid me across the dirt, inch by inch. He took my jowls in his calloused hands, tilted my head side to side to look into my eyes, my ears, and at my neck. Then he pried my mouth open. I twisted away and snapped my teeth shut, but he appeared to be done with his inspection. He was not, however, done with me.

He hooked a bearish arm around me and carried me inside his house, where I got the first bath of my life. I should have hated every minute of it. But in truth, I liked it. Liked the warm water washing the dirt from my fur and cleansing the fetid sores on my neck.

Gently, he dried me with towels, patting around my face and neck and massaging me vigorously over my back and tummy. Then he took a cotton ball and, dousing it with a clear liquid, dabbed it over my sores.

It stings!

I threw myself against the back of the tub, which only made him laugh. He dug his fingers in my mane and applied more of the firewater.

After that, he took me into the kitchen, where he took sausage links out of the refrigerator. He diced them up and cooked them in a pan, then sat down at the table and ate some from a plate. But the rest he left in the skillet. Which he put on the floor for me.

Trust is won in small gestures.

And what a fool I was to have thought that a handful of sausages meant that he pledged his loyalty to me. Because after that he took me on a ride in his truck.

And car rides for me have never, ever been good.

I puked up every last sausage bit. But he kept driving. If this day was going to end badly, I would at least leave evidence that I had been there.

—o00o—

This time, I was thrown in the kennel runs at the shelter, where the other adults were kept. Evelyn was not there when the farmer brought me in to the shelter. Instead, I met Aaron — and I loathed him instantly. He never looked into my eyes. His voice was flat, his movements sluggish, bordering on lazy. He did as little as possible, making a show of it when visitors came through, then sitting back down at his desk to watch TV and eat nonstop when he was alone.

When the young couple came in two days later, he waved them toward the runs on the far end, where mine was. They stopped at each kennel, the woman clutching her man whenever a dog barked loudly or jumped at the door, then grasping the chain link and making little kissy noises whenever the dog hung back. Disinterested, I slunk to the back of my kennel and curled up into a ball.

They stopped at my door and peered in.

"Is that the one he was talking about?" the young man said. His diamond-studded earrings flashed in the cold fluorescent light. Dark hair framed a hardened face. Swirling lines of color, a design of some kind, began at the sides of his neck, disappearing beneath the collar of his white T-shirt.

"Yeah, Mario, I think so. It's the only Border Collie here."

I am so not a Border Collie, I wanted to say.

"Looks kinda scrawny."

The girl, barely a woman, tilted her head observantly. Jet black ringlets bobbed with every movement. Her clothes were impossibly tight, surely not comfortable. Even less practical were the golden, spiked heels on which she balanced. "Just young. Maybe underfed."

Older than my years. And starved.

"Sure you don't want that silver-blue pit bull back there? That's a rare color. We could make some stud money off of him. He'd make a good guard dog, too. Keep you safe when I'm not home."

"I want a smart dog, like in that movie *Babe*. Not a Cujo."

"I don't know, Ariella. This one doesn't look like much of a watchdog to me."

"You said —"

"I know, I know. Just trying to help you reason things through, babe. You need to learn to make decisions with your head, not your heart. Smart choices."

"You saying I'm dumb?"

"Christ, no, baby girl. I'd never do that. But I know dogs. And I just want the best for you."

Pouting, Ariella tugged at the strings of his hoodie. "Whose birthday is it, anyway?"

Mario held his hands up in surrender.

She snuggled close, laying her head on his chest. "I know I can always count on you to take care of me."

His hands went around her back, then slid down over her plump buttocks. He whispered something in her ear and she purred in response.

I tucked my muzzle beneath my paw and closed my eyes, hoping they'd get the message. Mario took a firm hold of her elbow and guided her away.

Relieved, I stretched out on the cool concrete. The urine smell was stronger here than in the puppy room, since Aaron was so slow to clean it up. Already my newly washed fur reeked of some other dog's piss.

I was half asleep when the *click-click-click* of Ariella's heels rang out. Stopping in front of my kennel, she fished around in an oversized black leather bag and brought out a long, pink, satiny leash. Then she took out a collar, glittering with jewels.

It was so not me.

Aaron flipped up the latch for her with a breathy grunt. He flicked a hand at me, indicating for her to go in. Behind him stood Mario, arms crossed, his dark flinty eyes staring me down, challenging me.

A person's eyes, I was learning, told me everything. In a glance, I could sense the slow boil of anger that was Mario, the bland indifference that was Aaron, and the flighty fickleness of Ariella.

Ariella clipped the leash and collar together, then held them out to me. "What do you think, huh? Wanna come home with me, pretty boy?"

Not really.

If she and Mario were a pair and living with her meant being glared at by him, then no. Absolutely not. I would rather stay here in this piss-soaked purgatory. At least Aaron wasn't a bother. Nor did he look like he kicked puppies for sport.

I backed into the corner, pressed my face to the unyielding

cement wall. She slipped the collar over my head and ran a hand down my neck. Her long nails raked at my chest. In spite of myself, I leaned into her touch. No one had ever scratched me there. Ever. I felt ... delirious.

Against my better judgment, I walked out of the kennel with Ariella. I sat in the backseat of Mario's black sports car, my neck stretched forward to seek Ariella's magic fingers. But she was busy combing through her purse, which contained a hundred items of fascination for her.

One arm dangling out his window, Mario drove home at breakneck speed, the music from the speakers booming so loudly it vibrated the car's frame.

As car rides went, it turned out not to be any better than the others. With car rides, I had figured out, it was all about the destination.

—o00o—

My new home was nicer than any of the others had been, and whenever it was just Ariella and me, life was, well, not great, but good enough. She always remembered to feed me, my water dish seldom went dry, and there was a basket of toys and bones tucked in a corner of the living room. At first, I wasn't quite sure what to do with them, or if I was even allowed to chew on them or carry them about. But Ariella encouraged me to take them and seemed content with my behavior when I was gnawing on a bone.

The first day I was with her, Ariella called me Brutus, after a cat she once owned. It was an insult, but what say did I have in the matter? The next morning she changed my name to Chip, but by afternoon I was Chester, and by evening Charlie. Within the first week, I had been called by no less than ten different names, none of them Echo.

In the end, she named me Buddy. As in, 'Hey, Buddy.' Mostly, I think it was because she couldn't remember the last thing she'd decided to call me.

Whenever she wasn't working, Ariella took me on walks. Always once a day, but sometimes twice. Although never for very long, because she *always* wore high heels. That was one human fashion trend I'd never fathom.

The only problem was that Ariella worked. A lot. And Mario didn't like that. He complained about her hours, the chores that were not done, all the suppers she did not make for him. It was sad that what made Ariella so happy, only built resentment in Mario.

"Hey, babe." Mario walked out of the bedroom, his eyes heavy with recent sleep. It was midmorning and Ariella and I had been up for hours. His boxer briefs hung loosely on his hips. His chest, hard with muscle, was clean shaven. He often spent hours in the spare bedroom, lifting weights and then looking at himself in the full length mirror on the closet door. Clearly, he was in love with himself. "Why don't you stay home today? I have some things in mind I'd like to do to you. Things I *know* you like."

"Can't. I have to work."

"Twelve hours every day? That job more important to you than I am?"

"My job pays well, Mario." She braced her hands on her waist, defiant. "I can buy my own clothes and —"

Dark eyes flashing, he grabbed her wrist and yanked her against his chest. "I can buy you things, babe. Why don't you just let me take care of you?"

She struggled against his grip as she pushed a hand against his chest. "What can you buy me with a part-time job, huh? Your paycheck doesn't even cover the rent."

Something in him snapped. He shoved her against the kitchen counter. Before she could recover, he grabbed her arm, twisting it behind her.

"Let go! You're hurting me."

"You hurt me every day you walk out that door. You think it's a game to make fun of my manhood. Not my fault I can't find a fulltime job. You think I haven't been trying?!"

I scurried behind the couch. Life, so far, had taught me to preserve myself. Yet something else was stirring within me: the need to protect those I cared about. Unfortunately, I didn't know how to do that. I was not brave. Bravery meant boldness, the ability to act without regard for one's own welfare. If I protected Ariella, I would put myself in danger.

Then I thought about the pig, and how I had run from the Grunwalds' house before Earl came out the door and found us. And I regretted that. I truly did.

"Please, let go, Mario. Please," Ariella whimpered. "I just meant that my job's important to both of us. I wasn't putting you down. Honest."

He bunched her hair in his other fist, turning her away from him as he slammed his hips into her from behind to pin her against the counter. Bending over her, he pressed his mouth to her ear. "Am I important to you, babe?"

Ariella was crying softly now, her small sobs broken by groans of pain as Mario forced her arm farther.

"Am I?!" he screamed.

She stiffened at the force of his words, her eyes shut tight. "Yes," she whispered.

I crept forward, my heart breaking for her. She had been kind to me and tolerant of him; he had been possessive of her, manipulative, domineering — and even jealous of me. Why couldn't she see that? Why was she even with him?

"Do you love me, baby girl?"

"Y-y-yes."

"Say it."

"I love you, Mario."

"Do you want to make me happy?"

"Yes."

"Then you're staying home today, right?"

Her head moved in an almost imperceptible nod.

He loosened his hold on her gradually, but before he let her go, he told her, "Get your phone. Call in sick. Tell them you have the flu and might be out for a few days."

"A few —?"

"Just do it. You *don't* want to make me unhappy." This time he didn't yell or hurt her. The flatness of his tone delivered the threat quite plainly.

Ariella complied, telling her boss exactly what he had told her to. When she ended the call, he took the phone from her and tossed it across the room. It bounced off a wall and hit the floor, breaking into pieces.

"There," he said. "They won't bother you now."

She kept her eyes on the phone as he unbuttoned her blouse and slid it from her shoulders. Every time his fingers brushed her skin, she shuddered. I slinked closer, my head low, watchful. Mario buried his mouth in the space between her breasts, lapping and sucking greedily like a pup at its mother's teat. Ariella gasped and bit her lip. What was he doing? Whatever it was, she didn't seem to be enjoying it. Was he … was he *biting* her?

A growl rumbled in my belly. I wasn't even sure where it came from. I just knew I didn't like what he was doing to her. Hell, I didn't like him, period.

Mario's eyes shifted to me, but only for a moment, as his fingers wandered down to her skirt, shifting it downward.

I growled louder.

"Shut the dog in the bathroom, Ariella," he said.

"Why?"

"I don't like how he's looking at me. Besides, what we do is none of his goddamn business."

"He's okay, Mario. Just leave him alone."

"Fine. I'll do it." Shoving her onto the couch, Mario came at me.

But there was no way I was going to let that mean bastard separate me from her. Not if she was in danger.

As his hand came down, I jumped up and sank my teeth into the meat between his thumb and first finger. And I held on, clamping my jaw tighter. I wanted to hurt him, just like he'd hurt Ariella.

Pummeling my ribs with the fist of his free hand, he yelled at Ariella to get me off of him, but she just stood there, lost in shock. With each blow to my chest, it became harder and harder to breathe. My jaws were tiring, too, and my feet sliding on the smooth tile floor as he jerked his arm back. I needed to adjust my bite. So I let go of his hand, ducked low, and bit him in the calf.

Dumb move on my part. Because it was just enough time for him to grab a skillet off the counter and swing it at my head.

I staggered backward, my head ringing, then stumbled and fell.

I saw two of everything, then three, four …

From a distance, I heard Ariella screeching, "No, Mario! No!"

A belt went around my muzzle. I felt myself lifted up.

The next thing I was aware of was being in the back of Mario's sports car, music banging around me and rattling my bones, the car bumping over a rough road, and then …

A rush of warm air. Sunlight bathing me. Growing stronger. Hotter. Brighter.

The smell of crushed grass. Lilacs.

Birds … singing.

chapter 13

Hannah

Hannah saw dogs everywhere. On TV, in magazine ads, sitting on porches as her family drove to town, and walking down the road with ladies in high heels. She even saw them in the shapes of the clouds and random patterns of the bathroom floor tiles. There was nothing she wanted more than to have a dog and the day she got one would surely be the best day of her life.

Since coming home, a strange thing had happened to her. Not 'strange' as in bad. Just new and different. Too much of anything still overwhelmed her, but when it came to animals, she felt a new relationship to them. A connection, although she couldn't quite put her finger on why that was so. Except that sometimes she thought she heard them speak to her. Not that they said words out loud. But whatever they were thinking, she heard it in her head, as if their thoughts were hers, too.

She wasn't entirely sure she liked that.

And so, Hannah ignored the voices, turning her face away when she heard them, busying herself with other important matters, like cutting out all the pictures of dogs she could find in her mommy's magazines and pasting them to a piece of cardboard she'd ripped from the box their new dishwasher had come in.

"Hannah." Jenn knelt beside her, admiring the collage she'd created out of dog pictures. "I need to talk to you about something."

Hannah flipped through a magazine she'd already looked through twice, just in case she'd missed a picture. There was an ad with kittens in it, but she didn't want a cat. They were too snooty. Even the barn cats.

"Kindergarten starts this fall for you. They're having sign-ups over at Faderville Elementary, where your Gramma Lise used to teach. It's a nice school, with a big playground and lots of other kids. Maybe some of them could be your friends? You'd like that, wouldn't you?"

No, Hannah hadn't missed anything. There were no more dog pictures. She could cut out things a dog might like, like food or toys or a little kid's swimming pool, but that wasn't the same. It was cheating. Still, she'd been through the whole stack of magazines and didn't have nearly enough to fill up her big cardboard square. This just wouldn't do. Maybe if her daddy brought the newspaper in, there'd be something in there?

"Hannah, are you listening to me?" Jenn sat back on her bottom and blew out a puff of air. "No, of course you're not." Gently, she took Hannah's chin in her fingers and turned her daughter's face toward her. "We need to go to the school. Mrs. Watley wants to talk to you. She'll ask you some questions, simple things like counting and ABCs. Stuff you already know. You need to answer her, okay?"

Why was her mommy interrupting her to talk about school? "Maura goes to school," she said, trying to get her mother back on track.

"I know. And you will, too, next year, sweetie. Isn't that exciting?"

She scrunched her mouth up to show her disapproval. "Nope."

97

"Oh, now, don't be such a sourpuss. Bet you'll make a lot of new friends."

Gripping the glue bottle tightly, Hannah stared blankly at her. This was getting frustrating. She only needed one friend — a dog. Besides, she didn't particularly like other children. They didn't understand her, just like she didn't understand them. Anyway, what was the point of going to school when you could learn things at home?

"Oh, Hannah, look." Jenn pointed at the white glob of glue pooling on the floor in front of Hannah. "Can you help me clean this mess up? We don't want anyone stepping in it and getting stuck now, do we?"

Hannah hated cleaning up, but she did it anyway. Because more than she disliked cleaning up, she didn't like her mommy getting upset with her. So she tore a few paper towels from the roll, swiped it through the gooey puddle, then threw it in the trash and went outside.

"You're not done, Hannah," her mother said.

But Hannah was already on her way down the front steps, looking for her daddy to see if he had the newspaper yet.

Down the road by her Gramma's house, a low silver car stopped, music booming from inside. A man got out, laid something in the ditch, then got back in his car and sped away. *How strange*, she thought, but quickly forgot about it when she saw her daddy out on the lawnmower, going back and forth, making long symmetrical stripes across the yard.

While she waited for him to finish, she sat down beneath her favorite tree and drew dog pictures in the dirt.

—o00o—

"Hannah, lunch is ready!" Jenn called from the kitchen window.

Hannah was almost done waiting. Her daddy had just put the

tractor in the shed and was walking toward the mailbox. She'd wanted to get the newspaper herself, but she wasn't allowed by the road. Besides, out by the mailbox was where the school bus picked Maura up and Hannah didn't want a school bus to come and take her.

"Hannah?" Jenn stepped out the door, then said to her husband, "Hunter, bring her inside when you come in, will you? She's been out there watching you mow the whole time. Who knows what's on her mind?"

Smiling, Hunter waved at Jenn and went on down the lane. Hannah went to the picket fence, watching. This was as far as she was allowed to go. Her parents had said they'd put the fence up when she was little to keep her from running out onto the road. She didn't remember ever doing that.

Hunter walked up to the mailbox and looked inside. He pulled the paper out, tucked it under his arm, and turned back toward the house. But before he started up the lane, he paused, looking down the road toward Gramma Lise's. He began walking that way. A few steps later he broke into a jog.

Standing on the bottom board of the fence, Hannah waited, her impatience mounting. Grasping a picket, she swung her body side to side. She wondered why her daddy was running away with the newspaper that she needed. More than that, she wondered what he was running to. Gramma Lise and Grampa Brad were not walking down the road. Their sheep appeared to all be safe in their pasture. There was nothing there, as far as she could see.

After disappearing from view behind a clump of trees, Hunter reappeared briefly on the other side before bending down. He stayed there for much too long a time. Hannah swung side to side harder. She felt the nails of the board loosen, but she went on swinging. What was he doing?

Finally, he stood and started back. When he got to the other side of the trees, Hannah could see he had something big, fuzzy, and dark draped between his arms. He turned down their lane. The board popped loose. Hannah stopped swinging. She was too mesmerized by what she saw in her father's arms to move.

A dog! He was bringing her dog to her!

She let go of the broken board and hopped down. Unable to contain her excitement, she jumped up and down, up and down, up and down.

"Hannah," her mother began, "what are you —?"

But Jenn stopped cold as Hunter stepped through the gate. She pressed a hand to her chest. "Oh, no. Is he …?"

"Still breathing," Hunter made his way carefully up the steps. "Pulse is faint, but regular."

Jenn held the door open for them. "I'll get your bag out of the truck."

"As soon as you do that, find Maura. Have her keep Hannah in check, will you?"

By then, Hannah had stopped jumping. Something was wrong with her new dog. Terribly, terribly wrong. His eyes were closed. He was sleeping, but the kind of sleep it was hard to wake up from. Like after her accident. And there was blood coming out of his nose.

She followed Hunter inside as he laid the dog on the kitchen table and then probed him gently all over. When Jenn came in and set his bag down, he took a light out and pried the dog's eyelids open to shine it in his eyes. The dog moaned and tried to lift his head, but he wasn't very strong.

"Did he get hit by a car?" Jenn said.

"I suppose it's possible, but it looks more to me like someone hit him with something and dumped him by the road."

"How awful. Who would do that to a dog? I hope the monster gets his due." She stroked the top of the dog's head. "They say animal abuse is the first sign of a serial violent offender." Then, as if she suddenly remembered Hannah standing there, she said, "I'll fetch

Maura from her room."

Hunter's back was to Hannah. Without making a sound, she tiptoed to the table. For a while, she watched her daddy looking inside the dog's mouth.

He glanced at her, smiling sadly. "I'm going to patch him up, okay? Then we have to figure out who he belongs to."

Which seemed like such an odd thing to say, because he was their dog now. Whoever had left him like that didn't want him very much.

Hannah stroked the dog's head with gentle pets, like her daddy had taught her to do with Gramma's baby lambs. The dog's eyes opened a crack, as if he'd been waiting for a sign that she was there.

"I'm Hannah," she said.

His breathing was faint, but she heard him like a faraway whisper: *Echo*.

"I like that."

"Like what, sweet pea?" Hunter asked.

"His name."

"Oh." Hunter blinked at her. "What is it?"

"Echo. His name is Echo. Like when you make a sound in the hills and it comes back to you."

Taking out a syringe, Hunter filled it with liquid from a tiny bottle, then tapped at it to get the bubbles out. He explained to Hannah that this was to make the dog sleepy and not hurt so much, until he got better. "Have you seen him before?"

"Nope."

"Then how do you know his name? He's not wearing a tag."

"Because he told me."

Her daddy's eyes said he didn't believe her. Just like he didn't believe her about the bird or the fish. But it was pretty obvious to her by then. Other people didn't hear these things. Only Hannah did.

Jenn walked in with Maura.

"Who told you what, sweetie?" Jenn said.

Hannah pressed her lips together. Jenn and Hunter looked at each other. He leaned his head toward the hallway and her parents went and stood there together. They lowered their voices, but Hannah wasn't deaf. She could still hear them.

"She says the dog's name is Echo."

Echo was mostly black, with white on his paws and chest and a thin white stripe on his nose. His fur was shiny, like a blackbird's. He was kind of skinny, like Hannah, with long legs. What she liked most about him was his poofy little bobtail. She just wished he felt better.

"How —?" Jenn began.

Hunter held up a finger. "She *says* he told her his name. She also told me that on the day of the accident, a bird and a fish spoke to her."

Jenn tried to hide a smirk, but couldn't. "So she's St. Francis of Assisi now?"

"She's definitely dog-obsessed."

"I've noticed." She gestured toward Hannah's half-done picture board. "What do you suppose brought this on? I know she gets hooked on things, but there's usually something that sets it off."

For a few moments, Hunter didn't answer. Hannah stared hard at him. Was he going to remember his promise? For weeks now, he'd been avoiding talking to her mommy about it, even though he kept saying he would. And now he'd found a dog. A dog just for her. A dog that needed her as much as she needed him.

She laid her head on top of Echo's chest and listened to him breathing. His fur tickled her cheek.

"I ...I may have promised her a dog when she was in the hospital."

"You what?!"

Hunter shushed Jenn, then nudged her into the living room.

"You want to know something weird?" Hunter said to Jenn, his voice low. "Maybe it's just coincidence, but this dog looks an awful lot like the one we saw when Hannah went missing from the campsite. You know — the one that was carrying Faustine, before dropping the toy and running off?"

Leaning sideways, Jenn peered into the kitchen. "Now that you mention it … I suppose it could be. But wasn't that dog smaller, kind of scrawny?"

"A half-grown puppy. Remember, that was almost six months ago."

"Hunter, don't read too much into that. Anyway, the last thing we need is a dog. Maybe when she's a little older …"

Hannah couldn't hear them after that, but her mommy didn't sound happy. That was okay. She didn't have to be. Echo was her dog. She would take care of him. They would look out for each other.

Her parents returned to the kitchen, bustling about.

"Maura, will you keep an eye on Hannah for a few minutes?" Hunter said. "Your mom is going to help me take this dog to my clinic, where I can do some X-rays and —"

"Is he going to die?" Maura blurted, her face twisting in disgust as she caught sight of the blood pooling on the table.

Hannah's head snapped up. She stared at her sister in horror. Was there something they weren't telling her?

"Maura!" Jenn corrected.

"What? You have to admit he doesn't look too good."

"Go sit with your sister in the family room. Let her pick the movie. Gramma Lise will be here any minute. I'll be back in less than an hour, all right?"

"Yeah, yeah." Maura peeled her little sister away from Echo. "Come on, squirt. You get to watch your favorite movie again. Yay. One more round of *My Neighbor Totoro*. Magic seeds and a cat-bus and kids with eyes too big for their heads."

She pulled Hannah toward the basement stairs, but her little sister writhed out of her grip, watching as their mother held the door open and Hunter scooped Echo up in his arms. The door shut behind them. Hannah rushed to it and pressed her nose to the glass, watching as her daddy pulled away in his truck and her mommy followed behind in her car.

She stayed there even after Gramma came. Even after her mother returned home. Stayed until she saw her daddy's truck pull in the driveway hours later.

With a weary sigh, he ruffled her hair and pulled her up into his arms. She rested her head on his broad shoulder.

"Echo's going to be okay, sweetie. He's going to be okay," he murmured into her ear. "But he'll need to stay in the animal hospital for a little while, all right?"

Hannah nodded. She should have felt better then, but she didn't. Echo needed her.

"Maybe Mommy can bring you to see him in a few days. Right now he's pretty bruised up and tired. He needs to rest. Like you." He set her down and turned her shoulders toward the hall. "Go on, now. Get ready for bed."

Reluctantly, Hannah trudged to the bathroom, where Gramma Lise helped her change and got her started brushing her teeth. Then her grandma rejoined Jenn and Hunter in the kitchen. Toothbrush still in her mouth, Hannah tiptoed to the end of the hall.

"His mandible is fractured, but thankfully there doesn't appear to be any cranial damage. Maybe a slight concussion, but nothing serious. He's missing a couple of teeth now."

"Was he micro-chipped?" Lise asked.

"No. Nice collar, but someone had unclipped the tags. Like they didn't want anyone to be able to trace him. Judging by the injuries, the dog wasn't hit by a car. No, I'm more sure than ever that someone struck him."

"With what?"

"Who knows? A bat? A shovel, maybe? They walloped him one

good blow. Just thank goodness they didn't keep at it."

Lise's cell phone rang. "Excuse me, it's Brad. He's been on patrol tonight. I'd better take this." She stepped out onto the back porch to talk to him.

"So what happens to the dog now?" Jenn asked Hunter. "And I don't mean his medical treatment."

"I'd be afraid to put an ad in the paper for a lost pet. And given what he's gone through, taking a chance on relinquishing him to the shelter ... I couldn't do it, Jenn."

"So you're saying you want to keep him?" She waited for him to answer, but he couldn't seem to find the right words. "Hunter, you know how she's been with animals. She doesn't mean to hurt them. She doesn't think things through. There's a disconnect. We've talked about it before. She's just too young to understand the implications of a single action. Besides, it's only going to break her heart worse if we have to give the dog up later. Better to do it now."

"Jenn ... we can't. I promised her. Anyway, she's not the same kid she was before —"

"So you keep reminding me. Fine. Suit yourself. Just remember that I'm on record as saying this is not one of your best ideas, Hunter."

"Don't worry. If anything happens, I take full responsibility."

Hannah hurried back to the bathroom to finish brushing her teeth. As she rinsed her mouth out, she heard her grandma come back in the house.

"Brad says they took some man into custody for domestic violence tonight. The guy was pretty riled up, despite the fact that he had a gunshot wound to his leg."

"His wife shot him?" Jenn said.

"Girlfriend, I think. He was getting a little too rough with her. He stepped out of the house for a while, and when he came back she was standing there with a gun and told him to get out. He tried to take the gun from her, and, well …"

"Hah, serves him right."

chapter 14

Echo

Sometimes where you end up is where you were supposed to be all along. Even if you didn't plan on going there.

I hadn't expected to find myself with another family. I could have been content with Ariella, even with her long work hours, had it just been her. Although I had never felt any special bond with her, at least I was well cared for. But Mario had made his opinion of me clear and it hurt that Ariella had not saved me or stood up for herself. Maybe she didn't feel that she could.

I had tried to stand up for her. I had finally tried. And all it had gotten me was a pan upside the head and another car ride to hell.

Only, this time it hadn't ended all that badly. I mean, I hurt like the bloody bejeebers — I couldn't open my jaw or chew. Even swallowing water was *hard*. There was a hole in my gums where two teeth used to be and I was pretty sure I wasn't going to grow any new ones there.

My head. Oh my head. Hours after I woke up fully, my brain was a fuzzy mess, like the inside of one of those stuffed toys Ariella gave me. Hey, I had to rip one open to see what was inside — and then a second one, just to see if it was the same. My nose was swollen, so I couldn't breathe through it. My balance was off. All I had to do was tip my head and the room spun and flipped around me.

Yet the first time I opened my eyes after Mario threw me out of the car … that was the first time I fell in love. She was small, young, with pale yellow hair and tiny hands and eyes as blue as the sky on a cloudless winter day. A human child, which should have thrown me off because the only children I'd known so far had been mean to me, but she was … different. In a good way. A kind way.

Different like me.

She spoke softly and moved slowly. Her name was Hannah. It was the only word I heard before I drifted mercifully off.

Hannah …

—o00o—

How disappointing when I came to that the first face I saw was not Hannah's, but some older man's. Not *old* old, but a grown man. With serious, questioning eyes and a gentle touch. Something about his voice and the look in his eyes was vaguely familiar, as if I already knew him, but of course I didn't. I was sure I'd never seen him before. And yet …

He did all sorts of things to me, like poking the soft parts of my belly and putting tubes in me where tubes shouldn't be, sticking needles in my skin and sometimes taping them to my front legs so they stuck, other times injecting me with a magical liquid to leave me feeling like I was floating above myself. I learned to look forward to those injections — not that I liked getting stabbed with sharp objects, but they took away the pain that, when it returned, turned me inside out with misery.

He kept me in a metal box of some sort, with a wire door on one side. Like the ones the cats were kept in at the shelter, only bigger. I didn't have the energy to stand and look about, but I was vaguely aware of a bright row of lights above and more cages across from where I was. I heard other animals, and sometimes human voices, but it was all as if in a dream.

Had Hannah been a dream? An angel? I began to wonder.

Days drifted by in a fog. Nights, marked by the absence of those bright lights, came and went. My strength and clarity of mind returned gradually, until I could sit up and look out to see the other animals across from me, looking equally scared and unhappy. The days had never seemed so long. Not even when I was sitting in the backyard at the Grunwalds', waiting for winter to end.

Was this all there was to life? Pain, disappointment, crushed hopes, unrelenting boredom? Why did humans fail so horribly in their care of me? Why did they even insist on bringing me into their already dysfunctional lives? And was it even possible that somewhere out there was a person who could love me for who I was?

When I had looked into Hannah's eyes, I thought I saw that love, felt it, if only for a moment, but then … this. As much as I wanted to be left alone sometimes, even I wanted to be loved by that special someone.

Apparently, it was not to be. Life was meant to be endured, not enjoyed. The tough survived. The soft got the crap beat out of them.

Still, I couldn't help but hold the slightest glimmer of hope that there was something more in store for me. That I was meant for some purpose greater than I could yet comprehend.

In front of me sat a bowl of cold gruel. It was my puppyhood all over again. The sandy-haired man, the one who controlled the magic water, had put it there earlier, urging me to eat. Why bother? My stomach was empty, but I wasn't truly hungry. Although he'd removed the tube that went down my throat, the effort required too much energy. Even though I could move my jaw now, it was still very sore.

My tongue felt thick. Drool dripped from the corner of my mouth, dampening the fur of my neck. Swallowing water was like gulping down stones. I remembered what that was like — I'd tried it as a puppy and quickly learned a rock in your gut meant a belly ache and then a painful poop. Now *that* was something I hadn't done in days.

I rested my muzzle between my paws, but after a few minutes my jaw began to throb. The magic was wearing off. Where was he when I needed him? Couldn't he just put the magic liquid in a bowl and let me lap it at will?

The dull throb grew to a sharp, constant pain, stabbing upward through my skull. I rolled over onto my right side, the metal cage bottom cool even through my layers of fur, hoping that the sensation would pass, but it only grew worse. Along with it, my agitation mounted.

Where was he? Had I been forgotten again?

Lifting my head, I looked around the room. A young woman hurried past with a mewling kitten cradled in her arms. I whimpered, trying to draw attention to myself, but the kitten's soft cries soon turned to an otherworldly yowl. They disappeared into another room, but the kitten's bawling drowned out everything. Human voices tried in vain to soothe the poor creature, but it persisted.

The sound cleaved at my skull like a dull machete whacking away at bone. The river of euphoria that had coursed through my veins for days ebbed and faded away, leaving in its wake pain so raw that my only urge was to lash out against it. A wail of anguish rose up from somewhere, piercing deep in my ears, scraping away at nerves.

My gaze slid around the room. They were all watching me: the chubby old Labrador in the bottom cage, the wiry-haired mixed breed above him, a Siamese to the left. The cat flattened her ears, the mutt cocked his head, and then … the Lab opened his mouth and began to howl along with me. Soon, we were a chorus, bemoaning our imprisonment, relaying our pains, sending a message into the world that we were one and we would not be silenced anymore.

The young woman marched into the room, kitten-less. "Stop. It," she snarled. "Stop it, now."

They all went silent. Except for me. I had something to say. My needs needed to be met. My howl broke apart into a bark. *Bark, bark, bark, bark.* Breathe. *Bark, bark, bark* —

"What is wrong with you, huh?" She approached me, concern replacing irritation.

Bark. Breathe. *Bark, bark* —

"Kim, what seems to be ...?" The Magic One stopped mid-sentence.

I barked louder.

"I don't know. I think the kitten set him off. But why won't he stop?"

The Magic One pulled a phone from his pants pocket, jabbed a finger at it several times, and put it to his ear. "Hey, it's me ... Everything's good. Really good. I just wanted to tell you that you can bring her here any time... Yes, now's fine. Hannah will be very, very happy... Uh huh. Bye."

Hannah? I stopped barking. If there was one thing better than the floaty feeling I got from magic water, it would be seeing Hannah.

—o00o—

The day I went home with Hannah was the first good car ride of my life. It was a fresh start. The beginning of something wonderful and glorious. A journey to paradise.

Those feelings were so against what life had thus far taught me to expect that I tamped them down whenever they threatened to overtake me. What proof did I have that this bond would last? That she and the Magic One, whose name I learned was Hunter, wouldn't just toss me out the moment I became an inconvenience? That there was such a thing as a Forever Home?

Still, I wanted to believe it was possible. And when I gazed into her eyes, I knew that no matter what happened, that she would always love me with all her heart.

That was a lot to take stake in, especially when I had nothing to go on except the way she looked at me, the way she wrapped her arms around me as I sat shaking in the backseat, the way she laid her head over mine and whispered, "I love you, Echo."

What more did I need?

Yet my nerves got the better of me. As Hannah started up the front steps to their home, the two of us joined by the leash, my legs locked up. She slipped nubby fingers beneath my collar and tugged, but I couldn't move.

This was all so ... new. So unbelievable. From the clean inside of Hunter's truck, to the bacony treats that Hannah had hand-fed me at the clinic, to the big, well-kept yard stretching to either side of the house and the sheep grazing in the distance. It overwhelmed all my senses. Every noise, every movement sparked an overload of new information that I had to process. How could I sort the familiar — the flock of crows alighting in the trees, the wind rushing down from the hills, the sun high overhead — from all that I had never seen before and did not know?

Hunter held the front door open, waiting. Inside stood an older girl and a woman.

"Why isn't he moving?" the older girl said.

My body trembled. Flushed with embarrassment, I fought the urge to run. Where was my newfound courage?

With more patience than anyone had ever shown me, Hannah sank down to sit on the bottom step next to me. "It's okay, Echo." She took my face in her hands and kissed me on the nose. "I don't like new places, either."

Then she twisted at the waist and said to her father. "We'll stay

112

here for now."

Hunter looked at the woman. Arms crossed, she nodded and they all went inside. Except Hannah, who stayed with me.

We sat there for hours, the warm summer air thick around us as the sun dipped behind the ragged hills, the lightning bugs flickering across the lawn. Hannah's mother, the woman, brought her dinner and set it on the porch behind her. Hannah crawled to the end of the leash to reach it. She tore the corner from her grilled cheese sandwich and put it on the ground.

"For you, Echo," she said.

Sniffing, I crept closer. My mouth watered. My stomach growled. I stared at it for a long time before I took it. It melted on my tongue. She put another piece down, then another. Before I knew it, we were sitting right next to the front door. I wasn't shaking any longer. Curiosity begged me to look through the screen door inside the house, so I did.

Hunter looked down at me from inside. "Good work, Hannah. You made it ten feet in just under two hours. Is he ready to come inside?"

"Yah, I think so."

That night I slept beneath Hannah's bed. It was the closest I could be to her and yet still feel safe from all the newness. Eventually, my sleeping place became the rug beside her bed. There, I had a clear view to the door. No one could get to Hannah without first stepping on me.

I followed her everywhere, a silent shadow standing guard. The leash became a forgotten thing that was taken out of the closet and used only when we went to public places, and then more to comply with public expectations than to keep me within range. Hannah and I were bound to one another more strongly than any rope, chain, or length of leather could ever manage.

For weeks, I lived with the fear that Mario or Earl or Mavis would show up to claim me, and life would go back to being a series of letdowns. Yet with each passing day, that fear faded and trust grew.

—oO0o—

Hannah and I spent most of our summer under the Crooked Tree. Hunter had bolted a swing from the sturdiest branch of the taller bough and Hannah spent hour upon hour kicking her legs up high and flying toward the clouds, then falling back toward earth again. Ever watchful, I lay between the sprawling roots, one eye always open, fighting sleep as she tirelessly swung and climbed and skipped and cartwheeled.

One day, the McHughs went on a picnic in the park. When they were done eating, Jenn urged the girls to go play. Maura leaped up and joined a circle of other children lobbing a softball in a circle, laughing and chatting. Hannah, however, lay down beside me, her head tucked against my chest, her hand wound in my leash.

Next to the merry-go-round, a dark-haired boy sat with a small fawn and white puppy in his lap. I wasn't sure yet what to make of other dogs. I hadn't been around any since I was a pup, and even then it was only other puppies. I stretched out beside Hannah, watchful.

"Hannah," Jenn began, rubbing her daughter's back, "why don't you —?"

"Honey, she's fine." Hunter picked up the paper plates and set one down in front of me with a half-eaten biscuit and handful of carrots on it. The rest he stuffed into a plastic bag. "She *has* a friend now. Don't push it."

I gobbled the biscuit down in two gulps, then inhaled the baby carrots. I'd never known such food existed. Heck, I could have lived out of what was in the McHughs' trashcan, although they threw out a lot that Hunter proclaimed wasn't 'good for dogs'. I begged to differ.

"I just thought," Jenn said, "maybe Echo could use a friend."

"Did you not hear him growl at that German Shepherd we passed on the trail? I'd say he'd rather not have other dogs in his space. It's probably best that we respect that." He gathered up the empty cups and dumped them in the trash bag. "You know, he and Hannah are a lot alike. That's why they get along so well. And she's doing a great job taking care of him, don't you think?"

One brow arched, Jenn gave him a sidelong glance. "Honey, I could set my clock by Echo's feeding times. Yesterday, I put his food bowl in the dishwasher and Hannah about had a conniption when she couldn't find it for his breakfast time."

One side of Hunter's mouth crept upward.

Jenn slapped him lightly on the thigh. "What?"

"Nothing."

"Don't tell me 'nothing'. You were thinking something. What is it? Spill."

He gave a half-shrug. "Just ... well, they make a good pair, don't you think?"

Hannah turned her head toward her father and, throwing an arm over me, snuggled closer.

"Yeah, yeah, yeah. You were right, okay? Is that what you want to hear?" Jenn lay back on the picnic blanket and rested her floppy sunhat on her face to block out the sun. "They belong together. Like peanut butter and jelly. One without the other's just not right."

"Yeah, I felt that way about Halo."

"Who?"

"The dog I had growing up. When we had to move up North for a while, leaving her behind was devastating. But then she returned — and saved my life. Have I told you that story before?"

"Let me think ..." Pushing her hat back, Jenn made her hands into fists and unrolled her fingers one at a time. "Yes, you have. About a dozen times." Rolling toward him, she kissed his cheek. "And it gets better every time you tell it."

He sat up with a start. "I almost forgot."

From the pocket of his jacket, which had been lying next to the picnic basket, he took out a ball covered in bright yellow fuzz. Standing, he tossed it from hand to hand. As I watched it land in his palm, I saw him not as a man, but a boy, about Hannah's age. A boy with Hunter's eyes, lobbing a yellow ball into the sky. And I remembered, or thought I did, chasing that ball over crisp autumn leaves, and bringing it back again and again, until ... he fell to the ground, not breathing.

Concern overcame me. I rushed at him, knocking him to the ground, and lathered his face with licks, only to discover it was not Hunter the boy lying lifeless on the ground before me, but Hunter the man, very much alive and not at all happy with my overly zealous behavior.

"Whoa, there! Get off." Pushing me away, he wiped his cheek against his sleeve. "Calm down, will you? I haven't even thrown it yet."

I looked at his hand. The ball was still there, cupped in his palm. But peeking from the V-neckline of his polo shirt was the pucker of a scar, right next to his heart.

chapter 15

Hunter

Hunter stood on the front porch, one hand cupped above his brow as he stared into the afternoon sun. At the far west corner of their property, across the road, an older man was unloading boxes from a rental truck. Earlier that day, Jenn told him, an even bigger truck had arrived and a troop of burly men had taken furniture and appliances into the house.

Jenn came out the front door to stand beside him, swishing flies away with her dishtowel. "How long has that place been vacant?"

He took the glass of sweet tea she offered and drank it halfway down. He'd just had a farm call two miles down the road, so when he was done he stopped at home for a late lunch. It was still forty minutes until he had to be at his next appointment. "Hmmm, Old Man Harmon died about this time of summer two years ago, didn't he? I heard probate was a mess. That reminds me — we need to make sure everything's spelled out in our will."

"I take it he didn't have one?"

"Harmon? Nope. And three greedy daughters, to boot. House

itself isn't worth much as it is, but it's a nice piece of property."

"Well, maybe he'll fix it up. Whoever *he* is." They watched for a while, flies buzzing around them, sweat dripping down the fronts of their shirts. Jenn fanned herself, then rolled her short sleeves up over her shoulders. "Say, you didn't happen to see a woman over there, too, did you? A wife, or maybe an older daughter?"

"No, why?"

"I just thought it might be nice to have someone to talk to during the day."

Finishing his tea, he set his glass on the porch rail. "You can't talk to an older gentleman?"

"It's not the same, Hunter. I was hoping someone would move in there that, you know, might be closer to our age. Maybe a nice couple with kids that we could invite over for dinner now and then. I love the country, but sometimes it would just be nice to actually see living, breathing human beings, instead of sheep and cows."

She started to go inside, as if expecting him to follow, but Hunter went down the steps and turned around. "Want to go say 'hi' to our new neighbor?"

"Oh, I don't know, Hunter. He's probably terribly busy. We should wait a week. Let him settle in, don't you think? Besides, a lot of folks move to the country because they want to be left alone. He doesn't need some nosy neighbors butting into his business."

"Or maybe he's hoping we'll introduce ourselves so he has someone to borrow a cup of sugar or gallon of lawnmower gas from when he needs it? I'm never sure what the protocol is. Does the new neighbor come over and say 'hello'? Or is that our responsibility? I say we take the initiative." He beckoned to her. "Come on, Jenn. It'll only take a minute. If he's buried in boxes, that's the perfect excuse for us to bow out of there. If we wait and show up next week when everything's unpacked, he might ask us to sit down for a cup of coffee." He reached for her hand. "What do you say?"

Tossing the dishtowel over the railing next to his empty glass, she took his hand. "All right. I suppose you have a point."

They were halfway down the lane when Jenn pulled up. "What about Hannah? We can't just leave her —"

"Relax, Jenn. We won't go inside. We should be able to see her from his front porch. But if it makes you feel any better, run and tell her to stay put for ten minutes. Anyway, Echo's looking out for her. I doubt he'd let anyone jump out of their car and kidnap her."

A look of horror flashed over Jenn's face, as if the notion were a real possibility.

"Or ..." Hunter added, "you can ask her to come along and meet him? But you know how that's likely to go over."

Glancing toward the Crooked Tree where Hannah was playing, she huffed a sigh. "It won't."

"Sooo?"

"I'll be right back."

Two minutes later, Hunter and Jenn crossed the road. On the other side, Jenn turned to look back toward the tree. Hannah was still crouched over a pile of dirt.

"What exactly is she doing?" Hunter asked.

"Speaking to the ants." Jenn gave him a slanted smile. "Because, you know, they have a lot to talk about and no one ever listens."

Just then, the new neighbor came out his front door. He took a step back, as if he had just walked through the wrong door. Fine wrinkles framed a pair of deep brown eyes, and dark, nearly black hair was threaded with silver along his temples and sideburns, making him look to be in his mid-sixties. His slacks were pleated and he wore a crisp button-up shirt. He also had a meticulously trimmed goatee. Very metropolitan, Hunter thought. Not quite the look one would expect of someone who'd relocated to the outskirts of Faderville, Kentucky.

The man's face tightened. "Can I help you?"

Hunter gathered from the tone that the question was merely a courtesy and he had no intention of helping them with anything. Maybe ever.

"Uh, no, not really. We live next door — well, across the road — and just wanted to say 'howdy'." Hunter went up the steps and extended his hand, figuring it was best to at least make the gesture and then excuse themselves as quickly as possible. "I'm Hunter McHugh. I run the Samuels Vet Clinic in town. This is my wife, Jenn. She used to be a bank manager, but is busy raising our two daughters now."

"Hi." Jenn waved politely, but remained at the bottom of the porch stairs.

The man stared at Hunter's outstretched hand, then quite reluctantly clasped it without making eye contact. "Hello, Dr. McHugh." His eyes flicked to Jenn. "Mrs. McHugh."

"Please, that's too formal. You can call us Jenn and Hunter. Or Hunter and Jenn. They're interchangeable."

The man leveled an insistent gaze at Hunter. "If you'll excuse me ..."

"Do you need some help?" Before even seeing her expression, Hunter could sense Jenn's inward sigh. He grinned at her in apology, then looking back toward their neighbor, stuck his hands in his pockets and shrugged. "Sorry, I don't know what to call you."

"*Mr.* Menendez."

Hunter raised his brows in question. "Jack Menendez?"

"No."

"Frank? John? Bill? Ted?" Hunter forced a laugh, hoping the guy would lighten up. He was a tough nut to crack.

"If you want to run a criminal records check on me, it's Hector Arturo Menendez. Heck, for short. My parents were Cuban, but I was born here. Now again, if you'll excuse me ..." He brushed past Hunter and went down the steps without so much as nodding at Jenn.

She tossed Hunter a 'What the hell?' look. He rolled his eyes, then hurried to catch up with her as she made a break for it.

"Bye, Mr. Menendez," Jenn offered with a wave from halfway down the driveway.

"Bye, Heck." Hunter spun around, walking backward a few steps. "If you need anything, don't hesitate to call. We're in the phone book. Or just stop by. Anytime. Don't be a stranger."

Heck gave a perfunctory nod as he took a box from the rental van and went back inside.

When they were back in their own driveway, Jenn slapped Hunter on the arm.

"What?" he said.

"Satisfied?"

"It was worth a try. Maybe he'll warm up, eventually."

"I'll consider him a good neighbor if he doesn't throw wild parties and collect junk cars." She grabbed the dishtowel from the railing and flung it over her shoulder. "Fetch Hannah, will you? I need to go into town to pick Maura up from softball practice. The girls have a dental appointment in an hour."

"Hah, good luck with that." Maura would be fine, as usual, but Hannah could go either way. She didn't mind the dental instruments; it was the assistant having their hands crammed in her mouth for more than a few seconds that could set her off. Checking his watch, Hunter realized he had a quick farm call to make that afternoon and needed to be on his way. He trotted over to the tree where Hannah was. She was gazing up into the branches.

"What are you —?"

She pressed a finger to her lips.

For a good long minute, Hunter searched among the leaves. He saw a couple of birds there, robins maybe, but nothing else. Crouching down to scratch Echo behind the ears, he waited for a couple more minutes. Every time he looked into that dog's eyes, he couldn't help but think he'd known him for a long time already.

He glanced at his daughter. Hannah hadn't changed positions. He wasn't even sure she'd blinked since he came over.

"Honey, I really need to —"

"Shhh!" She flapped a hand at him. "Listen," she whispered.

He did. All he heard was an occasional chirp from overhead. Somewhere in the distance a tractor hummed. Another hay cutting. It had been a dry year. They'd be lucky to get a third. Farther away, cars zoomed along the state highway.

"Hannah, I have to go. And Mommy wants you to come inside to get ready to go. Is it something important?"

Finally, she looked at him, the narrow space between her eyebrows creased as if she were angry with him for breaking the silence. She pointed somewhere up in the tree. "The baby. It's going to try to fly, but the mom and dad are worried. They don't think he's ready."

"Ah, I see. All parents feel like that when their kids leave home for the first time. Come on. We need to go. Mommy's taking you to get your teeth checked. There's a new toothbrush in it for you if you're good." He lifted an arm toward the house in encouragement. It could be hard to redirect Hannah when she had her mind fixed on something even as simple as this. She couldn't leave one thing and come back to it later without some kind of closure. "Tell you what — I should be back before you. I'll check for the baby bird then. If he's sitting on the ground, I'll put him back in the nest, okay?"

He didn't even know where the nest was, but he had to say something to get her moving.

Although she didn't seem entirely convinced, Hunter was able to get her away from the tree and see her off with Jenn. After that, he drove to the east side of Adair County to Tommy and Beth Appleton's farm to tend to their goats. Tommy used to do all of the hoof trimming, worming, and vaccinating himself, but at eighty-two he was too stiff in the joints to manage it by himself anymore. So nowadays he just called on Hunter to do the brunt of the work while he handed him the hoof nippers, paste, and syringes.

When Hunter returned home, he let Echo out of his kennel to do his business while he watered the tomato plants. As Australian Shepherds went, Echo was pretty typical: mentally and physically active, a decent watchdog, and a little on the quirky side. He was black and white, which was a less common color combination for the breed, but everything else about him was Aussie, right down to his bobtail. The one trait he seemed to lack was any working instinct. Hunter had introduced him to his mother's sheep on three occasions so far and the dog hadn't displayed a lick of interest. In Hunter's eyes, it wasn't critical, but it would have been nice to have a dog that could have helped with livestock when needed. At any rate, he was a good companion for Hannah, and that was even more important.

A strange scrabbling noise drew Hunter's attention and he went around the corner of the garage to find Echo pawing at the bottom of Hannah's empty kiddy pool. Hunter pressed the lever on the hose nozzle and shot a stream of water in Echo's direction. The dog snapped at the water playfully. It took a good five minutes, but Hunter was able to fill the pool up. While he finished watering the garden, Echo dunked his head into the pool water and snorted bubbles. Eventually, the dog lowered himself fully into the water to lay in it. He didn't leave the pool until Hunter began walking toward the Crooked Tree.

As Hunter stopped to inspect the ground near the tree, Echo rolled his shoulders in a giant shake, flinging water over Hunter's front.

"Hey!" Hunter turned his face away until Echo was done. "A little warning next time, okay? Crazy Aussie."

As far as Hunter could see, there was no baby bird beneath the Crooked Tree. Craning his neck, he looked up into the tangle of branches. It took some time, but he finally spied the robins' nest. Both parents were sitting beside it, cocking their heads at him. He surveyed the area one more time. No sign of any baby bird.

Hunter was about to head on inside to see what he could make for dinner when he noticed Echo sitting on the far side of the tree near a clump of grass. Echo tipped his head side to side, his ears cocked as if listening. Hunter had an idea about what had his attention.

More down than feathers, the baby bird rested between Echo's paws. Hunter nudged Echo away and looked more closely. The eyes were closed, the mouth fixed open in a last gasp. He poked it with a finger. The body was cold, already stiffening. It was dry, so Echo hadn't had the poor thing in his mouth. No, the little bird had fallen. Not ready to fly, just like Hannah had said.

He fetched a shovel from the garage and scooped up the little body, then buried it in the garden next to a pepper plant as Echo looked on. To make it less obvious, he retrieved the rake next and smoothed the freshly upturned dirt, then scratched at a broader area down the row of peppers. Not that Hannah would have a clue there was anything buried belowground, but she often took notice of the oddest details, so Hunter wasn't taking any chances.

Together, he and Echo went in the house. Just as he opened the refrigerator door to peer inside, a text from Jenn came through:

On our way home soon. Burgers on plate, middle shelf, fridge. Tater tots and corn in freezer.

It was Tuesday. How could he forget? Hannah had to have tater tots on Tuesdays.

After preheating the oven and putting the burgers on, Hunter set the table and put out the condiments, placing the ketchup bottle squarely in front of Hannah's plate. The whole time, Echo watched him astutely, golden-brown eyes following Hunter's every movement as he spoke to the dog. Hunter often talked to the animals he was treating in a low, calm voice as a way of soothing their nerves, but with

Echo it almost seemed like he understood every word and that, if he could, he'd talk back. The dog already had an impressive arsenal of commands that he followed: sit, down, stay, come, off … All the usual. But almost daily, Hunter would take one object, repeat its name, then mix it in a pile of other things and ask Echo to bring it.

"Bring me the Frisbee," he'd say, and Echo would flip through the pile until he found it, then drop it at Hunter's feet.

To test him, Hunter would go through a list of items. Eleven straight was the record so far. When Echo tired of the game or got confused, he would resort to fetching his favorite toy — a squeaky giraffe, similar to the stuffed one called Faustine that Hannah still slept with.

Echo was easily the smartest dog Hunter had ever known. Since Halo, that was.

Car tires crunched on gravel. Jenn was home with the girls. Hunter mussed the hair on top of Echo's head fondly, then poured the drinks, put the food on the table, and sat down to wait.

Jenn and Maura tromped through the door wearily, stopping at the sink to wash their hands.

"Hey," Hunter hailed, "how'd it go, sport?"

Maura twisted her face, her lower lip drooping noticeably on one side. "Can't feel my tongue."

"Cavity." Jenn slid into her chair and arranged pickle slices on her burger. "Her first and only so far, though."

"Well, that's not so bad, then," Hunter consoled. "In our day, back when we drank Kool-Aid by the gallon with every meal, most every kid had a mouthful of silver-filled molars. Kids these days aren't going to know what dentures are." He scooped a ladle-full of corn onto his plate. "Where's Hannah?"

"She insisted on checking under the Crooked Tree for some baby bird," Jenn said. "If she doesn't come inside soon, I'll go get her."

Hunter cringed. Hopefully, once she didn't find anything, she'd be satisfied that all had gone well and let the whole episode go. He slid twelve tater tots onto her plate and then took some for himself.

Two minutes later, she plodded through the back door and plopped down in her chair, staring sullenly at the tater tots. She didn't even bother to arrange them in three rows of four — or maybe it was four rows of three. There was a difference.

"What's up, sweet pea?" Hunter was prepared for this. He'd dealt with two deceased hamsters when Maura was little, before Hannah came along. "You look a little sad."

Hannah didn't even look up from her plate when Echo rested his chin on her knee. "It's gone."

"What is?"

"The baby bird."

"Ah, right. Maybe it flew away? I think I saw a small robin over in the hedge row when I came home. It took off across the field." Sometimes little white lies were necessary, he reasoned.

Hannah's face hardened as she turned her gaze on him. Her breathing grew more audible as she forced breaths through pinched nostrils. "It died."

"Why do you say that?" Hunter bit into his hamburger. She was only guessing.

"You buried it in the garden, Daddy."

He stopped in mid-chew, suddenly aware of the sinking feeling in his stomach. How could she possibly —?

"They told me so," Hannah added before he could ask. Not that he was going to, although he did wonder how she'd come to that conclusion.

Finishing his bite, he washed it down with a swallow of almond milk. "Who told you?"

"The mommy and daddy. They saw you pick it up with a shovel and carry it to the garden and put dirt on top of it."

Stunned, he set his glass down. Jenn and Maura had stopped

eating and were staring at Hunter like he'd just been caught stealing the Halloween candy early. Hannah glowered at him. Even Echo had his intense golden eyes fixed accusingly on Hunter.

There was no way out of this, except to tell her the truth. "Okay, yeah, I, uh ... I found him, actually Echo found him. He was already dead. So I gave him a proper burial." He reached his fingers across the table toward Hannah's, then turned his hand over. "I'm sorry, sweet pea. I didn't want to upset you. It happens to a lot of baby animals in the wild."

Ignoring his apology, she pushed her plate back, got up, and trudged out the door. The screen door banged behind her. Jenn got up and watched her through the kitchen window.

"She's sitting under her tree, again," she said. She opened the door and ushered Echo out to look over her. "Wonder how many meals she'll miss before she breaks down and eats something?"

"Could be days," Maura muttered. "If I did that, you'd —"

"Don't," Jenn warned. "Hannah's not like you. You're a whole lot easier to reason with." Sitting back down at the table, she said, "How did she know that?"

Hunter knew. He was convinced of it now. Yet there was no way he was going to say it out loud. Just like he didn't tell people certain things about himself, like passing through a long tunnel toward a white light or seeing dead people. He cornered a spoonful of corn and munched it down. "Lucky guess, I suppose."

But one glance at Jenn told him even she had her suspicions.

—o0Oo—

Later that night, when Hunter found Hannah asleep under the Crooked Tree and carried her to her bed, her lashes fluttered in half-wakefulness. He put Faustine on her tummy. She folded an arm around the giraffe in a light hug and he pulled the blanket up to tuck her in.

"Hannah, I don't want you to ever be sad. You understand?"

Her blond locks rustled against the pillowcase as she nodded. "But you lied. You and Mommy always tell me it's bad to tell lies."

"You're right. I did and I shouldn't have." He tapped the button on her alarm clock and the sound of a babbling brook came from it. The thing had two dozen different white noises on it and for whatever reason Hannah found this sound calming. It helped her fall asleep. Hunter would have thought, given her experience nearly drowning, that it would be the last thing she'd want to hear, but whenever he tried changing it to something else, like birds chirping or falling rain, Hannah clamped her hands over her ears and started making a noise that was half shriek, half moan.

Anger and blame were gone from her face. She gazed at him softly, relaxed but fighting the pull of sleep. There was something he had to say to her before she drifted off. Something she had to understand.

"You remember when you told me after you fell in the river how you heard the bluebird and the fish talk to you?"

Her eyelids snapped open briefly as she nodded.

"Well, each of us has something very special about us. Something different. And sometimes we're so different that it's hard for other people to understand us."

She wrinkled her nose at him. Clearly, *she* didn't understand *him* right now. He may as well have been speaking Mandarin. She wasn't good at catching implications. He needed to be more direct.

"It's okay if you tell me, or maybe even Mommy. But when animals talk to you, Hannah, you probably shouldn't tell anyone else, okay?"

"Why?"

"Because other people can't hear them, sweet pea. They'll think you're making it up."

"But I'm not." She dangled her hand over the edge of the bed. Echo licked her fingers, as if to remind her he was there, then he lay down in his usual spot on the braided rug.

"I know, I know. It's just ... Just don't, okay? You'll understand why when you're older." A thought flickered through his mind. What if he got Hannah a book about Dr. Doolittle? On second thought, he decided against it. It would only encourage her to cultivate her ability.

For now, the more she kept this special talent under her hat the better. Especially since she was starting kindergarten in two weeks. That alone was bound to be traumatic for the entire family.

And to think, he'd been the one to talk Jenn out of home-schooling her. Maybe that was one argument he should've let her win.

chapter 16

Hunter

Moonlight flooded the room in a silver haze and the lightest of breezes parted the curtains. Hunter lay in bed, his back to his wife, listening to the rustle of sheets. She couldn't sleep either, apparently.

A week had gone by since the baby bird incident. That meant they were a week closer to Hannah heading off to school. Jenn had tried to be strong about it, but Hunter could sense her anxiety. Working with Hannah had been her life for the past several years. It was hard to hand that responsibility over to someone else.

Meanwhile, Echo's presence had been a godsend. With that dog at her side, Hannah was the confident little girl she'd been developing into before the accident. Away from the dog, she was once again the little girl afraid of her own voice. If anything ever happened to Echo …

Turning over, he ran a hand from Jenn's shoulder to her elbow, then slipped his arm around her waist. "I know you're worried, honey. And it may not go perfectly, but if we don't do this —"

"She's come a long way, Hunter." Jenn rolled onto her back to stare up at the ceiling. "I remember when they told us she might never talk." She scoffed. "They were *so* wrong."

He traced a finger over her collarbone, resisting the urge to plant a kiss at the base of her throat. She was beautiful. Still. Even after fifteen years he never got tired of waking up next to her. But now wasn't the time for passionate overtures. She needed reassurance. "You've done a great job with her, Jenn."

"Not me. *She's* done a great job. She's special, Hunter. And I don't mean that in a backhanded compliment kind of way."

"What *do* you mean?"

For several moments she didn't answer. "After the accident, I kept thinking she'd never catch up to where she was before that, but look at her now. She's changed so much. She wasn't even home a week when she started reading on her own. Reading, Hunter. Not just sounding things out, but saying whole words on sight. She's ahead of where she should be at this age, but whenever I take her to have her tested, it's like this door closes and they can't get anything out of her."

While Jenn had had great success teaching Hannah to read, write, and do basic math, getting her to connect socially was another matter entirely, and one that frustrated her to no end.

"I don't know what to do to change that," she continued. "It doesn't matter how smart she is. God, she could be a savant, for all we know. I'm starting to think she is. But if she won't talk to anyone besides us ..." She grabbed the pillow from behind her head and screamed into it. "Arrrrgh!"

"Hey, hey, hey." Hunter pushed the pillow away and brushed the hair from her face. "We have to be patient, all right?"

She slapped both hands to either side of her head. "At first they were saying mild autism, and then sensory processing disorder, but every once in a while they throw out Asperger's syndrome , which lately they've latched onto ... I mean, how am I supposed to deal with her if I don't know what her problem is?" Both hands flew up to cover her mouth. Slowly, she lowered them. "Ohhh, I didn't mean it like that. I just meant —"

"You don't have to explain yourself to me, Jenn. I get it. But maybe we need to stop looking at what she isn't and accept her for what she is. It could be a whole lot worse, you know. Every time I see a parent pushing a kid with severe disabilities around in a wheelchair, it hits me just how lucky we are. Hannah's healthy. She's highly functioning. She's smart. She can do anything a normal kid can do. She just doesn't know how to handle herself socially. She'll learn how, but it's going to take time. Anyway, a lot of famous people have had Asperger's."

"Really?" Jenn sat up, the lines in her face softening. "Like who?"

"Thomas Jefferson."

"Oh, no way. He was not. He was just freakishly brilliant."

"Mozart." He'd been doing his research ever since the last child development specialist bantered about the Asperger's label.

"Now that one I can believe."

"My point is, we need to stop —"

"You mean *I* need to stop."

The curtains snapped as the breeze from outside picked up. Clouds had crawled across the moon, shutting out its light, and there'd been a definite drop in temperature since they tried to go to sleep two hours ago. "Fine, *you* need to stop stressing about this. Just because she's different doesn't mean —"

"Should I get her lined up for piano lessons? Or maybe violin? You can tote a violin around anywhere, but they sound so screechy when someone's just starting out on one. What do you think?"

"Ask her."

"Ask Hannah?"

"Sure. She might not be interested in either. Have you ever seen her get enthralled with the classical radio station when we're driving somewhere and you're flipping through all the stations?" Hunter got

132

out of bed and closed the window just as rain began to pelt the side of the house. "Try whatever you want, Jenn. But don't push her. If she has some special ability ... *if* she does, it may take a while to come out. And it may not be what we expect or hope for."

Grabbing a shirt, Hunter headed for the door.

"Where are you going?"

Lightning flickered through the window, followed by the low rumble of distant thunder. "Downstairs to read for a while. I don't want to keep you up. Good night."

"Night, Hunter." Jenn slid back under the sheets. For several moments they stared at each other, something unspoken hanging in the air.

What Hunter didn't say — would never say — was that Hannah needed to go off to school for them as much as for her. Ever since she was a year old and they'd had a hard time making eye contact with her, their lives had revolved around Hannah. Everything was always about Hannah. Just having Echo around had freed them of some responsibility for having to watch or entertain her every single moment.

It wasn't enough, though. Hunter was ready to let her go out into the world. It was Jenn who needed to let their little fledgling take wing.

They couldn't protect Hannah from the world forever. She needed to learn to deal with it on her own terms.

—o0Oo—

The limb lying across the fence was as big around as Hunter's waist. He grabbed it, pushing up, while Brad put a shoulder into it from farther up. No matter how they leveraged it, no matter which way they pushed, it wasn't budging.

Last night's storm had generated sixty-five mile per hour straight line winds that had peeled the roofs from several barns in Adair

County, downed power lines, and toppled two semis on the interstate. The winds had left a swath of destruction from Elizabethtown to Knoxville. Fortunately, no one had been hurt, but their weather was all over the national news.

It had kept Hunter up half the night. He'd gone outside at first light to discover a dozen shingles missing from the roof and their trash cans on the far side of the hayfield next to the house. He never did find the lid for one of them. Jenn and Maura headed off to Somerset where the storm damage had been negligent to stock up on groceries. Jenn was convinced if she wasn't first at the store, they'd sell out of stock and the kids would go hungry.

When Lise called an hour later, Hunter went right over to help clean up, Hannah and Echo riding gunshot, since they were all up early too anyway. Several old growth trees had come down in the storm — one across the driveway and two had taken down sections of fence — and he and Brad were trying to move what they could through sheer manpower. It quickly became clear, however, that they were going to need to get the chainsaws out and cut some logs.

Brad put on his earphones and safety goggles, and pulled the starting cord on his chainsaw. Standing near the barn, Hannah clamped her hands over her ears and darted inside, where her Gramma Lise was. Echo trailed after her.

Mere moments later, Lise ran out of the barn, waving her arms in the air as if trying to flag down an airplane. "Brad! Hunter!"

Brad turned his chainsaw off and set it on the ground, then removed his earphones. "What is it?"

"The sheep — they're gone!"

"How?"

"The light pole fell and took out a section of stock panel. I didn't even think to look in the small arena this morning to check the fence. There was just so much else going on."

"Any idea where they went?" Hunter said.

"Judging by the tracks, they headed off to the creek. It was a cow pasture once, maybe thirty years ago, and pretty wide open, so we won't have a hard time finding them. But half the fences were taken down at some point. Beyond that, it's nothing but woods and wild hills."

"I'll get the ATV," Brad said. "Between the three of us, we can round them up."

"You'll have a hard time of it down there," Lise said. "The creek bed cuts pretty deep into the earth and takes a lot of bends. You'll no sooner get around to the far side and they'll disappear into a gulley and race off in the other direction. And if anything has spooked them, they could have already split in half a dozen different directions. There's no telling what the situation is until we get over that line of hills and take a look."

Hunter glanced toward the barn. Hannah stood in the open doorway, Faustine dangling from one hand, Echo at her knee. "I wouldn't count on three of us. Someone needs to watch Hannah. Rounding up a hundred sheep like that could take us hours."

Lise's gaze drifted to Echo. "Times like this I wish Halo was still around." She tilted her head, mulling the possibilities. "Hey, what if —?"

"No," Hunter levied. "Don't even go there. Just because Echo's an Australian Shepherd doesn't mean he knows a sheep's head from its butt. I'm afraid he didn't get the herding instinct gene. Last time I brought him into a pen with sheep, he hid behind me, shaking. He'd probably just as soon eat their droppings as herd them. Hell, if he even got up the courage to approach them, he could very well chase them all the way to Lexington. Then not only will you have lost your entire flock, Mom, but Hannah will have lost her dog."

"So you're saying 'no'?"

"Very perceptive of you."

"That's a shame. He's such a smart dog."

135

"I'd say we could call on the Listons with Spin, their Border Collie, to help," Brad said, "but they're in Illinois visiting their daughter. Is there any way you could call Jenn back home, Hunter? Maybe Maura could keep an eye on Hannah and with Jenn's help we could get this job done in no time?"

Hunter rubbed at his neck, lost for a solution. "I wish, but it'd take her a good hour to get here — and that's if she answers her phone right away. Knowing Jenn, she probably has her phone turned off."

"Think you could try?" Lise said. "You can stay here with Hannah until Jenn gets back. Maybe Brad and I will be able to get something done? If nothing else, we can figure things out while we call around for more help. This just might take a village."

Satisfied they had a plan for now, Brad went off to the spare barn to gas up the ATV, while Lise made a few phone calls to neighbors on the other side of the valley and down the road. There had been no sightings, which was a bad sign.

Sitting at the kitchen table with Hannah, who was arranging her carrot sticks in some kind of geometric pattern, a break from her usual neat rows, Hunter regretted not having exposed Echo to livestock more, but there really hadn't been a need to. The last Aussie his mom had owned died a few years ago. Since then, she hadn't even entertained the prospect of getting another dog. Brad was only months away from retirement and they wanted to travel while they were still young enough to get around. Having a dog would make that more difficult.

Hannah slipped Echo a carrot underneath the table. He sniffed it, then took a nibble. Soon, he was crunching away and begging for more.

"I saw that," Hunter said.

"Mommy says carrots are okay for dogs."

He couldn't argue with that. But he hadn't meant what he said as any kind of admonishment. He was merely teasing. Sometimes jokes were lost on Hannah.

The rumble of the ATV sounded just outside, then stopped. Brad strode into the kitchen, pools of sweat already darkening his shirt under his arms. He tickled Hannah's neck, but instead of giggling, she hunched up like a turtle pulling into its shell.

A few moments later, Lise came in and pulled a couple of water bottles from the fridge. "Calvin Rowe isn't answering his phone and the Minards are busy fixing their own fences."

"Gus said he could be over in an hour or two." Brad took one of the bottles from her. "Looks like it's just the two of us for now. Time for a roundup. Let's go, cowpoke."

Hunter didn't like not being able to help. Yet he couldn't just park Hannah in front of the TV and trust that she was going to stay there. He'd left a message with Jenn, but so far she hadn't answered. Knowing Hannah, she'd suddenly feel the need to wash her hands, then decide a bubble bath was a good idea and dump the whole box of Calgon into the tub while watching the bubbles overflow onto the floor. It had happened just last week. Thank goodness Jenn had walked in before Hannah stepped into a tub full of scalding water.

As Brad and Lise started out the door, Hunter stood. "You know, I was thinking maybe I could ask our new neighbor, Heck, to keep an eye on Hannah so I can help you guys. I saw his car when we came over. I'm pretty sure he's home."

Lise shrugged. "Sure. It's worth a try, I suppose."

"You go ahead and see if you can locate the flock. I'll walk Hannah over and ask. If she's standing right there with me, it'll be hard for him to say 'no'." Even so, given Heck's cold reception of them last week, he wasn't sure Heck would agree to watch Hannah. Or that it was a good idea, given that he didn't know anything about the guy. But with Echo along to supervise, Hunter felt reassured.

Echo nudged Hannah's leg. A carrot dropped from her fingers

onto the floor. He snarfed it down, then stretched out at her feet.

No, that dog wouldn't let anything happen to Hannah. Even if his life was at stake.

—o0Oo—

"Just remember, you need to keep an eye on Echo. Make sure he doesn't get into anything, okay?" Hunter eyed his daughter sternly. Really, he'd said that to make sure Echo always had Hannah in his sight, not the other way around. When she didn't acknowledge his question, he took her small jaw in his hand and turned her face so he could look into her eyes. "Okay, Hannah?"

Shifting side to side, she nodded. They were only standing on Heck's porch and already she was growing anxious.

"What did I just tell you?" he prompted. He'd learned to have her repeat things to make sure she understood. Sometimes her mind was a million miles away.

She twisted her face away. "Watch Echo."

"Good. Now let's see if Mr. Menendez will let you watch TV here while Daddy helps Gramma and Grampa. I'll come back in an hour and check on you." Actually, he couldn't promise if he'd be back in an hour, but Hannah wasn't likely to notice the time. Besides, he wasn't even sure if she could read a clock yet. He'd have to ask Jenn when she got home.

Hunter knocked on the door. No one answered. He knocked again, waited. Hannah was rocking on her feet, swaying like a tree in the wind. Heck's car was still in the driveway. And the TV was on. He checked his phone for texts, just in case he'd missed the little beep. Nothing.

Stepping away from the door to peer in the picture window, he called his mom. "Any sign of them yet?"

"Yeah, they're exactly where I suspected. I don't think any have wandered away from the group, but I won't know until we get them back in the pens and accounted for."

"Any luck getting them headed back toward the house?"

"Not yet. They're light, Hunter. Practically wild. They're spooked, too. It's like they found themselves outside the fence and reverted to their ancestral roots. Trying to do this with two people is just impossible. And the ATV is only scaring them more, even though they're used to seeing Brad ride it around the farm. You'd think a spaceship from Mars had landed in their midst."

"I'll be there as soon as I can, Mom. I know Heck's here, but he hasn't answered the door yet."

"Maybe he's indisposed, Hunter?"

"Fat chance." Hunter pressed his face to the glass. "I can see the bathroom from here. Door's wide open. Pretty sure there isn't a second one in this house."

"Give him a break. It's not like he was expecting you. Besides, a lot of people don't shut the bathroom door when they're in the house alone. You're going to feel pretty foolish when he comes out and sees you staring into his bathroom as he's zipping up his fly."

She had a point. Hunter stepped back to the door and pounded on it with the heel of his fist. "Call you back as soon as I figure things out, okay?" He ended the call and slipped the phone in his pocket, muttering, "Who is this guy, anyway? Some sort of hermit? A famous screenwriter escaping Hollywood? Kind of rude to ignore a neighbor in need. Geesh, you'd think —"

"I was in the garage."

Hunter wheeled around to see Heck standing on the other side of a crepe myrtle at the far end of the porch. He could smell the paint thinner from fifteen feet away.

Wiping his hands on a rag, Heck came around to the steps. He had on a pair of overalls covered in dabs and smears of various paint colors. "Did you say you needed something?"

139

For a moment, Hunter wanted to melt into the floorboards. Calling his neighbor a rude hermit was slightly more embarrassing than catching sight of him zipping up his pants while coming out of the can. "Sorry, Heck. I, uh, was getting a little flustered. My mom's sheep got out after the storm. She could use some help —"

"I don't know the first thing about sheep."

A dry laugh escaped Hunter. "Uh, no. That's not quite the favor I was going to ask."

Heck came up the steps slowly, looked down at Hannah, who was twisting side to side as she hugged Faustine. Echo surveyed him with a guarded expression, as if he hadn't quite made up his mind about the man.

"Don't know much about kids, either. Or dogs."

"I hate to ask. I'm kind of in a bind here. The quicker I can get out there to help, the better. Otherwise she could lose the entire flock. You could just sit Hannah here down in front of the TV, maybe with some paper and a pencil. She doesn't talk much. Well, usually she doesn't talk to strangers at all. I mean, you're a stranger to her, not me. But she —"

"Excuse me," — Heck turned his head partway, as if to hear better — "what did you say her name was?"

"Hannah. Her name's Hannah. It would only be for an hour, hopefully. Well, I can't promise that, actually, but it would take that long at least for us to —"

"The dog, too?"

Was he saying he would? Or that the dog was a deal-breaker? "Yes, they're kind of a two-for-one deal. Hannah doesn't go anywhere without Echo."

"Even school?"

"We'll figure that out in about a week." Hunter waited for him to say more, but Heck just stood there blank-faced, like he was waiting for them to get off his porch. "Look, sorry to bother you. I'll just wait till my wife gets back, whenever that will be. Have a nice day." He couldn't help but let the sarcasm leak through on that last bit. This guy was about as warm as a freeze-pop. He took Hannah's hand and started past Heck.

"Is *Sesame Street* okay?"

Hunter stopped. "Pardon?"

Heck gestured toward the front door. "I don't have a satellite dish and I can only get four, sometimes five stations, but I think PBS is one of them. Figure they probably have a children's program on this time of day. Although I've never really checked, so I don't know for certain."

When the idea of first asking Heck to watch Hannah had popped into his head, Hunter had thought it a reasonable solution to a dire situation. But the more he talked to the man, the less sure he was. Jenn would probably skewer him for leaving Hannah with someone they had barely spoken to, especially after their initial encounter. Yet one look at the gaping hole in the fence from across the road here told him he didn't have much choice. Still ...

Hannah tugged at his hand. This was a bad time for her to have to use the bathroom.

"Daddy?" she whispered.

"Yeah, sweet pea?"

"Echo says it's okay."

He sank down on his haunches to meet her eye to eye. "What do you mean? Okay for what?"

"For me to stay here. That Heck's okay."

Reaching out, Hunter stroked the dog's neck. "How would he know, sweet pea?"

"He can see it." She pointed to her eyes. "Here."

The fact that she had spoken in front of a stranger was enough to dumfound Hunter.

"Dr. McHugh ..." Heck began. "Hunter, is it? I understand your reservations. I wasn't particularly receptive to your visit the other day. The fact is that I moved out here for the peace and quiet. I was also very tired from packing and unpacking. I may not have a lot, but at sixty-seven, well, you don't have as much energy as you used to. Or tolerance, for that matter. But I'm not one to turn away someone in need. She can stay until your wife comes home, or until you find your sheep. The dog, too. But don't think this is a standing offer, understood?"

Straightening, Hunter extended his hand for Heck to shake. "Okay, thanks."

Heck kept his hands at his sides. "I have a thing about germs. As soon as the kid and dog are gone, I'll probably break out the bleach." The corners of his mouth turned up in a weak smile.

Great, Hunter thought, a germophobe who doesn't like kids or dogs. What could go wrong?

The door latch clicked behind Hunter. Hannah had already let herself in and turned the TV on. This was unusual. But if things were going his way for once, he wasn't going to question it.

chapter 17

Echo

Faustine propped up next to her, Hannah sat on the end of the couch closest to the door. She never looked at Heck directly, but every time his back was turned for more than a second, she stole a glance. Amazingly, she showed very few of the nervous habits I'd seen her display around other strangers. Probably because he just handed her the remote control, then went about his business, cleaning the kitchen. He didn't ask her questions, or offer her snacks, or sit uncomfortably close. He simply acted like she wasn't there.

A long time passed, though, before Hannah changed the station from a baseball game to a nature program about penguins in Antarctica. She didn't pay much attention to the person speaking from inside the TV, but whenever they showed the birds, every part of her went still, as if focusing on the sounds the penguins made.

I was stretched out on the floor in front of her, my eyes closed, halfway to sleep, when Heck's shoes scuffed softly near me. I pried one eye open, watching. He settled himself in the recliner and watched the rest of the program with her in silence until the credits scrolled up from the bottom of the screen.

Then he said, like he was the only one in the room, which he was probably used to being, "Emperors get all the attention. You'd think they were the only penguins in the world."

As slowly as snow melting on a cloudy day, Hannah turned her face from the TV toward him. He, in turn, looked at her. An understanding passed between them. An agreement of sorts, that Emperor penguins were indeed highly overrated. The significance of the moment was not lost on me, but Heck and Hannah were less aware of it. To them it was simply a natural progression, a breaking down of walls, like when most humans shake hands or say 'hello'.

The credits ended and a woodworking show came on. Disinterested, Hannah began to fidget. Heck removed himself from the room, gathering laundry from a hamper in one of the two bedrooms, then lugging it into a small room next to the kitchen where he turned dials and punched a button. The washing machine started up with a splash and a gurgle.

Hannah took the opportunity to change the channels, stopping on an old western, where the cowpokes were rounding up a large herd of cattle. Whenever they panned the herd of lowing cattle, Hannah's face took on a deep intensity. Heck even drifted past the doorway once, paused to make sure all was well, then wandered back to the bedroom with an armload of freshly dried sheets.

When the cattle drive scene ended and the movie switched to a saloon full of boozing cowboys and women in frilly costumes, Hannah lost interest. Her gaze wandered around the room. It was relatively austere, as if Heck were afraid too many things would anchor him there interminably. The only non-functional items in the room were the books in the short bookcase on which the TV sat and a row of paintings on the wall leading to the kitchen.

For the longest time, Hannah sat transfixed by the paintings, each a subtle wash of bright colors. Close up, the delineations between the objects in each picture were blurred. But from a distance the colors came together in shapes and patterns to create images so vibrant they appeared more real than any photograph I have ever seen. While she remained hypnotized by the paintings, Heck mopped the kitchen floor, wiped down the counters, and put a second load of laundry in.

Hannah was still sitting in the very same spot when Hunter knocked at the door.

"There you are!" he remarked with obvious relief.

Upon hearing his voice, Heck came out of the kitchen and let him in. I went up to Hunter and sniffed his pants legs, then his hands. He smelled strongly of those fluffy white creatures I often saw farther down the road. Sheep, he called them. I wondered what good they were as pets if they weren't allowed in the house. Judging by their scent, they clearly pooped and then laid in it. Which would explain why they were kept outdoors.

"How was she?" Hunter asked.

"How was who?" Heck joked dryly. "Oh, her. Forgot she was even here. She's been mesmerized by the TV ever since you left."

"Unbelievable."

"Why would you say that?"

"Because I was sure she'd have a meltdown."

Brows raised, Heck tipped his head back. "You expected her to be a problem when you left her here?"

"No, no ... Well, maybe. You never know with kids." Bending forward to put himself in Hannah's view, Hunter reached a hand out to her. "Ready to go, sweet pea?"

"She has Asperger's," Heck said. It wasn't a question.

Taking Hannah's hand as she stood, Hunter straightened. "How could you tell?"

"It's not difficult — if you know the signs." Heck glanced toward the front door, an indication that Hunter had overstayed his welcome already. "I hope you got all of your mother's sheep back, Dr. Mc—"

145

His face twitched. "I mean, Hunter."

"Believe me, it wasn't easy. I'm going to be sore in places tomorrow I didn't even know I had muscles in." His free hand wandered to his back, kneading at the base of his spine. "And I'm sure I'm going to need an adjustment after getting knocked flat on my tailbone — twice." As Hunter went by the paintings, Hannah twisted around to extend her view of them. "Come on, Hannah. Mommy and Maura will be home soon. We don't want to miss them."

Then to Heck, he said, "Thanks, again. If you ever need anything, I owe you one."

Hunter had one foot out the front door when Heck called out.

"Just a moment." Heck held up a finger to signal for Hunter to wait. A minute later, he returned and handed Hannah a postcard-sized painting.

"I thought Hannah might like this," Heck told Hunter. "She spent most of her time today watching a documentary on penguins."

Enthralled, Hannah held it in both hands and studied it. Eventually, she tilted it downward for me to see, pleased with her gift. It was of a bird perched on a rock by the water, with a stubby body, white in front and a deep bluish-black from head to tail over the rest of it, and flippers where its wings should be.

Stooping to peer at it more closely, Hunter pointed to a scribble in the lower corner. "You painted this?"

"My wife, Sophia, and I took a trip to Tasmania about twenty years ago. They usually aren't found there, but we were lucky that day. She took a picture of him, then I painted it later. Much later. It's a watercolor of a little blue penguin. The penguin world's best kept secret."

"I don't know what to say, except ... thanks. If there's anything I can do for you, just —"

"You already said that. Besides, there's no need to thank me. It was just sitting in a box. I have a lot of unopened boxes full of things

I'm not quite sure what to do with anymore." His voice trailed away, leaving much unsaid.

Behind his pupils hung a cloud of sadness. I wanted to nuzzle his hand, to be there for him in that moment when memories crept up and took hold, but just as quick as the urge arose in me, a curtain drew down over his eyes. He blinked repeatedly, bunched his cheeks in a perfunctory smile, and bid Hunter and Hannah goodbye.

He didn't acknowledge me, but then, he didn't need to. He'd been kind to Hannah. And anyone who was good to Hannah had my full respect. We didn't need rituals or formalities. Just small acts of friendship and moments spent in comfortable silence.

Just as Hunter pushed the screen door open, I dashed back to the couch and grabbed Faustine, returning in time to scurry out the door before it banged shut.

—o0Oo—

"Sorry I didn't answer the phone." Jenn put the box of cereal in the cupboard and closed the door. "They were still cleaning up that semi mess on the interstate. Traffic was stop and go for miles. When you called, it was just starting to move again and I didn't want to take my eyes off the road to look for the phone. You have no idea the havoc that a truckload of tomatoes can cause. And then everybody and their brother was at the same store. Guess I should have gone down an exit or two."

"Doubt it would have made a difference." Hunter lined the cans of vegetables up on the pantry shelf.

I had no idea where all the food came from, but marveled at how organized and well-stocked they kept their supplies — and wondered why they required so much variety. It seemed like a lot of extra work to me.

Jenn must've noticed me watching her, because she pulled a box from a grocery bag and rattled it before her. "I didn't forget you."

Treats? A breakthrough. I rushed to her feet and sat obediently. She was softening to me, finally. She put the box up on the table, unopened. Tease.

"The storm was all over the national news," Hunter said. "They've been talking about it non-stop. You'd think there wasn't anything else going on in the world."

"Must be a slow news day."

"I guess." With a grunt, Hunter plopped down on a kitchen chair and planted his elbows on the table. "Lots of property damage, but no fatalities reported."

"Well, that's good. I suppose it could have been worse. Next time they mention a line of storms like that coming, though, remind me to take them seriously. By the way, you look pretty beat. What've you been up to?"

"What haven't I done? Picked up the yard, hunted down the trashcans. Thank goodness it's Sunday and I didn't have to go in to the clinic, or else I don't know how I would have gotten anything accomplished. After all that, Mom called to tell me they had trees down across the driveway and over the fence."

"Oh, no." Placing a can of pop on the table, she sat across from him.

I stared at the biscuit box, then looked to her, then back to the box. She was preoccupied with sipping her drink. It wasn't until I nudged her with my nose, snorted, and looked at the box again that she took out a biscuit and gave it to me. These humans were easy to train. She was, however, easily distracted from meeting my needs. She would need constant reminders.

"Brad and I were using the chainsaws when Mom came rushing over and told us the sheep were out." Hunter then went on to tell her about how it took the three of them almost two hours to get the sheep away from the creek bed and into the barn, how Brad had rolled the

ATV once, and how the flock had run straight over Hunter twice before he could get out of the way. "It would have been much easier with a dog to help."

"I'm sure it would have …" Slowly, she lowered her drink. "Hey, exactly what was Hannah doing while you were playing cowboy?"

He looked away. "Oh … Heck watched her. It was no big deal. She was really good for him and I told him if he ever needed a favor to just let us know." The corners of his mouth flipped up into a nervous grin. "That was really nice of him, don't you think?"

Even I could see the storm building behind her eyes.

She stood, palms flat against the table. "What were you thinking?!"

Sucking his chin back, he blew out a burst of air. "I was thinking I didn't want Mom to lose several thousands of dollars and years' worth of work if her sheep ran off."

"And you put Hannah at risk for that?" Clutching the edge of the table, she leaned forward. "A bunch of sheep?"

He matched her stance. "How was I putting Hannah at risk, huh? Explain that to me."

Glancing toward the stairs, she lowered her voice. "Are you serious? We don't know anything about that man."

"That's not true. We don't know much. But I'll tell you what I found out about him today. He reads the classics: Dumas, Hugo, Dickens. He has bookshelves crammed full of the stuff. He keeps a tidy house, as in cleans with bleach and dusts the top of his refrigerator. And he paints, Jenn. Watercolors, mostly, but it's brilliant stuff. Hannah was fascinated with his work and when he talked about it, it was like a door to the universe opened for her. I've never seen her eyes so lit up."

Jenn's eyes narrowed as she considered it. Her shoulders relaxed. She sat. "Paintings? Really? You know, in one of the online groups I was in for parents of children with autism and Asperger's there was a thread about art and music therapy. I thought about using that with her, but I don't know the first thing about how to draw, or paint, or play the piano."

"Maybe he'd be willing to teach her?"

She bit at her lower lip. "Maybe we should get to know him better first?"

Hunter came around the table and drew Jenn up and into his arms. "I'll make a point of it. Although something tells me it'll be like squeezing blood from a stone."

Eyes half closed, she put her cheek against his chest. "So, you got all the sheep back?"

"Every last one." He lifted her chin with a single finger and kissed her lightly on the mouth.

"Then I suppose it all worked out okay." Giggling, she kissed him back. "I always knew you were Superman."

"I am. Would you like me to show you my superpowers?"

With a wink, she tugged the hem of his shirt from his pants. "Oh, I think I already know what they are."

chapter 18
Hannah

Hannah sat in the backseat alone, clutching her backpack to her chest. Her mommy had told her it was a twenty-minute ride to school. To Hannah that seemed like a terribly long time. She couldn't imagine making this trip all year long, twice a day. But her mommy had decided to drive them, because the bus ride was more than twice as long and she didn't want Hannah to ride on the bus. Which made Maura very mad.

"Why can't *I* ride the bus?" Maura complained for the tenth time. "Lindsey gets on two stops after me. I'm missing out on all that time I could hang out with my best friend."

"You'll have classes together," Jenn said. "Besides, I need you to walk Hannah inside the building and make sure she goes to the right room. When we were there for open house, I wasn't really sure she was paying attention. Whenever she gets confused, she tends to just shut down."

"Lindsey and I have one class together. One. Plus lunch. But that doesn't count, because the cafeteria's loud and there are like a *million* people in there and the lunchroom monitor is always barking at you to get in line, sit down, shut up, turn your trays in … It's like a fricking prison."

"I'm sure it's not that bad."

"So can I ride the bus tomorrow?"

"I don't know. Maybe next week."

"Next week?! You're kidding, right? Please tell me you're kidding. Nobody has their mom drop them off except the kids who aren't allowed to ride on the bus because they get in trouble too much." Maura snuck a look at Hannah. "And kindergarteners."

"Maura Irene McHugh, you know that's not true." Jenn gave her oldest daughter a warning glare. "You can be the big sister for one week. *One* week. Hannah needs you to show her around. And I need you to keep an eye on her. Part of growing up is accepting responsibility. Remember that when you want to go to the school dance next month or hang out at the football game with your friends."

"So you're saying I have to do this?"

"You don't *have* to do anything."

"Unless I want to go to football games and stuff."

Hands gripping the steering wheel, Jenn arched one eyebrow ever so slightly.

"Fine," Maura huffed.

The car slowed as Jenn turned into the drop-off lane for the school building. Hannah noticed her mommy was even more nervous than when they went to the psychologists. All morning long she'd fussed about every tiny detail, making sure Hannah wore the clothes she'd laid out, eaten every bit of her breakfast, combed her hair, brushed her teeth. There wasn't even time to sit with Echo under the Crooked Tree. If it was this frantic every morning, she didn't want to go to school. Not today. Not ever. Just thinking about it made her sick to her stomach.

More than being surrounded by other people and the hurried

rituals of mornings, the thought of not being with Echo upset her. With Echo, she could be herself. She could watch the ants under the tree swing build their mounds of sand, or study the way that rocks thrown into a puddle made ripples, or lie on her back in the grass and watch the clouds roll by, no two of them the same. Echo knew when to lean against her so she could put her arm around him, when to just be in the same room, and when to go off on his own. He knew when to race ahead of her in encouragement and when to walk dutifully behind, quiet and observant. He also knew when to keep a watchful eye on strangers and when to accept them. She was never good at understanding people outside her family. She was never sure what they expected of her or thought about things if they didn't say what they meant. And so she just said nothing, sometimes pretending they were not even there, always hoping they would ignore her. Or better yet, go away. Having Echo at her side gave her one less thing to worry about. She didn't know what she would do without him. Especially today.

She unzipped her backpack partway and slid a hand inside to stroke Faustine's topknot. She still took Faustine most places, but Faustine didn't talk to her like Echo did. Echo was the one who'd told her that Heck was okay, and he'd been right. No one had ever given her a gift as special as the picture of the little blue penguin. Every night before she went to sleep and every morning when she woke up, she gazed at the picture for a long, long time, thinking of how beautiful it was, how up close the colors looked like random blotches, but from farther away they formed a perfect image, alive with color. She knew Heck had painted it himself. Someday she'd ask him how he did it. Because she wanted to paint like that, too.

"Hannah," — Maura snarled at her — "you can't take Faustine to school."

"Why not?" Hannah asked. Her parents hadn't told her anything about not taking her stuffed animals. Was it against the rules? Had they forgotten to tell her?

"Because someone could steal her, that's why."

The thought of that horrified Hannah. But she didn't want to leave her at home. Faustine was a comfort to her. Faustine had been there when she'd fallen in the river. And in the hospital when she'd woken up. Faustine had slept with her every night of her life that she could remember. They'd already made her leave Echo behind. Her daddy had taken him to work with him early that morning. She wasn't about to abandon Faustine, too.

"I'll keep her in my bag," Hannah said defiantly.

"Suit yourself," Maura snipped.

The car came to a complete stop. Maura had jumped out and slammed her door before Hannah could even unclick her seatbelt. She was small enough that she still had to sit in a booster seat, but from her higher vantage point she could see all the other children in their new school clothes, swarming along the sidewalk, swinging their backpacks and lunch bags. They were all so much *bigger* than her. And when Maura opened the door, it was so noisy outside. All that talking. Feet stomping. Screaming with joy as they shouted to their friends. Busses rumbling. Cars honking.

Hannah clamped her hands over her ears to shut it out. She closed her eyes. Her body swayed back and forth. Each time she came back, she hit the back of her seat harder. *Thump, thump, thump.*

Her seatbelt loosened. Light hands brushed her bangs from her forehead.

"It's all right, sweetie. It's all right." Jenn leaned in to the backseat and hugged her, but only for a second. "You can take Faustine with you. I'll text your teacher and let her know it's all right. I'm sure she won't mind. You're going to be in a special class called a resource room. There won't be as many students in there, okay? It'll be quieter, I promise." Then she inclined her head toward the sidewalk. "And your sister's going to walk you in this morning. Then when school's over, she'll be waiting in the hall for you. Everything's going to be okay. You'll see."

But her mommy didn't act like everything was okay.

"Maura!" Lindsey Yates weaved her way through a sea of kids going the other way to the front doors. "I thought we were on the same bus? I was confused when I got on and couldn't find you."

"Hey, Linds." Maura hugged her. "We can talk at lunch, okay? I have to help my sister this morning. It's her first day of school."

"Oh, cool." Lindsey peeked in the back of the car. "Hi, Hannah." All smiles, she waved at Hannah, then started back in the other direction as she called to Maura. "See you at lunch."

Jenn helped Hannah out of the car, then Maura took her hand and pulled toward the double glass doors. Hannah stood rooted, every muscle in her body stiffening in resistance.

"Just follow me, squirt," Maura said with forced calmness. "I know this place inside and out. It's not as scary as it looks from out here. I know. I felt exactly like you do my first day here."

Hannah doubted that. Maura talked to everybody. She always knew what to say and how to act. Hannah could never sort that out and was sure her sister didn't understand how she felt. But she went with her anyway, even though her tummy was doing flips, because everyone expected it of her.

All week long, her parents and Gramma Lise had been talking to her about school. Talking *to* her, because Hannah had nothing to say. She was only going because they told her she had to.

The next thing Hannah knew, she was sitting at a desk staring at a big white board with lots of scribbles and pictures on it. The whole room was filled with pictures and letters and numbers. If she just focused on one thing at a time, some of them made sense. But mostly it was a whole lot of too much.

She stared down at her hands, folded on the desk before her, so the other children wouldn't talk to her. One came by, asked her the same question several times, then tapped her on the shoulder. Hard. Hannah screwed her eyes shut and laid her head down.

Go away. Go away. Go away.

Her teacher, Mrs. Ziegler, told the other student to take his seat and not bother Hannah anymore. His name was Patrick Mann, which Hannah thought was odd because he was a little boy, not a man at all.

It wasn't until snack time that Hannah looked up. While the other kids sat in a circle in the back of the room, eating their crackers and pretzels, Hannah took her backpack with Faustine inside and sat on a stool by the bookcases. Right next to the gerbil's cage. It wasn't Echo, but at least it was an animal and not a person. Mrs. Ziegler didn't say anything to her about not sitting with the other kids.

Her mother had packed eighteen crackers. Hannah arranged them in four rows of four and ate the two extra ones. When she wanted another, she had to reconfigure her pattern. The more crackers she ate, the more difficult it became. Odd numbers were more challenging, so she had to think ahead each time she put one in her mouth.

The other kids were being so noisy. She didn't understand why they had to shout so much. Mrs. Ziegler was constantly reminding them to be quiet and sit still. Especially Patrick Mann. So she told them if they could all be quiet for the next ten minutes while they finished their snacks, she would let them watch a movie. She didn't even say what it was, but it was enough to make them stop talking and fidgeting.

In that span of cherished silence, Hannah heard a voice. A very small, almost frightened voice.

Tail. Tail.

She snuck a look around her. There was no one within ten feet of her.

Boy.

Where was the voice coming from? It wasn't from the back of the room. Her stomach rumbled; she decided to ignore the voice and eat.

Three rows of three. To Hannah, this was the perfect arrangement. If she ate one more, then —

Bad.

This happened all the time to her. Sometimes she could never figure out where it was coming from. It also didn't make sense most of the time. She picked up two crackers and with the other hand, rearranged the rest in three rows: two, three, two. This pleased her and opened up new possibilities. Not every row had to have the same number.

Hurt!

This time she turned her head toward the sound. Squatting next to the bars inside the cage was the class gerbil. Franklin, Mrs. Ziegler had called him. He wrung his tiny paws nervously, staring at her with eyes like black chips of glass.

Tail hurt.

"Who hurt your tail?" she thought. But to Hannah her voice sounded as clear as if she were speaking out loud.

Boy.

"Which boy?"

For a while, Franklin didn't answer. He began to groom himself, rubbing his tiny paws over his tongue, then parting his fur with them. After a few licks, he scurried over to an alfalfa cube and nibbled awhile before Hannah heard him again.

Bad boy.

"Of course it was a bad boy. Which one?"

Just then, Mrs. Ziegler instructed the other students to take their seats, but to remain quiet. They scattered through the rows, some almost running to their desks, others taking their time. Patrick Mann bumped her stool, laughing. Hannah put her foot down just in time to keep it from overturning.

That boy. Pull tail.

Glaring at Patrick Mann as she went to her own desk close by,

Hannah watched him bounce like a kangaroo. Once he was in his seat — halfway at least, because he never could quite sit still — he swiveled around to look at her. When she didn't stop staring, he made an ugly face. Except it didn't mean anything to Hannah. Was it supposed to be funny? Playful? Or mean?

One thing she did know was that he had pulled Franklin's tail. Franklin then told her more. That it had happened before the school day started, while Patrick Mann's mother and Mrs. Ziegler were standing in the hall talking about his ADHD, whatever that was. He had reached inside the cage, lifted Franklin up by his tail, and swung him repeatedly. No matter how hard Franklin tried, he couldn't get his mouth close enough to Patrick Mann's fingers to bite him. And he wanted to. Badly.

The whole time the movie was playing, Hannah stared at Patrick Mann. It took him awhile to notice, but when he did he made more faces. When that brought no reaction from Hannah, he started to get mad.

"Make her stop looking at me!" he told Mrs. Ziegler.

The teacher shushed him, because the movie wasn't over. But she kept an eye on Hannah.

Finally, when Mrs. Ziegler was putting the screen up and had her back turned to the class, Patrick Mann got up from his chair and marched over to Hannah. He bent over, his face just inches from hers. "Stop it, you freak!"

Mrs. Ziegler whipped around. "In your seat, Patrick. Now," she said in a barely raised voice. As he scampered back to his desk, she approached Hannah, stopping in line of Hannah's view to Patrick. "Eyes forward, Hannah. It's not polite to stare."

All the other children, eight of them, were now watching Hannah. Instead of turning her head to look at the big white board at the front of the classroom, she laid it down on her arms and turned her face to the window to gaze outside.

At lunchtime, the rest of the kids rushed to line up. Hannah didn't move. When the others left, Mrs. Ziegler came over to her.

"Is something wrong, Hannah?"

Hannah didn't answer. Everything was wrong. This place. The other kids. She wanted to go home.

"Did Patrick do something?"

If she didn't tell Mrs. Ziegler, he'd probably do it again. She nodded.

"What did he do? Did he call you a name? Hit you?"

Hannah shook her head.

Mrs. Ziegler crouched down beside her. "I know you don't like to talk, but you'll have to tell me."

Crooking her finger, she beckoned Mrs. Ziegler in close. "Patrick Mann pulled Franklin's tail."

Her teacher's forehead creased. "Ohhh, I see. That is bad. So you saw him do this?"

"No."

"Someone else did and they told you?"

"No."

"Then, how do you know?"

"Franklin told me."

And just as soon as she said it, she remembered what her daddy had said to her, that she shouldn't let other people know that she can hear animals.

Mrs. Ziegler stood. "You are imaginative, aren't you? Animals can't talk, Hannah. Even as much as we'd like them to. Heaven knows I'd love to know what my cat is thinking when he starts racing around the house at three in the morning."

Somehow Hannah made it through the rest of the day. But what a terribly long, awful day it was. She waited until all the other children had left the classroom before she gathered her backpack up and unzipped it partway. There was Faustine, looking up at her. Mrs.

Ziegler wouldn't let her take her backpack with her when she had to go to the bathroom. So she'd spent the rest of the day holding it in, not wanting to leave Faustine, but afraid someone had stolen her the one time she did leave her.

Maura was in the hallway waiting for her. When they got outside and were standing by the curb, waiting for their mom to pull up, Hannah told her sister about how Patrick Mann had dangled Franklin by his tail and that Franklin had told her this. She figured it was okay to tell her sister.

"He did not, Hannah. Animals don't talk."

"I didn't say he talked, exactly."

"Then how did he 'tell' you, huh?" She flashed the air quotes before her.

"I don't know. I guess I just heard it inside my head."

"Right. ESP. Now I know you're lying."

Maura's words were like a slap to the face. Hannah felt their sting. "I'm not lying!"

"Then tell me what I'm thinking."

"I can't." Backing away, Hannah's voice grew smaller. She should never have told Maura, or Mrs. Ziegler. Her daddy was right. No one would understand. "It doesn't work like that."

Maura wagged a finger at her. "You can't tell me because you make stuff up, that's why."

Heat crept up Hannah's neck. She was angry and hurt. Why was it so hard for people to believe her?

When Jenn pulled up to the loading area and the girls got in, they were both silent. Maura slammed her door, then immediately put her earplugs in and cranked the music on her iPod. In the back, Hannah was doing all she could to keep the tears in.

"Well," Jenn began, looking from one girl to the other, "you both made it through the first day."

Neither answered.

"That good, huh? If either of you want to talk about it later …" Jenn slipped the gearshift into drive and pulled out onto the road.

Hannah wasn't going to say anything. What was the point when no one was going to believe her?

—o0Oo—

Hannah couldn't lie. Lying was just wrong. Every morning after that, she would lie in bed, thinking she'd tell her mommy that she didn't feel well, but when her mommy came by to wake her up, she couldn't do it. And whenever she tried to tell her outright she didn't want to go back to school, her mommy said she had to. It was the law. Hannah didn't want to break any laws.

So she went. And almost every day, Franklin told her something that Patrick Mann had done to scare or hurt him. But if Hannah told Mrs. Ziegler this, she wouldn't believe her. Somehow, she had to get Franklin away from Patrick Mann for good.

On Thursday, Mrs. Ziegler said Franklin needed to go home for the weekend with someone who would feed and care for him. Hannah volunteered. The next day, she took Franklin home in his cage. That night she set him next to her penguin picture. Echo, tipping his head from side to side, watched him go around and around on his wheel.

Maura stopped in the doorway. She always wore an oversized sweatshirt and a pair of shorts to bed, which didn't make sense to Hannah because they weren't pajamas.

"Why did you bring a rat home?" Maura said, pulling the ponytail holder from her hair and combing her fingers through it.

"He's a gerbil. And Mrs. Ziegler said I could."

"Whatever." She rolled her eyes. Franklin paused on his wheel to gaze at Maura, then began spinning it again. The little wheel made a low whining sound. "Is he going to make that noise all night?"

Hannah watched Franklin intently, his tiny legs churning. She

161

liked the sound. As long as it wasn't too loud. It meant that Franklin was busy and happy, not cowering in fear from Patrick Mann's abuse. She'd bring him home every weekend if her parents would let her, although she knew that other kids in the class wanted to take him home, too. Then it struck her: What if Patrick Mann wanted to take him home?

No, she couldn't allow that. Who knew what would happen to poor, frightened Franklin?

As she lay in bed that night, she began to plot. She'd make sure Patrick Mann never hurt Franklin again.

chapter 19

Hannah

The next morning, Hannah told her mommy that she wanted to go to the pet store in Somerset to get Franklin some treats and a new bone for Echo, because he had lost his favorite one. She was pretty sure it was under the couch, but she didn't mention that. Technically, it wasn't a lie, because Echo couldn't find it, so to him it *was* lost. Since they had to make a trip to the big grocery store anyway, Jenn agreed.

Right before it was time to leave, Hannah hurried up to her bedroom, saying she'd forgotten Faustine. Just in case Maura walked by, Hannah shut her bedroom door. She put on her purple hoodie and then took Franklin from his cage. He yawned, having been up half the night spinning, munching on seeds, and burrowing through his cedar shavings. She slipped him in her front pocket, then grabbed Faustine off the bed and hurried downstairs.

Every once in a while during the drive to Somerset, Franklin would shift from one side of her pocket to the other. Once, he even poked his head out. Hannah was afraid her mommy would look in the backseat at her just when he was doing this and figure things out, but she didn't seem to catch on at all.

When they arrived at the pet store, Hannah stuffed both hands inside her front pocket to keep him inside. While Jenn was busy picking out a squeaky toy and a bone for Echo, Hannah snuck away to the small pet section. There were three banks of glass cages and aquariums. The first and biggest of these was full of fish. Hannah tried to listen, but they didn't have much to say except, 'Food, food' and 'Get out of my way'. The second held a row of lizards, turtles, and snakes. She could hear nothing at all from them and was glad for it.

The last section was where the mice, rats, hamsters, and gerbils were. Hannah looked in each one, searching for gerbils that looked like Franklin. Finally, she found some. What Hannah couldn't figure out was how to open the cages.

"Would you like to hold one?" A young woman with blue-streaked hair and a nose piercing stood next to her. She had on a blue polo shirt and a name tag that said 'Bella'. Hannah could read that much. Last year, she'd taught herself on the computer how to sound out letters. She could read much better than anyone knew, even her parents. She just didn't see a reason to make a big deal out of it.

Turning away, Hannah shook her head and continued to stare at the cage before her. She hoped that Bella would go away, but for several minutes the woman poked around in the cages, adding cubes of alfalfa and refilling water bottles. Hannah watched her flip a latch and pop the screen top open, then reclose it.

It took forever for Bella to leave. The whole time, Hannah kept checking to make sure Franklin was still in her pocket, then looking down the rows, expecting her mommy to come and tell her it was time to go.

It was now or never. She flipped a latch up. Just as she dug her hand in her front pocket, Jenn came around the corner.

"There you are! You ready to go? I'll let you pick out your favorite cereals today. I can never remember which ones you —"

"That's not the right kind," Hannah said softly, hoping there was no one else nearby who could hear her. She didn't like people listening to what she said. "Echo likes peanut butter."

Jenn glanced down at the package of mint-flavored bones in her basket. "Oh, I didn't think it mattered. Anyway, I thought these would make his breath smell better. Kind of like your toothpaste."

"Peanut butter," Hannah repeated.

"Okay, then." Jenn took the bones from her basket. "Peanut butter it is. Maybe you should show me."

"I'm busy."

"Doing what?"

Hannah shrugged. "Just looking."

"You stay right here. Don't go anywhere, you understand?"

Wishing she'd hurry up and go, Hannah nodded.

As soon as her mommy was gone, Hannah took Franklin from her pocket, kissed him on the head, and put him in the gerbil cage. She almost pulled him back out when another gerbil started squabbling with him. Soon, however, they were sniffing each other and getting very friendly. Hannah pressed her forehead to the glass, watching. What were they —?

"Hannah?"

Hannah froze at the sound of her mother's voice. It took her a few moments to realize that the banging in her ears was the sound of her own heart. She took a step back, her breaths coming in shallow pants. Her knees were shaking. She sucked in a lungful of air, held it, then let it out.

"Hey, I saw a squeaky toy on sale and thought Echo might like it." Jenn tipped the basket to show Hannah the bones and squeaky, then bent down alongside her to peer into the cage. "Oh my. Looks like they're trying to make babies. I wonder if they know they have a boy in there with all those girls? They usually separate them." Straightening, she pursed her lips thoughtfully. "You know, he looks *just* like Franklin, don't you think?"

Did she know? Was she waiting for her to tell the truth? Should she lie? Could she?

Hannah grabbed her mother's hand and pulled toward the cash register.

They got all the way through the grocery store and back home before Hannah's elaborate ruse threatened to unfold.

—o00o—

"Mom?" Maura held the kitchen door open for them. "Franklin's gone."

Jenn set the sack of groceries on the kitchen table. "Are you sure, Maura? He's not just hiding under his bedding?"

"That's the first place I looked. I even looked under Hannah's bed and dressers, in her closet, and all the rooms upstairs." Maura's eyes slid to Echo, who was running circles around Hannah, his rear end wiggling like Hannah had been gone for months, not mere hours. He had the new squeaky toy, a pink elephant, in his mouth. *Squeak, squeak, squeak.* She narrowed her eyes at him. "When I was walking by her room, I stopped to check on him, and Echo was lying on the rug next to the cage. The door to the cage was open. The dog is tall enough to reach it, you know."

Jenn's mouth slid into a frown. "Ohhh, Echo. You didn't."

"Didn't what?" Hunter entered the kitchen. He searched through the closest sack. "Did you remember to get the turmeric? I was going to make that new recipe tonight. Thought we'd try something new and exotic."

Echo poked his nose at Hannah's pocket.

Is he in there? I smell him. Can I see? Where did you go? Can I come next time?

Hannah pushed his nose away. "Stop it, Echo," she mumbled.

"It appears Echo may have had a snack," Jenn informed her husband. "As in small, furry-tailed rodent appetizer."

"No, really? He was with me almost the whole time — except for those few minutes I stepped outside to take out the trash." Emptying a grocery bag, Hunter placed the vegetables in the refrigerator. "Maura, why didn't you tell me?"

"I just now figured it out. I've looked everywhere."

"Help your mom bring the rest of the groceries in." He shook his head at Echo. "We'll form a search party once they're all put away. Meanwhile, I'll put Echo in his crate."

They were all blaming Echo for something Hannah had done. Guilt ate a hole in her stomach. She hung her head. This wasn't going like she'd planned at all.

An hour later, after they'd scoured the house, Hunter declared Franklin officially lost. No one seemed mad at Echo, though.

"Did you forget to shut your bedroom door when we left, Hannah?" Jenn asked her.

She shrugged. Well, she didn't actually forget. It was all part of the plan. But she didn't think they'd suspect Echo of being the cause for Franklin's disappearance. If they chose to believe that, though …

As long as they didn't punish Echo for it, everything would be all right. It was done. Franklin was at the pet store now. Safe from Patrick Mann.

—o00o—

Monday morning, Jenn went in to see Hannah's teacher. Returning the empty cage, she explained the unfortunate incident.

"It's all right, Hannah." Her teacher patted her lightly on top of the head. "These things happen."

167

Inwardly, Hannah breathed a sigh of relief. It didn't look like she was going to get in trouble. Either Mrs. Ziegler really believed what her mother said, or she was just being nice and underneath she was really mad. Hannah could never tell.

Three days later, a white mouse appeared in Franklin's cage. Afraid for him, Hannah went home and told her parents what had really happened to Franklin. Echo was forgiven, but her mother scolded her for not telling the truth. Later, when Hannah went down the stairs to get a drink of milk before bedtime, she overheard her parents talking as they sat on the couch in the living room.

"You can't honestly believe her, Hunter."

"How do you know she didn't see that boy do something to the gerbil?"

"Because she told her teacher she didn't. How do *you* know she didn't make the whole thing up?"

"Why would she do that, Jenn?"

"Maybe she just doesn't like this Patrick kid. For all we know, he looked at her wrong, or cut in line in front of her. It could be one of a million things." There was a long pause, and then her mother spoke again. "You knew I didn't want her to go to school with other kids. She wasn't ready for it, Hunter. It hasn't even been two weeks and already she's making up stories trying to get some other kid in trouble. We need to nip this in the bud before it gets any worse. I'm going to speak to the school psychologist tomorrow."

"Jenn, don't. Not yet."

"Give me one good reason why."

Faustine in her arms, Hannah peeked around the doorway. The only light in the room came from the glow of the TV. They had the sound turned off. She was afraid to go up the creaky stairs while they were quiet; they might hear her.

"When I was little, about her age," her father began, "I ran away."

"You never mentioned that. How long were you gone?"

"I'm not sure exactly. Most of a day, I think."

Jenn rested her head on Hunter's shoulder. "Why did you run away?"

"Mostly because I couldn't cope with what happened to my dad and grandfather. When I watched the tractor roll, crushing both of them … it was more than I could deal with. But also because my mom had sort of 'checked out'. She was pregnant with Cammie then, dealing with my dad's messed up financial affairs … She was doing the best she could, but being the kid, I wanted her — the adult — to fix everything, and she couldn't. It sent me into a spiral of emotional shock. And I felt … no, I *believed* somehow the accident was my fault. That I should have stopped him before the tractor slid. That Mom was mad at me. Although that was probably just transference. Really, I was mad at myself — and angry at the world in general. So I ran."

"Are you afraid that's what Hannah will do?"

"I'm saying kids cope in unpredictable ways. They're more complicated than we realize. There's a lot going on under her quiet exterior. And there's no telling what she may do next."

"I don't know about you, but I can't take much more excitement. Days like this, more than anything, I just want her to be *normal*. Like Maura."

Hannah stopped listening. She'd heard enough.

Carefully, she tiptoed up the stairs. In her room, she climbed under the covers with Faustine. Sadness filled her, weighing her down. She wanted to draw far into herself, somewhere dark, where she could be alone …

Sitting up and pulling a throw from the foot of her bed, Hannah dragged it over to the closet and opened the door. She sank to her knees, scooted in, and burrowed in the far corner behind a pile of shoes. The dress with sunflowers on it that Gramma Lise had given her after she got out of the hospital hung down, brushing the top of her head. If she moved it, it would be out of the way, but this way it partially hid her in case anyone looked in there for her. She crouched into a ball and tugged her blanket to her, but it caught on the door.

As she began to unravel it so she could close the door, a black face appeared in the crack of light between the door and jamb. Echo's orangey-golden eyes gazed at her soulfully, as if asking if he could come in with her. His whiskers twitched as he sniffed her shoes.

Hannah patted the floor next to her and Echo squeezed himself between her and the wall. The blanket was just big enough to cover them both. Except their heads — they had to breathe.

She didn't remember waking up later, or putting her jammies on, but in the morning she woke up in her bed, Echo asleep on his braided rug beside her.

For a few minutes, she was sure it was a Saturday, but then she heard Maura taking a shower.

No, darn it. It was a school day.

—o0Oo—

Hannah had been calling her Dr. Lemon until she saw her name on the wall outside her office at the school that day — Dr. Cynthia P. Liming. Close, anyway.

For the better part of an hour, Hannah held out, not saying anything as Dr. Liming asked her question after question. Dr. Liming even offered her some paper and crayons and told her to draw pictures of whatever she wanted. So Hannah drew shapes and patterns: squares divided into more squares, and then circles in rows that from farther away took on the appearance of other shapes, like triangles. The whole time, she wondered if not saying anything was as bad as lying.

Eventually, it occurred to her that if she told Dr. Liming everything, they just might let her stay home from school.

It turned out to be a big mistake to tell Dr. Liming that the sparrow outside the window told her about the principal, Mr. Sloan, visiting Mrs. Ziegler's room every day after school and pulling the blinds.

That afternoon, when her mommy came to pick her up from school, they went straight from her classroom to Dr. Liming's office. Hannah was told to wait at a low table in the adjacent room while her mommy talked to Dr. Liming. The door between the rooms was made of frosted glass and Jenn hadn't pulled it shut tight, so it was still open a crack — which meant Hannah could both see and hear them.

Dr. Liming sat behind her desk, two paper notepads and a computer tablet before her. Elbows planted on the armrests of her big chair, the psychologist steepled her fingers together before her. "I'm concerned that Hannah may be having, well," — her voice lowered in volume — "delusions, Mrs. McHugh."

Meanwhile, Hannah busied herself drawing circles inside of circles inside of circles.

"Delusions?" Jenn leaned forward in her chair. "Like what?"

"Does she tell you that animals talk to her?"

"Well, yes, that's why I suggested she see you."

By now, Hannah was adding color to the circles. She couldn't make her fingers work as fast as her brain, but she tried. She needed more colors than the sixteen that were in the box. And the crayons were fat nubs. There was no sharpener. It was hard to make the colors go where she wanted them to.

"Has she said anything else to cause concern?" Dr. Liming said more quietly. As if Hannah, fifteen feet away, couldn't hear.

Bored with her patterns, Hannah started on something else. This one would be special. Different from the others.

"Concern?"

"Obvious untruths, Mrs. McHugh. Things that would cause you to be concerned for her safety or your family's."

"It's not like … Look, she's not a danger to anyone. I just think her imagination is vivid, that's all. I think she *thinks* she hears them talk to her. That she imagines it."

"And you consider that 'normal'?"

"I'd be worried if she *didn't* have an imagination. You know, I get that Hannah is different, Dr. Liming. But you have no idea how far she's come in the past few years. The fact that she's even been talking to her teacher, or you, is monumental. It's going to take time for her to learn to fit in. There are going to be bumps along the way, I get that. But having you suggest that she's some borderline paranoid schizophrenic with violent tendencies isn't going to float. You need to go back and study your textbooks. She's a highly intelligent five-year-old with Asperger's syndrome. That doesn't make her a freak who you need to slap labels on so you can shove her aside."

"I wasn't suggesting that. Far from it. I just thought we should discuss this in more detail, so we can make the right choices."

"Choices? What do you mean? Hunter and I spoke to both the principal and the teacher before the school year started. We all agreed that the resource classroom was the best place for her. Mrs. Ziegler told me not two days ago that she's doing just fine — except for the gerbil incident. But come on, she's five. Five-year-olds have a different way of reasoning, right?"

After pushing her tablet away, Dr. Liming said, "I think you and Dr. McHugh should discuss whether public school is the right place for Hannah right now. You might want to consider a private tutor. I'd suggest a special school, but the nearest ones that deal with her specific needs are in Lexington. In time, when her social skills have improved and her … her imagination is more under control, maybe she could re-enter the local school system."

This was going well, Hannah decided. Telling Dr. Liming everything *was* finally working just like she'd figured. Maybe tomorrow she could stay home after all?

She colored a few more circles, then stood up to eye the picture from a little farther away. Not perfect, but she was pleased with it for her first try.

"No," Jenn said. "You are not getting rid of her that easily. She hasn't hurt anyone, she doesn't disrupt class, she follows rules, and she gets her work done. Hannah will stay in school."

What? Hannah flipped around. *No!*

She glared at them through the crack. This couldn't be happening. What had gone wrong?

Dr. Liming craned her neck sideways as she spied Hannah. She got up from her giant chair and opened the door to look past Hannah. "What is that on the table, Hannah?"

A picture, she thought, like all the rest. Was this woman really that stupid, or just playing dumb to make her feel better because they'd been talking about her?

Jenn retrieved Hannah's latest artwork from the little table. She looked at it for a long time before placing it on Dr. Liming's desk. "It's a bird."

Not just 'a' bird, Hannah thought. A penguin. A little blue penguin. Couldn't they tell? Maybe she hadn't drawn it as well as she'd thought.

Flipping her reading glasses down, Dr. Liming brought the paper close to her face to study the detail. "This is … amazing. It's not just a crayon drawing. She's done it with dots. Like the pixilation in a photo."

"Hannah, this is beautiful." Jenn smiled at her daughter before turning to Dr. Liming. "So, do you still think she doesn't belong here?"

"Mrs. McHugh, it appears I was, quite honestly, mistaken. I'd say Hannah is gifted in ways we don't yet know. In fact, I retract my earlier suggestion. She should stay in Mrs. Ziegler's class. I'd like to continue to meet with her, however." Sitting back down, she swiped a finger across the screen of her tablet and began typing away. "Maybe we could allow her to sit in on Miss Wellington's art class?"

Hannah pressed her palms to the seams of her jeans. The last thing she wanted to do was come here and 'talk' to Dr. Liming again. She wanted to rip the picture from her desk and tear it up.

This had all gone terribly, horribly wrong.

—o0Oo—

All that night and the next morning, Hannah dreaded going back to school. Maura no longer escorted her to her classroom, so she took as long as possible to walk there. In less than half a minute, the bell would ring. She planned to linger outside the door until the last possible second, but something caught her attention.

Standing in the nearly empty hallway was Mrs. Ziegler, shaking a finger as she spoke sternly to Patrick Mann. "I saw you this time, Patrick. You cannot treat animals that way. If you had a tail, I'd swing you from it right about now. Go on to Mr. Sloan's office. March!"

Patrick Mann sneered at Hannah as he stomped by.

Turning to watch him go, Hannah shifted the straps of her backpack and felt Faustine slide to the left.

"Let's go inside, Hannah." Mrs. Ziegler held an arm toward the door to the room. "Class is about to start."

Hannah stepped inside the classroom. The bell clanged just above her left shoulder, sending a jolt of adrenaline through her heart. Eight pairs of eyes turned to gawk at her.

If Patrick Mann had finally gotten in trouble and Mrs. Ziegler believed her now, why didn't she feel any better about being here?

chapter 20

Hunter

Flexing his fingers on the handle of the knife, Hunter drew the blade toward him. The fibers of meat separated and little curls of steam rose up from the pot roast. "What did she say?"

Maura held her plate out as Hunter piled a second helping on it. Across from her, Hannah speared her carrots with her fork one by one, alternating left and right, as she took them from the row she had created between her meat and potatoes. She'd also molded her mashed potatoes into a mountain range, of sorts. Hannah was always the last one done at dinner because she had to arrange her food into works of art. Lately, her creations were becoming more elaborate.

"Turns out that little boy, Patrick Mann, was teasing the class mouse after all." Jenn filled Echo's water bowl at the sink and then sat down. "Mrs. Ziegler caught him doing it."

"So, our little Hannah here was right about Franklin, then?" Leaning back in his chair, Hunter patted his stomach. He was stuffed full. A little well of pride bubbled up inside him. Hannah had done the right thing, even if her solution had been a little extreme. Then again, what did they expect from a five-year-old?

"Appears so." A smile broadened Jenn's cheeks as she reached over and patted Hannah's wrist. Flinching at her touch, Hannah went on stabbing her carrots. "Honey, I don't know how you knew, but the important thing is those animals are safe because of you. Next time, you make sure and tell us everything, okay?"

Hannah's lips tightened. "But I did."

"I know — and we should have believed you."

"Even the part about Franklin talking to me?"

The smile faded from Jenn's eyes. Her hand fell away from Hannah's wrist. "Well ..."

Hunter shot her a warning glare.

"Sure," Jenn said. Her conviction was lacking, but Hunter was pretty sure Hannah hadn't picked up on it.

Until Hannah smacked her fork flat on the table and tucked her chin to her chest.

"No, you don't believe me. No one does." And then she shoved her chair back and stomped out of the kitchen and up the stairs. Her bedroom door banged shut.

Echo scrambled up from his place beside Hannah's now empty chair. He ambled to the bottom of the stairs to gaze after her. After a few seconds, he came back to sit beside Jenn, sniffing the air as he tried to detect if she had any scraps for him.

Jenn shooed the dog away and gave Hunter a 'what the hell?' look. "Can't I say anything right?"

"Her feelings were hurt," Hunter said. "You know how she hangs onto things. Give her five minutes to brood about it, then take her plate upstairs and apologize to her."

"Apologize? For what? Sometimes I think it doesn't matter what I say." After moving the empty serving bowls and pots to the sink, Jenn took the dishwashing soap from the cabinet underneath. "Besides, if tomorrow she tells us little green men landed in the backyard and offered her a ride through a wormhole to another galaxy, are we supposed to believe her then? Seriously, I don't know where this is coming from, but I don't want her thinking she can go on about talking animals in front of anyone and everyone."

"It's a phase, Jenn. Hannah's had a rough year. Dr. Pruitt said the effects of the trauma could manifest in a number of ways."

Groaning, Maura clamped a hand to the side of her head. "Here we go again," she muttered. "Hannah, Hannah, Hannah."

Both Hunter and Jenn looked at their oldest daughter, as if suddenly aware of her presence.

Maura slid her plate back and flattened her palms on the table. "Does anybody care that *I* had three kills in my volleyball game today? Coach Rawlings says I made the difference between losing that match and winning. He also says maybe if I go to camp this summer and get better at my overhand serve and learn to block, I could get a scholarship for college. But I'd really have to train hard and hire a strength trainer and do everything I could to get my name out there, like play in select traveling leagues and stuff." She lifted her chin and looked from one parent to the other. "So ... can I?"

"Can you what?" Jenn asked, the irritation in her voice as pointed as the prickly thorns on a cocklebur. Flipping the faucet lever up, she squirted a long stream of dishwashing liquid into the sink.

"Go to camp? This summer in Indianapolis. Of course, someone would have to drive me up there. But it would get me out of your hair for a week. Then you could focus on Hannah the whole time."

"Of course you can go," Hunter said. "But not because we want to get rid of you."

A light scoff escaped her. "If you say so."

"Maura," — Jenn flipped around to glare at her, suds clinging to her hands — "that's enough!"

"Sorry," Maura shot back snidely. "But it *would* be convenient for you."

Jenn tensed visibly. Bubbles dripped in foamy clumps from her fisted hands onto the floor.

As soon as they resolved Hannah's issues at school, Hunter would be sure to set aside some time just for his oldest daughter. In the meantime, Jenn had to understand that Maura's jealousy wasn't unfounded. "Jenn, she has every right to feel —"

"Don't. You. Start." Jenn jabbed a finger at Hunter three times. "Quit being the peacemaker, for once."

"What?" Where was this coming from? Maura was being an obnoxious tween and while he didn't expect Jenn to tolerate it, why was she coming after him now? He made an effort to keep a lid on his emotions. Right now he just didn't want it to turn into a shouting match that Hannah was likely to overhear. "I'm just saying that here we have a daughter who is doing her best to *be* her best. You have to take that into account and —"

"I take it Maura didn't tell you she got detention today for talking back to her teacher?"

Maura slumped, her body threatening to slide under the table, her indignation replaced by a smoldering air of betrayal. She'd obviously confessed to her mom earlier, but Hunter was sure she hadn't told him because even though Jenn was the one to act stern, she never did much to reprimand the kids beyond a burst of shaming. Hunter was the one who would have levied Maura with a week's worth of grounding — and she knew it. Still, she wouldn't misbehave without reason.

Hunter's glance slid to Maura. Then he turned his gaze back on Jenn. "While I don't condone misbehavior of any sort, if she's acting out, it's probably because —"

A knock, so soft that it almost went unheard, sounded at the front door. Hunter and Jenn looked toward the door, but Maura kept her head down. Tension hung thick in the air. Finally, Echo trotted to the front door to peer through the sidelight. He gave a soft 'woof,' then ran back to Hunter as if to escort him to their guest.

"That's odd," Jenn said, her fuse temporarily snuffed. "He barks at everyone except your parents. And since when do they stand out there and wait for an invitation?"

Rising, Hunter rolled his shoulders in a shrug. "Let's find out, shall we, Echo?"

He had no idea who it could be. They rarely had visitors this far out in the country. Recently, Jenn had told him that having a dog had made her feel safer in their house. Echo may not have been very intimidating as a guard dog, but he was as good a watchdog as any. Except now.

Echo's bobtail wagged in a tiny, almost imperceptible circle. He pranced on his white sock feet beside Hunter all the way to the door, always two steps ahead as if to tell him to hurry up.

A vaguely familiar face, distorted by the intersecting lines of the decorative oval window of the front door, stared back at Hunter. Apparently, Heck Menendez had made a favorable impression on Echo. Hunter opened the door.

"Dr. McHugh." Heck had his hands shoved deep in the pockets of his bulky winter coat. He was a full five feet back from the door.

"Hello ... Heck." A frigid wind bit at Hunter's nose and he had the sudden urge to pull the hood of his sweatshirt over his head. He swept an arm toward the living room. "It's freezing out there. Come on in."

"I don't want to intrude." Heck glanced toward his house, his body turned sideways as if to make for a quick exit. "It's probably your suppertime."

"You're in luck — we just finished. And anyway, I need to shut the door and I'm not coming out there."

Heck blinked several times. Finally, he came inside, but just far enough for Hunter to shut the door.

"Now," Hunter said, "what can I do for you?"

"Who is it, Hunter?" Jenn came to stand in the open doorway to the kitchen, wiping her hands on her pants legs. "Oh … hi." Her voice dipped at the end, as if she'd been expecting someone with a giant Publishers Clearinghouse sweepstakes check — not the grumpy next-door neighbor.

"Mrs. McHugh." Heck's voice was equally lacking in enthusiasm, but it was hard for Hunter to tell if that was because of Jenn's lukewarm reception or just the way Heck was in general.

"So …?" Hunter turned to face Heck again. "You needed something? I'd invite you in for dessert, but we don't have —"

"Dessert, yes. Funny thing. I was gathering the ingredients to make a German chocolate cake from scratch when I discovered I'm fresh out of eggs. I never run out of eggs, but this morning I made myself an omelet and apparently used the last of them. Forgot entirely." Heck touched a gloved hand to his thick, dark hair, threaded with the barest hint of silver. "Age creeping up on me, I suppose."

"Do we still have some, Jenn? I haven't checked in a few days."

"Sure, plenty." She tipped her head, one brow raised ever so slightly, as if she sensed Heck was just making an excuse to drop in. "How many do you need, Heck?"

"Four … if that's not too much to ask?"

"Not at all," she replied as she went into the kitchen, her tone noticeably friendlier now. The soft whoosh of the refrigerator door opening sounded, followed by a drawer opening and closing.

Hunter and Heck stood looking at the doorway, waiting for her to reappear. When she didn't, Hunter broke the silence. "Special occasion?"

"Pardon?"

"Just wondering why you're making a cake. Our girls would have cake every day if they could, but we try to reserve them for birthdays. Not so much because of the calories, but because if you give Hannah too much sugar you pretty much have to peel her off the ceiling and it's impossible to get her to go to bed."

"Ah, yes, a birthday." Heck glanced at the family photos arranged in a giant grid on the wall above the couch.

"Yours?"

"No." His words came out so soft Hunter barely heard them. "My wife's."

Since Heck lived alone now Hunter assumed he was a widower. It was an awkward subject to broach, but Hunter was curious. "So, your wife, when did she —"

"Here you go!" Jenn strode into the room with a basket handle looped over her wrist. The eggs were tidily cushioned in a tea towel. She handed the basket to Heck. "I put six in there. That way if you need eggs before you get to the store again, you have a couple extra."

He held the basket at arm's length for a few moments, as if he were going to thrust it back at her. His lips parted, remaining open while his mind worked at a thought. But all he could manage was a nod and: "Thank you."

Five seconds later he was out the door. Jenn and Hunter shared a glance.

"Don't you dare let him pay us back in eggs, Hunter." She marched back into the kitchen.

Hunter followed her, but before he could tell Jenn about Heck's wife, Maura blurted out, "You won't believe what I heard the other day." Before either of her parents could reply, she got up, plate in hand, and went on. "My friend Linds is friends with Izzy Pinkerton and her aunt's hairdresser said that she heard Mr. Menendez was a fugitive from Columbia. Something about a drug cartel."

Crossing her arms, Jenn turned away from the sink. "Oh, really now? Your friend's friend's aunt's hairdresser?"

"Yeah, but that's not all." Maura put her plate and silverware on the counter. "She heard he moved here because he was being investigated for transporting Mexican immigrants over the border in a

181

van, mostly girls my age and younger, to be used as child slaves. But they couldn't prove anything, so he went where the media wouldn't bug him. Which is here — Nowheresville, Kentucky."

"Funny how he doesn't have an accent, since he's from Columbia," Hunter said jokingly. "Or is it Mexico?"

"He's probably been here awhile. I bet he took some lessons to get rid of his accent. Foreign actors do that all the time."

"Maura Irene McHugh," — Jenn took her daughter by the shoulders and imparted her sternest look — "you shouldn't spread wild rumors like that. How would you feel if someone said something about you that wasn't true and then four more people repeated it? Pretty soon, everyone in Faderville would have their own version of things."

"But it could —"

"But nothing. I know for a fact that the hairdresser you're talking about, Brandy Janssen, claimed to be the love-child of Cher and Elvis."

Maura's forehead creased. "Who?"

Rolling her eyes, Jenn let go of her daughter. "Never mind. Just don't let me catch you repeating that, okay?"

"Ooookay, sure." Maura gathered her backpack from the mudroom to go up to her room. "But why does he live alone out here?"

"Lots of older people live alone, Maura."

She started for the stairs. "Yeah, but he's just ..." — she shrugged a shoulder — "kinda weird."

Hunter tapped her arm as she went past.

Maura spun around. "What?"

"You're grounded."

"For calling him weird? Geez, sorry. I take it back."

"For talking back to your teacher."

"How long?"

"Until further notice. I'm calling your teacher tomorrow to get her side."

Deflated, Maura trudged up the stairs and closed her door — firmly, but not quite a slam.

Jenn put a hand on her hip. "For a while, I thought you were going to take her side."

"Just because I understand why she's acting out, doesn't mean I'll excuse it."

They spent the rest of the evening in quiet domesticity — Hunter at his makeshift desk at the coffee table, and Jenn toting laundry upstairs in between bouts of prodding Maura to finish her homework. Hannah never did come back downstairs to finish her supper.

The girls had been put to bed and Jenn and Hunter were snuggled up on the couch watching their favorite reality talent show when someone rapped at the front door.

"That *has* to be Heck," Jenn said lowly.

Hunter went to the door. When he opened it, Heck was already halfway down the driveway, the beam of his flashlight lighting his way back home.

For a few moments, Hunter couldn't quite figure it out. Then he looked down. There, sitting in front of the door, was a cake — or three-fourths of a German chocolate one, actually — neatly encased in a plastic container. Hunter picked it up. Taped to the top was a note:

'My wife would have wanted to share this with you.'

"Thanks!" Hunter called, but the wind swallowed his words and Heck kept on walking down the road.

chapter 21

Hannah

Every day, Hannah thought about ways she could get out of going to school. Mrs. Ziegler was nice enough, but Hannah wasn't comfortable with the other children. She didn't understand them, didn't like all the noise they made, and was never sure if they liked her or not. Every time they whispered to one another, she wondered if it was something about her. She heard things, words, snatches of conversation, like: 'strange', 'weird', 'always alone', 'why doesn't she talk?', and 'is something *wrong* with her?'

If anything, being at school was worse than she ever imagined it would be before she started going. All the noise and motion and goings-on made her jittery and nervous. It was so hard to concentrate. At home, it was calm and quiet. She could think there.

What if she did something bad? Would they tell her not to come back to school, then? It would have to be really bad. Patrick Mann had tortured Franklin, yet he hadn't been kicked out of school. True he wasn't allowed anywhere near the new mouse's cage and he spent a lot of time at the principal's office, but it was almost as if he actually liked the extra attention that acting out brought him.

No, Hannah didn't want people to notice her, for good or bad reasons. She especially didn't want her parents to be upset with her.

The only way out of having to go to school was to get sick. Hannah avoided washing her hands. She only pretended to take her vitamin in the morning, hiding it in her mouth until her mommy looked away, and then slipping it to Echo. She stopped washing her hands. When it got cold, she didn't put her coat on until someone made her. But nothing seemed to work. She didn't get sick. She could've faked a tummy ache or sore throat, but that, again, would be lying.

After that first visit with Dr. Liming, Hannah was more confused than ever. Both her parents sat her down that night and told her to keep it to herself if animals spoke to her. Not telling someone, they said, wasn't the same as lying, in this case. It was *so* confusing.

Things only got worse when, in November, her parents decided it was time for her to ride the bus with Maura. Her mommy was starting back at work part-time, and so the extra time she'd be afforded by not driving Hannah to school made her schedule easier.

Patrick Mann was not on Hannah's bus, but there were a lot of older kids: fourth, fifth, and sixth graders. Not only were they big and loud, but bossy. Hannah sat in the front, right behind the bus driver, Miss Beverly. It was the only safe place she could find. Her sister didn't want to sit with her and she had no friends. When they got to school in the morning, she always waited until all the other kids got off the bus before going inside. Miss Beverly never said anything more to her than 'Have a great day', and that was just fine with Hannah.

During recess, Hannah always stayed inside and drew pictures. Before any of the other kids came back, she hid them, because she didn't want anyone to see what she was doing. She never felt her pictures were as good as she wanted them to be. Especially not after her mommy and Dr. Liming had mistaken her little blue penguin for a common bird, as if it were a sparrow or crow.

Then one day, they had a substitute, and it was raining and too cold to go outside for recess, so Mr. Panki-Something-or-Other — Hannah wasn't sure since he'd only mumbled his name once and hadn't written it on the board — made them all go to the gym. Hannah wanted to let him know she always stayed in the room while Mrs. Ziegler graded papers, but she didn't know him at all, so she didn't say anything.

Knots of snakes formed inside her tummy as she entered the gymnasium. When she realized she'd left the room without her backpack — and Faustine — panic filled her chest.

She glanced at the clock on the wall. Twenty-two minutes until they went back to the room. Sound bounced off the concrete block walls and metal rafters, ringing inside her ears. Kids were running back and forth, lobbing basketballs at the hoops, jumping rope off to the side. Others stood in clumps, talking and laughing. Occasionally, one would glance at Hannah, then say something to the person beside them.

A girl, small like Hannah, came up to her. She was black-skinned with the prettiest chocolate brown eyes Hannah had ever seen. "Hi, I'm Lexi."

Hannah looked down at the ground. The noise in her head rose to a deafening hum.

"Want to play with me and Josie? We're being Disney princesses."

What Hannah wanted was to sit down. Everything around her was tilting left and then right, then left again. She shook her head 'no'.

"Okay. If you decide later you want to, we're right over there."

Hannah was vaguely aware of Lexi leaving. Voices filled her head, blending together in a confusing buzz. She turned toward the wall, hands over her ears.

"Hannah, are you okay?" Mr. Panki-Whatever asked.

"Leave her alone," someone else said. "That's just the way she is."

She had to get out of there. *Now*. A quick look around told her all the doors were closed. If she pushed one open and ran out, they'd come after her. Better to just disappear.

It took all her self-control and courage to slowly work her way around the outside of the gym and up onto the stage. Kids were not supposed to be up there, but luckily no one had noticed her so far.

She crawled under the bleachers, where it was dark and dusty. A beetle scampered between the metal bars of the framework, startling her. A few moments passed and she saw no more of the bug. She pushed on, deeper, farther, somewhere safer. She went as far underneath as she could, where she wouldn't be seen. And there she tucked herself into a ball, with her arms covering her ears and her eyes shut tight.

It was better there. There was room. Less going on. If she imagined being at home, out under the Crooked Tree, with the birds singing and the sheep bleating, the voices faded away.

Even after it got quiet in the gym, she stayed. She was too afraid to come out. When they found her, *if* they found her, she'd get in trouble. And trouble was one thing she did not want to cause.

Yet it was also what just might get her out of there.

—oO0o—

The school day was only halfway over when Hannah climbed into the backseat of her father's truck. Echo was there, his limpid golden-brown eyes overflowing with love and sympathy. She wrapped her arms around him, tears falling softly on his shiny black fur.

Things would have been so much better if Echo could go to school with her. Then she'd never be afraid, because Echo would always protect her and make everything all right. But that wasn't going to happen. No, they'd make her go back to school alone, where she didn't fit in, where there was too much noise and too many people.

187

A 'panic attack', Dr. Liming had called it. Whatever that was. Hannah only knew it was a different way of being sick. Like there was something inside your head that was wrong. Which only made her feel even more different than she already did.

Hunter started the truck, but he didn't drive anywhere yet. He just let Hannah cry and hold tight to Echo. She wished he would just take her home. She didn't want to talk about today.

I'm here, Echo said as he licked the tears from her cheek. *I'll always be here for you.*

"I know," Hannah whispered.

Leaning out from the headrest of his seat to hear better, Hunter said, "What's that, sweet pea?"

Hannah pressed her forehead to the window, her face away from the school building. "Nothing."

She closed her eyes, hoping he'd think she was going to sleep, but it was hard to keep from sniffling. She couldn't shut the tears off, no matter how hard she tried.

"I'm not mad at you, Hannah. Mr. Pankiewicz isn't mad, either. You couldn't help it. We know that." He took a tissue from his glove compartment and dried the tears from her face, then gave her an extra one so she could blow her nose. "We just need to figure out what triggers it and find ways for you to learn to cope with it, because we don't want it to keep happening to you, okay?"

Hannah nodded, even though what he said didn't make much sense to her.

"Can I stay home until then?"

Hunter laughed. "I don't think so, sweet pea. Mrs. Ziegler will be back tomorrow, anyway. I'm sure she'll let you stay in the room during lunch and recess, like usual. You'll be fine."

Fine? Hannah wasn't so sure about that. Even thinking about school made her queasy.

—oO0o—

The next morning, Hannah woke up early. Not out of excitement, but dread.

Puffs of warm air brushed against her arm. A tongue, long and wet, slid over her wrist.

"I love you, too, Echo," she said in her quietest voice. And she did. More than anything.

Echo hopped up on the bed and squeezed himself next to her. Her mommy had said he wasn't allowed on the furniture, so he never got on her bed. But this time Hannah didn't make him get off. She wrapped an arm around him and buried her face against the dark fur of his ruff.

They lay like that for an hour, drifting in and out of sleep, until Jenn's footsteps sounded softly in the hallway. Hannah gave Echo a nudge and he jumped off the bed.

Jenn cracked open the door. "Rise and shine, monkeys."

When neither of them stirred, she came into the room. Echo was curled up on the rug, one eye open, and Hannah was trying to lie as still as possible. Then Jenn shook her gently. When Hannah slid farther under her covers, her mother peeled them away and told her in no uncertain terms to get dressed and come down for breakfast.

The ride to school was both too short and too long. Maura skipped getting on the bus to ride with them, but didn't complain about it.

That day was worse than the one before. Maura walked her to class early and all the way to her desk before leaving. Hannah lay her head down on the cool surface. Her heart raced. She couldn't make her lungs expand. She was dizzy.

With every kid who entered the room, the noise grew louder and louder, banging in her ears. She covered her head with both arms and squeezed tight. And now her stomach felt funny.

Mrs. Ziegler tapped her on the back. "Hannah, are you all ri—"

Abruptly, Hannah leaned to the right, away from Mrs. Ziegler, and threw up her breakfast.

Patrick Mann, sitting three rows away, stuck his tongue out and made a gagging sound. "Oh, gross!"

Mrs. Ziegler covered her mouth with her hands and mumbled between her fingers, "I'll have the nurse call your mother."

—oOOo—

Her mother didn't say a word all the way home. Just sat up front, her hands tight on the steering wheel, spine rigid, never once looking back at Hannah.

When they got home, Hannah went straight to bed. She wasn't sick, or tired. But she didn't think her mother wanted to talk to her right then. All this time she'd wanted to not have to go to school and just stay at home with her mommy like she'd always done, but now that she was home, it wasn't the same anymore.

Echo tried his hardest to comfort her and get her to play, twice dropping his squeaky giraffe in her lap, but Hannah ignored him. Eventually, he drifted away. She was barely aware of the click of his toenails fading away in the upstairs hallway and then the soft padding of his feet as he went down the stairs.

For a time, Hannah tried to draw, but a heavy feeling in her tummy distracted her. None of her toys interested her. She looked out the window for an animal to watch, but the only birds she saw were tiny dots in the distance. She had already read all her books several times. Perhaps there were some in Maura's room she could read? As she tiptoed through the hallway, she heard the snick of the back kitchen door and her father's footsteps.

"I'm *so* glad you're finally home," Jenn said.

"Lucky you, Tommy canceled on me. The newborn kid he was so

worried about finally got up on her feet and was bucking like crazy. All's well at the Appleton goatery." His keys clinked as he tossed them on the counter. "So what's up? You look pretty frazzled."

"Sit down. Let me make you a pot of coffee. I'm about to unload."

"Oh, boy. Hannah?"

"Who else?"

A few feet beyond the landing, out of sight, Hannah sank to the floor, brought her knees to her chest, and pulled her T-shirt down over them. She knew she shouldn't be listening, but this was about her.

She had caused this problem. She just didn't know how to fix it.

chapter 22
Echo

I wanted so badly to make Hannah feel better. I did my best to make her notice me — nuzzling her hand, tilting my head, turning in circles as I wagged my hind end, offering my favorite, most beloved and sacred toy, the squeaky giraffe — yet she wanted nothing to do with me. The look in her eyes was distant, pained, troubled. My own heart ached for her, even though I didn't fully understand what had caused her hurt.

So many times, it was like she could read my thoughts, but today it was as if she weren't even in the room right there in front of me.

Unable to help her, I drifted from the room and down the stairs, finally claiming my spot beneath the kitchen table.

"You look like you could use a hug." Hunter held his arms wide for Jenn.

She collapsed against his chest, like a knot of frustration unraveling at his touch. Then, eyes shut, she squeezed him tight.

Eventually, he was able to pry her away and sit at the kitchen table. As Jenn poured him a cup of coffee, it all came out about

Hannah's day and how Jenn had to leave work to pick her up from school.

"And the nurse said she was fine?" Hunter's spoon pinged against the inside of his cup as he stirred.

"Fine as in not sick. No fever, no stomachache. But the moment the nurse began to walk Hannah back to class, she started to dry heave."

"Ah, I see." He lowered his voice. "Sounds psychosomatic. Did she say anything before she left for school this morning?"

"Nothing at all."

"Meaning she didn't *volunteer* anything — or you didn't ask?"

"I was afraid if I did, it would make her even more anxious than she already was."

"Okay, I see your point. Maybe she's afraid of having another panic attack?"

"Maybe." The dryer buzzed. Jenn rose and went into the laundry room next to the kitchen, her shoes clopping over the tiles. She popped the dryer door open and began unloading it. "Did you talk to Mr. Sloan or Dr. Liming about Echo going to school with her?"

I lifted my head from my paws. She banged the dryer door shut and came back into the kitchen, a laundry basket at her hip.

"I did," Hunter replied. "Turns out, it's more complicated than I originally thought. It could be done, but the training would take months. And at the end of it all, if he didn't pass the certification, he couldn't go."

Lowering the basket to the floor, she sat across from him. "We don't have months."

"I know."

"You have to understand, Hunter, this isn't just about Hannah." She began folding, then setting each item on top of the table. "It affects our whole family. Me more so than you. All these years I resisted going back to work because I thought I needed to be here for her. And it did work. For her, at least."

Hunter grabbed a crumpled T-shirt from the basket to help her and snapped the wrinkles from it before flipping the sleeves back and creasing it down the middle. "Jenn, she wouldn't be where she is now without you. She's light years ahead of other kids her age."

"Academically, maybe. But socially? Hunter, she can't cope with being in school. Not yet, anyway. Dr. Liming mentioned a new school for the gifted opening next year in Danville. The Finley Academy, I think. The bank has a branch there. I could transfer. It's just ... I don't know ..." She tossed a facecloth back at the basket, as if even that task required too much concentration, but it missed and landed on the floor.

I crept forward, picked it up in my mouth, and sat in front of her. She took a hold of it and I tugged back. All this talk was boring me. They both needed to lighten up. Play a little. Rolling her eyes at me, Jenn spat the word 'Out' and yanked it from my teeth so hard I was afraid she'd dislodged a canine. One flick of my tongue told me all my teeth were still there.

Jenn marched to the washing machine, threw the washcloth inside, and returned to the kitchen, pausing at the sink, her attention drawn by a few dirty dishes that had been there since yesterday. "I don't know if it's the kids, the teacher, or just being away from home." She ran the faucet and dumped a glob of dish detergent into the sink before setting the dishes inside it. "Anyway, it's freaking her out. Two months ago, I'd have just said, 'Fine, let her stay home'. But it's not that easy. I've gone back to work and ..." Her shoulders bunched up.

"Go on, Jenn," Hunter urged calmly. "No sense keeping it bottled up."

The heel of her hand pounded downward on the faucet handle. She flipped around. Curling her fingers into fists, she tucked them under her armpits and cast her eyes to the ceiling. "Damn it, I feel guilty for saying this, but" — she met Hunter's eyes, a mixture of resolve and regret warring behind her own eyes — "I *like* it. I like being with people my own age and making friends and being appreciated by customers. Today I helped this young couple secure a loan for their first home. It made me feel really good to be able to help them. Besides, I used to go stir crazy sitting out here in the middle of nowhere with no one to talk to except a five-year-old. If I go back to homeschooling Hannah, then I'm stuck doing it for who knows how long. I know this sounds insane coming from me, especially since I'm the one who was against sending her in the first place, but —"

There was a long pause, during which Jenn's lip drooped. She sniffed several times, took a tissue from her pocket, and blew her nose. Hunter rose and went to her. Gently, he took her hands in his and murmured in her ear.

She looked at him, her eyes glimmering with the promise of relief. "You will?"

He nodded. "Yeah."

"It's a lot to ask."

A tear spilled down her cheek. He whisked it away with his thumb, then brushed his lips to her brow before leaning his forehead against hers. "Honey, they adore Hannah. You know that. I'm sure they'd love to help out."

"But I don't want to take advantage of them just because they live next door."

His hands slid from the tops of her shoulders down her arms, until he held both her hands in his. "Asking family for help when you need it is not taking advantage of them. That's what they're —"

She broke away from him and sat down again, facing away from him. "But Brad's retirement was a big deal. He's been counting down the days for the last six months. I don't know. It's too much to ask." Looking down at her lap, she lowered her head and shook it. "Don't."

Reclaiming his own seat, Hunter sat back, the chair frame creaking as he pressed his weight into it for support. "Got any other options?"

"Short of me disrupting my career again? No." Jenn plucked another washcloth from the basket and wrung it as she let out a long sigh. "Okay. Go ahead. Ask. At least it'll give us time to figure things out."

"Look, we knew we were in for some trials at this stage. We just didn't know what. We'll get it all figured out eventually. In the right environment, Hannah will thrive. We can look into the Finley Academy some more. Maybe that's a better option."

She laid the washcloth on her knee and smoothed it. "You're right. You *always* are. I kind of hate that about you." Her frown quivered, then twitched upward into a grin. "I love it, too. I can't imagine navigating this crazy life without you. You're good at what you do, great with the girls, and a godsend to me when I can't think straight."

Hunter scooted his chair around the table and touched the pad of his thumb to her cheek, collecting another tear. Then he kissed her there, until she turned her mouth to meet his.

This was where I got uncomfortable. I forgot to mention this because, frankly, I don't like to talk about it, but within a month of joining the McHugh family Hunter took me 'on a ride' to his veterinary practice and, well … He poked me with a needle, which I assumed was just another vaccination. After drifting off happily to sleep, I woke up pretty stiff 'down there'. Yeah, snip-snip.

Pity, I was just coming to an age where I felt the need to sow my oats, although I hadn't yet had the chance to do so. A couple of weeks earlier, I had desperately wanted to, though, when I caught a whiff of that pretty German Shepherd at the softball park. Apparently, her owner was clueless as to the desirability of her dog's condition. The lady was more than happy to let me say 'hello, how ya doin'?', but when I proceeded to hug her bitch (and yes, that's what we call the fast girl dogs), who was a little on the tall side for me, I struggled to express my urges. But hey, I was determined, and I may have gone a little nuts. Hunter yanked me off and mumbled something about getting me 'fixed' soon. Fixed? Was I broken? Now I knew what he meant.

Anyway, I was neutered now, but I still understood what was going on right in front of me. Although they were discreet about it, Jenn and Hunter were two *very* affectionate humans. They mated frequently in their bedroom, which would have made me wonder why they didn't have more offspring, except I figured Hunter was probably 'fixed', too.

It always started with Hunter's hand on her back, drifting downward, a prolonged kiss, their bodies rubbing against each other … Seemed like a lot of unnecessary prelude to me, but hey, I'm a dog. We don't waste time when it comes to copulation.

Now here they were, pawing at each other as if I weren't even in the room, staring at them, trying to send them ESP about my appetite. The usual routine at this point for them was to break it off, sneak upstairs, and disappear for an hour or so. But it was broad daylight. Hannah was upstairs, still listening, perhaps, and Maura would arrive home on the bus at any time. Besides, I was due for my afternoon biscuit.

Standing, I sneezed loudly and followed it with a groan, hoping to get someone's attention. Hunter's eyes flicked to me, his lips still touching Jenn's. Evidently, mating with her was more pressing than feeding me, because he shut his eyes again as he slipped a hand under the front of her shirt.

She caught his wrist and pulled away, breaking the kiss. Hunter's subsequent glare practically burned a hole in my head. As if it were my fault he'd forgotten to feed me or that Jenn was preoccupied.

"You know what else?" Jenn leaned back to gaze at Hunter. "I've always had this feeling, deep down inside, that Hannah has something truly special to contribute to the world. Just dang if I can figure out what that is."

Tugging at a belt loop on her slacks, he laughed. "Yeah, maybe by the time she's thirty we'll figure that out." His head tipped to the side. "Wanna go upstairs?"

A smile teased at the corners of her mouth. She bit her lip, obviously tempted.

I planted my rump and, pulling my paws in close to my chest, sat up. When neither of them looked at me, I barked. I managed to balance perfectly for a moment, before tottering sideways.

"Awww." Totally ignoring Hunter, Jenn retrieved a peanut butter biscuit from the tin on the counter. I sat up again, this time balancing longer. She flipped it in an arc and I snatched it in midair. "Did you teach him that?"

"Unfortunately, yes." Hunter's cell phone rang. He glanced at the display. "Speak of the devil. It's Mom. I have to grab some paperwork out of the truck, so I'll talk to her out there. Be right back. Remember where we were."

While he was busy outside, I managed to bum three more biscuits off of Jenn. Hunter never gave me more than two. In the future, I resolved to hang out at Jenn's feet more often while she was in the kitchen. This could be lucrative. I folded to the floor, then rolled over onto my side.

"You play dead, too?" Jenn took yet another biscuit from the tin. *Score!*

Palm up, she extended the treat. A blast of cool air rushed in as the door was flung open. Her hand hovered above my head, just out of reach. I stretched my neck, sniffing.

"Nuh-uh," Hunter said. "He's had enough."

Jenn's fingers curled over the treat. With a shrug, she tossed it back in the tin. My stomach gurgled in protest.

"So what did she say?" Jenn said.

"Not the permanent solution I was hoping for. They can watch her this Monday and Tuesday, but it seems Brad surprised Mom with a cruise. They're flying out Wednesday."

Jenn shook her head slowly. "No, just … no."

"Yes. They're off to the Bahamas for two weeks."

"And after that?"

"Uh, yeah, well, they can't. Seems Brad realized he wasn't ready to retire yet. He just needed a less stressful job. Come next month, he's the head of campus security at the community college. And Mom's going to remain part-time at the clinic. They said they talked about it and decided that people who keep working have more social connections and live longer."

Jenn's body slumped in disappointment. "So what are we supposed to do with her? We can't lock her in a closet. And I refuse to send her to that school in Taylor County like they suggested at first. She's gifted, not mentally challenged." Her fingertips moved in slow circles over her temples. "I suppose I could take a day or two off of work, but that's all. I just started there. Is there any way you can rearrange appointments or bounce clients over to Doctor Timowski for the rest of next week?" She flipped her hand up. "No, wait, never mind. If you don't work, you don't get paid. We may need that money for some kind of special school that can deal with her issues. Except that there's nothing even *close* to what she needs in this county. Maybe we could hire a nanny? Or a manny? That's what they call them, right?"

"Jenn, Jenn." He rubbed her arms consolingly. "We don't have to figure it all out this moment. We have a few days to think things over. For now, we need to stay calm and —"

"We? You mean me." She pushed his hands away. "You tell *me* to 'calm down' like all I have to do is flip a switch and suddenly I'm all Zen. Like I can just summon forth rainbows and unicorns by popping Skittles. It's not that easy, Hunter. Everyone keeps analyzing Hannah's situation, but this has totally mucked up *our* life, too."

Jaw clenched, Hunter sucked in a breath. "Remember she almost died, Jenn. No, she *was* dead — and Dr. Townsley brought her back to us. I'll take her as she is, rather than not at all."

Jenn looked away.

Clearly, he hadn't wanted to go there, but he'd said it anyway. Hannah was Hannah. Brilliant and baffling all in one. There was no changing her.

His hand wandered up her cheek to brush the hair from her forehead. "This is a setback. That's all. There are people who have it far worse than we do. We need to keep it all in perspective. Okay?"

Nodding, she glanced at him, then lowered her eyes.

He folded her to his chest and held her, stroking her back. Minutes passed, in which he rocked her in his arms and she wept softly against his checkered flannel shirt.

Often, what I noticed about them was that the tenderest moments occurred when they said nothing at all. Moments like this. Mario and Ariella's love — if one could call it that — had been like a fire blazing out of control, consuming them both. And the Grunwalds ... if there had ever been any love between Mavis and Earl it was expressed solely by the fact that they had allowed one another to go on living.

The tears now gone, Jenn splayed her fingers against Hunter's chest. "See, this is why you're good for me. You keep me sane. *You* hold this family together. I love you, Hunter McHugh. I love Hannah, too. I really do. It's just —"

"Shhh, I know, I know. I suppose if raising daughters was easy, we wouldn't appreciate the good days as much as we do."

I sighed then. I really did. This was what I loved about this family. Why I never wanted to be with any other. And why everything I had gone through before I met them only made being with them that much more meaningful.

I would do anything to keep them safe and whole and happy.

chapter 23

Hunter

Hannah was in the same place and position that Hunter had left her almost nine hours earlier: her rump on the top step of her grandparents' porch, her chin balanced on the heels of her hands, elbows firmly planted on her knees. She was still wearing the same sullen scowl, too.

And judging by the way Brad shook his head as he leaned wearily against his rake, his second day of watching Hannah hadn't gone any better than the first.

Hunter climbed down out of his truck and shut the door. He hesitated for a few moments, pretending to check his phone messages before he went to Brad, who always had this vigilant air about him that made Hunter feel like he somehow knew that he'd gone five miles per hour over the speed limit on his way there.

Hind end waggling, Echo ran to Hunter. He skidded to a halt to sit at Hunter's feet and tapped his thigh with a pleading paw.

"Come here, boy." Hunter patted his chest. As Echo reared up, bouncing on his hind feet to get closer, Hunter ruffled the dog's mane.

"At least someone's happy to see me."

"That makes two of us," Brad said as he approached. He propped his rake against a fence post and pinched the brim of his baseball cap in greeting. Brad didn't wear hats because he was losing his hair. He had a head full of it, a blend of dark brown and pepper gray. After almost thirty years as a deputy and then sheriff, he said not having something on his head felt like the equivalent of showing up in public buck naked.

"How'd it go?" Hunter asked. "Same as yesterday?"

"That would've been nice. At least yesterday she ate something."

"Hunger strike, huh?"

"Yep. I even made her favorite — square crackers with square bits of cheese. I made sure they were perfectly symmetrical. Did I miss a memo? Is she into circles now? On some paleo diet?"

"Not that I know of. So, no lunch?"

"Not even a snack. She must be dying of hunger. Couldn't lure her into the kitchen, so I brought her out a tray and an extra coat. Put the food back inside after a while. Your mom's always harping on me about food poisoning when I forget to put the leftovers in the fridge."

One of Brad's fleece jackets was draped over Hanna's shoulders. It was a little on the cool side today, being November, but the sun was out and there wasn't much of a breeze. Still, not the kind of day you'd want to stay outside in for long.

"Bathroom breaks?" Hunter commanded Echo to 'go get Hannah' and just as he was told, Echo bounded to her. Ten feet away, he slowed, lowered his head, and crept up to her submissively, the clear message being that he bowed to Hannah in all matters. Despite the fact that Echo was slathering her with kisses, Hannah did little more than flinch in acknowledgment.

"Twice. She did have a glass of milk early on. Guess she didn't want to pee her pants."

"Sorry she's being so difficult."

"I wouldn't say she was 'difficult'. But I did worry about her. She has a history of drifting off, so I made sure I kept her in my sights." Brad glanced over his shoulder at her. "Have you taken her to, you know, *talk* to someone?"

"This is Hannah we're talking about. She doesn't do deep, meaningful conversations. She doesn't even do small talk most of the time."

"True. It's just … well, the way she's acting kind of makes you wonder what all went on at school lately. I'd hate to think the worst, like some sort of abuse, but you never know. In all my years of law enforcement, I learned that some of the nicest people have the most diabolical motives. Even bullying can have a big impact on kids. Words are powerful weapons."

The thought of anyone preying on one of Hunter's children sent his protective traits into overdrive. "I hadn't given it much thought, actually. Do you think it's possible?"

"Hard to say. I don't want to make you start believing something happened that didn't. Just throwing it out there. Anyway, like your mom's said plenty of times, Hannah's complicated. She processes things differently. Which begs the question: what are you going to do? She's stuck in some kind of funk. Hate to see her this way."

"To tell you the truth, Brad, I have no idea. Jenn and I have been brainstorming like crazy. She'd made so much progress this year after the accident. And now …" His hands shoved deep into his pockets, Hunter turned and began walking toward the porch, Brad following. "Our options in this area are too limited. Jenn's torn between staying home again and helping Hannah get through this, and remaining at her job. She's checking with Human Resources at corporate headquarters to see if she could take a leave of absence while we work things out. I told her we'd find a permanent solution, but right now, I can't for the life of me see what that might be."

"Lise and I have been talking and we can just cancel our —"

Hunter wheeled around and stopped in front of him. "No."

"Why not, Hunter? Family is important. It's a small sacrifice to make."

"I don't want you to change your plans, that's why. Hannah will come to work with me the rest of the week. Next Monday, we're seeing a child psychologist in Nashville who specializes in children with special conditions like hers. Dr. Liming at the school pulled some strings to get us in. It may not solve our current problem, but we're hoping it will give us some answers — although getting Hannah to open up is a little like asking for the key to Fort Knox. Could be we'll have to guess our way to the answer."

Nodding, Brad patted Hunter's upper arm. "Well, good luck there. And I mean that."

"Yeah, I know you do." The ping of metal on metal drew Hunter's attention. Farther down the road, on the other side, Heck Menendez heaved upward on a post driver before smashing it downward, slamming a skinny T-post into the ground. Hunter cupped a hand over his brow to shut out the glare of the sun. "What's he doing over there?"

Brad squinted. "Not sure. Putting in a new mailbox maybe?"

"If he is, it's the flimsy kind. He hasn't learned yet, has he?"

"Apparently not."

"I'll stop by on my way home and tell him. It's the neighborly thing to do, I suppose."

"By the way, looks like we'll be missing Thanksgiving this year. I'm really sorry about that."

"Don't be. You two haven't had a vacation since … Gosh, it's been years, hasn't it? Go. Enjoy yourselves."

They said goodbye and Brad went inside the house.

"Come on, sweet pea. Time to go." Hunter retrieved Hannah's book bag from the bottom step, where he'd set it earlier that day. It was still zipped, as if she hadn't taken anything from it. He checked inside. Yes, Faustine was still there, along with Hannah's favorite Shel Silverstein book. He slung it over his shoulder, thankful there wasn't anyone around to see him sporting the pink and purple flowery backpack. He held out his hand for his daughter and pulled her to her feet. "Maura will be home soon and Mommy's bringing pizza home for supper. You like pizza, right?"

As he expected, Hannah said nothing. Just slogged along with her head down, toes dragging. He knew there was a reason she'd gone silent, but he didn't have the energy to delve into it right now. That day alone he'd already turned and birthed a breech calf, flushed the ear canals of a Bloodhound, had his hand pinched in the beak of a disagreeable African Grey parrot, wormed and vaccinated five pygmy goat kids, and diagnosed progressive retinal atrophy in a beloved Cocker Spaniel — and that was just before lunch.

Once Hannah was secured in her booster, he opened the passenger side door. Echo hopped into the co-pilot's seat, his ears perked forward. He'd enjoyed trailing along with Hunter while Hannah had been in school. The frequent comings and goings of visitors at the clinic had made him far more accepting of strangers than he had been when they first got him. They would never know his history, but Hunter guessed that his early months had not been good ones. It was a testament to the dog's resiliency that he had not only attached himself to a child who was sometimes challenging, but that he carried himself with such a calm and contemplative air. Echo was like an old soul who had discovered his calling, that of the family dog and a child's best friend. A simple calling, yet a noble one.

After Halo, he'd been too busy with vet school for a dog. Then along came Maura, then Hannah ... Later, fate had delivered this black and white Aussie right to him, just when he was most needed. Now, Hunter couldn't imagine being without a dog. So many times, he'd look at Echo, Echo would look back at him, and he'd get this powerful sense that he'd known the dog far longer than Echo had been alive.

Hunter pulled into the end of Heck's driveway and turned his truck off. "This'll only take a minute," he said to Hannah, before getting out. Then he walked over to where Heck was eyeing his T-post. On the ground beside him was a smashed in mailbox.

"Leaning a little to your left," Hunter said.

Laying the post-driver on the ground, Heck dragged his jacket sleeve across his forehead to mop away the sweat. "So you stopped in to critique my post-driving abilities?"

"Actually, I came to warn you that with that flimsy thing, you'll probably end up retrieving your mailbox from the ditch on the far side of the road by next week."

"Is vandalism a favorite pastime around here?"

Hunter shrugged. "I suppose there are worse things a teenager could do besides whack at mailboxes with baseball bats."

"So what do you suggest? A P.O. box?"

Smirking, Hunter raised a finger. "You know, I never thought of that. I suppose if you went downtown every day, it's a good option. But you don't seem like the sort to me who gets out much."

"I worked in downtown Louisville for thirty-seven years at a pharmaceutical company. I've been out as much as I ever want to be. Battling rush hour traffic on a daily basis was not my ideal life. Retirement has its perks."

Now it made sense why he'd move out into the middle of nowhere.

"A pharmaceutical company, huh? So you were a pharmacist?"

"Research chemist."

"Ah, now that's interesting."

"Not really." Heck picked up the post-driver again. "Now, do you have a level with you? Because right now this post will have to do. Until I can hire a handyman to —"

"I can help you."

"Help me?" Heck looked at him as if Hunter were suggesting they go tubing down the Amazon.

"Sure. I can run to town, pick up a wooden post, some cement mix, a steel mailbox, some two-by-fours ... What we do in these parts is just build the sucker so sturdy that it takes the fun out of it. Last thing some drunken teenager wants to do is explain to his parents why he's in the emergency room with a broken arm. It won't be pretty, but —"

"They're drunk when they do this?"

"Or high. Or both."

"And exactly how do you know this?"

"It's been going on since I was in high school."

Heck eyed him suspiciously.

"No, I never ..." Hunter waved his hands before him, but Heck was already marching off toward his garage, the post-driver propped on his shoulder, making him lean to that side.

He was about to follow Heck into his garage when he noticed Echo with his nose pressed to the inside of the truck window, steaming it up. Hannah was watching him, too. He let them both out, then took Hannah's hand and went to the garage. Who knew how long this was going to take? Heck hadn't answered him yet and he wasn't leaving until he either said, 'Sure, thanks' or 'Leave me the hell alone'.

The overhead door was closed, but the side entrance was open, so Hunter went in there, Echo trotting close behind them.

He wasn't expecting what he saw: canvases on easels, shelves full of paints and paint remover, brushes, palettes ... Most of the canvases were blank, some had sheets over them, but there was one in the corner with a photo clipped at the top of the easel.

Tugging at his hand, Hannah led Hunter toward it. It was the first time in days that she'd interacted, and so he let go of her hand as he took everything in. There were a few garden tools clustered up front by the overhead door, but for the most part Heck had turned his garage into a studio.

Hannah reached out and touched the painting before Hunter could stop her.

"Hannah, no!"

"It's all right, really." Heck set the post driver against the wall. "As long as her hands are clean, I don't mind. She's just curious. Besides, it's dry."

Hannah brushed her fingertips over the swirls of color, tracing a streak of pink from one end to the other. Then she stepped in close, her face just inches from the painting.

Hunter stared in awe. The scene unfolding in dashes of paint was of a Western landscape with geologic formations, awash in reds and oranges beneath a cloudless sky. It was stunningly beautiful.

"Zion National Park," Heck said from behind them. "My wife and I used to travel during summer break. She was a teacher, but at heart she always wanted to be a photographer. I dabbled in painting over the years, but it wasn't until I retired last year that I took it seriously." His eyes softened as he gazed at the photo above the painting. "Never put your dreams off, thinking you'll get around to them someday. You never know what could happen. There might not even be a someday."

But Heck, Hunter noticed, wasn't looking at the photo anymore. His sights were fixed toward the window, gazing off into the distance. Certainly, Hunter had wanted to know more about Heck — he was his neighbor now, after all, and might be for years more — but this moment was almost too personal, hinting at emotional wounds not fully healed. There was only one thing to do at a delicate time like this — change the topic.

"So, uhhhh," Hunter began clumsily, "I can run to the hardware store right now, if you want. Be back in forty-five minutes. Have your new mailbox up before suppertime. Sound okay? You can just reimburse me for supplies. The labor's free."

A distinct 'V' formed between Heck's dark, bushy eyebrows. "Why?"

"Why what?" Hunter repeated, baffled.

"Why would you do that for me? Any handyman I know would charge twenty-five dollars an hour. Or more."

"You must've come from a rich neighborhood. Anyway, folks around here look out for each other. We don't keep track of favors."

"Just the same, I would feel obligated to return the favor."

"Only if you wanted to. I won't hold you to it, I promise."

Once again, Heck hadn't really answered him. By that point Hunter figured he probably felt awkward asking for help, so Hunter decided he was going to do it anyway.

He was getting ready to gather Hannah up when he realized she'd drifted to another easel and had lifted up the sheet covering it. This one was of a valley filled with rows of tulips. Two gardeners were bent over the rows, gathering flowers into baskets at their hips.

Echo lay down beside her, his chin resting on his paws. Hannah began pressing her fingertips to the dabs of paint. Before Hunter could reach her to pull her hand away, she'd lifted a dry brush from the easel ledge.

He plucked the brush from her and set it back on the easel. "Come on, Hannah. We have to go to the store."

"She can stay," Heck said.

"What? Why?"

"I'm sure your errands will go more quickly if she stays here."

Heck had him there. It wouldn't be impossible, but it would take a good while longer. "Are you sure? I mean, you can't let her out of your sight, not even for a minute."

Heck brought Hannah a stool, then a little wooden tool box filled with brushes. He propped a piece of thick paper onto a small easel and then retrieved tubes of paint from a waist-high shelf.

"Acrylics," he told Hunter. "They dry fairly quickly, but they're more forgiving than watercolors. Not as messy as oils, though."

Hannah had already grabbed a brush and was waiting raptly for Heck to squeeze the paints onto a palette for her.

"If you hurry up," Heck prodded, as he pulled a stool up beside Hannah, "she won't even know you're gone. But if you're worried, you can leave the dog here. From what I've seen, he's rarely more than ten feet from her unless he's with you."

Hunter didn't move.

Taking a pair of reading glasses from his pocket, Heck set them halfway down on his nose and peered at Hunter over the top of the rims. "Look, I noticed her sitting on your parents' porch all day. She didn't look happy. This interests her. I think if you tried to drag her away from it before she had a chance to try it, you'd have a very disgruntled young lady on your hands."

He couldn't have been more right. And it *had* been a hectic day. A few minutes by himself in the truck or at the store would be a welcome gift.

Besides, by the looks of things, Hannah had already made the decision for him.

Maybe school wasn't what she needed to grow and thrive. Maybe what she needed … was this.

—o00o—

Heck stood just inside the front door of Hunter and Jenn's house, rain dripping from his boots onto the already soggy welcome mat, a pumpkin pie cradled in his arms.

"Not my best crust. It's a little brown around the edges. I left it in the oven a few minutes too long." He looked down at it, then grimaced slightly as he held it out to Jenn. "So I made an apple pie, too. It's on the back seat of my car. I had too much to carry to walk here. Besides …" — he glanced out the front picture window — "it's a little damp out there."

"Why, thank you, Heck. Crust looks about right to me. You're too hard on yourself." Jenn took the pie from him, then brought it to her nose and inhaled deeply. "Oh my. It smells heavenly. If this is subpar for you, I can't imagine what your best is like. Maybe you should be on *Top Chefs*?" She ducked into the kitchen to set it on the counter, passing Hunter.

"Hey there, neighbor!" Hunter gripped Heck's hand to shake it. Heck practically cringed at the contact, so Hunter let go. He figured when he asked him to Thanksgiving dinner a couple of weeks ago that Heck would offer up some excuse not to come, but surprisingly he'd accepted. Maybe the guy did crave some human interaction after all? "We saved a place for you at the head of the table."

"Uh, well, I …" Heck pulled at the fingers of his gloves, but not like he was going to remove them completely. More like he didn't know what to do with himself.

"Now, you aren't going to beg out on us, are you? Really, everyone's been looking forward to having you." That probably classified as a little white lie. When Hunter told Jenn he'd invited him, she'd been a little annoyed that he'd done so without asking her first. Hunter had played the pity card, stating that he knew Heck was going to be alone that day and inviting him was the neighborly thing to do. Maura had wrinkled her nose at the news and mumbled something about 'weird' and 'a loner'. Hannah had expressed little more than mild curiosity, which in her case was a positive sign. It was going to be awkward, Hunter knew that. But the only way to get to know people was to get past those initial stages. Besides, Hunter had an ulterior motive in inviting him. "You do remember what we discussed, right?"

"Word for word," Heck said. "When do you plan on bringing it up?"

"No idea." Hunter held out his hands. When Heck didn't budge,

Hunter prompted him. "Can I take your coat?"

"I was going to say I need to get the other pie, but it's a veritable Noah's flood out there."

"There's an umbrella in the basket behind you."

Heck turned around to find Echo sniffing the umbrella, as if to point it out for him. "Oh, thank you." He unfastened the snap and opened it partway. "I'll be back in a moment, then."

Just as he went out the door, Jenn appeared at Hunter's side. "Okay, I wasn't thrilled at first that you'd invited an extra guest for Thanksgiving without asking me first, but on second thought, I'm glad you did. That pumpkin pie looks and smells delectable. Did you see the fancy crust? And he's got another pie in the car? The man must've been up before dawn, baking away." She peered through the sidelight of the front door, her hand on the knob, waiting to open the door for Heck. "Besides, the table does seem kind of empty without Brad and Lise taking up their usual spots."

"It was the only opening they had to get away until who knows when."

"Yeah, I get that. And in their shoes I'd probably have done the same thing. Anyway, makes me feel kind of good that he's here instead of sitting alone with a TV dinner, watching the Macy's parade. The kids should get to know him better. Maura, for one, needs to give her imagination a rest."

Which was exactly what Hunter wanted to happen. Heck was a little icy around the edges, but beneath that cool exterior was a decent guy. He was sure of it. All he had to do was give Jenn the chance to see the same man he'd come to know recently. So far, so good.

Echo waited by the front door until Heck came back in, but Hunter suspected it was more because of the yummy-smelling food Heck was bringing in than anything.

Once Heck was settled at the big dining room table, Jenn and Maura started bringing the feast out while Hunter tried, in vain, to engage him in conversation. Heck was a master at one-word answers. Hannah performed her usual chore of laying out the silverware beside each plate in order of length — knife, fork, spoon.

The spread was impressive: an eighteen-pound turkey with orange-cranberry-walnut stuffing, garlic mashed potatoes, skillet-cooked green beans with bacon, Greek salad, flaky biscuits, and a bowl of berries and real whipped cream. Hunter was proud of himself. Admittedly, he'd gone a bit overboard, but he'd relished the endeavor. Thanksgiving dinner would usually have been prepared by his mom, but with her and Brad being out of town, Hunter had stepped in, chasing Jenn back to bed that morning so she could get some much needed rest. It was his first turkey and amazingly, he hadn't under- or overcooked it.

Jenn scooped herself up a big dollop of mashed potatoes before passing the bowl to Maura. "Heck, Hunter tells me you're a painter. How long have you been doing that?"

He finished chewing his bite of stuffing and dabbed at the corners of his goatee with a napkin. "Just over a year."

"Is that all? You must have done some artwork before that — drawing, sculpting, photography?"

"No, not really."

"Sophia took the pictures," Hannah blurted out. She corralled her peas into a perfect circle, before herding them onto her spoon three at a time to eat.

"What pictures? And who's Sophia?" Jenn asked Heck.

Everyone but Hannah was looking at him, waiting to hear more, but not wanting to ask anything outright. Hunter had never mentioned anything to Jenn about Heck being married before because, honestly, it just hadn't come up. He realized now that was a mistake, information Jenn would have considered critical.

Heck busied himself slicing his turkey into bite-sized pieces. "The paintings I do are from photos my wife, Sophia, used to take." He pointed to a serving bowl next to Hunter's plate. "Could you pass me the gravy, please?"

Sensing Heck's reluctance to talk about his wife, Hunter redirected the topic as he passed the gravy along. "So, Maura, when did you say your first basketball game is?"

From there, the conversation was a little livelier, although none of it involved Heck. Until he set his fork down to the left of his plate.

Hannah stood, her gaze fixed on his fork, her forehead scrunched. "That doesn't go there."

"I'm sorry," Hunter began. "She —"

"No, no." Heck raised a hand to stop him. "It's all right. I used to be the same way, wanting everything to have a place and an order." He glanced at Hannah's silverware and immediately rearranged his to match. "Like this?"

Hannah nodded and calmly sat back down, then went back to eating her peas by threes.

Jenn gave Hunter a look of astonishment. He shrugged. This was his chance to get his plan back on track.

"Hannah, sweet pea, do you want to show Mommy that picture Heck was helping you paint?"

She popped the last of her peas into her mouth. "Nope."

"Why not?"

"It didn't turn out right."

"Show her anyway. You might be surprised. I bet she'll think it's pretty amazing."

"Okay." She slid her chair back and ran up the stairs. Thirty seconds later she was at Jenn's side, holding the painting in front of her.

"That is *so* cool!" Maura said, which in itself was a huge compliment.

At first, it was obvious that Jenn wasn't sure what it was. Patches of blue and purple were interrupted by the faintest streaks of white.

Little stars of yellow and green and orange were scattered throughout.

When she took it from Hannah and held it at arm's length, her mouth fell open. Up close, there were patterns of color that in themselves were vivid enough to capture one's attention. But from farther away all the bursts of color and squiggly lines came together to reveal the outline of a dog.

"This is Echo," Jenn uttered in amazement. She complimented Hannah before turning her gaze to Heck. "How did you teach her to do this? It's Echo, but it's ... I don't know, like she's looking through a kaleidoscope at him."

"Mrs. ... Jenn, I didn't teach her anything. She has a gift. A rare gift. I simply gave her the tools. I showed her how to mix colors, how to load her brush, then I let her loose. This was actually her third attempt. She was quite dissatisfied with the first two. They ended up in the trashcan. I don't think she could transfer to the paper what she saw in her mind right away. We had the paper on an easel, but the colors kept running. I had offered her acrylics, but she prefers watercolors, which are probably the most difficult to master. So finally, I turned on some Tchaikovsky and we set the paper on a flat surface and this ..." — he nodded toward the painting she held — "is what transpired."

Jenn's hand drifted to just above her heart. "This is amazing. Thank you, thank you."

"Does she like Tchaikovsky?" Hunter asked.

"If insisting that I play it on a loop for three hours is any indication, then yes."

Joyful tears flooded Jenn's eyes. She kissed Hannah on the cheek, then handed the picture back to her. "This is much too nice for the refrigerator, Hannah. Can you set it in the living room on the side table by the front door? I'll check to see if I have a frame for it later and if not I'll pick one up tomorrow. And Maura, can you and Hannah fetch some dessert plates, the pies, and some extra forks for us?"

When Hannah and Maura left the room, Jenn turned her attention to Hunter. "So, when were all these art lessons going on?"

"While I was building Heck's mailbox."

"And that took how many days?"

It was clear to Hunter that while she was astonished at Hannah's talent, she also wasn't thrilled he'd kept this secret from her. He had to think quickly before this devolved into something ugly. "Just one, but he also needed help putting some shelving up and fixing a stuck window and —"

"Your husband has been invaluable to me," Heck offered, rushing to his rescue. "I'm afraid I'm not very good with power tools. If left to my own devices, those projects might never have been completed. I offered to occupy Hannah while he was busy. It turned out rather well, don't you think?"

Her eyebrows flicked upward. Any steam that might have been building dissipated. "It did, yes. Thank you, again, for letting her use your paints and brushes."

Still, Hunter wasn't sure what to make of her reaction. It seemed a little too polite.

Heck lifted his water glass as if to take a drink, but set it back down. "I should thank you, really." When she returned a quizzical look, he continued. "Ever since I had to set up house without Sophia, I've been, well, a bit of a hermit and not always in the best of moods, to put it mildly. Seeing Hannah become so absorbed in using color to create the pictures in her mind … It fills me with an awe I haven't known for years." Blinking, he looked away for a moment. Then, his tone intensifying, he added, "Hunter tells me Hannah had some difficulties adjusting to a classroom setting and that you decided to withdraw her from school, but haven't resolved the issue of what to do with her until she can enter another school next year."

"That's right." She eyed Hunter sideways. "Why?"

"If you're amenable to the idea, I'd like to step in and watch

Hannah until then. It would give me something to do besides read and paint. Of course, I'd be more than willing to continue with any ongoing lessons with her. I'm no expert in early childhood education — that was my wife's expertise, really — but I think it would be good for Hannah. And for me."

Sitting back in her chair, she wagged a finger between Heck and Hunter. "You two have talked about this already, haven't you?"

"Look, Jenn," — Hunter pushed his plate back — "this just sort of happened. Remember how you say 'Everything happens for a reason'? Well, maybe Heck moving here was meant to be? If Hannah has a special gift and Heck can help her unlock it, why don't we give it a try, see what happens?"

Arms crossed, she swung her left leg over her right, her foot tapping in the air. She glanced toward the door to the kitchen, where the sound of plates being set on the counter indicated dessert was imminent.

"You could stay at your job," Hunter added, trying to tip the scales.

Jenn gave him a piercing glare. "Laying it on a little thick, aren't you?"

Hunter threw his hands wide. The ball was in her court now. Jenn didn't like to be pushed into anything.

Just then the girls came into the room, Hannah carrying two plates and Maura juggling three.

Heck cleared his throat. "Take as long as you need to think about it." He picked up his fork as Hannah set a slice of apple pie in front of him. "I'll certainly understand if you're not comfortable with the arrangement."

"I don't need to think about it." Jenn got up from the table. "I've already made up my mind."

She went into the kitchen, leaving Heck and Hunter to exchange a glance.

"What was that about?" Maura placed a pie slice where her mother had been sitting, then sat down with hers and began shoveling.

Shaking his head, Hunter gave Heck an apologetic look. "Sorry, I thought —"

Jenn returned, carrying a small stack of school books. She set them down next to Heck. "Now, she's a bit behind, but not too far. And this will only be until late May, so if you could work with her through Christmas, she should be all caught up. How long you have to spend on her assignments each day depends on how quickly she works, if at all. Short stints are best, but if she's focused, go with —"

She stopped, suddenly aware that both Hunter and Heck were staring at her.

"What? You thought I was going to say 'no'?" She rolled her eyes at them, shook it off, then said as she left the room again, "Be back in a second. I have to grab the curriculum notes, so I can explain them to you. I hope this isn't too much all at once?"

"Not at all," Heck replied after her.

Hannah watched her mother dart up the stairs, then looked at Heck. He winked at her, ever so slightly, and she grinned back at him.

chapter 24
Echo

A series of plinks and hums, blending, quickening, going up and down in pitch, drifted from the small device on Heck's counter. I tilted my head, trying to figure out what exactly was making the noise. It was like the TV, but without pictures or words. I folded back and settled on my belly, studying the little square machine intensely.

Finally, it dawned on me that the sounds were a means of communication I was familiar with. Lifting my snout, I let out a plaintive howl.

A-woo-woo-wooooo!

"He likes it." Hannah patted me on the head, then claimed her chair next to the window.

We were having lunch at Heck's kitchen table. Like every lunch, Heck played music from a little black device on the counter. It was very different from what Maura, Jenn, or Hunter listened to. There were no words to it, but something about it was much more dramatic.

"This is by Vivaldi." Heck turned the volume up. "It's called "Autumn". There are actually sonnets that go with it, but they're much more moving in Italian than English."

"What's Italian?"

"Just a different way of speaking. People in other parts of the world have different names for everything than we do. It's said there are sixty-nine hundred languages in the world today, but that's a matter of conjecture that linguists argue extensively. Does one count dialects separately? What about dead languages? And are older versions of the same language, such as Olde English, different from modern versions? If you and I went back to the Middle Ages, chances are we'd have a hard time understanding them. One could debate ..." His voice trailed off as he noticed Hannah staring at the plate of lunch meat he was holding. "I've lost you, haven't I?"

She nodded, her eyes still on the plate.

Setting the plate down, he spread the remaining sandwich fixings on the table. Every day, he put out different cheeses and meats, leafs of lettuce, sliced tomatoes, and a variety of condiments. Some days he had turkey and Swiss with Dijon mustard. Others he had roast beef and cheddar with mayonnaise. He never ate the same sandwich two days in a row.

And just like she did every day, Hannah put a slice of Colby cheese onto her white bread, then topped it with a piece of ham so thin you could almost see through it. Never two slices, never whole wheat bread, never Swiss or Cheddar cheese. For a full minute that day, though, she eyed the tomato slices before sliding one onto her sandwich. It wasn't like Hannah to be spontaneous. Change was something she seldom embraced. This was monumental.

A slice of cheese dangled from her hand under the table. I snarfed it down. It was no secret that she fed me at mealtimes. Heck saw her do it every time and never said a word.

Heck touched a finger to his earlobe. "If you listen to the music, Hannah, you can hear the leaves falling."

She shut her eyes. Her hands drifted into the air, fingers

outspread as if she were reaching for something just beyond her grasp.

"I see them," she whispered.

Heck smiled. He didn't smile often, or for very long, but sometimes things that Hannah did made him smile.

When they were done eating, Hannah asked if they could paint now.

"Soon, Hannah. But I promised your mother that we would read out loud today. Did you bring any books with you?"

She nodded and ran into the living room and fetched her book.

"Hmm, Shel Silverstein's *Falling Up*. A fine book. Delightful poems. But didn't we read it yesterday, and the day before that? I should think you'd have it memorized by now. Would you like to read one of my books, Hannah? I have so many of them, just sitting in boxes, unloved, ignored."

She looked unconvinced.

"Why don't you at least go check the boxes in the spare bedroom while I clean up? If you don't find anything you like — and there are hundreds of books to choose from, everything from cookbooks, to travel guides, to the classics, to mysteries — then we'll read from your book again. Agreed?"

Her head bobbed in a 'yes'. I trotted after her down the hallway. The door was already cracked, so she nudged it open fully.

A room *full* of boxes confronted her. A few, nearest to the door, had been opened, revealing books of various sizes. Hannah pulled out an assortment, some with pictures inside, some just words. Then one by one, she began to sort them into piles by relative size, biggest books on the bottom. She had five different piles going when she stopped and began rearranging them by the colors on the outside.

Frankly, if any of those other boxes contained books, I was afraid this would go on forever. I found a cozy corner next to the register and curled up, preparing for a long nap.

Heck appeared in the doorway. "Just one, Hannah. Don't worry about sorting them. I'll do that later. I need to put the trash out right now, but I'll check on you again in five minutes. Bring one book out to the living room then. We can always read the rest some other day."

He left and Hannah slid one book aside and put the rest away. Despite what Heck had said, she checked some other boxes. From one, she lifted out an old camera case. From another, several women's blouses. From a third, a pair of women's boots. Then, from yet another, she pulled out a pearl necklace.

My eyelids were getting heavy. I yawned, but Hannah took no notice. I thought she might lose track of time and go through the whole lot, when she took out a framed picture.

As she stared at it, it was as if the world around her faded away. Something in it held her captive.

"Hannah?" Heck called from elsewhere in the house. "It's time."

The picture pressed to her chest, Hannah went to the living room, me ambling sleepily behind. She stopped at the entrance to the room, a question framing behind her eyes.

Heck was rearranging pillows on the couch, his back to her. "I thought I'd show you more about how to do watercolors this afternoon, since I know you like them so much. They're more difficult to —" He stopped talking when he turned around and saw the picture she held.

"Who's this?" She turned the picture around so he could see. It was a black and white photograph of a woman, young, fair-haired, pretty in a girl-next-door kind of way. "Is this your mommy?"

He breathed a laugh. "No, although I can see where you'd say that. It's an old picture." His gaze took on a far-off, somber look, as if recalling days gone by. "It's my wife. Was … Is …"

Her steps slow, her expression curious, yet compassionate, Hannah approached him. "Did she die?"

Sinking onto the couch, he shook his head. "No, but she's not really here. I mean … she doesn't remember anything. Not even me."

He took the picture from Hannah as she sat beside him. His fingertips grazed the woman's hair, then paused on her lips as he sighed wistfully. "That happens when you get old, sometimes. Only it happened to her earlier than most."

Hannah scooted closer, leaving a gap of only a few inches between them as she peered at the picture with him. "How did it happen?"

His shoulders lifted in a shrug. "Not an accident or a tumor or anything, if that's what you're asking. She just started forgetting one day. Things like where she left her glasses, what time she was supposed to be at an appointment ... I didn't think anything of it at first. She was always very busy, teaching and helping out in the community, and when you're busy like that, it's a lot to remember. One day she couldn't remember where she parked her car. She called the police, saying it had been stolen. It had been in the garage all along. Then she left a pot on the burner and went on an errand. When I got home, the kitchen was filled with smoke. At that point, I realized I had to be with her every minute. One night ... one night I woke up, found her in the kitchen, and she looked at me and grabbed a skillet, ready to hit me, because she thought I had broken into the house ..." Frown lines carved deep into the crevices around his mouth. "She didn't know who I was — and I knew it was time."

"For what?"

"To let go, I suppose. I couldn't take care of her any longer by myself. We lived in a very busy neighborhood. She could've walked out the door and gotten lost or wandered into traffic and gotten hit. Even worse was the possibility that if she found the car keys, she might cause an accident and hurt someone else. So I made the decision to place her in an assisted living facility. It was the hardest thing I've ever done." With each sentence, his shoulders sank lower, as if the weight of it all was bearing down on him. "She grew up in Faderville when she was little, about your age, so that's why I chose to come here with her. Her sister, Maria, still lives in the area. I was hoping that being here would spark memories, but it hasn't."

A few moments elapsed in silence — Heck sorting through a quagmire of emotions and Hannah struggling to comprehend it all. Finally, Heck straightened his spine and exhaled loudly. "Do you know that place called Fox Hollow, this side of town?"

She shrugged.

"It's where mostly old people live, people who need a lot of help getting around, or a nurse to look after them. That's where she is."

Hannah's eyes lit with understanding. "My Aunt Cammie works there!"

"So you've been there?"

"Once. To see Aunt Bernie."

I tilted my head at her. The name sounded familiar, although I couldn't quite place it.

"It's very sad there," Hannah added.

"It is. I visit Sophia twice a week still, even though she doesn't know who I am, or that I was there just a few days before."

"I'm sorry she doesn't remember."

"Me, too. But I try to use those times to talk about things we used to do together. It makes me realize how lucky I was to have met her. Not many people would put up with me."

"*I* like you, Heck."

"I like you, too, Hannah."

Something told me that what was developing between them was stronger than 'like' and more like love. But humans can be shy about expressing that emotion. Dogs never are. If we love you, there will be no doubt about it.

"Sophia's a pretty name," Hannah said.

"I think so, too."

"How did you meet her?"

"Nothing out of the ordinary. We met in high school when her

224

family moved to Louisville, but I was two years older and we'd only gone on a few dates when I was drafted. Me, in the army. Can you imagine that? Anyway, we wrote to each other for a while, when I was fighting in the war, but one day her letters started coming back to me unopened. Turns out her family had moved several more times. Still, she never married and neither did I. I suppose we never gave up hope of finding each other again. And then, almost twenty years later, we met again through mutual friends. Three months after that we were married."

"Did you have any kids?"

"No, we didn't." Heck squeezed his eyes shut for a moment. "But Sophia was always good with children. You would have liked her."

Tucking a leg beneath her and twisting sideways so she could face him, Hannah gave Heck a quizzical look. "*Would* have?"

"The way she used to be." He studied his fingernails briefly before getting up from the couch. "I was just thinking, before you walked into the room, that maybe we should just go paint something. When I'm feeling melancholy, it helps to lift my spirits." He held out his hand.

Hannah stared at it as if he'd just offered her a handful of rusty tacks. Except for me, Hannah didn't like to make physical contact with others, not even with her parents.

"What if Mommy asks what I read today?"

Grinning, he tipped his head. "I have just the thing." He went to the back bedroom and came out a minute later with a travel guide full of pictures of a place with a castle and roller coasters and palm trees. "This is a book about a magical place called Disney World. Have you ever been there, Hannah?"

"Nope."

"Every child should go there once in their lives. After we do some painting and clean up, we'll read about it. Maybe combine it with a geography lesson on the state of Florida, as well as some history about Walt Disney himself. And you know what? You may keep it. It even has a map, so you can find your way around. Maybe you can convince your parents to take you there. Okay?"

"Okay." Hannah placed her hand in his and he pulled her to her feet.

—oOOo—

That afternoon Hannah painted a picture of Sophia. From memory. But it wasn't black and white. It was alive with streaks and patches of pinks, yellows, blues, and greens, and Sophia was standing in a field of flowers, just like the one in Heck's painting.

Heck's eyes misted over as he stood behind her, watching her add the finishing touches. "She's wearing pearls," he said quietly.

"Do you like it?" Hannah asked.

"It's the most beautiful painting I've ever seen." He turned away, his breath a quavering sigh. He pulled his shoulders up high. "Why don't we go back inside, Hannah? I need to start sorting through those boxes. Most were Sophia's belongings. Someone else could probably make good use of them. After all, what am I going to do with fifteen skirts, half a dozen high heels, and several strings of pearls?" He flashed a joking smile, although his eyes were still sad. "Don't answer that, by the way."

They cleaned up the paints hastily, but before Heck could delve into sorting through his boxes — the same boxes that had been sitting around since the first time Hannah and I stayed with him when Lise's sheep got out — Hunter arrived to take Hannah home for the day.

While much of the past year, by all accounts, had been rough for Hannah, there were some highlights to it. For one, she and Heck were forming an unusual but very strong bond.

Then there was me. You might think I would feel like a third wheel, but that was never the case. I did miss my days with Hunter,

226

but there were many times he had to either leave me in the truck while out on calls or behind a baby gate at the clinic, a place I never much cared for anyway. I had never warmed to all the noise and commotion there, not to mention the continuous string of strangers and nervous animals mewling and barking and squeaking.

On days I spent with Hannah, I was always right beside her. And that was where I would always choose to be.

But sometimes, even when life is exactly as we want it to be, it doesn't stay that way. In a heartbeat, it can all go away.

chapter 25

Echo

A favorite part of my day was feeding the horses with Jenn after she got off work. Today, however, we were doing our chores a little early while Hannah took a nap in her bedroom. Instead of Hunter picking Hannah up around four, Jenn had picked her up a little after one, explaining to Heck that she had the afternoon off.

If Hannah was confused by the change in routine, she didn't mention it, but we dogs are very aware of such things. If you forget to wake up at dawn on the weekends to let us out, we will snort in your ear until you do. Being the dog I am, though, I forgot about the disruption in our usual schedule the moment we stepped into the barn and a hundred wonderful smells — horses, manure, hay, and dirt — filled my nose.

Somewhere, I caught a whiff of field mouse among the straw bales. I had my nose buried in between two stacks of it when Hunter walked in. Jenn was bundled up in her coat and wearing mud boots, scooping feed into the horses' buckets.

"Hey," he said. "What's up with the cryptic text message?"

I bounded over to him, my hind end wiggling, but he ignored me, which only made me try harder. When I jumped on the front of his coat, he pushed me off. I skulked away, wondering if I'd done something wrong. It wasn't like him to dismiss me without a proper greeting.

Although my beginnings had consisted of people who disappointed and betrayed me, lately my life was full of nothing but good and honest people: Hunter and Jenn, Hannah and Maura, Brad and Lise. Even Heck. None had ever raised a hand against me, or yelled at me, or forgotten to feed me. Not even Jenn, who at first had seemed reluctant to have me in the house and constantly with Hannah. And so I never let the chance pass to let them know how much I appreciated them. I licked their hands at every opportunity, didn't cause trouble, never chewed on anything that had their scent, and watched over them as if their lives depended on it. But sometimes, apparently, they forgot that. Like now.

Jenn finished filling Cinnamon's bucket, then put the scoop back in the feed sack before turning around. She leaned against a support post, her face a mixture of concern and confusion. "I learned something today that has me rethinking things."

"Like what?" Hunter asked. Normally at this point, he'd pull her into a hug and give her a long, noisy smooch, but something about her stance must have warned him off. "Did Maura get into trouble at school again? She's been pretty good since —"

"It's not Maura." Jenn went out the barn door and headed toward the house, Hunter close behind.

Cinnamon stomped a hoof on the ground as I passed her stall. Clover snorted at me, big globs of horse snot spraying down on me. The horses and I had an agreement — I ignored them and they looked down their noses at me. Actually, I was smart enough to know if I annoyed them, they could flatten me with one good kick, so I stayed the hell away. I'd been stepped on once. Nearly broke a toe. That was

229

enough. Besides, there was something about being in one of those confined stalls that didn't sit well with me, although I could never quite understand why. I also had this inexplicable fear of horse blankets and being smothered by them.

"Then who?" Hunter said.

At the back door, they both scraped their shoes on the welcome mat before going into the kitchen. I slipped in just before Hunter closed the door.

"Hector Menendez, that's who."

Chuckling , Hunter helped her take her coat off and hung it on a hook. "Did he make her listen to Rossini, instead of Tchaikovsky? Or introduce her to the horrors of impressionism?"

"I'm serious, Hunter." Jenn grabbed a Diet Coke from the fridge and took a swig. "I think we may have rushed into this arrangement with him … and maybe we should put a hold on it for now."

He shrugged his coat off and draped it over the back of a kitchen chair. But he didn't sit down yet. "Where is this coming from, Jenn?"

"Hunter, he could be a child molester, for all we know."

He slapped a palm lightly on the table. "Oh, come on, Jenn. That's ridiculous. What on earth would make you think that? I know he was a little standoffish when we first went over to say 'hi', and he can be a bit of an oddball, but —"

"A little standoffish? A *little*?" She set her drink down firmly on the counter, then glanced around to make sure Hannah wasn't lurking close by. "He did everything but tell you to fuck off — and that's only because his generation doesn't have that word in their vocabularies. I mean really, Hunter, I didn't think we'd have to agree that it was a bad idea to let someone that we hardly know watch our kids. That's just common sense." She put her pop back in the fridge, shutting it so hard the bottles in the door rattled. From the drying rack beside the sink she grabbed a spatula and waved it around. "Like what does he, or did he, do? Is he divorced, widowed, never married? I mean, he never really said. At least not that I know of. And is he Catholic, Methodist, a Druid? Republican, Democrat, Libertarian?"

"Well, he's a retired pharmaceutical chemist, I assume he's widowed — and who cares what religion or political party he is? Seriously, you're making a big deal out of nothing. And if you don't have something to back it up, we need to drop it. Now."

Smacking the spatula down on the counter, she drew a deep breath. By now I was cowering under the table. I'd seen Mario lose his temper, and Mavis throw shoes at Scowler. It always started like this. I knew when to take cover.

Jenn jabbed a finger at Hunter. "Don't you *ever* tell me I'm overreacting, Hunter." She took several more ragged breaths before sitting down. "While I was standing in line at the grocery during my lunch break, I grabbed a newspaper and started skimming the headlines. Buried on page seven was a piece about a bunch of kids who've disappeared from the Louisville to Lexington area over the past twelve years. Until now, all leads went nowhere: no suspects, no witnesses, no clues, no bodies. Yesterday they found the remains of a six-year-old girl in the woods less than two hours northwest from here, along the highway near Frankfort. They estimate someone had buried her in the hillside about four years ago." Her tone went flat. "She had no clothes on."

Hunter didn't say anything. He just went and put his arms around her shoulders from behind, resting his chin on top of her head. "That's an awful thing to happen to anyone's child." His lips grazed the crown of her head. "But we can only protect them so much, Jenn. Bad people are going to find ways to do bad things. Meanwhile, if we don't let ourselves trust anyone, we rob our kids of the chance to meet new people and get out into the world to experience wonderful things. You know, my mom used to shove me out the door and tell me to be back by supper. We didn't have cell phones or GPS trackers. And our parents didn't orchestrate every minute of our days with schedules and practices and play-dates. They just let us be kids."

Jenn peeled his hands away, got up, and paced to the door, then back, her arms crossed.

"Jenn, she's going to meet all sorts of people throughout her life. Most will be nice. A few will be mean. And I pray she never meets anyone who's anything like the monster who hurt those missing children — but sometimes we just have to trust that everything's going to be okay."

He waited until she met his eyes to speak again. "Don't put suspicions over on Heck Menendez just because he's new in town and we haven't read his autobiography yet. My gut tells me this is a decent guy."

"I can't, Hunter. You need to keep her away from him."

"Why? Give me a good reason."

Sitting, she studied her fingers, laced together on the table before her. "I talked to Nancy Schwartz at work this morning, the realtor who sold Mr. Menendez the house. She said he moved here from Frankfort."

Hunter looked like he wasn't sure what to make of that morsel of information. "He never said anything about living there, but so what? You'll have to give me something better."

"I checked online. There were two similar missing children cases that have gone unsolved from two and three years ago. Just outside of Frankfort."

Scoffing, Hunter shook his head. "So you're judge and jury now, based on hearsay and a cursory internet search? Honey, you can't —"

Jenn shot up from her chair so fast it nearly toppled over. "Hannah can't go to Heck's anymore, Hunter! End of story. Don't try to talk me down from this. I'm taking a leave of absence starting tomorrow."

Then she went from the room, stomping all the way to their upstairs bedroom.

On my belly, I scooted closer to Hunter, concerned about him. I didn't like that Jenn was upset, either. In the time I'd been with Hannah's family, no one had ever acted this way — scared and worried and angry. It was like there was a cloud full of lightning hovering inside the house, charging the very air around it with electricity.

Hunter scratched between my shoulder blades. "You think old Heck's all right, don't you, Echo?"

Yeah, but what could I do to make things right? I'd say that humans are dumb, only they aren't. They just over-think things sometimes. If only they'd trust their instincts. Listen to their hearts.

Life's really not as complicated as they make it. All you need is a little kibble, a warm place to sleep, and someone to rub your belly.

And a squeaky toy. There is no joy in life without squeakies.

While Hunter worked on unclogging the downstairs bathroom drain, I ambled into the living room in search of a quiet corner to curl up and nap in. What I found instead was Hannah, hugging a pillow as she sat in Hunter's oversized recliner.

She'd heard every word of her parents' argument.

chapter 26

Hannah

It would be easier this way. Hannah didn't want them to have to worry about what to do with her. She didn't care if they'd be mad at her. They obviously hadn't cared about her feelings when it was decided she'd no longer go to Heck's every day, even though being there, watching Heck paint, and listening to him tell her about how to blend colors and pay attention to the light, had been such a source of fascination for her. It was like her whole world had taken on new meaning — and now that was being taken away from her.

She knew exactly what she was going to do.

Right before bedtime, she took her shoes off, added an extra pair of fuzzy socks, a sweatshirt, and another pair of jeans over the leggings she'd worn that day, and slipped her long, fuzzy nightgown over top. Then she climbed into bed, pulled the covers up to her neck, and waited for her father to tuck her in, just like he always did.

The door latch clicked as Hunter turned the knob. Her face toward the door, Hannah watched through one barely open eye, her right one. She kept the left shut tight, to make it look as though she'd already fallen asleep.

A square of light fell upon the floor, widening as Hunter quietly nudged the door open. The light from the hallway fell over Echo's curled up form. The dog twitched an ear, yawning.

Hunter lingered at the threshold, his face half-hidden in shadow. He watched Hannah so long, she was having a hard time staying still.

Her heart twisted. She'd miss him. Terribly. But this was for the best. She may have been angry at her mom for forbidding her to go to Heck's anymore, but she was just as disappointed that her father hadn't come to her rescue and defied her mother.

On bare feet, Hunter tiptoed to Hannah's bedside, bent down, and laid the lightest of kisses on the crown of her head. In that moment, she almost threw her blankets off and wrapped her arms around his neck, eager to confess everything, but she resisted.

Tomorrow, things would be better.

For her. For Heck. For everyone.

—o0Oo—

Hannah hadn't had any trouble waking up early. She was too afraid she'd oversleep. Besides, thinking had kept her awake most of the night. That and being hot because she was wearing three layers of clothes. Mostly, she thought of all the things that could go wrong. Her plan only went as far as how she was going to sneak away. After that, she was pretty much winging it.

The pipes downstairs clunked and rattled as Hunter got in the downstairs shower. Just like he did every morning, Echo lifted his head, stretched, then got up and left the room. That was Hannah's cue. She slipped from her bed and wiggled free of her nightgown. Inside the nightgown, she stuffed a long pillow, then placed it under her blanket, bunching it up until she was satisfied that it would look like she was still asleep underneath.

235

She dug through the pocket of her coat, which she'd left draped over the back of her desk chair the night before. The letter crinkled as she unfolded it. She read it to herself one more time, to make sure it would make sense to whoever found it. She didn't know how to spell all the words, but she'd done her best to write them like they sounded.

Mom and Dad (and Maura),

I am going ~~were~~ ware I wont be a problum. Heck wood never hurt me. He is my frend.

Love you (still),
Hannah
P.S. Win I get a job, I will call you.

She smoothed out the creases and put the letter on top of her desk. From under the bed, she dragged her backpack out. She had no idea how long two boxes of square cheese crackers would last her, but she didn't have room to carry more. Unless …

Faustine's topknot tangled in her fingers as she lifted her out. She gave her giraffe one last hug and put her on top of the nightstand next to her bed. She didn't have time for long goodbyes. Anyway, in two weeks, she'd turn six years old. She didn't need stuffed animals anymore. They were for babies. And she was old enough to take care of herself. She'd prove it.

As Hannah turned to go, something on her desk caught her eye: the shell necklace Maura had given her in the hospital. She'd only worn it for special occasions, which meant not often, but she treasured it. It was a reminder that even when Maura was snotty to her or cranky, she still loved her little sister. Maura had taught her how to ride a bike and always shared her books. Most of all, Maura looked out for her. Hannah snatched the necklace from where it lay and tucked it in her coat pocket.

Before going out the door, she paused beside her nightstand and looked at Heck's penguin painting. She picked it up, then set it back down. No, she couldn't take that with her, either. She didn't want anything to happen to it.

At the bottom of the stairs, she peeked around the corner. Echo was lying at the end of the hallway by the bathroom, his eyes closed. Good. She didn't want him making a fuss and alerting anyone. Besides, he'd probably ask what she was doing and she wasn't up for a conversation right then.

On fuzzy sock feet, she stole across the kitchen floor, pausing just long enough to stash a third box of crackers in her backpack. As she wrapped her small hands around the doorknob, she took one final look around. It was the last she'd see of her house, but she didn't regret leaving. By this time tomorrow, she'd be making all her own decisions.

And maybe, a month from now, they'd give up looking for her and have a life free from the trouble of having her around.

She grabbed her boots from beneath the bench beside the door, pulled the hood of her coat up, and went outside. It was barely light out. A fresh dusting of snow blanketed the ground. To the left, over by Heck's house, a slice of pinkish-orange rimmed the far-off hills. Cold air stung her face.

Her boots felt warm as she slid them on and pulled the zippers up, but she just as quickly realized how numb her fingers already were from the cold. She'd forgotten to pack any gloves. They were just inside the door, in a basket on the other side of the shoes.

Her hand on the knob, she turned it slowly.

Thump!

Her heart catapulted into her throat. She snapped her head up to stare into golden eyes. Echo's breath fogged the inside of the door's window. He cocked his head at her.

What are you doing out there?

"Go away," Hannah said between clenched teeth.

Are you going somewhere? School, maybe? Can I come with you?

"No, no, and no."

But I want to be with you.

"Not today. Now get off the door before Daddy sees you."

He lowered his muzzle toward his chest, disappointment plain in his face. A tiny wrinkle formed between his eyes, as if he knew something was not right.

Forget the gloves, Hannah decided. She turned and ran before she could change her mind, glancing over her shoulder to make sure no other lights had flicked on in the house and that no one was watching her through a window.

The only sounds that morning were the frosty grass crunching beneath Hannah's feet and her bursts of breath as she gulped in air so cold it hurt her lungs. At the garage, she went through the side door, leaving it open for a few moments while she oriented herself to the dark confines. Gradually, her eyes adjusted and she shut the door behind her.

The tailgate of the truck was high, almost to her chest, but she'd scaled it before. Clambering up on the bumper, she lifted the handle. It clicked open. Before the weight of it knocked her down, she jumped back down. Carefully, she lowered the tailgate, hoping to slide inside, but there were two big metal boxes in the way and behind them a stack of feed. She knew she couldn't move any of them. The only way in was over.

Climbing onto the now open tailgate, she tried the handle on the cap. It turned easily, the window lifting with a gentle nudge. Once inside, she had a new problem: how to shut the tailgate.

The window would be easy, but the tailgate was almost too heavy for Hannah to close from inside by herself. But more than that, there were other, bigger problems. Her arms simply weren't long enough to sit inside on her knees, reach over the top, and lift it up.

She hadn't thought this part through. Although she'd sat in the back of the truck while riding the half mile down the road to Gramma and Grampa's many times, her daddy had always closed the back for her. Now she had to do it on her own and it wasn't nearly as easy as he'd made it look.

For five minutes, Hannah tried every way she could think of to close it. Finally, she scooted over to the side where she could hold on to the edge of the cap. Fingers hooked securely, she leaned out and clamped her other hand over the top of the tailgate. With one great heave, she flipped it up and slammed it shut. So loud, anyone standing within a hundred feet of the garage — or even in the back of the house — could have heard it.

Breath held, she listened for the stomp of feet, expecting someone to call out. They'd find her there, scold her, give her a long talk, and confine her to her room for months. Things would be worse than ever.

Seconds passed. A minute. Nothing happened, thankfully. It was just Hannah by herself in the back of her father's truck, like she'd planned. On her way to somewhere else.

As quietly as she could, she closed the window of the cap. Then she burrowed behind the sacks of feed and coils of rope and veterinary supplies, where she curled up and waited, using her backpack as a pillow.

While she lay there, her hand wandered to her pocket. She drew out the shell necklace and put it on, her fingertips running over the polished shells as she counted them, one by one — fifteen in all. Five, five, and five more.

Thirty seconds later, she remembered she hadn't eaten breakfast. So she opened one of her cracker boxes and counted out six crackers. She had to make her three boxes last. Just as she popped the fourth one into her mouth, she bumped her elbow on a plastic jug of iodine.

The last two crackers in her hand fell, lost in the tangle of an electrical cord. Reluctantly, she got out two more, reminding herself to be more careful. She couldn't waste any.

Waiting was always difficult for Hannah. She had a hard time keeping her mind quiet. Harder still was trying not to move. If she moved, she'd make noise and if Daddy came in and heard her, her plan would be ruined. She'd gotten this far. She couldn't risk discovery now.

So she counted in her head, all the way up to a hundred. First by twos, then by fours and fives. She could do threes or sixes, or even sevens, but they wouldn't fit neatly into a hundred. She'd either have to stop before that or go over, and that just wasn't right. No one had ever taught her this. She had figured it out by herself. Tens and twenties worked, but they went rather quickly.

She was on thirty-seven, counting backward by ones, when the garage door clicked and began to hum in its tracks. Daylight wedged inward from outside.

A moment of panic gripped Hannah. What if her daddy opened the back and saw her? She hadn't thought to cover herself. So she grabbed the closest thing she could find — the rope — and laid it on top of herself. It smelled like hay. And she was pretty sure there were bits of cow poop embedded in its fibers.

The truck door opened and Hunter tossed something onto the seat. Hannah exhaled in relief. He hadn't looked. Then again, he hadn't started the engine yet.

Her father's work boots pounded on the concrete, then paused next to the rear wheel. Through the tinted side window, Hannah saw him squinting into the sunlight, a cup of coffee cupped between his hands to warm them.

"Echo," he called. Dog toenails clicked on the garage floor, then stopped. A paw scratched once on the outside of the tailgate. "What *are* you doing? Get off there. You're not riding in the back. No way, no how. And since when did you start stealing Hannah's school papers? Give that to me." Turning around, Hunter went back and thumped on the inside of the front door. "Up here."

Once Echo was inside, Hunter started the truck. It lurched into reverse.

As the tires hit the chipped gravel of the road, the sound of music from the radio rose above the noise. The truck bumped over potholes, jarring Hannah's bones. She pulled herself into a ball, cushioning her head with her arm and wishing that she had brought a blanket.

She had no idea where she was going or how long it would be before she could get out. All she knew was that home was getting farther and farther away.

Soon though, very soon, her family would be free of her. She would no longer be a burden to them. And *that* would free her.

—o00o—

Hannah awoke with a start. The truck wasn't running. They were parked somewhere. But where?

She listened for the sound of voices, or cars driving down a busy road. Anything that would tell her where they were. But it was quiet. *Very* quiet.

Cautiously, Hannah pushed the rope away and sat up to peer out the side window. With the darkness of the tinted windows, it would be hard for someone outside to see her unless they were really close. She almost felt invisible.

It was full daylight now. A bright day for December. The truck was parked on a muddy gravel driveway, to the back of a cluster of barns. Animal pens made of stock panels and heavy metal tubing gates connected the two closest buildings. A dozen nanny goats milled about in one of the pens, dipping their heads in a wire feeder to pull out flakes of hay. To the other side of the truck, a patchwork of pastures sprawled where there were more goats, some of them half-grown kids.

This must be the Appletons' farm. She'd been here with her father once before, but only long enough to drop off some medicine. If that was right, it was clear on the other side of the county.

How long had they been here? And what was the closest town? And where was the highway from here?

More importantly, where was her father and when was he coming back?

She wasn't going to wait to find out.

Hannah crawled over the feed sacks and opened the rear window. Slowly, so she wouldn't make any noise. The goats heard her, though, and turned to watch. She hiked a leg over and lowered herself to the bumper. So far, so good.

Knees bent to absorb the shock, Hannah leaped to the ground. She landed softly, but in a puddle. Cold water seeped through the seams of her boots, soaking her socks and feet before she could step free.

She surveyed her surroundings. No sign of anyone. Only the goats.

On the other side of the driveway, the ground sloped away to open pastures dissected by miles of fence and hills yellow with winter-dead grass. Curving around the barn was the lane leading to the house, she remembered that much. She turned around, her eyes following a path with two barely worn tire ruts that twisted right and then disappeared behind a stand of trees.

Forest. Miles and miles of forest. She could hide there until her father left, then take the lane past the house, back out to the road, and follow it until she came to a town or found another truck she could stow away in. The farther away she went, the harder it would be for anyone to find her.

Maybe the path into the forest went somewhere and she wouldn't have to go by the house? She could find out.

Hoisting her bag over one shoulder, she started toward the woods. The goats rushed at the corner of their pen. The voices started, soft and polite at first:

Who are you? Who are you?

Apples? Carrots? Hay?

What do you have for us?

Who are you?

Hannah froze. If she ignored them, they'd stop, surely. She went on, her steps quickening as she tried not to look at them.

Hey! Come back!

Feed us!

Scattered bleats quickly rose to a clamor.

'Shut up!' she wanted to yell. They were going to ruin everything for her. But they wouldn't stop. Their cries rang in her ears, demanding attention. Any other day, she would have spoken to them and fed them treats. But not today. Not now.

Pushed onward by their incessant demands, she ran. On and on. Until her lungs burned and her heart threatened to explode and her legs grew heavy.

Her feet began to drag. She stumbled, uprighted herself, and kept going. She could still hear them, even as she dove deeper and deeper into the woods. If Mr. Appleton and her father had been alerted by the noise, they would have noticed the goats watching the spot where the lane plunged into the forest. The thought of it sent a jolt of energy through her. So she picked her feet up and ran faster.

The lane grew rougher, the ruts deep with muddy clay, rocks scattered everywhere. Junipers and brambles crowded the path, lashing out at her arms with spiky thorns and prickly needles. Slowing to a walk, she took to the swath between the tire tracks, even though the grass was taller and thicker there.

Her heart thumped in her ears. Casting a glance behind her, she realized she could no longer see the house or barns. Just as she turned to look forward again, her foot caught on a root. Momentum propelled her forward, her knees buckling as she flailed a hand out. She caught herself before she could go face down, but a sharp impact, like a hammer striking her kneecap, sent waves of pain up through her leg. She tumbled sideways, rolling onto a patch of wet leaves.

When the pain ebbed, she dragged herself forward onto a mound of gravelly dirt. She'd fallen on a rock and torn her jeans. The rip was several inches long. She'd even managed to tear her leggings underneath. Blood seeped from the scrape there.

A moment of weakness pulled at her. She could go back now, make up some story that she'd wanted to go on rounds with her father. But it was possible she might still get in trouble. *Big* trouble. Then, all her plans would be for nothing. The problems she was causing would still be there. And now she was only adding to them.

No, she couldn't give up now. She wouldn't.

Determined, Hannah pushed herself up from the damp ground to gimp on. Around her, the trees grew denser and the hills taller. The path became more rugged as it wound between tree trunks and climbed craggy hills. Hooking her thumbs under the straps of her pack, Hannah kept going, looking for the road at the other end.

But then, just when she thought she might be safe and well on her way to freedom, she heard feet clipping rapidly through the grass behind her.

It wasn't the steady plodding of two human feet, but the galloping of an animal in pursuit.

Moments ago, Hannah had wanted nothing more than to fold to the ground and rest, but she forced herself into a run again, propelled by fear.

She didn't feel cold or tired anymore. Only afraid of what was behind her. What it would do to her. She couldn't stop, couldn't rest, couldn't give up.

She pumped her arms hard, gulping in air.

The animal was closing on her.

She didn't dare look. Wouldn't. It would cost too much time.

Ahead, the trees parted in either direction. The road dropped suddenly. She plummeted, barely staying upright, and landed in a little stream, water halfway up her shins. The rocks in the streambed were slippery. She slid sideways and threw a leg to the side. But she kept going.

No sooner had Hannah cleared the stream than she heard a splash behind her. She scrambled up the short incline and headed for the nearest tree. She was good at climbing. It was her only chance.

With one strong leap, Hannah grabbed a branch and swung a leg up and around. Seconds later, she was straddling the branch, face down. She pulled her feet up to squat on the branch, glancing above her for some way up higher. There was another thick branch a-bove her, just out of reach. She placed her right foot on a smaller branch and tested her weight on it while gripping a furrow in the bark. It held, although the fullness of her backpack made it hard to judge her balance, and she stepped up. Twisting back around, she curled both arms over the bough and pulled herself up. Now safely perched up high, she braved a look down at the ground, fighting a wave of dizziness.

Out of the corner of her eye, a black blur appeared, bounding over the bank of the stream.

"Echo?" she said.

Her dog bounced on his feet far below, his bobtail wagging his whole hind end. He yipped joyfully.

"Go away," she commanded in her sternest voice.

Why? He bounced higher.

"Because I don't want you to come with me, that's why."

Ears flattened, he lowered his head, still looking up. He fixed her with sad eyes, the color of autumn leaves. His eyebrows twitched back and forth, like he was thinking, but didn't know what to say.

The branch was broad enough for Hannah to sit comfortably on. She pulled her knees to her chest and hugged them tight. The warmth that had risen in her body from running was now dissipating. She felt cooler. Through the tangle of branches, she could see the clouds thickening in the sky to the west.

"I said 'go'."

Echo rocked back on his haunches to sit, a signal that he wasn't going anywhere.

Darn him, Hannah thought. If he didn't skedaddle off, her daddy would come looking for the dog and find her sitting there in that tree. She had to keep going, hitch a ride to another town, and then another maybe, until she was far enough away that nobody would know who she was. But how was she supposed to do that with a dog?

"I mean it. Go away," she said between gritted teeth.

No.

A lump formed in her throat. She forced the words past her tongue. "I don't need you."

He looked away abruptly, as if she'd just struck him with her fist. His head sank and soon his body followed, collapsing to the ground. Slowly, he lifted his eyes.

But I need you. Don't go, Hannah. Please, don't go. What will I do without you?

Her heart crumpled in on itself, like a paper bird crushed in someone's fist. She tried to be strong, to think of something mean to say that would make him slink back to the truck and let her go on her way. Yet no words came to her.

The longer she sat on the branch above him, the stronger the feeling grew. He was her friend. Her *best* friend. Nobody understood her like he did.

She needed him, too. Probably more than he needed her.

chapter 27

Hunter

Hunter tucked the vials of blood into his case and brushed the bits of straw from the front of his denim coveralls. "You should know soon which ones are bred, Tommy."

"They had *all* better be." Tommy Appleton slid the pipe stem from one side of his mouth to the other. "That new buck cost me an arm and a leg. Not to mention the drive down to Georgia to fetch him."

"Hope it was worth it. You've invested a lot in these goats." Hunter gathered the last of his implements and stepped through the gate before another mischievous young doe could butt him in the back of the knees. These were Tommy's Boar goats and over the years he had traveled far and wide competing at goat shows and fairs across the country. The money, he'd confided to Hunter, wasn't in selling them for meat, but in breeding stock.

"What do I owe you, Doc?" Tommy followed him through the barn door and out into the crisp winter air.

"Come on, Tommy. You know the drill. I'll send you a bill.

Eventually." Hunter walked briskly. If he stopped at home long enough to change clothes and shower, he could make it to Maura's basketball game before the first quarter was halfway over. She'd gone straight from volleyball to making the basketball team. He was proud of her and had promised himself that he'd make a point of letting her know it from now on.

"It's a wonder you make any money doing this. Last time you said that, it was two months before you even mailed the darn bill."

"Not my doing. Jo Middleton was the receptionist when Doc Samuels was there. She does things at her own pace." Which meant glacial, but Hunter didn't say it out loud. Jo may have been a slow worker, but she had a rapport with the clientele that stretched back to the mid '70s. "Besides, we have a deal. I don't tell her how to file the papers; she doesn't tell me how to do a C-section on a Bulldog."

They stopped at the back of Hunter's truck. He hooked his fingers in the latch of the tailgate, only to find it wasn't completely closed. He must've forgotten to slam it hard enough last time he shut it. He set his case in the back, but kept the vials with him. The feed sacks had shifted to the side and a coil of rope was strewn atop boxes and bins. Eventually, he ought to straighten this mess out, but there always seemed to be something more pressing to do.

A smile creased Tommy's leathered face into deep folds. "Thanks a bunch, Doc."

They clasped hands, then Hunter looked around the barnyard for his trusty companion. He thrust his tongue between his lips and let out a shrill whistle. "Echo! Come on, boy. Time to go home."

A dozen goats raced from inside the barn out into an adjacent pen and started bleating. Hunter waited a few more seconds before whistling again. He took a quick look in the cab of the truck as he set the vials down, just to make sure the dog wasn't in there, although he remembered Echo loping along behind him when they went into the main barn and sniffing at the mineral blocks stacked next to a round bale of hay.

"Maybe he's around to the side?" Tommy posed. "Big ol' manure pile over there. You know dogs."

There was no sign of Echo hanging around the manure pile, or the feeding troughs, or the chicken coop. Where could that dog have gone? He was barely ever more than thirty feet from Hunter. He'd never wandered off before.

Tommy began calling out Echo's name, too. Pretty soon, Tommy's wife, Beth, had joined them in scouring the property.

Hunter was standing by the dock that reached out into the old swimming hole when his phone vibrated in his pocket. It was Jenn calling. She rarely phoned him during work hours, restricting herself to texts that he could answer at his convenience. Must be important. He pushed the button.

"Hunter?" The pause that followed was enough to make him sink to his haunches and brace his elbows on his knees. He could hear her breathing, rapid and frantic. "Oh my God. I don't know where to start."

"Honey, what is it?"

"This *can't* be happening. It can't. It just can't."

"What are you talking about? Is Maura okay? I know her basketball game doesn't start for another hour, but —"

"It's not Maura!"

"Hannah?" Cold sweat broke out on his forehead and the center of his chest. Unable to move, he stared at the frozen pond, fixing his gaze on a bubble of air trapped beneath the thin layer of ice. The question, when it finally came out, sounded airy and hopeless, even to his own ears. "What happened?"

A grievous sob sounded on the other end. And then, "She's gone."

Shock compressed Hunter's ribs. "Gone?"

"Missing, Hunter. She's missing. We can't find her anywhere."

That morning, while he was waiting for his coffee to finish brewing, he'd cracked open her door and seen her sleeping form bunched under the covers. Then he went downstairs, where he'd found Echo waiting by the back door. Usually, the dog would follow him around the house in the mornings from the time he stepped out of the shower. Then, when he let him out and went to his truck, Echo had come running with what appeared to be one of Hannah's school papers in his mouth. The dog had never chewed on or stolen anything from any of them. He'd slid the paper under the front seat to keep it safely out of Echo's reach, so he could return it to Hannah later, but the whole sequence of events was quite out of character for Echo. There was a lot about this day that was anything but normal. How could both Hannah and Echo go missing in one day?

Hunter stood and started back toward his truck. "You checked with my parents, right?"

"They were the first people I called. They just got back in town yesterday and they haven't seen her."

"Did you check in all the barns? The garage? My parents' outbuildings?"

"Yes, of course we did."

"The Crooked Tree? I wouldn't put it past her to climb up too high and get stuck."

"Yes! I told you. We looked *everywhere*. Faustine is still sitting on top of her nightstand. If Hannah had wandered off, she would've taken Faustine with her. Hunter, what if ... what if someone *took* Hannah?"

"Honey, please don't think the worst. Remember, Hannah has a history of just drifting away." He didn't want to ask the next question, but he knew he had to. The last time he'd put it off had very nearly cost Hannah her life. "Did you call the sheriff?"

"I did," she bit the words off. Hunter sensed she was going to lash out at him again, but he expected that. Jenn was very emotional.

Her girls meant the world to her. But stupid questions had to be asked if he was going to get up to speed on this.

"So they're already looking for her? They've notified surrounding law enforcement?"

"Sure, I guess. But right now Brad's across the road, talking to Nate Bowden, the new sheriff."

"At Heck's, you mean? Why? Did you tell them Hannah might have gone over there to paint?"

"No, Hunter. They're taking Heck in for questioning."

Hunter stopped at the back of the Appletons' house, where Beth was standing on the back porch, putting a knit cap and gloves on. Beside her was her oldest grandson and one of her daughters. He held up a finger to let her know he'd talk to her in a minute, then turned away, lowering his voice. "What? Why?"

"Why do you think, Hunter? Maybe those rumors Maura was talking about … maybe there's a grain of truth to them?"

No, she was wrong. It couldn't be. Not Heck. "I'm on my way home, Jenn."

After putting his phone away, Hunter turned to Beth. "If you could keep looking for Echo for me …?"

Nodding, Beth stepped closer. "Is everything all right at home?"

"Family emergency. Sorry, I have to go."

"We'll call you. I'm sure your dog just —"

Hunter didn't hear the rest of it. His mind was miles ahead of him already.

Maybe by the time he got home, they'd have found Hannah asleep behind the straw bales in the horse barn. He had to hope.

chapter 28

Echo

Her arms around my neck. Her nose buried in my fur. The sweetest things I've ever known.

A dog without his person is only half a dog. If that.

When I fled from the Grunwalds and was on my own, those endless days and weeks when I sat at the shelter, all that time at Carol and Ed's when I was small, after my siblings left — I had felt nothing then but alone and empty, even as I tried to convince myself of how independent I was. It embittered me to people. Made me reluctant to trust them.

The day Mario hit me with the skillet and left me for dead on a country road, *that* was the worst day of my life. And the luckiest. Because it brought Hannah into my life and opened my world to love. I belonged to the McHugh family. I was a piece of their whole. Without me, they were incomplete.

How could I make Hannah understand that it was also true for her? I knew she was trying to run away because she saw herself as the cause of recent problems, but she had to have faith that things would work out. Hannah's parents loved her. Not more or less than Maura, but differently. Like you can love cookies just as much as you love bacon.

Hannah's challenges were also her gifts. Her parents were smart enough to know that. Heck had also recognized that gift and taught her how to capture it, shape it, and share it with others. Which was probably why Hannah didn't want to go home. Because they had taken away her friend. A friend she could see just down the road. A friend who had shown her more purpose and opened her eyes to more wonders than anyone else in her whole life.

I could relate.

Yet there was a lot that I still didn't understand, like why they had forbidden her from going to Heck's in the first place. We dogs may not always comprehend the complexities of human relationships, but we see what is so plain to us, like the way someone hangs their head in shame; a quiver of fear in their hands; the bitter drawl of loathing in their voices; the way their eyes light up when a loved one walks in the room; the sad longing when they leave. When it came to how the McHughs perceived Heck, I saw a spectrum, a disparity so grave that it left me bewildered.

Hannah, of course, loved him. It was a love stemming from admiration, from a connection of like souls, and from gratitude. Hunter desperately wanted to trust him, but his wife and oldest daughter's contrasting sentiments left him confused in loyalty and doubting his own intuition.

If there's one thing we dogs know, it's always trust your gut. Always. Objective analysis is highly overrated. Reasoning is better left to lawyers and scientists. And sometimes Border Collies, but don't get me started on that.

Anyway, I digress. Jenn was acting out of fear. Guilt, too, although she didn't realize it. She wanted to be there for Hannah, but she also wanted to have a life of her own. Maura, on the other hand, was boiling with jealousy. Ever since Hannah had been born, much of her parents' attention had revolved around her little sister. Lately, it was even worse. And most recently, Hannah was developing a talent far beyond anyone's expectations. Heck showered her with attention through his patient instruction. Her parents praised every creation. At first they pinned the crayon drawings to the refrigerator with magnets, then they taped them to the kitchen wall, and now they were framing her watercolors and hanging them in the hallway. Meanwhile, Maura — hardworking, athletic, almost-never-been-in-trouble Maura — was brushed aside unwittingly.

What was she to do but turn the tables on Heck and rob her attention-mongering little sister of all that was important and special to her? Everything but me, that is. Then again, Maura *had* tried to cast blame on me for Franklin's disappearance.

Right now, I was all that Hannah had. I couldn't convince her to go home, but I could stand by her, make sure she was safe and loved, if only by me, a dog.

A shiver rippled through Hannah's tiny frame. Her shoes and socks were wet from jumping in the creek. Her pants all the way up to her knees were soaked, too. In the time since she had climbed down from the tree and huddled next to me, the sun had vanished, its shining face replaced by low, brooding clouds. A damp wind gained force, plying frigid fingers beneath my thick fur. I curled up in Hannah's lap as she sat cross-legged, doing my best to keep her warm. But it wasn't enough. Her shivers grew more violent. We needed to get moving. Find shelter.

I escaped the comforting circle of her arms and whirled around. Her cheeks were ruddy and her eyes red from cold. Pulling her knees in tight, she rested her chin on them, lip quivering.

She looked so … lost. Probably because she was.

Hopping backward a few steps, I bowed low and barked. Anything to entice her to move about, get the blood flowing through her body. She turned her head sideways to lay her cheek on her arm. Head low, butt high, I growled playfully, my nub wagging.

She laughed. Not a belly-deep, unfettered laugh, but a small one. Her cheeks bunched in a weak smile as she slowly got to her feet. I bounced farther away, leading her on. She moved stiffly the first few strides, but soon she was loping alongside me.

For miles we walked in silence, our only objective to keep going. Often, I looked around me and inhaled deeply, trying to memorize the landscape by sight and smell. But one tree looks much like another, even to a male dog. Which gave me the idea eventually — hey, better late than never — to mark as many as I could. A habit which annoyed Hannah greatly.

"Stop it," she said. "How can you pee *that* much?"

She didn't understand. It was better than leaving a trail of bread crumbs that birds could swoop down and eat. So I lagged behind on occasion, peeing at more random intervals, spraying only a few drops on the trunks so I could make my urine last as long as possible. My tank was emptying. All this walking and peeing was making me thirsty.

As for smells, the wind was making that hard. I couldn't pick up any scents, save for those close to the ground. Other animals had passed here, but what kind I had no way of knowing. On the many calls I had gone with Hunter, I had seen plenty of cattle, goats, and sheep, as well as a few horses and llamas. But these smells were none of those.

The lane dumped out into an overgrown pasture, crowded with scrub brush. We followed the tire tracks some more, until suddenly they weren't tracks anymore. We stood on what was probably a deer path, the way ahead marked by barely bent stems of growth and an ever-thickening forest. When had we left the path?

We circled right, crossed our own path, veered left, backtracked when we were confronted with a fallen tree too big for either of us to get over, then climbed a hill to go around it and rejoined the deer path.

Chin raised, Hannah gazed at the hills ahead. Then she looked at the hills behind us. I was sure they had grown bigger. The trees were also more densely packed, and thicker, and taller.

As sure as if she had been here before, Hannah tromped on.

We had no idea where we were going, but it didn't matter. We were together.

—o00o—

We were lost.

As in, no sign of civilization, whatsoever. Just us two dummies, bumbling along through the wilderness. Pretending we knew what we were doing when we were just hoping to get lucky.

Talk about stupid.

But I wasn't about to tell Hannah that. No matter what, from a dog's perspective, the human is always right — even when they aren't. It's some sort of pact that we're sworn from birth to uphold. I don't remember putting my paw print on the dotted line, but who am I to question the Code of Canine Loyalty?

So I followed her. On and on. Uphill, downhill. Except I was pretty sure the hills were now mountains. Over stream, through trees and more trees, under an old railroad bridge spanning a dry creek bed.

At some point, Hannah followed a trail that went up high and then along an overhang. Her steps were slow, because they were so small, but she plowed on with the determination of a soldier. At the lip of an outcropping, she stopped and sank to the ground to dangle her boots over the ledge.

Less confident that the rocks beneath us would not crumble and fall away, I hung back, crouching behind her. Hannah unlooped the straps of her backpack and settled it in her lap. She pulled out a box of cheese crackers. Square, of course.

Counting them out into her palm, she formed a stack. I couldn't tell how many, but clearly it had to be something exact. She pinched three off the top and offered them to me. I turned my nose away in denial. Hannah needed her strength more than me.

She shrugged — "Suit yourself." — and stuffed all three in her mouth at once.

The first snowflake that fell landed in her hair. I watched it sparkle as she tilted her head to look in the box, then melt from the heat of her body. More snow tumbled down as Hannah munched away. Flakes so big and fluffy that in the distance they looked like balls of cotton being tossed from above.

The wind had stopped. It was so quiet now. Breathtakingly, powerfully quiet. Like there was no one else in the whole world but us two. Which could very well have been the case.

There was not one road, one house, one building anywhere in sight. We could see only the deep greens of the pines and the blended dull grays and browns of the deciduous tree branches, layered one against another, stretching for miles and miles and miles. Snow piled thick upon limbs, etching their forms in webs of pearly white. Here and there, the side of a mountain cut away to reveal sheer walls of stone, some of them soaring high.

Fingers pressed together as if she were holding a brush, Hannah dabbed at an imaginary piece of paper, painting in the sky the shapes and colors that formed in her mind. Her wrist flicked back and forth, occasionally dipping to wash out her 'brush' and then pick up more color.

In the distance, a crescent of pale yellow shone just above the horizon through lightening clouds. The day was almost over. Night would come soon — and under cloak of darkness would also come the cold.

Shivering, Hannah plunged her bare hand into the box. Her mouth dipped in a frown.

"Gone," she whispered hoarsely as she tossed the box over the ledge. I didn't look, couldn't hear it fall, but Hannah leaned forward so far, watching it, that my heart plummeted. I sat up, about to take the back of her coat in my teeth to keep her from falling. But before I could, she pulled her knees up, scooted back, and stood.

"Let's go. I'm thirsty."

So was I. And I'd long since run out of anything inside me to pee. Unfortunately, it was a long way down to any creek bed and we hadn't seen one for hours. Not since Hannah had scrambled up that tree.

But Hannah, being Hannah, marched on with a purpose all her own. Toward a vision that only she could see.

My duty was to stay at her side. Protect her. Because who knew what dangers we might meet in this vast and rugged land?

chapter 29

Hunter

"What the hell is going on?" Hunter stormed at Brad. He'd driven to Heck's house first. It seemed like the most logical place to get answers. Jenn wasn't answering her phone.

Brad motioned him over to the side of the driveway. Three Adair County sheriff's deputy cars were parked in the driveway. Nathan Bowden, the new sheriff, had just gone inside Heck's house, as deputies wearing latex gloves carried out objects in plastic bags and put them in the trunk of one of the cruisers.

Hunter jabbed a finger in their direction. "They're collecting evidence? Of what?!"

Putting an arm over his stepson's shoulder, Brad walked him farther away. Hunter went reluctantly, his head craned to watch the comings and goings in the house.

"Hector Menendez told them to take anything they wanted," Brad said, "that he didn't have anything to hide. I agree the search is a bit overboard, especially since no warrant's been issued, but Jenn —"

"How could she point the finger at him, Brad? And why? What

makes her think he did *anything* to Hannah?" As soon as the words were out, Hunter wanted them back. Did Jenn know something he didn't? What if Heck —?

"She saw him put a large trash bag into the trunk of his car sometime after you left this morning. Shortly after that, Heck drove off. When Jenn discovered Hannah was gone and went outside looking for her a little over an hour later, Heck pulled back into his driveway."

A shot of lead dropped through Hunter's gut, tearing apart his insides. Maybe there was more to this than he thought. But there'd never been any indication, any proof that Heck was anything but a regular, decent guy. A widower restarting his life, wanting nothing but a peaceful existence. Things had gone so well between him and Hannah. No, as much as he loved Jenn, she'd assumed too much.

"So the first thing she did was accuse Heck? Come on, Brad. You know Hannah. She could be anywhere — asleep in the hayloft, stuck in a tree somewhere ... The last time she ran off, it was because she thought she heard a bird talking to her."

"Yeah, I know. We're on it. I explained it to Nate and told him their efforts would be better spent combing the area for Hannah. He already called out two canine units from adjacent counties. They're on their way. The fire department is organizing volunteers as we speak. The community has pulled together in an incredibly short time. Pretty amazing, really, what folks will do for their neighbors."

"I appreciate it, Brad. I do. It's just that ... this ..." He waved a hand at the sheriff's cars lined up. "It's not right. We need to find Hannah. Not initiate a witch hunt."

Curving a hand around the back of his neck, Brad nodded. "I agree. This should be about finding your little girl. And they're going to do that, Hunter. They will. But right now, like I said, Heck's cooperating fully."

"Tell me, Brad, not in your professional opinion, but based on your gut. Do you think they have any reason to suspect Heck? I mean, Hannah hasn't been gone for more than a couple of hours. So Heck put something in his car, drove somewhere, and came back. So what? There could be a hundred explanations for that."

"There could be, but ..." Brad gave a telling half shrug. "It's circumstantial, yes. But in cases like this, it's best to explore all leads, no matter how much we don't want to believe the worst possibilities."

Worst? Hunter was trying to let it all sink in. And yet he resisted. How could everything in his world change so damn fast?

"Where's Jenn?"

Brad tipped his head toward Hunter's house. "Home. With Lise and Maura. Nate told them it would be best if they stayed there, so if any news came we'd be able to find them."

Hunter started toward his car, but Brad hooked a hand around his elbow to stop him.

"It's been hard on her, Hunter. Don't blame her for what's happening to Heck. She's beside herself with worry. No matter what, remember that this is about Hannah." He clasped Hunter's shoulder, squeezing. "Remember."

How could he forget? The entire ride here from the Appletons' — normally a thirty-five-minute drive, but he'd done it in twenty-six, all the while hoping that the state patrol didn't pull him over — all he could think was that there had to be some logical explanation for where Hannah was. Somehow, the pieces would snap together and they'd find her. Or clues about where she was, at least. Right under their noses, probably. But he'd been disappointed to arrive here and see that was obviously not the case.

A commotion on the front steps drew Hunter's attention. There, four deputies were escorting Heck out in handcuffs.

Hunter bolted forward.

"Hunter!" Brad called.

But there was no way Hunter was going to let them do this to his

261

friend. He got to the sheriff's car just as Heck scooted into the backseat, his arms bent behind him.

"Stop! Wait!" Hunter shouldered his way past the two deputies bringing up the rear. He wedged himself between Heck and the door before they could shut it. "Heck, what's going on here?"

A wry smile crossed Heck's mouth. He spoke softly, calmly, but there was an underlying worry to his voice. "They're just going to ask me some questions, Dr. McHugh. That's all."

"Like this?"

"Everything will be fine where I'm concerned. Trust me."

"Don't talk to them without a lawyer, Heck. Don't."

"I considered that. But they'll see soon enough this is all a grave misunderstanding. The sooner I give them a statement and clear my name, the sooner they'll move on." He shifted his legs to face front, the seat creaking beneath him. "Don't worry about me, Doc. Let Echo help you find Hannah. That dog's your best bet."

Drawing back, Hunter nodded. He lifted a hand in a goodbye as they shut the door, but Heck kept his eyes forward, his face devoid of emotion. The car pulled away, followed by another cruiser.

"Believe me," Hunter muttered to himself, "if I knew where Echo was right now, I'd set that dog loose and let him lead us right to Hannah."

The two cars drove off into the distance, leaving behind more questions than answers. His mind numb, Hunter drove the short distance to his house. He parked next to the kitchen door, not bothering to put his truck up in the garage. If any news came about where his daughter was, he wanted to get there as quick as possible.

The back door swung open and Jenn came to stand on the back steps, waiting for him. Her eye sockets were red, like someone had punched her in both eyes repeatedly. For a moment, she swayed, holding herself. Then, her shoulders crumpled forward and she collapsed to her knees, covering her face with her hands.

Just the sight of her, rocking back and forth, sobbing like her world had ended, dampened Hunter's hope.

chapter 30
Echo

It was a strange little house, a shack really. Barely tall enough for a full grown man to stand in. The outside a faded red, now mostly gray. The lower right corner of the door clawed at and chewed through by some wild beast. Flaps of tattered canvas covered the glassless windows.

How anyone could live here was beyond me. But it was definitely a house. A tiny, dilapidated house. It smelled of humans, overlain with the urine and feces of some large varmint, although a long time had gone by since any people were last here.

Empty bottles littered the floor. A torn potato chip bag lay beneath a broken folding chair. The cans they'd left behind were rusty, save for two smaller ones with pictures of fish on the outside. Hannah pulled the tab on one and sniffed it. A rancid odor drifted down. She curled her lip, then flung it out the window, where it thunked against a tree trunk. I was hopeful when she opened the second one. Her nose wrinkled. She dipped her pinkie inside, tasted it.

"Yuck! You can have it."

The open can on the floor before me, I approached it skeptically.

It smelled strongly … of fish. Oily, salty fish. I feasted on it.

Darkness enclosed our little shelter. The wind gained force, rattling the door on its crooked hinges, beating at the canvas flaps. We had to huddle down next to the ground to escape it, but in the corner it wasn't so bad. Snowflakes drifted in through the windows and swirled through the opening in the door to pile up on the far side of the room.

Hannah's body trembled. I curled around her as best I could, but I, too, was cold to the bone. It hadn't been so bad when we were moving all day, but we both needed rest. Hannah had taken a pair of socks from her backpack and put them on her hands like mittens. With them, she mopped the tears from her cheeks.

That was how I fell asleep, curled up next to my girl, her sniffles soft in my ears.

—o00o—

My mind was so slow to register my surroundings, that when I awoke it took a long time before I remembered where we were and how we had gotten there. Somehow, I had stopped shivering in the night, although I had woken many times, my toes aching from the cold. A bubble of warmth had formed between Hannah and me, the scant heat of our bodies shared.

I snuggled closer to her, rubbing my muzzle against her chest. She didn't move, except for the slight expansion of her ribs. I wanted to get moving, so we could warm up and find someplace better than this, but I let her sleep on, because I was too stiff to move.

Golden light spilled through the tiny windows, its brightness making the room look far cozier than it felt. In summer, this place would have looked so very different.

As the day brightened, I decided it was time to go. I licked Hannah's face, but she didn't respond. She looked so tired and worn.

265

So frail.

I shoved my nose in her armpit and snorted. When that brought no reaction, I swiped my tongue across her mouth. Several times.

I began to worry. Why wasn't Hannah waking up?

So I barked. Loud and strong. My mouth inches from her ear.

She started with a jolt, her head snapping up. She pushed herself up on an elbow to glare at me.

"Don't scare me like that, Echo! Never again."

Yeah, well, it worked, didn't it?

She scrunched her mouth up. Her lips were cracked at the corners, her nose red and chafed from rubbing it. Her skin had a pallor I had never seen on a human before. Ghostlike, almost.

Yes, we dogs see ghosts *all* the time. What do you think we're barking at when we stare off into a dark corner of the yard, our hackles raised?

Hannah opened her second box of crackers. This time I took what she offered, even though the crackers made my mouth drier than it already was. Truth be told, I could've eaten the whole box by myself, but halfway through Hannah closed the top flaps and stuck it back in her pack.

I whined. I couldn't help myself.

"We have to make them last, Echo."

Why? I'm hungry. Aren't you?

She smoothed the hair on top of my head. Her sock-mittens smelled of fake cheese. "Because I don't know how far it is to Disney World, that's why."

I cocked my head at her.

"My Aunt Emily told me she auditioned to be a princess there once. I figure that's as good a job as any. And maybe then if I make some money, I can buy paints and brushes and then I can sell my paintings. I don't know how much they're worth, though." She shrugged. "A dollar or two? Maybe five, you think?"

How was I supposed to know? I wasn't even sure what a dollar was good for. Hunter was always counting his dollars, then folding them up inside a couple of pieces of leather and tucking that in his back pocket. Once, at the drive-thru, I saw him give the girl inside the window a bunch of dollars. She gave him French fries. Therefore, dollars equaled French fries.

It took some prodding, but Hannah finally got herself up and out the door. Actually, it kind of fell off when she nudged it open. Two steps beyond the door, we both stopped, awestruck.

Crystals of ice clung to every surface, glittering like fallen stars in the sunlight. I squinted against the brightness. Hannah slogged over to a fallen tree and scooped a handful of snow into her sock mittens. She bit at it, smiling as it melted in her mouth. I ate mouthfuls of snow, the cool liquid running down my throat, filling me with a burst of energy.

Onward we went on, renewed from within. For a while, at least.

—o00o—

Stuck. That's what we were.

We must have stared at it for a good hour, sitting up on the mountainside, looking down at the silvery ribbon as it twisted through the valley and disappeared around a faraway bend. A river, broad and deep. Just like the one into which I'd once been thrown. Maybe it *was* the same one? Water raced between its stony banks, its crashing and splashing more than a babble, but not quite a roar.

Neither one of us seemed compelled to move toward it, or even to try to find a way across. From where we were sitting, it looked pretty much impossible.

On the other side, two ridgelines away, there was an obvious swath through the trees. A road, maybe? It would be worth checking out, but … yeah, the river. Kind of in the way.

Anyway, I didn't like to go swimming. For obvious reasons. But I wasn't quite sure what Hannah's hesitation was. I'd heard Jenn and Hunter talk about Hannah's 'accident' in hushed tones more than once. A couple of weeks after I joined the McHugh family, they went on a picnic to a state park. There was a lake there. At first Maura had wanted to claim a table overlooking the water, so that afterward she could take her shoes and socks off and go wading. But Hannah had started to hyperventilate, and so Jenn told Hunter to drive on to the picnic grounds in the woods. Once again, Maura's wishes had been overridden by her sister's needs.

Hannah slapped her socked palms together, then rubbed at her arms. White puffs of vapor drifted in the air before her as she exhaled. Shoulders hunched, she tucked her hands under her armpits. Her teeth clattered, no matter how hard she tried to clamp her jaws together to fight the shivers that had overtaken her.

If for no other reason than to warm herself, she rose and started down the slope toward the river. I was sure if I stayed put, she'd stop and come back. Yet I watched her back getting smaller and smaller between the tree trunks, her backpack making her look like a tiny beetle navigating its way through stems of grass.

I woofed, but she kept on going. So I barked again, louder, several times.

She twisted at the waist to look over her shoulder at me. And just as she did so, a packed mat of leaves slid beneath her clunky boots. She flung her arms outward, but her feet flew from under her. She hit the ground, her tiny body sliding downward over slick clay until it collided with a small boulder, then crumpled at its base.

I raced toward her, rocks and saplings blurring past. But the closer I came, the more apparent it was.

Hannah wasn't moving.

—o00o—

Hannah's hand lay palm down against the earth, her arm stretched above her head.

I sniffed at her upturned cheek, smudged with reddish-brown dirt, then snorted softly into her ear. The barest of moans rose from her throat, followed by my name.

"Echo?" She lifted her head to gaze at me through damp lashes. A single tear spilled from the corner of her eye and splashed onto the ground. "I don't want to go to Disney World anymore. I want to go home."

I lay down beside her and tucked my muzzle between her neck and shoulder.

Me, too.

She pulled her knees beneath her, until she was sitting, then stretched her legs out and brushed the dirt from them. "But I don't know the way. Do you?"

I hung my head, ashamed.

No.

I'd tried to mark our trail, but I'd done a poor job of it and after several hours I'd lost our scent in the wind. I could try to retrace our path, but we'd been gone over a day now and there was an even bigger chance that we'd end up more lost.

We could follow the river. But upstream or downstream? Either choice could be wrong. Our best bet was to find that road in the distance. Even if it was only a driveway or a long country road, it would have to lead to another, busier road eventually. Yes, we had to cross the river somehow.

As if she'd been thinking the same thing, Hannah scanned the river. Not far downstream, a thick tree spanned its width. Its limbs had long since been stripped clean by raging spring waters. At its very end, a few feet from the far bank, the tree dipped into the water. And there, a tangle of broken limbs clustered, caught up by what remained of the tree's branches. Climbing over might be hard, but at that point the water looked only a couple of feet deep.

Hannah looked at me. "I'll go first."

I followed her the rest of the way down the hill. At the bank, we stood a few minutes longer, trying to summon our courage. Had it been a wide, sturdy bridge, we would have raced across it. Had it been a log lying across a dry ditch, we would have both taken our chances at falling. But it was neither.

And yet it was our only chance.

Knees wobbling, Hannah stepped around the array of roots that remained and pulled herself up onto the weather-smoothed trunk, until she was straddling it backward. She scooted toward the other end a few feet, then stopped.

"Come on, Echo." She extended a hand. "I'll help you."

Below, the river flowed madly, its silty waters dark and deep. I inched closer, taking it all in, calculating my chances, theorizing on the many ways this could go terribly wrong. At the far bank, foam swirled in the little eddies formed by the debris trapped there. My confidence was diminishing by the second.

She wiggled her fingers at me. "If I can do it, so can you."

Easier said when you have two hands.

"Whatever. If that's your excuse ..." She swung her legs around to sit forward and began to scoot across, but she was barely a quarter of the way across when she looked down and froze.

I trotted to the tree, put my feet up and jumped. It took several tries, but I was finally standing atop it. Hannah lowered herself until she was practically hugging the tree. With the hump of her backpack, she looked like a turtle sunning itself. Carefully, she looked back at me, and smiled weakly.

"We got this, Echo."

Right behind you.

I gave a little woof of encouragement and she kicked her feet to

270

scooch forward, inch by inch.

The hard part for me was that the surface of the log had been smoothed over by the elements. I had no fingers to grip with. It wasn't soft like dirt, where I could dig my nails in. Every step was like walking on a curved surface of ice. So I let Hannah work her way across. When she was nearly to the other side, she looked back one more time

Just as our eyes caught and I took my first step, a strap of her backpack caught on the nub of an old branch and broke. The pack shifted abruptly on her back, sliding until the weight of it slipped from her right shoulder and slid down her arm. She caught the strap in her hand, her knees clenched to the log.

Her knuckles whitened. Its weight pulled her toward the gurgling water.

Let go!

Her fingers loosened. The backpack plunged into the greenish-brown murk. Water splashed up to hit her in the face.

More determined than ever, Hannah continued on, until she was at the end. Nimbly, she picked her way across the web of debris and was soon standing on dry land.

I ran, my toenails skittering across the narrow, sloping track before me. Then, with nothing more than my faith to guide me, I leaped —

Into Hannah's waiting arms.

With an *oomph*, I knocked her to the ground and then smothered her in kisses. She pushed me away just in time for us to both sit up and watch her backpack bobbing along down the river before it disappeared around a far-off bend.

We had no food left. We were cold and tired to the bone. My pads were cracked and Hannah complained of blisters on her heels. We didn't know where we were going — or if anyone out there was even looking for us.

But we never, ever gave up hope or abandoned that courage

borne of desperation.

Because who knew when we would need them even more?

—o00o—

The road was farther away than it had seemed from the mountainside. It took us half the day to get there. The ground was rougher, the trees denser. Several times we had to climb to a vantage point to gauge its position again. But we finally got there. And it turned out not to be a road, like the kind cars drove on, but a wider path. Yet it was something and it bore evidence of traffic: footprints, the human kind.

Not far from where we joined the path, we saw a sign. We walked to it. As much as I stared at it, I couldn't make any sense of it. There were no pictures. To me it was just slashes and circles.

Hannah's brow puckered as she sounded the letters out. "Norrrth … rim … traaaail. North rim trail. Main … main … A-C-C-E-S-S, whatever that is, road … eight … mmmyyy-less … miles ahead." She fixed me with a disgruntled stare. "That's a long way."

Maybe, but we'd already come pretty darn far.

But even one mile would be a marathon to us that day. We'd eaten the last of the snow that morning before it melted under a tepid sun. Our bellies were so taut with hunger after sacrificing Hannah's cheese crackers to the river gods that they no longer growled for food. The only message my body was sending to my brain was that I needed to lie down and sleep. For days. Preferably someplace warm. Which meant nowhere in sight. Hannah was tired, too. She stumbled along with her eyes half closed, her arms hugging her body. Our hearts, though, begged us impossibly onward — to home.

Yet we knew no better how we were going to get there than we did Disney World.

We followed the trail anyway. Better than staying put and blindly hoping someone would come to our rescue.

"We'll get to the road, Echo. Keep going until a car comes by. I'll wave at them, get them to stop … No, you run out into the road and lie down. I'll kneel right beside you, like you've been hit …"

No. Way.

"Okay, okay. It's just that I want the first car we see to stop for us." Halting, she turned to face me.

It was dangerous to stop going forward. Inertia is a powerful thing. The longer we stood there, her staring at me as thoughts struggled to form into words, the more likely it would be that we wouldn't move at all. And then … the corners of her mouth sank. Her lower lip twitched.

No, Hannah. Now is not the time.

She inhaled a shaky breath. "But —"

We need to go. To the road. Eight miles.

"Yep, only eight miles." She turned her head to look in the direction we'd been heading. "Cars drive down roads all the time, right?"

I waited, but still her feet didn't move. Silent tears trailed down her chapped cheeks. As much as I wanted to console her, wallowing and moaning about our predicament — the one that she'd caused when she decided to run away from home — wasn't going to solve anything. We needed to get to that road before dark, or it was going to be another hellaciously cold night. Come morning, one or both of us might just not wake up.

So I went on, not looking back. Expecting to hear the soft plod of her boots on the dirt-packed trail. She wasn't going to stand there alone.

Yet she did. Sniffling and moaning in between sobs. Feet firmly planted. But then her whimpers stopped abruptly. Which concerned me even more.

Don't look back, I told myself. *Keep going. She'll catch on, eventually.*

Against all reason, I slowed, turning to look back so I could figure out why she wasn't coming.

Hannah stood fixed in place, eyes wide. Directly between us, two half-grown black bear cubs raced, loping playfully along. One reached out with a paw to swipe at the hindquarters of the other. The cub in front twisted around to bat at its sibling in retaliation. They tumbled along the trail in Hannah's direction.

Hannah's gaze shifted from the cubs to follow a sound coming from her right, where something large was crashing through the underbrush. Her mouth opened in a silent scream.

Galloping from the tree-line was a full-grown mama bear, muscles rippling beneath a mantle of thick black fur. Claws sliced at the earth as she propelled her powerful bulk forward, until her shadow enveloped Hannah's frail form.

chapter 31

Hunter

From the moment Hunter learned that Hannah was missing, he had sensed she was in danger — but not for a second did he ever think Hector Menendez had anything to do with it.

Yesterday, he'd sat in his living room for hours, alternately staring at the TV and pacing to the back kitchen door, a sense that he'd overlooked something gnawing at his insides. No word came of Hannah. A quick check with the Appletons provided no leads as to Echo's location, either.

As Hunter studied the search teams gathering on his front lawn, it struck him like a blast of winter wind: Hannah was out there somewhere — alone, afraid, lost, cold. He prayed she would be found and returned safely to them as soon as possible.

This time last year, when Hannah had disappeared from their cabin, everything had happened so quickly. But they'd found her. *Found* her. This time, however, twenty hours had gone by — and not one clue.

Hunter was barely aware of the heat building in his palm as he held his cup of coffee. His coat unzipped, he drifted outside to where Nate Bowden was briefing his deputies on their plan for the day.

When he was done, Nate walked over and clapped Hunter on the shoulder. "We'll find her, Doc McHugh. I've got every available man on it."

Hunter nodded politely, but he couldn't summon a reply. He turned to go back in the house, then paused in front of his truck. A fresh dusting of snow coated its surface, glistening under a weak sun. He brought his cup to his lips, blew the steam from it, and sipped. The coffee was bitter. He'd forgotten to add cream and sugar.

A haze filled his head as he stared absently at the truck, trying to connect things that made no sense. Why had Echo been looking out the back window when he came down from his shower yesterday? And why had he brought him Hannah's school paper?

On the other side of the truck, about fifty feet away, footsteps crunched on crisp snow. Two deputies were milling about, going over what little information they had to go on.

"There's no way she just wandered off," the older male deputy said. "Someone put a nightgown over a pillow and stuffed it under her blanket to make it look like she was still asleep in bed."

"Do they think someone took her?" the woman said with grave concern.

"They haven't ruled it out."

"Hmmm, I don't know. How could a perpetrator have gotten inside the house without anyone knowing? There was no sign of a forced entry. And the mom and sister were there all morning. They would have heard something, wouldn't they?"

"Huh, you've got a point there."

There was a pause before the woman said something more. "Hey, do you suppose …?"

"What?"

"Suppose she ran away?"

It was hard for even Hunter to admit it, yet indications were that Hannah was the one who'd put the pillow under her covers and stolen away, either in the middle of the night or sometime that morning. But why? And more importantly, *how* had she slipped away without anyone noticing?

"You know how these things go —" the older deputy began, "the more time goes by, the less likely it is they'll find the kid."

A sickening unease roiled inside Hunter's stomach, pushing upward until it burned his throat from the bottom up. He stumbled to his truck and grabbed the front bumper, retching thin yellow bile. He clamped a hand to his abdomen, trying to hold it in, but another wave rolled through him. When he had nothing left in his gut to vomit, he steadied himself and started for the kitchen door.

Something stopped him dead. A set of smears inside the rear window of the cap. A place where the dust had been smudged away.

He splayed his fingers and pressed his own hand against them: four narrow streaks and the barest hint of a fifth, starting slightly lower down.

Hannah's handprint.

—o00o—

Two cheese crackers. Hunter studied them in his palm. He broke the corner of one, put it on his tongue, tasted it. Not stale. They had been left there recently. There was only one way she could have gotten in the back of his truck.

Why had it taken him this long to figure it out?

"Are you sure about this?" Brad asked. He'd run over from his house the moment Hunter called.

"Positive." Turning his palm over, Hunter dumped the crackers onto the ground. "It all makes sense now. She stowed away in the cap. Echo must've watched her leave the house and go out to the garage.

That's why he was looking through the back window of the kitchen. He also jumped at the tailgate after he brought me —"

Something else tugged at him, the sense that there was another clue within reach.

He flung open the door to the truck and shoved his hand under the seat, groping around. He pulled out a few receipts, the owner's manual, a gum wrapper ... And then he found it: a piece of paper, crumpled and soggy around the edges, where Echo had mouthed it. He smoothed it out, then skimmed it twice.

'I am going were ware I wont be a problem. Heck wood never hurt me. He is my frend ...'

Brad read the letter over his shoulder. "When did she write this?"

"Recently, I'd say. Echo brought this to me before we left for the Appletons'. I didn't think anything of it at the time. Thought it was just some random school paper from one of the kids that he'd picked up. So I shoved it under the seat, thinking I'd return it to them later. But then everything went haywire and I totally forgot about it." Hunter handed the letter to Brad, then pounded a fist against the side of the truck. "How could I be so stupid?! If I'd just been paying attention, we could be that much closer to finding Hannah — and Heck wouldn't have had to go through what he did."

"I'll tell Nate to redirect the search crews to the Appletons' place. I don't know how far she could have gotten in a day, but if they fan out from there and concentrate their efforts in that area, they'll be that much more likely to find her."

"Brad, their property abuts the national forest. She could be anywhere out there."

"Hey," — Brad folded the paper up and tucked it inside his jacket pocket — "we may not know exactly where she is right now, but at least we know where she started from." He took out his phone and called Nate, who was somewhere out of view. As soon as that was done, he laid a sympathetic hand on Hunter's shoulder. "This letter also removes any last trace of suspicion that may have been hovering over Heck. Everything he told us aligns with what we found out. Jenn said she saw him putting the trash bags in his car at approximately 9 a.m. Fifteen minutes later, the volunteer at the Goodwill store confirmed that a man fitting Hector Menendez's description dropped off ten bags of clothing, books, and jewelry at the store. Heck even waited long enough to get a receipt for tax deduction purposes. Shortly after that, the front desk at Fox Hollow confirmed that he checked in for a visitation."

"For who? I mean, not that it's any of my business ..."

Brad looked at him as if it should have been obvious. "His wife."

"Wife?" This was news. "Sophia?"

"Yes, I thought you knew."

Hunter shook his head. "No. He'd barely mentioned her. We assumed she was deceased."

"No, she's very much alive, but ... she has Alzheimer's. Cammie said he comes to Fox Hollow every Tuesday and Saturday religiously. Sophia grew up around here and has a younger sister still in the area, which is why he moved her here from Louisville."

"Frankfort, you mean?"

"No, he's never lived anywhere near Frankfort."

"You're sure of that?"

"One hundred per cent. He did say he looked into facilities for his wife in Frankfort, but also Danville and Campbellsville, I believe. But that's the only connection he has to Frankfort. Why?"

Hunter shrugged. "No reason."

Apparently, Jenn had been fed a major chunk of misinformation, which had, understandably, led her in the wrong direction. Damage control would have to wait, however.

They were headed back inside the house when Hunter's phone

beeped with a text. It was Beth Appleton.

'Still no sign of your dog. Sorry. Any news on Hannah?'

Hunter grabbed Brad by the arm.

"Call Nate back," Hunter told him. "Tell him she has her dog with her."

"Her dog? You never said anything about —"

"I didn't know until just now. He disappeared from the Appletons' farm yesterday when I was on a call there. If Hannah got out of the truck while I was in the barn, it makes sense that Echo would have followed her."

Nodding, Brad made the call.

A tiny surge of relief welled inside Hunter. Hannah may not have been safely at home yet, but at least, wherever she was, Echo was there at her side to protect her.

—o00o—

Half a day went by. It may as well have been a hundred years.

Daylight was fading. They'd found Hannah's and Echo's tracks leading away from the Appletons' goat barn, where Hunter had parked. A good sign. Dogs had been put on the trail, but a few miles later the tracks crisscrossed and they lost the lead. Since then ... nothing.

Hunter paced the floor — around the dining room table, back out to the living room, pausing at the picture window, then through the kitchen before beginning his laps again. Every so often, he'd stop in front of the fridge, stare at it as if unable to recall what it was for, then open it wide and stare some more, until he decided he wasn't hungry. And yet he found himself there again, staring at the last remaining can of beer in there for a good five minutes before shutting the door and opening the cabinet above the stove.

Bottles of gin, vodka, and rum tempted him. He and Jenn were only casual drinkers, their indulgence limited to rare dinner parties. But as he wrapped his fingers around a bottle of Captain Morgan and took it down, he understood how easy it was to take that first drink toward becoming an alcoholic. Even more than that, he understood why.

There was an ache inside him that couldn't be filled; it could only be dulled. Moments later he held a half-full glass of rum. He brought it to his lips.

The back door knob jiggled as a key was fitted into the keyhole. Maura opened the door.

"Daddy!" she said in surprise, her eyes skipping from his glass to the bottle on the counter.

Embarrassment flooding his chest, Hunter set his glass down. "What are you doing back, honey?"

"Gramma said I could come and get some of my things for the night. But then I figured maybe I'd just come back here and sleep. I miss you guys. Is that okay?"

"Sure, if you want."

Shutting the door behind her, she put her backpack in the mudroom. "Where is she?"

"Upstairs with a migraine. She's not dealing with this very well."

"Looks like she's not the only one."

If Maura was anything, she was honest.

He dumped the rum in the sink and put the bottle away. "We just got done having a long talk. She feels pretty bad about the mix-up with Heck."

Head hanging, Maura shoved both hands in her pockets. "Yeah, about that … I feel pretty cruddy, too." Then she raised her eyes, her voice a barely controlled jumble of emotions. "I shouldn't have said those things I did about him. It was mean and stupid and it's all my fault."

She threw herself against Hunter's chest. "I'm so sorry. I'm so sorry," she said, over and over again.

"Shhh, shhh. It's all right." Hunter cupped her head to his heart, smoothing her hair with his hand until she quieted. When her sobs ebbed away to sniffles, he handed her a tissue. "Why don't I fix you a hot chocolate, huh? I'll even put part of a peppermint stick in it. Then, if your mom's up to it, we can take her some chamomile tea with honey and you two can keep each other company."

She leaned back to look up at him. "What about you?"

"I'm going to make a quick visit to Heck's. Try to set things straight."

Not that it would bring Hannah back, but he had to do it.

—o00o—

"You didn't need to come over here." Heck lifted a hand toward the couch, as if inviting Hunter to sit, but the tone of his voice wasn't exactly welcoming, so Hunter remained standing just inside the door. "I'm sure Jenn needs you."

Hunter fingered the zipper of his coat, but didn't tug it down. "Maura's with her. They know I'm here."

More stoic than usual, Heck sat down in his recliner and started flicking through the channels, the sound on low. He stopped on a PBS program about Versailles, turning the closed caption on. "Why *did* you come?"

"To apologize," Hunter offered meekly. "I know it's too late to fix things, but I want you to know that Jenn feels really bad about what happened. It was a kneejerk reaction. If Hannah hadn't gone missing, she would never have —"

"Why isn't she here, then?" Heck said, his gaze still fixed on the TV.

"Because I talked her out of it. Jenn's pretty fragile right now. I told her to stay home with Maura and I'd handle this."

Hunter waited for a response, but Heck said nothing.

"Look, I just wanted to tell you how sorry we are." There was so much more Hunter wanted to say, but his thoughts were all over the place. At any rate, that was probably the gist of it. He'd hoped his visit would be more productive. Maybe Heck just needed time to process it. Or maybe he'd never forgive them and, honestly, Hunter couldn't blame him. "Well, that's all I had to say."

Heck looked at him, then, a profound sadness revealed in the depths of his dark eyes. "You're handling this better than I would, in your shoes. I've had two mixed drinks and a glass of wine today. She's not even my child. I feel like she is, though. Or a granddaughter, at least."

Hunter hadn't even thought about what Heck might be feeling about Hannah's disappearance. He sat on the couch across from Heck. "Hannah adores you. When she comes home …" His voice caught. He'd spent so much of the last two days being strong for everyone else that he had yet to fully give in to his own feelings. Fists clenched over his knees, he swallowed back his tears, but instead of giving in to them, he distracted himself by offering Heck some compassion. It made him feel less vulnerable. "Brad told me about your wife's condition. We didn't know, Heck. If there's anything we can do for you …"

"I suppose I never said anything because I don't like to burden others with my problems." When Hunter looked away, he rushed to add, "Now I'm sorry. That sounded rather callous."

"No, I kind of understand. I'm that way, too. Have been my whole life." Suddenly, Heck's reticence was a lot clearer to Hunter. He hadn't been the way he was because he was without emotion. Quite the contrary. He had more than he could deal with sometimes.

A pause opened up between them. They'd both said a lot in a few words and seemed to have reached some kind of understanding about each other.

Finally, Hunter said, "Echo's with Hannah."

Heck nodded once. "I heard. That's good."

They fell silent again, both pretending to watch as the camera panned expansive spreads of intricate shrubbery and marble fountains. Hunter had just shifted forward, ready to excuse himself when Heck spoke.

"We tried for years to have children."

Easing back against the cushion, Hunter stayed put.

"On her forty-third birthday, Sophia learned she was pregnant. Our prayers had been answered. There were complications, however. She was relegated to bed rest, but the baby still came early. A tiny thing. Blue eyes and a tuft of yellow hair, the exact same shade as her mother's. We never got to bring her home, though. Her lungs were too weak. In the end, she wasn't strong enough. Sophia was heartbroken. So we looked into adoption. Twice, it fell though. Eventually, we gave up hope. It was too late in life for us to think about raising a child." The TV cast the only light in the whole house. In its pale glow, Heck looked even older than his years. "I hope and pray they find her, Hunter. That little girl has so much to give to the world."

Nothing more between them to say, Hunter rose and went to the door. He wanted to tell Heck that hope, so far, hadn't brought his daughter home, nor had prayers, but he wouldn't say it out loud.

Just as he put his hand on the knob to leave, he paused. "What was your daughter's name, Heck?"

"Hannah," Heck said softly, as if calling to her in the quiet of the night. "Her name was Hannah. When you showed up at my door and asked me to watch *your* Hannah, I thought …" He shrugged off whatever he was about to say, then fixed Hunter with a pensive gaze. "Well, suffice it to say that if her name hadn't been the same I would have said 'no'. That would have been a great tragedy, because

I would never have gotten to know your little girl."

A beam of headlights arced across the wall of Heck's living room. He joined Hunter at the front door. An Adair County sheriff's car had pulled in the driveway.

Nate Bowden got out and came to the door, a lump of pink and purple tucked beneath his arm.

Opening the door, Hunter's hope dimmed as the realization dawned on him.

"Dr. McHugh," Sheriff Nate began, "they found her backpack in a river on the outskirts of Daniel Boone National Forest." He held it out, a damp, muddy nylon backpack, one strap broken and tattered.

His stomach coiling into knots, Hunter opened the zipper. Inside were a few extra articles of clothing, a travel book on Disney World, and a box of unopened cheese crackers, the cardboard container so saturated it was close to disintegrating.

"Any sign of Hannah?" Hunter uttered.

"Sorry, no. I'm afraid they've called off the search for the night, on account of darkness, but they'll be back at it first thing in the morning."

It was only a backpack. Only a backpack. Hannah was still out there, somewhere. She had to be.

"Go on home, Hunter," Heck urged, placing a hand on his back. "Jenn and Maura need you."

"I can't. I ..." Grief crashed through Hunter like a tsunami. Dropping the backpack, he covered his face with his hands. Morning was such a long way off. He tried to stop the torrent, but it slammed through him.

"I'll take you home," the sheriff offered, turning aside to let him by.

Still, Hunter didn't move. He couldn't. All he wanted was to wake up from this nightmare.

Heck put his hands on Hunter's shoulders. "Remember, she has

Echo with her. He wouldn't let anything happen to her."

As much as Hunter tried to take consolation in that, there were so many unknowns. They were alone and lost, without food or water — an almost six-year-old girl and a dog — in a mountainous wilderness that stretched for tens of thousands of acres on yet another frigid winter night. *How could they possibly survive that?* he asked himself.

Then he remembered a dog named Halo … and the lengths to which that one dog had gone to protect those she loved.

With a trembling hand, he wiped away his tears and followed the sheriff to his car.

chapter 32

Echo

They say that love conquers all. That it defies reason. Chases away fear. Makes anything possible.

It is, without question, the most powerful force in the universe — as it was that day when I saw the bear crashing through the brush and launching itself at Hannah.

I didn't stop to calculate the risks to myself or assess the situation. I simply acted. My only thought was that I had to save Hannah.

Or die trying.

Hackles raised, I hurtled myself forward, swallowing ground with fluid ease, my body a stone shot from a sling.

In the periphery of my vision, I saw the two cubs skitter off through the tall grass, hop over a fallen log, then turn to watch behind safe cover.

The mama bear, a beast more terrifying then any bull or boar or ram I'd ever seen, stood on her hind legs to tower above Hannah. The bear's jaws gaped wide. Her lips pulled back, revealing a jagged row of yellow teeth. She stretched her neck to bellow. The ground shook in the wake of her throaty roar. Claws outstretched, she swaggered forward.

Hannah's eyelids fluttered. Then her head lolled sideways. She crumpled to the ground, as if her bones had suddenly been yanked from her body.

The bear went down on all fours, turning its great maw sideways as it dove toward Hannah.

My feet left the ground. I sailed through the air, arcing high and long. And didn't stop until my paws slammed into the bear's shoulder. The jolt of the impact jarred me to my teeth. I bounced off, landing on my side a few feet from Hannah.

The collision was just enough to knock the bear off balance. But more than that, it diverted her focus from Hannah. Like it or not, I had that bear's full attention. I also had about two seconds to come up with a plan.

Hannah still lay motionless, her knees drawn up, head tucked to her chest like a turtle drawn into its shell. I leaped to my feet, placing myself between Hannah and the bear. My head was still ringing from the impact, but I readied myself for battle.

The bear shook her withers, letting out a yowl of rage. Then with a snort, she swung her head to level me with a murderous gaze. Steam billowed from her black nostrils.

A low growl rose from my belly. I bared my teeth and placed one paw forward. I was no coward. I would not run.

For a fleeting moment, as she took the first stride toward me, I reconsidered that. She was five times my size, maybe ten. She could crush my head in her jaws. But brute strength is not everything. Cunning and quickness are their own advantage.

I rushed at her, barking frenetically. Which angered her greatly. As was my intention.

She bounded at me, swiping a paw at my head. I jerked back, spun on my hind feet, then ducked in low for a bite. My teeth barely grazed her leg. Huffing, she flicked her paw at me. I felt the slice of a claw across my muzzle — and then the burn of cold air as blood welled to fill the tear in my flesh.

I dodged another swipe, then lunged again and again and again, my jaws snapping, pulling fur, spittle flying. That dark mass filled my vision, a mountain of muscle beneath sleek hair, black as blackest night.

Time raced by in a blur of madness. As much as I could, I tried to draw her away from Hannah, barking as I backed up, nipping at her hindquarters, her feet, her belly, steering clear of her head so I would not feel the vise of her jaws compressing my skull. But I felt her swat pummeling my ribs, her claws cutting into skin.

How long we went at it, I'm not sure. But at some point we stood apart, staring at each other, both of us heaving for air.

And then one of the cubs ambled across our path. It paused to gaze at me with soft brown eyes above a golden muzzle. Small round ears twitched in curiosity. Then, as if bored of the drama, it rubbed the topside of its head against its mother's chest, and bounced back in the direction of its sibling, still half-hidden behind the log. They both turned and went off into the woods, not bothering to look back for their mother.

She huffed twice more, gave me one last disdainful glance, and loped away after them.

I swear she had a limp now.

I watched until they were long gone. Stood guard. Alert. And enormously grateful that our brawl had not gone on one minute more. Because I don't know that I would have lasted.

Hannah stirred. She pried one eye open to look around.

"Are they gone now?"

I went to her, lay down beside her, and licked her face. *I think so.*

She touched a finger to my nose, then drew it back for me to see. "You're bleeding."

I'm okay.

"No, you're not. We need to get help."

I'll be fine.

Her arm curled around my neck. "Did I do the right thing — pretending to be dead?"

You did.

"You were brave, Echo."

Only because I had to be.

—o0Oo—

Our progress was agonizingly slow. Not because of Hannah. Because of me.

She was the one urging me on now. Patting her leg. Offering words of encouragement.

"We're getting closer. I know we are. We have to be. Soon, we'll get to the road and someone will find us. I know it."

I wasn't so sure. At this rate, we wouldn't reach the road by nightfall. And anything could happen between now and then.

The surge of adrenaline that had flooded my veins during the fight quickly wore off. In its place, I felt nothing but intense, bone-deep weariness. I didn't remember getting half the cuts or scrapes I now bore. When I first pounced on the mama bear and fell to the ground, I must have jammed my hip. Now I was dragging that leg, reluctant to put weight on it. Every time I flexed a joint or stretched a limb, it felt like my cuts were pulling open wider. My ribs ached to draw in deep breaths. Pain filled my head. And my mouth pooled with blood from a missing tooth.

Yet despite it all, I continued on. If not for Hannah, I would have dropped right there on the road, wretched and battered, too broken in spirit to go on.

Clouds so low they scraped the treetops rolled in. Wind buffeted our faces, prying icy fingers beneath my thick coat. Hannah kept her sock-mittens tucked beneath her armpits. Our only blessing was that the trail was smoother than the deer path we'd been following. My thirst, however, was draining me. My tongue stuck to the roof of my mouth. I could have drunk a lake dry.

We crested a small rise and found ourselves looking over the answer to our prayers. It was a brook, glittering with fast-flowing water.

We could have waded across it, but for one problem. Although the water wasn't nearly as deep as the river we'd had to cross by way of the fallen log, it had carved deep into the earth. Given my current state, jumping across was out of the question.

The trail led right up to it. Except that where once there had been a bridge there was now nothing, except for a few bits of framework jutting out into the rocky ravine.

Before I could even search for another way across, Hannah was jogging down the hill toward it. She reached the remnants of the bridge, leaned out to look over the front of it, then to the side.

I was only halfway there when she shouted, "This way!"

She motioned to me and went between the base of the old bridge and the rocky wall of the creek bed. Grasping a sapling rooted nearby, she stepped down onto a stone. But it was loose. Even under her slight weight, it wobbled. And then ... a tiny squeal escaped her throat as rock and earth gave way. Her hand ripped free of the sapling. Her body plummeted.

I half-ran, half-hobbled to where she had disappeared to gaze over the edge. At the bottom, a few feet from the narrow span of water, sat Hannah, one leg extended before her, the other tucked beneath her bottom. She rolled over onto her side, looked up at me ... and burst into tears.

My whimpers rose to a whine as I franticly searched for a safer way down. I paced the ledge, ten feet one way, ten another. Back and forth, back and forth, each time going farther, until I saw a place where the roots of a huge pine tree partially hid a broadening crack between a boulder and the dirt where the runoff from uphill ran. The channel was dry now, but suffocatingly narrow.

Into the shadowy crevice I plunged, drawn onward by Hannah's yowling sobs. Twice I had to wiggle my way through, the rock pressed so close, but somehow I made it to the bottom.

I ran along the water-slicked stones, my paws slipping with each stride, not even thinking to stop and drink. When I reached Hannah, she calmed visibly, but she was clutching her ankle. It hurt. Badly.

I didn't know what to do except to be there for her.

Once her tears stopped flowing, Hannah carefully removed her boot and sock. Her ankle was ten shades of purple, the bone surrounded by puffy flesh. Her forehead puckered in concentration, she wiggled her toes. When she tried to point them, she gasped in pain.

"Ow, ow, ow!" She bit her lip until the pain passed. Shaking her head, she looked at me. "I can't walk, Echo." Then, fresh tears sprang anew.

The warmth of my body being the only thing I had to offer, I huddled next to her. Snowflakes swirled around us, melting as they met the earth. Hours slipped vaguely by as we listened to the wind whispering through the little valley and rustling the tree limbs far above. Daylight faded. At least down here, out of the wind, it was a little warmer. But not nearly warm enough.

I drank my fill from the stream, trying to fool my belly into believing it was full, but the water was ice cold and tasted of dirt.

As I lay next to Hannah, the world around us darkening, the taste on my tongue brought back memories of the day that Ed stuffed me in the sack and tossed me from the bridge. After that, I had vowed to give my loyalty to no human being ever again.

Yet now, here, I could not leave Hannah's side. Her life meant more to me than my own.

That night was the longest of my life. I was almost certain it would be my last. Above, stars winked between broken clouds. Hannah's breathing slowed, became fainter. Once she finally drifted off to sleep, she didn't stir.

When the first light of morning came, I stared at her for an eternity, until I detected the barest movement of her chest. I licked her face vigorously, trying to rouse her. It wasn't until I shoved my nose at her bad ankle that she showed any sign of life.

Her breath caught. Eyelashes fluttering, she gazed at me dully. Her lips were blue, split, and bleeding at the corners.

"C-c-cold … Hur-hurt …" She let her eyes go shut again. Her lips parted. At first, nothing but a puff of air came out, then she looked at me one more time, only for a moment. "Go, Echo. G-g-get … help."

Her life depended on me.

One last kiss upon her cheek and I went, although every bone in my body, every sinew, every vessel screamed at me to lie down beside her and stay until we both ceased to breathe.

My heart, though … my heart echoed Hannah's words: 'Go. Get help.'

One thing a dog never, ever does is let his person down.

chapter 33

Hunter

Two nights had now gone by since Hannah and Echo disappeared. And with every hour that passed, Hunter's hope diminished even more. When Sheriff Nate showed up at Heck's to tell him they'd found Hannah's backpack in a stream almost twelve miles from the Appletons' farm, it was nearly altogether extinguished.

The morning had been silent, full of sadness and tension. He and Jenn sat alone in their living room. They hadn't said a word to each other since coffee, three hours ago. Neither of them dared give breath to what was inside of them. The hurt was too great.

Lise was upstairs with Maura, who was taking this as hard as anyone. Half of Faderville had been looking for Hannah and her dog. That morning, Hunter had even seen a segment on the national news. The search had been expanded, the number of volunteers doubled just within the past day. But all they had to show for it was a backpack with a box of soggy crackers and some extra clothes inside.

Jenn sniffled into her tissue and blew her nose for the thousandth time. Outside, another patrol car came up the driveway and parked outside. Twisting around to look over the back of the couch through the window, she watched as the officer got out and spoke to Brad and the sheriff. Brad nodded, glanced her way, then took the officer aside.

Breath held to keep the tears from bursting forth again, Jenn turned back around and hid her eyes behind her hands.

Hunter wanted to reach out, to hold her, but there was still so much unspoken between them that he didn't want to explore just yet. When Hannah had fallen in the river, she was quickly found. Then, there had been hope.

This time, though, it was different. In so many ways. And Hunter couldn't help but wonder if had they handled things with Heck differently, then maybe Hannah would never have run away. He blamed himself and that blame would sit with him forever if they didn't find —

There was a knock at the door. It may as well have been the tolling of a death knell.

Jenn and Hunter exchanged a glance. An officer at the door was never good. If there had been good news, someone would have phoned them from the field.

Hunter's heart crashed through his gut. Jenn didn't move, even though she was closest to the door. He rose to spare her the task.

His hand hovered over the knob. He didn't want to know, didn't want to hear it. But there was no avoiding it. Putting it off wasn't going to change anything.

He gripped the knob, felt the cold metal firm beneath his fingertips. He opened the door just enough to see Brad's worn and aging face through the crack.

Hunter looked down. He couldn't bear it anymore. It was like a hundred boulders had just been piled on top of him, crushing the air from his lungs, compressing his bones into dust. He wanted this over with. So he asked, "They found her, didn't they?"

"Hunter …" Brad pressed a hand on the door, forcing it open

wider, and stepped inside. "Hunter, Jenn. Both of you need to come with me."

Bracing herself against the arm of the couch, Jenn stood. "Why?" Her voice was as rough as sand paper from days of crying.

"Just ... come."

Hunter waited for Jenn. Then, with his hand lightly on her lower back, they followed Brad outside. Hunter did not feel the bitter cold or see the sun break through sullen clouds. He was dead inside, his body a barely functioning shell. Brad led them to the patrol car that had just arrived. He opened the back door, stepped away.

There, in the backseat on a rumpled blanket, lay Echo, motionless, his eyes closed. Bloody gashes marked his muzzle, back, and legs, the fur around them matted. He looked like he'd been chewed up and spit out by a vicious monster.

A great hole of nothingness opened up beneath Hunter, swallowing him whole. Why hadn't Brad just said it — that they'd found Echo's body? He could've spared them this morbid sight.

Then Brad leaned over Echo's still form, placed a hand upon his withers. "Hey, buddy. Wake up."

Wake up? Hunter stared harder. *Was he ... breathing?*

Echo's whiskers twitched. His nostrils flared ever so slightly. One eyelid was grossly swollen, but the other parted. A single golden eye pierced Hunter's soul. Moaning, Echo stretched a paw toward Hunter.

Tears obscured Hunter's vision, but he knelt down, found Echo's calloused paw, and rubbed a thumb over the top of it.

Hunter looked up at Brad. "Where ...?"

"I'll explain on the way." He nodded toward another cruiser. "Deputy Mortenson will take Echo here to Dr. Timowski's. The paramedics looked him over, said he probably needs some antibiotics and fluids, but mostly he's just worn out and dehydrated."

Jenn's hand alighted on Hunter's back. He met her eyes. They held the same question he had.

"And Hannah?" he asked Brad.

Brad grasped Hunter firmly by the arm and helped him to his feet. "They found her."

A single word hung in the air: *Alive?*

A smile graced Brad's face for the first time in days. Nodding, he looked from Hunter to Jenn. "She's a little rough around the edges, but she's going to be all right."

Suddenly, Jenn was in Hunter's arms, both of them laughing and crying at once. He rocked her and kissed her forehead, then rushed back into the house and called to Lise. She and Maura came running outside.

Soon, they were all hugging and crying and saying how they'd never stopped hoping. Whoops sounded from the neighbors who had gathered to help the McHughs. Deputies clapped each other on the back. Several people took out their phones and called friends and family, spreading the good news. A reporter signaled his cameraman to start filming and soon he was narrating the breakthrough as he stood in front of the McHughs' farmhouse.

Thumping his palm on the closed door of the cruiser, Brad sent the deputy off with Echo for treatment.

Aware of all the commotion, Heck came out of his house and stood on the porch. Hunter waved to him.

"They found her, Heck! They found her!" Hunter yelled. He wasn't sure from this distance, but he thought he saw Heck pump his fist. "Echo, too!"

As Hunter got in the back of Sheriff Nate's car, he noticed the reporter rushing toward Heck's house. He regretted everything they'd put Heck through. As soon as he could, he'd find some way to make it all up to him.

Maura piled into the back next to her mother and clutched her arm. Putting his right arm around them both, Hunter squeezed Jenn's knee with his left hand. Relief washed over them in waves.

So many moments, Hunter was sure they'd tell him Hannah was dead or gravely injured. And there was always the equally terrible possibility that she had vanished forever. But in the end, thanks to all the rescue workers — but most of all because of the courage and determination of one intrepid black and white Aussie — Hannah had been found.

Found!

As Sheriff Nate's car rolled onto the road, Brad, sitting in the front passenger seat, told them Hannah was at the hospital in Somerset where she was being treated for mild hypothermia and a badly sprained ankle.

"So where did they find her?" Hunter asked.

Brad met his eyes. "Somehow she'd made it all the way to Daniel Boone National Forest and onto the North Rim Trail. Turns out she'd seen a sign that said there was a road ahead and she was on her way there when she fell in a ravine and hurt her ankle. But the question isn't so much *where* they found her as *how* they found her. That trail hasn't been used for years. Not since a flood about five years ago washed out the bridge leading across it."

"How did they find her, then?" Jenn asked.

"Echo showed them the way."

Jenn's forehead creased. "How?"

"After Hannah fell, he stayed the night with her to keep her warm. This morning he left her, picked up the trail on the other side of the ravine and went three more miles to the main access road. Lucky for him, there were a couple of hikers from out of state who saw him. They'd seen the news this morning and recognized Echo from his picture. When they approached, he started barking and ran off a hundred yards or so. One of them stayed at the roadside and called 9-1-1, while the other followed the dog. Echo wouldn't let him get close enough for the man to catch him, so the guy figured he was leading him somewhere. And he was. Straight to Hannah. Echo *knew* what he was doing. He kept stopping, waiting for the guy to catch up, then running ahead."

"That's some dog you've got yourself, Doc," Sheriff Nate said with a wink.

"Yeah, I suppose so." There weren't enough superlatives to describe Echo. Plainly put, the dog was a hero. What a wonderful coincidence that of all the remote, twisting country roads in Adair County, whoever had left him for dead had done so right in front of their house. From the start, Echo had glommed onto Hannah like white cat hair to black slacks. And when duty had called, he'd put himself on the line and paid the price for it. "So, all the cuts. Do they know what happened? Hannah wasn't —"

"No, she doesn't appear to have been attacked. Echo must have protected her. Poor dog's had the tar beat out of him. He's cut up a bit. A few good gashes, nothing life threatening. My guess is a bear, judging by the claw marks."

Gripping the headrest in front of her, Maura leaned forward. "A bear, seriously?"

"Unless wolverines have invaded this part of Kentucky, yes, a bear." Eyeing Hunter in the mirror again, Brad raised a finger. "Last time I knew a dog that brave, it was your girl Halo."

Hunter's gaze drifted to the hills racing past. He remembered how Halo had stayed at his side when he had run away, just like Echo had stayed with Hannah. Then later, how she had found her way home when Tucker Kratz stole her. Soon after that, she had attacked Kratz when he held Hunter's family at gunpoint, saving them all as she risked her own life.

It was almost like Halo was still with him, looking out for his family.

Maybe, in a way, she was.

chapter 34

Hannah

Maura clamped her arms around Hannah and squeezed. "Don't you ever, *ever* go away like that again, hear me, squirt?" She let go as Hannah squirmed from her hold, but then took her little sister's face in her hands. "Do you know how worried I was?"

Biting her lip, Hannah stared at the needle taped to the back of her left hand, then followed the tube coming out of it all the way up to the bag hanging upside down on a hook beside her hospital bed. Truth be told, she hadn't thought much about it — until last night, as she lay numb with cold under a sky speckled with starlight, drifting in and out of consciousness. She *had* thought of her family then. Of how much she missed them, even after all the trouble she'd caused. In hindsight, maybe running away hadn't been such a brilliant idea. She had been thinking too much of herself and not enough of her family.

Hannah drew in a shaky breath. "I missed you, too."

Maura crushed her in an even tighter hug.

"I can't ... breathe," Hannah choked out. Her sister loosened her hold, then planted a kiss on her forehead before scooting carefully down from the bed.

Behind Maura stood her parents, Hunter with an arm over Jenn's shoulder and Jenn mopping away tears, which thoroughly confused Hannah. Why was she smiling *and* crying? Was she glad? Mad?

Hunter came to the foot of Hannah's hospital bed and peeled the blanket back. Bags of ice were taped to her ankle, which was propped up on pillows. Above the plastic bags, her puffy toes peeked, a bright purple bruise spreading from the base of her big toe to just above her swollen ankle.

"That's quite a number you did on your ankle, sweet pea," he remarked. "Does it hurt?"

"Only if I move it."

"Then I won't play 'This little piggy' with your toes for a while." Carefully, he replaced the blanket over her foot. "I suppose it wouldn't be fair to challenge you to a race right now, either, huh?"

It was a joke. She got that much. But Hannah didn't feel like laughing just yet. She was still waiting for someone to yell at her or ground her or give her a lecture.

"I'm sorry," she whispered, looking down at her hands as she clutched her blanket. Because she *was* sorry. Truly sorry. And she was willing to face whatever punishment her parents would give her.

Drifting to her, Jenn placed the tenderest of kisses on the top of her head. "We're just happy you're okay, sweetie. We love you soooo much."

Hannah looked into her mother's eyes. "You're not mad?"

"If I'm mad at anyone, it's myself. I jumped to conclusions about Heck. I shouldn't have. It wasn't fair to you or him."

"So he can still show me how to paint?"

"Yes. That and more. First, I have to apologize to him, okay? I caused him a lot of trouble and I'm not even sure he wants to talk to me at the moment, but if I can get it all straightened out, then yeah, you can spend as much time at Heck's as you want to."

Hannah wasn't entirely sure what her mommy was talking about. She looked forward to going back to Heck's, anyway. There were so many things she still wanted to paint.

"Hannah," her daddy said, "did Echo … did he fight with a bear?"

Cold fear flooded Hannah's chest. It all came back to her in a rush. One moment she was watching the cubs bounce and roll — and the next she was staring up at a bear so big and black it blocked out all the light in the sky. She'd tried to listen, to understand what it wanted from her, but all she sensed was rage. Panic had frozen her feet to the earth. She couldn't move or speak, could barely breathe. She knew she couldn't outrun it, so she collapsed to the ground, slowly pulling herself into a ball to protect her face. The banging of her heart in her ears was so loud she was only vaguely aware of the scuffle going on between Echo and the bear. All she could do was wait and hope. Wait and hope. Wait …

"Hannah? Hannah?"

A hand came to rest on her forearm. A few more moments passed before her eyes regained focus. Hunter lifted her chin with his fingers, turning her face to his. "Was it a bear, Hannah?"

Shaking her head, she held up three fingers.

"Three?"

She nodded. "Two little bears — and a really big one. But Echo only fought with the big one."

Jenn leaned against Hunter's side. "That was probably the mama bear, protecting her babies. Cubs stay with their mother through the first year. And around here, they don't always hibernate all winter long, but wake up to forage for food occasionally."

"But I wasn't going to hurt them or steal their food."

"We know that," Jenn said, "but the bear didn't. Sometimes mothers do crazy stuff if they think their babies are in danger — I know." She brushed Hannah's bangs back from her forehead. "They

302

said you can come home tomorrow, Hannah."

Home. Hannah couldn't wait. But ... had something happened to Echo? She vaguely remembered telling him to go for help, then he'd licked her face, trotted off a ways, looked back once ... and the next thing she knew, she was being lifted into the back of an ambulance.

She craned her neck to the side to peer down at the floor, scanning the entire room and out into the corridor. "Where's Echo?"

"At the animal hospital," Hunter said. Quickly adding, "He'll be okay once they stitch him up and give him some medicine."

A single, salty tear trailed its way from the corner of Hannah's eye, then down beside her nose and lip, finally dripping from her chin to land with a *plop* upon the pale blue blanket bunched in her lap. She rubbed its trace away with a fist, holding her breath to stave off more tears, but they came anyway. Soon, her vision swam in a waterfall of them, stinging her eyes.

"He's going to be okay, sweet pea," Hunter told her. "He really is. He chased the bear off. And when you fell and hurt your ankle, he brought help to you. He saved you."

She blinked at the wetness clinging to her eyelashes, pushing more tears over the brim of her eyelids. Snot filled her nose, making it hard to breathe. She sniffed it back, but it ran down her throat. After swallowing twice, she managed between blubbering breaths, "I ... know."

"Then why are you crying?" Jenn asked.

It was hard to find the words that expressed precisely what it was she felt: an ache emanating from the center of her chest so big, so intense, she felt like her heart might burst. But the more she thought about it, the simpler it was.

"Because I love my dog. More than anything."

If she were to write that down, she would write it all in capital letters, underline it five times, and draw stars all around it.

—oO0o—

Hannah kicked her legs out in front of her. Wind raced through her hair, teasing it from the elastic that held her ponytail in place. Lacy white clouds rushed at her, then fell away as her weight carried the swing back. For the briefest of moments, she hung suspended, looking down. Then her world reversed and the ground blurred past as momentum tossed her forward again.

Just as her arms and legs began to tire, Hunter walked across the yard and set down a duffel bag beside the Crooked Tree. Moving behind her, he pushed the seat of her swing as high as it would go. She laughed. Laughed so hard and so long her cheeks and stomach began to hurt.

Today was the first warm day of spring and while there were still no leaves on the trees, the sun was bright and warm upon her face. When Hunter reminded her it was almost time to go and he stepped away, Hannah let the swing glide on its own for a little while, then dragged her feet over the dirt until she came to a stop. A dull ache throbbed in her ankle, so she pointed her toes and moved her foot in a small circle. The doctor had showed her exercises so her ankle would get strong again. It was better, but sometimes it still bothered her.

Echo was lying at the base of the tree, his muzzle resting on his paws, his rear legs stretched out behind him like a frog. Two long pink scars were still visible, going from the top of his nose to just below his right eye. Her daddy had told her that hair would grow over those in time, but she kind of liked them. They reminded her how brave he'd been and that if he hadn't fought the bear off, she might not be alive at all. Which made her wonder about something ... Something very serious. She didn't want to think about it at all, but she couldn't help it.

"Daddy?"

"Yes, sweet pea?"

"How long do dogs live?"

Hunter crouched beside Echo and stroked the top of his head. Groaning, Echo closed his eyes. Soon, he rolled over on his back and spread his legs wide, exposing his belly. Hunter scratched all the way from inside Echo's rear legs to his chest.

"Not long enough," Hunter finally said.

Hannah came to sit beside them, Indian style. "So, not as long as people?"

"No, not as long as people."

"How long?" She was insistent. It was important to know.

"A breed like this? Twelve or thirteen years, generally. Sometimes a few more, sometimes less."

Adding the numbers in her head, she quickly came to the conclusion that she didn't like it. Not one bit. "Best friends should live longer."

He didn't say anything, just nodded.

"But where do they go after they ... after they stop living?"

"Do you believe people go to heaven when they die, Hannah?"

She didn't know. So she thought about it. They had to go somewhere. "Yes, I think so."

Her father stood and she stood with him. A frown of disapproval tugged at his mouth. Bending over, he wiped the dirt from Hannah's knees.

She tugged at his sleeve as he straightened. "Do they ever come back?"

"Come back?"

"From heaven?"

"Dogs or people?"

"Both, I guess."

He gazed at far-off clouds, a smile slowly teasing at the corners of his lips. "I don't know, Hannah ... but I'd like to believe they do."

"Good, because if Echo can't stay forever, or at least as long as I'm around, I want another dog just like him. Well, maybe not *exactly* like him. It's okay if it's different. Maybe a girl dog, instead. Or a little dog. Or a brown one. But a good dog. It has to be a good dog. A really good dog."

As she said that, it occurred to her that all dogs were good. They just needed to meet the right person who would love them for what they were.

Echo sat at her feet, love and admiration evident in his golden-brown eyes.

"Hunter?" Jenn called. Standing at the rail of the front porch, she slipped her arms into her denim jacket, then began buttoning it up. "There you two are. Almost time. Fifteen minutes."

He raised a hand. "Got it! We'll be there." Picking up the duffel bag, he glanced at Hannah and then Echo. "You two ready?"

Hannah hesitated. She was and she wasn't. Too bad Echo couldn't come with them.

Together, they walked across the yard, Echo running circles around them, as if he had exciting adventures of his own ahead. But then, Echo acted that way every day.

At the edge of the property, where a narrow footpath squeezed between a row of forsythia bursting with golden blooms, Echo sat and waited obediently. When Hunter gave the okay, they crossed the road and strolled up Heck's driveway. He was there on the porch, wearing charcoal-colored corduroy pants and a gray tweed jacket.

"Just in time," he said, taking the duffel bag from Hunter. "Echo and I are headed to Fox Hollow for a visit — if that's all right with you, Hannah?"

She nodded. "You have my present, right?"

"I do. Nicely wrapped for transport. We wouldn't want anything to happen to it before she sees it."

They followed Heck inside. He set the bag beside the sofa. Echo lay down next to it, sniffing along the zipper. Inside, Hannah had stuffed Echo's favorite things: his squeaky giraffe, his elephant, two balls in case he lost one, three bones of different flavors, and the braided rug to sleep on, along with a sack of kibble and two dishes. She'd wanted to pack more for him, but her mommy had said that was probably enough. He didn't need to scatter too many of his things through Heck's house.

Hunter took a piece of paper from his pocket and handed it to Heck. "I've written down the details of our trip, including our flights and accommodations. Brad and my mom will take care of the horses, but if you could check the mailbox for us, that'd be great." He pointed to the bottom of the paper. "My cell number is —"

"Don't worry, Hunter. Jenn went over everything with me yesterday, including how much and when to feed the dog."

"Oh, all right, then." Hunter squatted down, so he could look Hannah in the eye. "It's time."

Hannah scrunched her mouth up. "Do we have to go?"

"Aren't you the one who wanted to go to Disney World?"

Well, yes, but when she asked about it, no one told her you couldn't take your dog into the park unless it was a service or therapy dog. Echo had months of training left before he could earn his vest that would allow him to go to school with her and other places like restaurants and stores and doctors' offices.

Hannah didn't want to say goodbye, though. It sounded too permanent. Going to Echo, she held up seven fingers. "This many sleeps, Echo, and I'll be back. I promise."

With a whimper, Echo raised himself up on his hind feet and hooked his front paws over her shoulders, almost knocking her over. He tucked his muzzle in the crook of her neck. Her arms went around him in a hug. Soon, she felt his wet tongue sliding up and down her cheek, tickling her ear.

"I'll try," she said to Echo. "But I'll still miss you."

"You'll try what?" Hunter asked her.

"He said I need to be brave."

307

"You already are, Hannah. At six years old, you've survived more than some people ten times your age. But I'd be okay if you were a little less brave sometimes." Hunter took her hand in his as they turned to go. "You know, I'm kind of nervous about this week. Maybe you could stick a little closer to your mom and me, all right? I wouldn't want anyone to get lost."

"Okay." She tugged on his sleeve. "Do you want to borrow my map?"

"Your map?"

"Of Disney World. In case you get lost."

"Oh, yeah, sure." He winked at her. "Good idea."

chapter 35

Echo

There was sadness and loneliness in this place. A longing for things past. I sensed it the first time we walked into the reception area and saw the long hallways with their polished railings and aseptic floors, and then as Heck guided me past a large gathering area where an old man with a weathered face stared catatonically at a large-screen TV, oblivious to our passing.

It was our third visit to Fox Hollow in a week. Tomorrow, Hannah and her family would return from their trip to Disney World. As much as I had enjoyed my time with Heck, I was ready for Hannah to come home. Still, I was glad I had come to Fox Hollow. For all the sorrow contained within those walls, if you simply *listened*, there were stories to be heard ...

People spoke softly here, in voices worn from use. Their hands were gnarled and shaky, their spines sometimes stooped, their movements slow and stiff. Yet as we went by each room and I stole a peek, eyes rich with wisdom turned to gaze observantly at me, memories kindling in the depths of their hazy pupils.

"Ohhh, would you look at that?" said one elderly gentleman, leaning on his walker. "Just like my old boy, Shep. Best farm dog this side of the Mississippi."

"What a bea-U-tiful dog," another remarked with a toothless smile.

"Such shiny black fur."

"Pretty gold eyes."

"How handsome he is."

"How well behaved."

But more often than the compliments on my looks and manners, I heard, "I used to have a dog."

Oh, the stories that were contained in those few words: *I used to have a dog.*

We heard quite a lot of them in those few visits. Many more than once. How one Jack Russell Terrier had roused his family in the night and saved them from a fire. How a Labrador mix had been hit by a truck and found on the highway, barely clinging to life, then served for fifteen years as the Faderville firehouse dog. How one mutt of indeterminate heritage had helped raise nine children and fifteen grandchildren, patiently tolerating ear-tuggings and tail-pullings (those children were obviously no relation to the Grunwald twins). And how one tiny teacup poodle had been his master's ears, alerting him to an attempted burglary with his fierce yapping.

Then smiles would transform the residents' faces and tears dampen their eyes, and trembling hands drifted down to stroke my head and withers. Softest of all were Sophia's fingers. She knew the perfect place to scratch just below my ear and around to the base of my throat. But each time we visited, it went exactly the same.

"Sophia?" Heck would say after tapping lightly on the door, which was always open. "Sophia, would you like a visitor today?"

Sitting in her recliner, the one with the buttons that made it go up and down so she could stand more easily, she would tilt her head at me, smiling. "Ohhh, what a lovely dog. May I pet him?"

Then Heck would venture cautiously in, my leash tight in his hand, even though I never pulled at it or jumped on people. But the sadness and loneliness I sensed in this case came not from Sophia, but from Heck. He was so patient with her, so loving, yet he longed for what used to be.

"What's his name?" she'd ask, her feeble hand running over the dome of my skull and down my neck.

"Echo."

"And what's your name?"

He would smile, melancholy flickering in his pupils. "Hector Menendez, but you may call me Heck." Then with a sigh, "Sometimes you used to call me Holy Heck, just to tease me."

The comment would go without reply, no recognition evident in her face, as Heck would begin to tell her how they'd met, how they'd drifted apart, but later found each other again, and then about the day they got married, and how there was a thunderstorm and the lights in the church went out ...

But it was our most recent visit when something truly special happened. After years of not remembering any of her life with Heck and only bits of her childhood, Sophia suddenly interrupted Heck in the middle of his reminiscence and said, "On Gable Street — didn't the people behind us have a dog like this?"

Heck's cheeks twitched upward in a heartwarming smile. "Yes, yes, they did. It was smaller, with a bit more white and a tail, but very similar looking. Funny, even I didn't remember that until you mentioned it just now."

He asked what else she remembered, but just as quickly her mind drifted off again and she began talking about how warm it had been that week and how her friend down the hallway was having trouble with vertigo.

"Ah," came a voice from the hall, "I see she's regaling you with tales of Bernadette's inner ear problems."

Bernadette. Why did that name sound so familiar?

I looked to the doorway to see Mr. Beekman, dressed in a pair of crisp green scrubs. Tinker darted between his legs and ran up to me, her smooth, whip-like tail thumping against the carpet as she skidded to a halt in front of me. We'd met the first day I came here, and even though both of us had grown considerably since we met in the shelter, we remembered one another's scent. It had been an overwhelmingly joyful reunion and we still found it hard to contain our excitement every time we met. We lathered each other in licks and then sniffed each other in the usual places before Tinker rolled over on her belly. I nuzzled her snout, then dipped low in a play bow.

"Tinker, not here," Mr. Beekman reminded us firmly as he gently wrapped a blood pressure cuff around Sophia's thin arm.

We both hung our heads apologetically, but moments later Tinker had her paw on my shoulder, and so I butt-slammed her playfully. She sneezed at me, then sat innocently at Sophia's feet before Mr. Beekman turned around.

Heck and Mr. Beekman talked for a few more minutes about Sophia. She seemed completely unaware of their conversation. I'd noticed that unless someone made a point of calling her name and asking her a question directly, she was detached from the goings-on around her. Finally, Heck excused himself.

We went down the brightly lit corridor to the dining area, where Heck paused to look at the paintings hung along one wall. Several of them were Heck's, but the one that was drawing the most comments lately was a piece that Hannah had painted.

"This one reminds me of summer," said a very old lady from her wheelchair in front of it. She was heavier set, with bright red hair and loudly colored clothes that said she was not afraid of being noticed. There was something vaguely familiar about her voice, but I couldn't quite place it. She moved the joystick on her armrest to maneuver

312

closer to the painting. "It's so vibrant with all the tulips and the sunshine. I can practically smell the flowers she's holding. What a beautiful woman, too."

It was the painting of Sophia picking flowers.

Heck said nothing. He simply lingered there, gazing at the painting as if seeing it for the very first time. Hannah had given it to him a week ago before leaving for vacation. After Sophia fawned over it — although she didn't seem to recognize that it was her in the painting — she had suggested putting it in the dining area, so everyone could admire it. Which had turned out to be a good idea.

"That's my wife," Heck finally said. "Sophia."

The old woman shifted her joystick in a circle to turn around and face us. The moment she laid eyes on me, something plucked at the back of my mind. I went to her and sat politely, like I'd been taught.

"My name is Bernadette," she told us, "although most people just call me Bernie. You know, I used to have a dog like this, an Australian Shepherd. She had that same look in her eyes, like an old soul. Well, she wasn't mine. She belonged to a young man named Hunter McHugh. I used to live with his family. But that was a long time ago ... Do you know him?"

She reached out a hand and rested it on top of my head.

And then I remembered. A time before this. Another life, when I had another name ...

author's note

My dog Arrow, a black and white Australian Shepherd, is often mistaken for a Border Collie. She forgives the offenders, but wishes they would be more observant of the subtle differences between the breeds: her ears do not stand up, she does not crouch when moving toward something, nor does she move loosely in the shoulders. She also doesn't have a tail.

Arrow was only three weeks old, her eyes barely open, when she tried to climb out of her whelping box. On her first try, she succeeded. I lovingly scolded her and said her future owners would be getting a handful; I swear she told me her name and that *this* was her home. She stayed.

Her purpose in life is to let me know I am loved, adored, and worshipped. I welcome the devotion. Who else would think so highly of me?

Arrow's appetite for learning is hindered only by my poor attempts at dog-speak. Still, I am constantly amazed at what she does understand. She is, I have learned, a very observant dog that reads subtle body cues and tone of voice, more so than words. And that made me think — what a gift it would be if we could understand dogs as well as they do us.

But an even better gift would be if we got to meet our heart-dogs again. And again and again and again …

about the author

N. Gemini Sasson holds a M.S. in Biology from Wright State University where she ran cross country on athletic scholarship. She has worked as an aquatic toxicologist, an environmental engineer, a teacher and a cross country coach. A longtime breeder of Australian Shepherds, her articles on bobtail genetics have been translated into seven languages. She lives in rural Ohio with her husband, two nearly grown children and an ever-changing number of animals.

Long after writing about Robert the Bruce and Queen Isabella, Sasson learned she is a descendant of both historical figures.

If you enjoyed this book, please spread the word by sharing it on Facebook or leaving a review at your favorite online retailer or book lovers' site.

For more details about N. Gemini Sasson and her books, go to:
www.ngeminisasson.com

Or become a 'fan' at:
www.facebook.com/NGeminiSasson

Sign up to learn about new releases via e-mail at:
http://eepurl.com/vSA6z

Made in the USA
Middletown, DE
02 November 2024

63761225R00194